Also by Susanna Gregory

The Matthew Bartholomew Series

A Plague on Both Your Houses
An Unholy Alliance
A Bone of Contention
A Deadly Brew
A Wicked Deed
A Masterly Murder
An Order for Death
A Summer of Discontent
A Killer in Winter
The Hand of Justice
The Mark of a Murderer
The Tarnished Chalice
To Kill or Cure

The Thomas Chaloner Series

A Conspiracy of Violence
Blood on the Strand

THE BUTCHER OF SMITHFIELD

THE BUTCHER
OF SMITHFIELD

Susanna
Gregory

sphere

SPHERE

First published in Great Britain in 2008 by Sphere
Reprinted 2008

Copyright © 2008 Susanna Gregory

The moral right of the author has been asserted.

*All characters and events in this publication, other than those clearly in the public
domain, are fictitious and any resemblance to real persons, living or dead, is
purely coincidental.*

A CIP catalogue record for this book
is available from the British Library.

ISBN: 978-1-84744-062-4

Typeset in Baskerville MT by Palimpsest Book Production Limited,
Grangemouth, Stirlingshire
Printed and bound in the UK by
CPI Mackays, Chatham ME5 8TD

Sphere
An imprint of
Little, Brown Book Group
100 Victoria Embankment
London EC4Y 0DY

An Hachette Livre UK Company
www.hachettelivre.co.uk

www.littlebrown.co.uk

To Peter Carey

Prologue

The solicitor Thomas Newburne knew he was not a popular man, but he did not care. Why should he, when he had everything he wanted – a lovely mansion on Old Jewry, a pleasant cottage on Thames Street, cellars stuffed with fine wines, and more gold than he could spend in a lifetime? He glanced at the man walking at his side. People liked Richard Hodgkinson, because he was affable and good-hearted, but had his printing business made *him* wealthy, allowed *him* to buy whatever he fancied and not worry about the cost? No, they had not, and Newburne could not help but despise him for it.

'Let me buy you another pie, Hodgkinson,' he said, making a show of rummaging in his loaded purse for coins. He was aware of several rough types eyeing him speculatively, but he was not afraid of them. He was legal adviser to the infamous Ellis Crisp, and only a fool would risk annoying the man everyone called the Butcher of Smithfield. Cutpurses and robbers could look all they

1

liked, but none would dare lift a finger against the Butcher's right-hand man.

'I have had enough to eat, thank you,' replied Hodgkinson politely. 'It was good of you to invite me to spend a few hours with you.'

Newburne inclined his head in a bow. Of course Hodgkinson appreciated his hospitality. Newburne was the ascending star in Smithfield, and Hodgkinson *should* be grateful that the solicitor had deigned to acknowledge him, and spoil him with little treats. Of course, Newburne would have preferred to be with his one true friend, a shy, retiring fellow by the name of Finch, but Finch was off playing his trumpet to some wealthy patron, and so was unavailable. Newburne had not wanted to be alone that afternoon – it was much more fun spending money when someone else was watching – so he had asked Hodgkinson to join him instead. It was a good day for a stroll – the first dry one they had had in weeks, and they were not the only ones taking advantage of it. The Smithfield meat market was packed, a lively, noisy chaos of shops, taverns, stocks and brothels.

'My stomach hurts,' Newburne said, not for the first time during the outing. 'You said gingerbread would soothe it, but I feel worse.'

Hodgkinson looked sympathetic. 'You drank a lot of wine earlier, and I thought the cake might soak up some of the sour humours. Perhaps you should take a purge.'

Newburne waved the advice aside; the printer did not know what he was talking about. 'I shall have a bit of this cucumber instead. Cucumbers are said to be good for gripes in the belly, although I cannot abide the taste.'

'They are unpleasant,' agreed Hodgkinson. He pointed

suddenly, and his voice dropped to a low, uneasy whisper. 'There is the Butcher, out surveying his domain.'

Newburne glanced to where a man, hooded and cloaked as usual, prowled among the market stalls. Even Crisp's walk was menacing, light and soft, like a hunter after prey, and people gave him a wide berth as he passed. He was surrounded by the louts who did his bidding, members of the powerful gang called the Hectors. They were another reason why no one tended to argue with the Butcher of Smithfield, and even Newburne was a little uneasy in their company, although he would never have admitted it to anyone else.

'I am told he killed a man yesterday,' he said conversationally to Hodgkinson. He smiled, despite the ache in his stomach. The Butcher knew how to keep people in line, and Newburne fully approved of his tactics. It was refreshing to work for someone who was not afraid to apply a firm hand when it was needed. 'By that slaughterhouse over there.'

Hodgkinson swallowed uneasily. 'I heard. Apparently, the fellow objected to the way he runs things. I suppose that explains why Crisp's shop is so full of pies and sausages this morning.'

Newburne nodded, glancing across to where the emporium in question was curiously devoid of customers, although everywhere else was busy. He was never sure whether to believe the rumours that circulated regarding how Crisp disposed of his dead enemies. Most of Smithfield thought them to be true, though, which served to make the Butcher more feared than ever, and that was not a bad thing as far as Newburne was concerned. Frightened folk were easier to control than ones who were puffed up with a sense of their own immortality.

Hodgkinson shuddered, and began to walk in another direction, away from the Butcher and his entourage. 'Look! Dancing monkeys! I have not seen those in years.'

Newburne took a bite of the cucumber as he stood in the little crowd that had gathered to watch the spectacle. He was beginning to feel distinctly unwell, and thought he might be sick. He swallowed the mouthful with difficulty, and started to take another. Suddenly, there was a searing pain in his innards, one that felt like claws tearing him apart from the inside. He groaned and dropped to his knees, arms clutching his middle. He could hear Hodgkinson saying something, but could not make out the words. Then he was on his back, in the filth of the street. People were looking away from the performing animals to stare at him, although no one made any attempt to help. Hodgkinson was shouting for someone to bring water, but all Newburne cared about was the terrible ache in his belly. He could not breathe, and his vision was darkening around the edges. And then everything went black, and the printer's clamouring voice faded into silence.

Chapter 1

London, Late October 1663

A combination of chiming bells and hammering rain woke Thomas Chaloner that grey Sunday morning. At first, he did not know where he was, and he sat up with a jolt, automatically reaching for the dagger at his side. The realisation that he did not need it, that he was safe in his rooms at Fetter Lane, came just after the shock of discovering that his weapon was not where it had been these last four months, and it took a few moments to bring his instinctive alarm under control. He lay back on his bed, staring up at the cracks in the ceiling, and forced himself to relax. He was at home, not working in enemy territory on the Spanish–Portuguese border, and the bells were calling the faithful to their weekly devotions, not warning of an imminent attack.

He pushed back the blanket and walked to the window. In the street below, Fetter Lane was much as it had been when he had left the city back in June. Carts still creaked across its manure-carpeted cobbles, impeded that morning by the rainwater that formed a fast-moving stream down one side, and the Golden Lion tavern still stood opposite, its sign swinging gently in the wind and its sleepy-eyed patrons just beginning to emerge from a night of dark talk and conspiracy. The recently installed Royalist government was uneasy about the seditious discussions it believed took place in the many coffee houses that were springing up all over London, but Chaloner thought half the country's dissidents could be eradicated in one fell swoop if the Golden Lion was monitored – and probably half its criminals, too. He did not think he had ever encountered a place that was such a flagrant haven for felons and mischief-makers.

He almost jumped out of his skin when something brushed against his leg, and he reached for his knife a second time; but it was only the stray cat that had attached itself to him on his journey home from Lisbon. He assumed its affection was hunger-driven, until he spotted the remains of a rat near the hearth; the animal had evidently despaired of being fed and had procured its own breakfast. It rubbed his leg again, then jumped on to the window sill and began to wash itself.

Dawn had broken, and people were walking, riding or being driven to church. Chaloner supposed he had better join them, not because he had any burning desire for religion, but because he did not want to draw attention to himself with unorthodox behaviour. After a decade of Puritan rule, the newly reinstated bishops were eager to assert the authority of the traditional Church, and anyone not attending the Sunday services laid himself open to accusations of nonconformism. Like most spies, Chaloner tried to keep a low profile, and aimed to do all that was expected of him in the interests of maintaining anonymity.

The travelling clothes he had been wearing for the last three weeks were tar-stained and stiff with sea-salt, so he knelt by the chest at the end of the bed and rummaged about for something clean. He was horrified to discover that moths and mice had been there before him, and that what had been a respectable wardrobe was now a mess of holes and shreds. It was not that he particularly enjoyed donning splendid costumes, but his work as an intelligence officer meant that he was required to dress to a certain standard in order to gain access to the places where he needed to be. If he went to the Palace of White Hall – where the King lived and his ministers had their offices – clad in rags, the guards would refuse to let him in.

Eventually, he found a blue long-coat with silver buttons, knee-length breeches and a laced shirt that had somehow escaped the creatures' ravages. 'Lacing' was a recent – and to his mind foppish – fashion, and he disliked the sensation of extraneous material flapping around his wrists and neck, but at least it provided convenient hiding places for the various weapons he always carried. Over the coat went the sash that held his sword; no gentlemen ever left home without a sword. His hat was black with a wide brim and a conical dome, and looked unremarkable. However, it had been given to him by a lady he had befriended in Spain, and its crown had been cleverly reinforced with a skin of steel. In a profession where sly blows to the head were not uncommon, he felt it was sure to prove useful.

He stumbled over a warped floorboard as he headed for the door, and a quick glance around the rented rooms he called home – an attic chamber containing a bed, two chairs, a chest and a table, and an adjoining pantry-cum-storeroom – told him that the subsidence he had first noticed at Christmas had grown a lot more marked during the four months he had been away. A fire in the house next door was to blame, and he was surprised the city authorities had not ordered his building to be demolished, too. The roof leaked, his windows no longer closed, and there was a distinct list to his floor. He only hoped that if – when – it did collapse, he would not be in it.

He walked swiftly down the stairs to the ground floor, the cat at his heels. He did not tiptoe deliberately, but stealth was second nature to a spy, and his sudden, soundless appearance startled his landlord, Daniel Ellis. Ellis was standing in front of a tin mirror, trying to see whether his wig was on straight in the dim light of the hall.

'Lord!' Ellis exclaimed, hand to his heart. 'I did not hear you coming. I must be growing deaf.'

Ellis had been genuinely pleased to see his tenant return the previous evening. The speed of Chaloner's departure – which had barely left him time to pack a bag; he had actually missed the ship he had been ordered to catch, and had been obliged to pay a riverman to row after it – had left Ellis with the impression that Chaloner might not come back. And there had been rent owing.

Chaloner gesticulated upwards. 'Did you know the ceiling in my room—'

'There is nothing wrong with my house,' interrupted Ellis, in a way that told Chaloner he was probably not the first to complain. 'Rats have a penchant for wood, as I have told you before, and they always gnaw beams when folk leave their rooms unoccupied for long periods of time. Of course, now you have a cat, rodents will no longer be a problem.'

Chaloner could have argued, but the chambers suited him well for a number of reasons. First, the subsidence

8

had allowed him to negotiate a low rent, which was important to a man whose employer sometimes forgot to pay him. Secondly, Fetter Lane was a reasonably affluent street and its householders kept it lit at night – a spy always liked to be able to see what was happening outside his home. And finally, it was convenient for White Hall, where his master, the Earl of Clarendon worked.

'Some letters came when you were gone,' said Ellis, retrieving a bundle of missives from the chest under the mirror. 'I was going to give them to your next of kin.'

'You thought I was dead?'

Ellis became a little defensive. 'It was not an unreasonable assumption – you left very abruptly, and then there was no news of you for months. I heard you playing your viol last night, by the way. At least the rats did not eat that.'

Chaloner would not have been pleased if they had. Playing the bass viol, or viola de gamba, was the thing he had missed above all else during his time away. Music soothed him and cleared his mind when he needed to concentrate, and although Isabella – the lady who had provided him with the hat and other comforts in Portugal – had arranged for him to borrow an instrument, it was not the same as playing his own. He took the letters from Ellis as his landlord locked the front door behind them.

There were five messages, which included three from his family in Buckinghamshire. He opened these first and scanned them quickly, afraid, as always, that a missive from home might carry bad news. All was well, though, and his brother was only demanding to know why he had not written. The fourth note was from his friend, the surveyor–mathematician William Leybourn, inviting him to dine with him and the woman he intended to

9

marry. A date of the twentieth of July was scrawled at the bottom, and Chaloner wondered whether he might find Leybourn wed when he went to visit. He hoped so: Leybourn was always whining about not having a wife.

The fifth and last had been written just two days before, and was from a musician called Thomas Maylord. Maylord had been a close friend of Chaloner's father, and had played for Oliver Cromwell's court; when the Commonwealth had collapsed and King Charles II had reclaimed his throne three years before, Maylord had somehow managed to persuade the Royalists to keep him on. The letter was brief, and begged the spy for a meeting at his earliest convenience. The tone was curt, almost frightened, and very unlike the amiable violist. It was unsettling, and Chaloner supposed he had better find out what was distressing the old man as soon as he could.

St Dunstan-in-the-West was a large, stalwart church with a big square tower and a walled graveyard that jutted out into Fleet Street – much to the annoyance of carters and hackney-drivers, who tended to collide with it in foggy weather. It was full that morning, as people crowded inside to hear Rector Thompson preach a sermon about original sin. It was probably an erudite and well-argued discourse, but Thompson mumbled and there were so many babies and small children screaming that very little of his homily could be heard. Chaloner leaned against a pillar, folded his arms and thought that obligatory appearances at Sunday services was one aspect of home he had not missed at all.

Also bored, Ellis began to tell Chaloner about the foul weather that had beset the city while the spy had been away. Chaloner glanced around and saw the landlord was not the only one to be talking while Thompson pontificated in his pulpit. Behind them, two merchants discussed the imminent arrival of a consignment of French wine, while the man in front had his arms around two women, and was enjoying a conversation that was bawdy and far from private.

'You did not say where you have been,' said Ellis, when Chaloner made no comment on his dreary monologue of storms, rain and drizzle. 'Was it far?'

'I visited Dover,' replied Chaloner ambiguously. He was fortunate in that Ellis seldom quizzed him about the odd hours he kept, or the disguises he often donned. The landlord believed him to be a victualling clerk for the Admiralty, an occupation so staid and dull that few people ever wanted to know about it. Unfortunately, though, even Ellis's incurious nature was goaded into asking about a sudden and abrupt departure that had lasted nigh on four months.

'Dover?' echoed Ellis, scratching his head. There were lice in his periwig. 'In Kent?'

'The navy has business there,' hedged Chaloner. Careful phrasing meant he was not actually lying, because his ship *had* stopped in Dover before sailing for Lisbon. He supposed there was no reason why he should not tell people that he had been on official business in Portugal and Spain, but he had been trained to keep confidences to a minimum and, after a decade in espionage, it was a difficult habit to break.

'There is a big castle in Dover,' said Ellis, as if he imagined his tenant might not have noticed it. 'It will be our first line of defence when the Dutch invade. I was in the Turk's Head Coffee House last night, and it was

11

full of talk about the great flotilla of boats the Dutch is building, ready to fight us.'

'They do not need to build anything,' said Chaloner, who had spent several years undercover in Holland. 'They already have a great navy. And, unlike ours, it is manned by sailors who have been paid, and is equipped with ships that are actually seaworthy.'

Ellis shook his head. 'The government should spend more money on defending us from foreigners, and less on chasing phantom rebels in the north of England. Have you been reading the newsbooks? The new editor, Roger L'Estrange, wants us to believe that Yorkshire is trying to start another civil war. He is obsessed with men he calls "phanatiques".'

'Right,' said Chaloner vaguely, reluctant to admit that he had not seen a newsbook – an eight-page 'news-paper' produced by the government for the general public – since June *or* that he had never heard of Roger L'Estrange. He did not want to startle Ellis into an interrogation by displaying a total ignorance of current affairs.

'L'Estrange is something of a phanatique himself, if you ask me,' Ellis went on disapprovingly. 'Someone should tell him the newsbooks were *not* founded to provide him with an opportunity to rant, but to disseminate interesting information to readers. I want to know who has died, been promoted or robbed in *London*, not L'Estrange's perverted opinions about Yorkshire. And as for that piece about the Swiss ambassador – well, who *cares* what a foreign diplomat was given to eat in France?'

'True,' said Chaloner, supposing he had better spend a few hours reading, to catch up.

'I am pleased to see you home again,' said Ellis, searching

12

for a subject that would elicit more than monosyllabic answers. 'You said you might be gone a month, but it was four times that, and I was beginning to think you had decided to lodge elsewhere.'

Chaloner thought back to the blossom-scented June morning when he had received the message that ordered him to go immediately to White Hall. Such summons were not unusual from his employer, and he had not thought much about it. Like many politicians, the Earl of Clarendon – currently Lord Chancellor – had accumulated plenty of enemies during his life, and relied on his spy to provide him with information that would allow him to stay one step ahead of them. However, it had not been Clarendon who had sent for him, then dispatched him on a long and dangerous mission to the Iberian Peninsula. It had been the Queen – and no one refused the 'request' of a monarch, even though Chaloner had been reluctant to leave London. He smiled absently at Ellis, then made a show of listening to the sermon. Ellis sighed at his tenant's uncommunicative manner, but did not press him further.

When the service was over, the congregation flooded into Fleet Street and Ellis went to join cronies from his coffee-house. They immediately began a spirited debate about a newsbook editorial that described Quakers as 'licentious and incorrigible'; some thought the epithet accurate, while others claimed they would make up their own minds and did not need L'Estrange telling them what to think. Chaloner began to walk to White Hall, aware that his Earl would want to know he was home at last. The rain had stopped, although it had left Fleet Street a soft carpet of mud, and he was astonished by the lively bustle as traders hawked their wares. There had been few secular activities allowed on the Sabbath in Catholic Spain, and the contrast was startling.

'God will send a great pestilence,' bawled a street-preacher, who evidently thought the same. He stood on a crate in the middle of the road, and risked life and limb as traffic surged around him. 'There is plague in Venice, and He will inflict one on London unless you repent.'

'He has already sent one,' quipped a leatherworker's apprentice, as he staggered by with a load of cured pelts balanced on his head. 'Half the Court has French pox, so I have heard.'

People laughed, and Chaloner was impressed when the lad managed a cheeky bow without dropping what he was carrying. The preacher scowled at him, and muttered that God would be including cocky apprentices among His list of targets when the plague arrived in the city.

Chaloner hurried on, warned by a rank, acrid smell that he was approaching the Rainbow Coffee House, an establishment infamous for the 'noisome stenches' associated with its roasting beans. Suddenly, the door was flung open and a man stalked out. He was tall, lean and elegantly dressed, and a pair of outrageously large gold rings dangled from his ears. His handsome, but cruel, face was dark with fury, and he gripped the hilt of his sword as though he itched to run someone through with it. Chaloner thought he looked like a pirate – dangerous and unpredictable.

Moments later, the Rainbow's door opened a second time, and two more men emerged. Both were clad in the very latest Court fashions, although the spotless white lace that frothed around their knees and their clean shoes told

Chaloner that they had not sloshed through Fleet Street's mud that morning, but had travelled in style – carried in a sedan-chair or a hackney-coach. The shorter of the pair, who sported a long yellow wig, held a newsbook in his hand.

'"Personal lozenges by Theophilus Buckworth for the cure of consumptions, coughs, catarrhs and strongness of breath",' he read in a yell that drew a good deal of attention from passers-by. 'You call that news, L'Estrange?'

The tall man whipped around to face him, while Chaloner noted wryly that, for all London's vast size – it was by far the biggest city in the civilised world – it was still a small place in many ways. Ellis had mentioned a newsbook editor called L'Estrange, and suddenly, here he was. Not wanting to be caught in the middle of a spat that looked set to turn violent, Chaloner stepped into an alley, joining a soot-faced lad who was disposing of a bucket of coffee-grounds there. The youth scattered his reeking, gritty pile by kicking it, and the stench of decay told Chaloner that the lane had been used as a depository for the Rainbow's unwanted by-products for years. The coffee-boy pulled a pipe from his pocket and watched with interest as L'Estrange strode towards his tormentor.

'That particular notice had nothing to do with me,' he snarled. 'My assistant inserted it without my knowledge.'

'I see,' drawled the yellow-wigged man, exchanging a smirk with his dashing companion. 'So, you admit you have no control over what is published in your newsbooks, do you? That explains a good deal – such as why they contain all manner of dross about the Swiss ambassador's dinner in Paris, but nothing about the dealings of our own government.'

The coffee-boy grinned conspiratorially, and nudged Chaloner with his elbow. 'They have been at it all morning,' he whispered.

'At what?'

'Squabbling. L'Estrange edits the newsbooks – although *they* hold little to interest the educated man, except their lists of recently stolen horses; the rest is given over to L'Estrange's tirades against phanatiques. The fat fellow with the yellow wig is Henry Muddiman.'

'Who is Muddiman?' asked Chaloner, aware, even as he spoke, that this was a question which exposed him as an outsider. Unfortunately, it was true. His postings to spy overseas, first for Cromwell and then for the King, meant the time he had spent in London was limited to a few weeks. He was a stranger in his own land, which was sometimes a serious impediment to his work. He knew he could rectify the situation – but only if his masters would stop sending him abroad.

'Muddiman was L'Estrange's predecessor at the newsbooks,' explained the coffee-boy, looking at him askance. 'Everyone knows that.'

'Oh, yes,' said Chaloner, frowning as vague memories of the man's name and the nature of his business began to surface. Muddiman had produced newsbooks during the Commonwealth, and the King had kept him on after the Restoration. 'I remember now.'

'Muddiman was ousted for political reasons, and the pair now hate each other with a passion. These days, Muddiman produces news*letters*, which are different to news*books*, as you will know.' The lad shot Chaloner another odd glance, not sure if he was assuming too much.

'Newsbooks are printed,' supplied Chaloner, to show

16

he was not totally clueless. 'Newsletters are handwritten. Printed material is subject to government censorship; handwritten material is not.'

'Precisely – which means the news*letters* are a lot more interesting to read. Of course, Muddiman's epistles are expensive – more than five pounds a year! – but they contain real information for the discerning gentleman.'

From the way he spoke, Chaloner surmised that the boy considered himself familiar with 'real information'. He was probably right: coffee houses were hubs of news and gossip, and working in one doubtless meant the youth was one of the best informed people in the city. Chaloner edged deeper into the shadows when L'Estrange drew his sword.

'L'Estrange should learn to control his temper,' the boy went on, his tone disapproving. 'One does not debate with *weapons*, not at the Rainbow. We deplore that sort of loutishness, which is why he has been asked to leave. And Muddiman should not have followed him outside, either, because now L'Estrange will try to skewer him. You just watch and see if I am right.'

'You speak as much rubbish as you print,' said Muddiman, addressing his rival disdainfully. Chaloner was not sure he would have adopted such an attitude towards a man with a drawn sword, especially one who was clearly longing to put it to use. 'You are nothing but wind.'

'You insolent—' L'Estrange's wild lunge was blocked by Muddiman's companion, and their two blades slid up each other in a squeal of protesting metal. The Rainbow's patrons had seen what was happening through the windows, and friends hurried out to separate the combatants.

The coffee-boy tutted. 'There is not enough room in London for *two* greedy, ambitious newsmongers. One of them will be dead before the year is out, you mark my words.'

Bells were ringing all over the city, from the great bass toll of St Paul's Cathedral to the musical jangle of St Clement Danes, as Chaloner resumed his walk to White Hall. He threaded his way through the inevitable congestion at Temple Bar – the narrow gate that divided Fleet Street from The Strand – and headed for Charing Cross. Carriages with prancing horses ferried courtiers and officials between state duties and their fine residences, although judging from the dissipated appearance of some passengers, the duties had been more closely allied to a night of debauchery than to papers and committees.

Chaloner turned south along King Street, and entered the palace by the main gate. The porter was reading a leaflet that condemned the immoral activities that took place in and around Smithfield. However, seeing the rapt gleam in the man's eye, Chaloner suspected the lurid descriptions of the various vices on offer would do more to encourage the fellow to visit the area than to arouse any feelings of righteous distaste. Indeed, having scanned a few of the phrases on the back, Chaloner was tempted to go himself.

Once the porter had waved him through the gate, Chaloner's first inclination was to hunt out Maylord. The musician's letter had bothered him, and he wanted to know what had prompted the old man to pen such an urgent-sounding missive. But White Hall thrived on gossip, and the Earl of Clarendon would not be pleased to hear from some tattling official that his spy had finally returned home and had not made him his first port of call. So, as duty had to come before meeting old friends, Chaloner made his way to the Stone Gallery.

The Stone Gallery was a long corridor at the heart of White Hall. Its floor comprised sandstone slabs, like a cloister, and its arched windows further enhanced its monastic ambience. Its occupants put paid to any illusion of monkish virtue, though. The room rang with coarse laughter, because someone was telling an improbably lewd tale about the Duke of Buckingham's latest conquest. Some nobles wandered about in night-gowns and bed-caps, affecting exaggerated yawns to let everyone know they had been out carousing the night before. Others were dressed, but their clothes were so laden with ruffles, lace and pleats that even the more temperate of them looked debauched.

Chaloner walked the length of the chamber looking for his Earl, nodding to the occasional acquaintance, but the Lord Chancellor was not among the chattering throng, so he went to his offices instead. These comprised a suite of rooms overlooking the elegantly manicured Privy Garden. In a small, windowless room that was more cupboard than chamber sat the Earl's secretary, John Bulteel, copying figures of expenditure into a ledger. Bulteel was a timid, unhealthy-looking clerk who rarely spoke above a whisper and who always seemed on the verge of exhaustion. He smiled when he saw Chaloner, revealing brown, crooked teeth that probably gave him a lot of trouble.

'The Earl is not here, Heyden,' he said. 'It is Sunday.'

Thomas Heyden was Chaloner's favourite alias, and one he always used at Court. Because his uncle had been one of the men who had signed the first King Charles's death warrant, Chaloner was a name best kept quiet

19

until the frenzy of hatred against the regicides had faded. 'Is he at church, then?' he asked. 'Should I return tomorrow?'

'No, he will certainly want to see you today. He had your letter telling him you would be home before the end of the month, and said it would not be a moment too soon. He did not expect the Queen's business to take quite so long, and is not very pleased about it, to be frank.'

'He told me to go,' objected Chaloner. 'I wanted to stay in London.'

'I know that, but he resents the fact that you were not here when he needed you.' Bulteel raised his hand when the spy started to protest again. 'It *is* unfair, and I am not saying he is right – I am just warning you that you may face a cool reception when you meet. Do you remember where he lives? In the building called Worcester House on The Strand. You cannot miss it – it is a great Tudor monstrosity with some part that is always falling down.'

Chaloner was startled by the elaborate description of a house he had visited dozens of times. 'I have only been gone four months, Bulteel – not long enough to forget that sort of thing.'

Bulteel gave his wan, unhappy smile. 'It feels more like four years, but then time passes so slowly here, especially when His Lordship is suffering from the gout. It makes him terribly irritable.'

Grimly, Chaloner recalled that gout made the Lord Chancellor a lot more than just 'irritable'. 'He has been venting his temper on you, has he? Because he is unwell?'

Bulteel winced. 'His ailment has not plagued him as badly as it did in the winter, but his temper has not improved, even so. Watch what you say, and try not to be insolent if you can help it. You have a cynical tongue, and he is less inclined to overlook that sort of thing when his legs are hurting.'

As Chaloner turned to leave, the glitter of gold caught his eye; something had fallen between the wall and the table. When he bent to retrieve it, he found himself holding an elaborate pendant, which was studded with jewels that were probably rubies. He handed it to the clerk.

'I imagine someone will be missing this. Is it yours?'

Bulteel gazed at it in astonishment. 'It is Lady Clarendon's love locket! She lost it last week, and the Earl and I spent *hours* hunting for it. Eventually, he decided it must have been stolen. Well, actually, he thought *I* had taken it, if you want the truth. They will both be pleased to see it safe.'

'The Earl will owe you an apology when you give it back, then.'

Bulteel regarded it wistfully. 'I doubt he will bother. But you found it, so you should be the one to take the credit for its discovery. It will earn you his good graces.'

'Do you think I need his good graces?' asked Chaloner, shaking his head when the secretary attempted to pass the bauble back again. He did not want to walk out of White Hall with a valuable piece of jewellery; it was the sort of thing that landed men in trouble.

Bulteel smiled sadly. 'We all do. This *is* White Hall, after all.'

Chaloner was crossing the expanse of open space called the Palace Court, intending to visit Worcester House straight away, when he saw a man called Thomas

21

Greeting, who basked in the lofty title of Musician in Ordinary to the King's Private Music. Greeting was a handsome, grey-haired fellow in his forties, whose splendid attire and confident swagger made him more courtier than entertainer. He was in great demand as tutor to the wealthy, because he specialised in teaching the flageolet, which was an easy instrument to master. He was ambitious, greedy and Chaloner considered him deceitful.

'Heyden,' said Greeting pleasantly. 'What news?'

'What news?' was the accepted salute for anyone entering a coffee-house, and Chaloner supposed the musician was showing himself to be a man of culture by using it. He did notice, however, that Greeting's clothes were showing signs of wear up close, and that his elegant shoes needed re-heeling.

'I hear Theophilus Buckworth's lozenges are good for ensuring sweetness of the breath,' he replied flippantly, thinking about the altercation outside the Rainbow Coffee House.

Greeting raised his eyebrows. 'You have been reading the newsbooks, have you? It is scandalous that L'Estrange is allowed to fill them with rubbish such as that – men *do* spend hard-earned cash on the things, after all. Not me, of course. *I* cannot afford such luxuries, not on the salary White Hall pays me. I am all but destitute, if you want the truth.'

'I am sorry to hear it.' Chaloner knew how he felt – his own worldly wealth at that moment comprised sixpence. He only hoped the clerks at the Accompting House – who did not work on Sundays – would not be difficult when he went to claim his back-pay the following morning.

22

'I live in constant fear of arrest for debt,' Greeting went on bitterly. 'And I have been forced to move from my lovely house near Lambeth Palace to a hovel in Smithfield. Still, such is the lot of a lowly Court musician.'

'Speaking of musicians, have you seen Maylord today? He wants to meet me.'

Greeting's eyes narrowed. 'Have you been away? Yes, you must have been, because I have not seen you since that trouble involving the barber-surgeons last spring. You had some sort of set-to with Spymaster Williamson, and then you very wisely disappeared.'

Chaloner was bemused. 'You think I ran away?'

Greeting shrugged. 'I would, had *I* incurred Williamson's displeasure. Our new Spymaster is not a man to cross, and folk do so at their peril. Several bold fellows are now banished to remote villages for speaking their minds, although at least they are alive to reflect on their folly. Not all his enemies are allowed to live, so I have heard.'

'Williamson kills men he does not like?' Chaloner was not sure he believed it. Spymasters were powerful men, with a lot of dubious resources at their fingertips, but only a very stupid one would use them for personal vendettas, and Williamson was far from stupid.

Greeting looked uncomfortable. 'We should not be discussing such a topic, especially in White Hall. Nonetheless, I urge you to be careful. He does not like you – I heard him say so myself.'

'That was indiscreet of him,' said Chaloner disapprovingly. He could not imagine Cromwell's old Spymaster, John Thurloe, ever making such a comment in front of a loose-tongued man like Greeting. Of course, Thurloe's attitude to his work had been efficient and professional, and Williamson fell far short by comparison. 'What did he say, exactly?'

Greeting shrugged. 'Just that you were involved in the untimely death of a friend, and he resents you for it. I would stay low, if I were you.'

Chaloner hoped the Earl's next commission would allow him to do so. And while it was true that one of Williamson's cronies had met a violent end in Chaloner's company, it had not been the spy's fault. He felt it was unreasonable of Williamson to blame him for the mishap.

'Maylord,' he prompted. 'Does he still live on Thames Street?'

Greeting frowned. 'I had forgotten you and he were acquainted. He taught your father the viol, I understand, and was kind to you when you first arrived in London. He was a good man, and we all miss him. He died on Friday.'

Chaloner stared at him in shock. 'No! I do not believe you.'

Greeting's expression was sympathetic. 'It is true, although I sincerely wish it were otherwise. He died of eating cucumbers.'

Chaloner gaped at him. Like all Englishmen, he knew cucumbers could be dangerous when eaten raw, but he had never heard of anyone actually dying from them. And surely *Maylord* could not be dead? Chaloner had known him all his life, and loved the old man's sweet temper and innate decency. 'He died on Friday?' he asked, struggling to keep his voice steady.

'Friday evening. He had been asking after you, too.'

'Asking after me when? The day he died?'

Greeting shook his head. 'Earlier – when he and I

24

performed in Smithfield last Wednesday. He wanted to know if I had seen you, and was oddly distressed when I told him I had not.'

'Do you know why?'

Greeting shook his head again. 'But something was troubling the poor old devil, and it is a pity you were not here, because he clearly needed a friend. What do *you* think was upsetting him? Something to do with his music?'

'I have no idea,' said Chaloner, wishing with all his heart that he had been on hand to answer the old man's call for help. His fingers curled tightly around the letter in his pocket. 'And now I probably never will.'

Greeting was silent for a moment, then spoke softly. 'He recently left his Thames Street cottage and took rooms at the Rhenish Wine House in Westminster. He said his move was a secret, and his closest friend – who you will recall is old Smegergill the virginals player – said he would not even tell *him* where he had gone.'

'Yet he told you?' asked Chaloner, rather sceptically. He still found it hard to believe that Maylord would have chosen Greeting as a confidant.

Greeting was offended. 'Maylord liked me. When I asked him why he had left Thames Street, he told me he wanted to be nearer White Hall, but I am sure he was not telling the truth. I suspect it was all connected to whatever was bothering him.'

Chaloner regarded him unhappily. Maylord had loved his house, and would not have left it without good cause. The spy was deeply sorry that his friend had spent his last few days in a state of such agitation.

'I had better go,' said Greeting, when Chaloner did

not speak. 'The King has invited a party of mathematicians to meet him, and my consort – the little group of musicians under my direction – has been hired to play for the occasion. There is a fear that these worthy scientists may become tongue-tied with awe in His Majesty's presence, and we are commissioned to fill any awkward silences with timely noise.'

Chaloner watched him go, feeling grief settle in the pit of his stomach. He felt something else, too – resentment that circumstances had prevented him from being there for Maylord, and guilt that he had let down a friend. He took a deep breath and forced his thoughts back to his White Hall duties, and the Earl.

He left the palace, and headed for The Strand, where the south side of the road was lined with handsome mansions, and the north side was faced with shops and mean dwellings of the kind that were owned by the poorer kind of tradesmen. Worcester House was not the finest home in the area, but it was smart enough to provide an imposing residence for a lord chancellor. It was mostly Tudor, boasting a forest of twisted, ornamental chimney-pots, stone mullions that were stained black with age, and a massive iron-studded gate.

Chaloner walked up the path, which was bordered by viciously trimmed little hedges, and knocked on the door. He was shown into a pleasant, lavender-scented chamber overlooking the gardens and asked to wait. He expected the Earl to finish what he was doing before deigning to meet a mere retainer, and was surprised when the great man bustled in just a few moments later.

England's Lord Chancellor was a fussy, pedantic man, whose prim morals did not make him popular with the

26

dissipated Court; the younger nobles mocked his prudery, and he had earned himself a reputation for being a killjoy. His appearance did not help, either: he was short, fat and wore overly ornate clothes that did not suit his stout frame. He had grown bigger since Chaloner had left for Lisbon, a result of a sedentary lifestyle and the Court's rich food. That morning, he wore a massive blond periwig, with a dark red coat and matching satin breeches. Lace foamed at his neck, partly concealing his array of chins.

'Heyden!' he cried, touching the spy's shoulder in a rare gesture of affection. Yet as soon as it was made, he seemed to regret it, because he became businesslike and aloof. 'When did you return?'

'Last night, sir, but too late to visit you. You would have been in bed.'

'I doubt it,' replied Clarendon, indicating his spy was to sit next to him on the window-seat. 'I am up all hours with affairs of state. Do you recall that feud I was having with the Earl of Bristol? Well, after you had gone, he tried to impeach me *in Parliament*! He accused me of all manner of false crimes, but the House of Lords saw through his lies, and he is now banished to France.'

Chaloner nodded. He had heard the stories on his way home, and had been pleased: the flight of Bristol would mean one fewer enemy for him to worry about when he resumed the business of protecting his Earl.

'My fortunes are on the rise again, thank God,' Clarendon went on. 'But unfortunately, my *other* foes – namely the Duke of Buckingham and the King's favourite mistress – wait like vultures for me to make a mistake.'

Chaloner was not surprised; the Earl's aloof manners had earned him a lot of enemies in White Hall. 'I am sorry to hear that, sir.'

27

'Today, however,' said the Earl with an unfriendly look, 'we had better talk about you. You abandoned me shamefully in June. The Queen summoned you to meet her, and you accepted the assignment she offered without once asking *me* whether it was convenient for you to go.'

Chaloner was taken aback by this version of events. 'That is not quite true, sir. I told Her Majesty that I was not the right man for the task she had in mind, and pointed out that I had duties here in London, but you ordered me to do as she asked.'

The Earl glared at him. 'Well, of course I did when she was there, man! She asked if she might borrow you, and I could hardly refuse the request of a queen, could I? I am the Lord Chancellor, for God's sake – a servant of the Crown. However, you should have thought of a reason to decline, and I am angry that you did not bother. I feel it was a betrayal.'

Chaloner suspected the Earl saw betrayal everywhere after what he had been through with Bristol. But what had happened in June was not his fault, and he felt he was being unfairly accused.

'I did not ask to be summoned by her. I did not ask to go to Lisbon, either.'

Clarendon continued to glare. 'She noticed you because you had the audacity to smile at her on an occasion when she felt the city was hostile towards her. She asked your name, and I just happened to mention that you knew Portuguese – her native language – as a point of conversation. I did not imagine for a moment that she would demand your services. It was not what I intended at all.'

'No, sir,' said Chaloner, thinking the Earl should have

28

kept his mouth shut about his servant's skills, if he had not wanted him poached.

'And then news came about a fierce battle between Portugal and Spain, and she decided she needed intelligence from her own agent, a man she could trust. So off you went. She was pleased by what you did, by the way – uncovering that treacherous duke, who was undermining Portugal by feeding secrets to Spain – and I confess your reports were useful to me in determining certain points of foreign policy. But you should not have gone. *I* needed you here.'

Chaloner recalled the speed with which he had been dispatched – less than an hour to return to his lodgings, pack a few essentials and board the Lisbon-bound ship. He had rushed his preparations, because he had wanted a few moments to scribble a brief message to John Thurloe at Lincoln's Inn – what the Queen had asked him to do was fraught with peril, and he had wanted *one* friend to know what had happened to him, in case he failed to return. He had been right to take such a precaution, because the escapade had transpired to be one of the most dangerous things he had ever done. And in an occupation like his, where risk was an everyday occurrence, that was saying a good deal.

'You arranged my passage on that particular boat, sir,' he pointed out, stubbornly refusing to accept all the blame. 'Had you chosen a later one, we could have discussed—'

The Earl's scowl deepened. 'Lord, you are insolent! I am angry with you, but do you attempt to placate me with some suitable grovelling? No! You antagonise me with impudent observations about my past actions. I imagine you expect me to employ you again, but I am

29

not sure I want a man who so eagerly races off to do the bidding of someone else.'

'But you *told* me to go,' objected Chaloner, becoming alarmed. Because he had been a spy for Cromwell's regime, the King's government was wary of him, and would never employ him in its intelligence service. Luckily, the Earl was capable of recognising talent when he saw it, and was willing to overlook former allegiances. However, if he changed his mind, then Chaloner was in trouble, because no one else would hire him, and he was qualified to do very little else. 'Indeed, you *ordered* it.'

'As I said, I assumed you would be clever enough to devise an excuse that would keep you at my side,' snapped the Earl. 'I suppose you were seduced by the money she gave you for your expenses, and by the reward she promised you on your return.'

'Speaking of which, I have sixpence left. Do you think you could arrange an audience with her? The rent is overdue and the cupboard is bare.'

Clarendon looked a little spiteful. 'Her Majesty is unwell, and the physicians are not letting anyone see her at the moment, so you will have to wait. Let us hope her illness does not cause her to forget her promises. It would be a pity to have risked your life and livelihood for a profit of sixpence.'

Chaloner decided he had better change the subject before the disagreement saw him in even deeper water. 'Your secretary says there is something you would like me to do, sir. How may I help?'

'Does he indeed?' muttered the Earl venomously. 'Well, there is something, as it so happens.'

'What?' asked Chaloner, when his master did not elaborate.

The Earl waved his hand carelessly. Chaloner had learned this was a bad sign, and that a dismissive flap from the Lord Chancellor invariably meant his spy was going to be asked to do something that was dangerous, only marginally legal, or both.

'Have you heard about the new-style government news-books that came into being in August? One is called *The Intelligencer*, and it is published on Mondays. The other is called *The Newes*, and it comes out on Thursdays. They are edited by a man named L'Estrange, and Londoners complain that they are characterised by a marked absence of domestic news.'

'Before I left, the newsbooks had different names, and were edited by Henry Muddiman.'

'Things change fast in London,' said Clarendon point-edly. 'Sneak away for four months, and you will return to find nothing as you left it. But we are supposed to be talking about my business, not yours. *The Intelligencer* and *The Newes* superseded Muddiman's publications, and they are now the only two newsbooks in the country. Spymaster Williamson appointed L'Estrange to edit them. He made him Surveyor of the Press, too.'

'The posts of official censor and chief journalist are held by the same man?' Chaloner tried not to sound shocked. It was a deplorable state of affairs, because it meant any 'intelligence' or 'newes' printed would be what the government had decided the public could have. He was surprised Williamson had been allowed to get away with it. However, it certainly explained why the newsbooks contained nothing of home affairs – the government did not want people to know what it was up to.

The Earl shot him a rueful glance. 'It was not my idea,

I assure you. Of course I am happy for the general populace to be kept in the dark about matters it cannot possibly comprehend, but this is too brazen an approach. And it is having a negative effect, in that anything we publish now is automatically regarded as political propaganda and is taken with a pinch of salt.'

'And rightly so, because that is exactly what it will be. Williamson's decision is a foolish one. A man of his intellect should know better.'

The Earl sighed. 'Williamson ousted Muddiman with a shocking bit of deviousness, and appointed L'Estrange in his place. L'Estrange is totally loyal to the government, but he is too opinionated to be a good journalist. Muddiman is a far better newsman, and we should have left him alone.'

'I saw Muddiman and L'Estrange arguing today, about whether an advertisement for lozenges can be classified as an item of news.'

'I am not surprised – Muddiman has high standards of news-telling, while L'Estrange will include anything that uses up space. They differ fundamentally.'

'What exactly would you like me to do, sir?'

'L'Estrange visited me on Wednesday, and said one of his newsbook minions – a fellow called Thomas Newburne – is dead under peculiar circumstances. I would like you to look into the matter.'

Chaloner did not think that was a good idea. 'If Newburne was working for L'Estrange, then it means he was a government employee and his death will come under Spymaster Williamson's jurisdiction. Williamson already dislikes me, and will be angry if I interfere.'

'I am the Lord Chancellor of England, so you will interfere if I tell you to,' snapped Clarendon. 'I do not

32

care if Williamson is angry or not. Besides, I am sure he will conduct his own enquiry.'

'Will he not share his conclusions with you?'

'I would not trust them if he did,' snorted the Earl. 'The more I learn about Williamson, the less I respect his judgement. He is too devious for his own good, and I do not approve of him dismissing a respected newsman like Muddiman *or* the dual appointment he foisted on L'Estrange.'

'L'Estrange could have refused one of them.'

'You do not "refuse" Williamson! Besides, I do not think L'Estrange has very good judgement, either. I like the man, and consider him an ally, but he is not very sensible.'

Sensible men did not draw their swords as a means to resolving arguments, so Chaloner suspected the Earl was right. He considered the 'minion' whose death he was supposed to investigate. 'What happened to Newburne? How did he die?'

'He passed away at the Smithfield Market. Have you heard of it?'

'Of course,' replied Chaloner, startled by the question.

The Earl grimaced. 'You have spent so much time away that you seem more foreigner than Englishman most of the time. But let us return to Smithfield. Apart from being a venue for selling livestock, especially horses, it is also an area of great vice, where criminals roam in gangs. The biggest and most powerful clan calls itself the Hectors.'

Chaloner was not sure what the Earl was trying to tell him. 'Newburne was killed by Hectors?'

'Actually, no – at least, I do not think so. I was just trying to give you an impression of the area in which you will be working. Newburne was not killed by louts, as far as I understand the situation. He was killed by cucumbers.'

Chaloner's thoughts whirled in confusion. Surely it was unusual for *two* people to expire from ingesting cucumbers in such a short period of time – Newburne on Wednesday and Maylord two days later? Had a bad batch been hawked around London, or were Newburne and Maylord just gluttons for that particular fruit? He was careful to keep his expression neutral – no good spy ever revealed what he was thinking – as he continued to question Clarendon.

'Have you heard of any other cases of cucumber poisoning recently, sir?'

The Earl raised his eyebrows in surprise. 'No, but we all know they should be avoided, and I cannot imagine why Newburne should have been scoffing one. They are nasty, bitter things.'

'Have there been any other odd deaths lately, then?' Chaloner pressed. 'Inexplicable or—'

'Of course there have! This is London, and people die of strange things all the time. Why are you asking such questions? It is Newburne I want you to explore, not the entire city.'

'Because Newburne's death may not be an isolated event, especially if L'Estrange and Muddiman are embroiled in a feud. If there have been other incidents, it would be helpful to know about them before I start investigating.'

'I am sure L'Estrange would have mentioned other unusual deaths, if there were any. However, you will find Newburne's demise *is* an isolated event, so do not make it more complex than it is.'

'Why do you want to know what happened to Newburne, sir?' Chaloner's instincts – usually reliable – told him the Earl was holding something back. However, if he was going to be trespassing on Williamson's territory, then he needed the whole truth. 'Because of your friendship with L'Estrange? Because you want to antagonise Williamson? Or is there another reason?'

The Earl grimaced. 'Your blunt tongue will land you in serious trouble one day, Heyden. It is a good thing you are not a politician – you would be dead or disgraced in a week.'

'Newburne, sir,' prompted Chaloner, refusing to be sidetracked.

The Earl sighed in a long-suffering manner. 'Very well. During the wars, L'Estrange published some pro-Royalist pamphlets at considerable risk – and expense – to himself. He helped our cause immeasurably then, and I would like to return the favour now. I always remember my friends.'

There was a hesitancy in his reply that told Chaloner he still did not have the complete answer, but there was only so far he could push the man. 'Will you tell me what you know about Newburne?'

'He was a solicitor, employed by L'Estrange to hunt out illegal publications. You must have heard of him. It was he who brought about the saying "Arise, Tom Newburne".'

Chaloner regarded him blankly. 'What does that mean?'

The Earl became prissy. 'I use it as an expletive, although I avoid foul language, as a rule.'

'That is foul language?'

'Yes, when spoken with feeling,' replied Clarendon

tartly. 'And please do not offer to teach me a few epithets you consider more apposite, because coarse swearing is anathema to me.'

The interview was becoming a bit of a trial, and Chaloner was still tired after his long journey. Manfully, he tried to stifle his exasperation. 'Is there anything else?'

Clarendon rattled on as if he had not spoken. 'I am surprised you have never come across the saying, although I suppose you have not had much chance to familiarise yourself with London customs, given that you have not deigned to live here for more than a few weeks in the last decade. But what else can I tell you about Newburne? He was about fifty years of age, and very corrupt. He was unethical in a number of ways, but one of his most brazen was in taking bribes from printers and booksellers to keep quiet about pamphlets published without a royal license. Oh, and he had no hair.'

It was a curious combination of facts. 'Did you know him personally?'

Clarendon waved the fat hand again. 'I met him once or twice when I visited L'Estrange. His funeral is on Thursday, so you do not have many days, should you wish to inspect the corpse.'

'So, you think he was murdered,' surmised Chaloner. 'You do not think the cucumber killed him, or you would not suggest I examine the body.'

Clarendon frowned at the remark. 'I do not *know* if he died naturally, Heyden – that is what I want *you* to find out. Of course, you must ask your questions discreetly, because, as you pointed out, Williamson will not appreciate us interfering with a government investigation.'

Chaloner tried one last time to elicit the whole truth from the man. 'Is there anything else I should know?'

'No,' said the Earl briskly. He stood and rubbed his hands together; Chaloner did not think he had ever seen a more furtive gesture. 'You will want to question L'Estrange, of course, but you cannot barge in unannounced, so tell him you have just returned from Spain and Portugal, and that you have intelligence for his newsbooks. You must have learned something there that English readers will find interesting.'

Chaloner was pleasantly surprised. It was a good idea, and would allow him access to Newburne's place of work without arousing suspicion. 'I can think of a few odds and ends.'

'Good, although it would be a kindness to the government if these "odds and ends" were actually true. It is embarrassing when a snippet of information is printed, and it later transpires to be a lie – these things are difficult to deny once they are in the public domain, you see. And there is just one more thing before you go.'

'Sir?' Chaloner did not like the sly expression on the Lord Chancellor's face.

'L'Estrange is a man of fierce passions, and he despises phanatiques most of all.'

'Fanatics?'

'Meaning Puritans, Roundheads and regicides. So, watch what you tell him about yourself.'

Chaloner was bemused. 'I am none of those things, sir – especially the latter.'

'But your uncle was a king-killer, and the Chaloner clan is still full of dedicated Parliamentarians. No one in London knows your real name except me, Thurloe and your friend William Leybourn. Make sure it stays that way, because L'Estrange will kill you if he finds out who you are.'

'He is welcome to try,' muttered Chaloner.

The Earl did not hear him. 'You can start your investigation tomorrow. L'Estrange's offices are on Ivy Lane – that is near St Paul's, in case you do not know – and he will be open for business at dawn. Do not forget to keep me informed.'

Chaloner left Worcester House with a vague sense of unease. He was not particularly worried about L'Estrange, but he did not like the notion that there was something he was not being told. Was the Earl deliberately sending him half-prepared into a dangerous situation, to punish him for serving the Queen? Chaloner wanted to believe the Lord Chancellor was above such pettiness, but found he was unable to do so.

Chapter 2

Weak sunshine was beginning to slant through the clouds as Chaloner left Worcester House, and when he glanced down one of the lanes that led to the river, he saw a rainbow shimmering in the dark clouds above Southwark. The ground was sticky from the recent deluge, and a clot of rubbish had blocked one of the drains, so The Strand was flooded with a filthy brown ooze. Chaloner leapt to one side as a cart thundered past, spraying pedestrians with watery filth.

He walked towards Westminster, intending to pay his respects to the dead Maylord. There were at least two Rhenish wine houses in the area, which specialised in the sale of the dry white vintages that were produced around the River Rhine. He had learned from Greeting that Maylord's home was in the oldest of them, a large, venerable building on a narrow lane called Wise's Alley. It was four storeys high, and had vines carved along the front. It had been in the hands of the Genew family for at least sixty years, and was frequented by clerks from White Hall, as well as officials from the Houses of Parliament and the Exchequer.

As soon as he was inside, Chaloner's eyes began to smart. Because it was noon, the tavern was full of people enjoying their midday victuals, and it seemed that every one of them had a pipe; the smoke was so dense that Chaloner could not see the back of the room at all. Men, and a few women, sat at tables reading, drinking pale Rhenish wine, and eating chops or fish. The odour of seafood past its best combined unpleasantly with the stink of burning logs on the hearth and the patrons' wet feet. Someone had dropped a newsbook on the floor, so Chaloner retrieved it, shaking off the excess mud and water. It comprised eight small pages, and proudly declared itself as *The Newes, published for the satisfaction and Information of the People With privilege.* He turned to the back and saw it was printed by 'Thomas Hodgkinson, living in Thames Street, over against Baynard's Castle'.

Unlike a coffee house, there was no expectation for patrons to sit together and be sociable, so he found an empty table, instinctively choosing one where he could sit with his back to the wall. He ordered buttered ale – warm beer mixed with melted butter and spices – and paid for it with a token he had found in his pocket. A chronic shortage of small change had led many taverners to produce their own: they comprised discs of metal or leather that were widely accepted in lieu of real money. Although not strictly legal tender, most Londoners usually had several in their purses at any given time, and most respectable establishments accepted them.

Landlord Genew was a thin, unhealthy man in a clean white apron. It was said that he tasted every cask of wine that was broached, to ensure his customers were never served with wares that were anything less than the best. Chaloner did not think his devotion to quality was doing him much good, because his skin had a yellowish sheen and his eyes were bloodshot. Genew shook his grizzled head sadly when he learned what Chaloner had come to do.

'Poor Maylord. He owned a house in Thames Street, but moved here two weeks ago.'

'Did he say why?'

'He told his friends that he wanted to be near his work at White Hall, but he confided the truth to me. It was to avoid a cousin who visited him at inappropriate hours. He said she wanted to seduce him.'

Chaloner knew Maylord had no family, and wondered why the musician had felt the need to lie. 'Has she been to pay her respects to his body?'

'He lies in St Margaret's Church – my patrons do not like the notion of a corpse rotting above their heads as they drink, so he could not stay here – but the vergers say no kin have been, male or female. Many friends have, though. The vergers have been all but overwhelmed.'

'He was a popular man,' said Chaloner, assailed by another wave of sadness.

'Even that horrible Spymaster Williamson and his creature Hickes visited, although they were under a moral obligation to put in an appearance, because Maylord was a Court employee.'

'Do you still have his belongings?' asked Chaloner, wondering whether there was something among Maylord's possessions that might give some clue as to what had upset him before he had died. Although the notion of pawing through them was distasteful, he thought Maylord would not have minded, under the circumstances. 'Or have you already let his room?'

Genew was offended. 'Of course not! That would

be deemed as acting with indecent haste. They will remain *in situ* until his funeral next Saturday. It is only one of the attics on the top floor anyway, and the rent is insignificant.'

'Do you know if he was ever visited by a solicitor called Newburne?' asked Chaloner, keen to ascertain whether there was a connection between the two men, other than cucumbers.

'If he had, I would not have let him in,' declared Genew. 'Newburne had fingers in far too many rancid pies, and Maylord would never have endured an acquaintance with a fellow like *him*, anyway.'

'Newburne was involved in illegal activities?'

Genew became uneasy. 'Perhaps they were not illegal as such, but they were unpopular. He used to spy on me – to make sure I only provide *official* newsbooks for my customers to read. Had I bought others, he would have reported me to L'Estrange, and I would have been fined.'

When Genew had gone, Chaloner drank the buttered ale and read *The Newes*. Its front page was dominated by a harangue from the editor about a conspiracy of phanatiques in the north: *Well, gentlemen, after all this Noyse and Bustle, was there really a plot or no, do ye think? That's the plot now, my masters, to persuade the people that there was no Plot at all, and that all this Hurly-burly and alarme was nothing in the whole world but a Trick of State.* Chaloner grimaced. The country was still reeling from two decades of war and regime change, so the last thing it needed was someone in authority braying about conspiracy and rebellion.

Next came a detailed report about a 'sad bay mare with a long tail (if not cut off)' that had been stolen from Mr Sherard Lorinston, grocer of Smithfield. Anyone coming forward with information was promised to be

42

'well satisfied for his pains'. It was tedious stuff, and Chaloner soon lost interest.

The Rhenish Wine House also subscribed to a news*letter* service – the handwritten epistles that were not subject to the same censorship laws as printed news-books, so could contain all manner of items barred from the printing presses. The one that had been left on Chaloner's table was dog-eared and well fingered, indicating it had been read a lot. He saw from the date that it and *The Newes* had been produced the same day, but L'Estrange's official offering had clearly been received with considerably less enthusiasm than the handwritten one. He turned to the back page, and saw it came from the office of Henry Muddiman. The obvious preference for Muddiman's work to L'Estrange's productions indicated that the ousted editor represented a serious challenge to his successor.

'Do not believe everything you read in those things,' whispered a soft voice close behind him.

Chaloner pretended to be surprised, but the truth was that he had noticed someone attempting to creep up on him several minutes before. He also knew, from the clumsy way the man moved, that it was William Leybourn, mathematician, surveyor and bookseller of Monkwell Street, Cripplegate. Leybourn was Chaloner's closest friend in London, a tall, stoop-shouldered man with long straight hair and a hooked nose. He had gained weight since Chaloner had last seen him; his cheeks were rounder, and there was a distinct paunch above the belt that held up his fashionable silken breeches.

'How did you know I was here?' Chaloner asked, returning the surveyor's grin of greeting with genuine pleasure.

43

'We clever spies know how to find a man newly returned to the city,' said Leybourn smugly.

Chaloner ignored the fact that Leybourn was not really a spy – he only dabbled in espionage to help their mutual friend, John Thurloe – and began to assess how he might have been tracked down. 'You are wearing unusually fine clothes, so I surmise you were one of the party of mathematicians who met the King today. Greeting was playing there, and he told you we had met. He mentioned we had discussed Maylord's death, and you made the logical assumption that I would visit his home.'

Leybourn grimaced. 'You make it sound obvious, but it was actually an ingenious piece of deduction. I came as soon as I could politely escape from the King.'

'Why? What is the urgency?'

'You disappear for months, without a word of farewell, and you want to know why friends are eager to see you? Thurloe said you were gone overseas, but refused to say where, and I have been worried. Many countries boil with war and tension, and I doubt whatever you were doing was safe.'

'No,' agreed Chaloner ruefully. 'It was not safe.'

Leybourn clapped him on the shoulder. 'Well, I am pleased to see you home, and I have a lot to tell you. What do you think of the newsbooks, by the way? Or do you prefer the newsletters?'

'Do *you* read the newsbooks?'

Leybourn shot him an arch glance. 'Why would *I* read anything penned by L'Estrange? All he does is rant about matters he does not understand, hoping to earn Williamson's approval and be promoted to some other post beyond his meagre abilities. However, his newsbooks *do* contain notices about stolen horses, which is something in their favour.'

'You mean the advertisements?' asked Chaloner, startled. In Portugal, such snippets were printed at the end of the publications, in smaller type, but in L'Estrange's journals, they were prominently placed between items of news, which lent them an importance they should not have had.

'Most people ignore L'Estrange's pitiful excuse for editorials and *only* read the advertisements. For example, last Monday's *Intelligencer* told me that one Captain Hammond was deprived of a dappled grey gelding near Clapham. Now that *is* interesting.'

'It is?' Chaloner wondered if Leybourn was being facetious.

'Yes, for two reasons. First, it tells me Hammond is in town, which is good to know, because he owes me money. And secondly, I am now aware that I must commiserate with him when we meet. There is a great yearning for news these days, you see – it is a lucrative and booming business.'

'Is it?'

'Oh, yes. These last few months have witnessed a burning desire to know what is happening at home *and* overseas. Of course, if you want real news, you must subscribe to Muddiman's weekly letters.' Leybourn tapped the handwritten sheet in front of Chaloner with a bony forefinger. 'He is a professional journalist, not a pamphleteer like L'Estrange, and so can be trusted to tell the truth.'

'You cannot trust L'Estrange?'

'Of course not! He is the government's mouthpiece, and only fools believe anything *they* say. But suppressing

45

the news is not his only talent. It is his job to censor – which he thinks means "macerate" – every book published, too. You should see what he did to my pamphlet on surveying.'

Chaloner wondered what Leybourn could have written that was controversial; surveying was hardly a subject that would have insurgents champing at the bit. 'What did you do? Tell your readers how to build palaces that will collapse and crush unpopular courtiers?'

'It was almost entirely given over to technical calculations, and needed no editing from an amateur. But edit L'Estrange did, and the result was an incomprehensible jumble that made me look like a half-wit. And I am not the only one to suffer. There were six hundred booksellers in London a couple of years ago, but he fined so many of them for breaking his silly rules, that there are only fifty of us left. His vicious tactics have put many good men in debtors' prison.'

'He is unpopular, then,' said Chaloner, recalling how it was Newburne's task to report wayward booksellers to L'Estrange. It doubtless meant the solicitor – or 'minion' in the Lord Chancellor's words – was held in equal contempt.

'Very. He has gone into business with a fellow called Brome – using Brome's shop as a base for his vile activities. Decent man, Brome, although inclined to be spineless. I cannot imagine he is pleased with the arrangement.'

'He cannot mind that much, or he would tell L'Estrange to leave.'

Leybourn snorted derisive laughter. 'If he did, it would be his last act on Earth. Oh, I am sure Brome is making a pretty penny from L'Estrange, but he will not be happy about it. Money is not everything, after all. There is principle to consider.'

'You seem to know a lot about the situation.'

'People talk and I am a good listener. Why all these questions, Tom? I know one of L'Estrange's toadies – a fellow called Newburne – met an untimely end last week, but I hope you have not been charged to investigate *his* demise.'

'Why should you wish that?'

'Because no one was sorry when he died, and if he was murdered, then there will be a lot of men eager to shake the killer's hand. You do not want to be embroiled in that sort of thing.'

Leybourn's chatter had unsettled Chaloner, and it brought home yet again the fact that the Lord Chancellor was not a good master. Clarendon must have known about L'Estrange's unpopularity, but had not bothered to mention it. The spy wondered whether his initial suspicion had been correct: that the Earl was deliberately sending him into a dangerous situation to teach him a lesson for 'abandoning' him.

'We have not had a dry day since June,' grumbled Leybourn, glancing at the sky as they left the Rhenish Wine House. 'Will you walk to the Westminster Stairs with me, to see the river?'

Chaloner regarded him askance. 'What for?'

'It is the thing Londoners do these days. We have been near catastrophic flood so often, that we have all taken to gazing at Father Thames in our spare moments, to assess his malevolence.'

It was not far, and Chaloner and Leybourn were not the only people to stand along the wharf. The tide was going out, and the water was stained muddy brown from the silt that had been washed into it upstream. They watched a skiff struggling against the current, but not even the encouraging cheers from the Westminster Stairs could give the oarsman the strength he needed to reach the pier, and it was not long before he gave up and allowed himself to be swept back towards the City. His fare would be obliged to walk or take a carriage to his final destination.

Leybourn sniffed at the air. 'Can you smell cakes? There is a baker's boy. Would you like some knot biscuits? I shall pay, as Bulteel tells me you are no longer on the Earl's payroll.'

Chaloner sincerely hoped Bulteel was wrong. 'When did he tell you that?'

'When you first disappeared, and he was describing the Earl's fury that you had accepted a commission from another master. Do you want to borrow a few shillings? You are welcome, but please do not mention it to Mary. She does not approve of me lending money, not even to friends.'

Chaloner waved away the proffered purse. 'Mary?'

Leybourn grinned. 'My wife. I am the happiest man alive.'

'You are married? Why did you not tell me at once, instead of gibbering on about newsbooks and flooded rivers?'

'I was waiting for the right moment.' Leybourn's expression was dreamy. 'I have been wanting a wife for years, because I like the notion of permanent female companionship. Then, last July, Mary visited my shop, and it was love at first sight – for both of us.'

Chaloner was delighted for his friend, not least because

48

Leybourn's idea of charming a lady entailed regaling her with complex scientific formulae, thus giving her an unnerving insight into how she might be expected to spend her evenings as a married woman. Few risked a second encounter, and Chaloner had assumed that Leybourn was one of those men doomed to perpetual bachelorhood. 'When can I meet her?'

'I had better warn her first,' said Leybourn mysteriously. 'But you *must* promise to be nice.'

Chaloner regarded him in surprise; his manners were naturally affable, and most people liked him when they first met, even if his work meant they later revised their opinion. 'I am always nice.'

'On the surface perhaps, but you are often sullen and sharp. However, I do not want you to be *so* personable that she wishes she was with you instead of me. You can aim for something in between – pleasant, but no playing the Adonis.'

'I shall do my best,' said Chaloner, somewhat bemused by the instructions. He changed the subject before he felt compelled to ask why Leybourn should be worried about his wife's fidelity at such an early stage in their relationship. 'Can you tell me anything more about Newburne?'

Leybourn sighed. 'So, the Earl *did* order you to investigate that particular death. I thought as much when you started to quiz me about L'Estrange and the world of publishing. It is not fair: you are almost certain to get into trouble, given the fact that *everyone* despised Newburne.'

'Why was he so hated?'

'Partly because of his work for L'Estrange, and partly because he was so dishonest. A dangerous gang called the Hectors controls Smithfield, and he was its legal

49

advisor. Combined, they made him rich – so much so that he was able to buy a fine house on Old Jewry. He was also accused of being a papist, because he never attended church, but then it was discovered that he missed his Sunday devotions because he was too drunk to get out of bed. Have you never heard the injunction, "Arise, Tom Newburne"?'

'Is that what it means? My Earl said it was an obscenity.'

Leybourn laughed. 'He really is a prim old fool! Did he tell you that Muddiman bought cucumbers from Covent Garden the day before Newburne died? And here you must bear in mind that Newburne worked for L'Estrange – the man to whom Spymaster Williamson gave Muddiman's job as newsbook editor. Do not tell *me* that is not significant!'

Chaloner was thoughtful. 'If Muddiman did kill Newburne, then he was careless to let himself be seen buying the murder weapon. Of course, that assumes it was cucumbers that killed Newburne. I know traditional medicine says they can be harmful, but they are not usually considered deadly.'

'Newburne died at the Smithfield Market, while watching the dancing monkeys. Lord! I wish your Earl had given you something else to do. Newburne was loathsome, and only had one friend, as far as I know – a fellow called Heneage Finch. You can ask him what he thinks happened to Newburne. He lives on Ave Maria Lane, by St Paul's.'

Chaloner watched him eat the knot biscuits. 'You are getting fat.'

Leybourn almost choked. 'And you are thin – sallow, even. Did they not feed you in France?'

Chaloner smiled at the transparent attempt to discover where he had been. 'Not very well.'

50

'Mary prepares a wonderful caudle of wine, eggs, barley and spices. Unfortunately, that is all she can make, so we are obliged to send to the cook-shop most days, and she does not like housework, either. But we are very happy together, despite her . . . domestic shortcomings.'

She sounded singular, and Chaloner's interest was piqued again. 'When were you wed?'

'We are not *wed*, exactly.' Leybourn sounded defensive. 'But we live as man and wife, because when you are in love, you do not need the Church to sanction your devotion. You did not marry Metje, although she inhabited your bed most nights.'

'I did not say—'

'And I wager you availed yourselves of plenty of pretty . . . Danish ladies when you were abroad, too,' Leybourn went on relentlessly. 'Hoards of them, and not one escorted to the altar.'

Chaloner was taken aback by what amounted to an unprovoked attack. 'Steady, Will,' he said, ignoring the surveyor's second attempt to find out where he had been. 'I am not condemning you.'

'Everyone else is, though,' said Leybourn sulkily. 'Well? Tell me about your latest love. I know you have one. I can tell.'

Chaloner's brief but passionate attachment to the lovely Isabella – a Spaniard working for the Portuguese – had been blissful, but his false identity had been exposed when he had trapped the duplicitous duke, and he doubted he would ever see her again. It was a pity, and he raised his hand to touch the hat she had given him, with its cunning bowl of steel.

'Who disapproves of your arrangement?' he asked, declining to talk about her.

Leybourn sniffed. 'Thurloe, my brother and his wife, most of my customers. But I do not care. Mary may not be as pretty as your Metje, but she is mine and she loves me dearly. You never have trouble securing yourself ladies, but it is different for me, and I intend to keep this one.'

'Then I wish you success of it,' said Chaloner soothingly. He watched Leybourn fling away the last of the biscuits, which were immediately snapped up by stray dogs. 'And now I should pay my respects to Maylord before more of the day is lost.'

It began to rain as Chaloner and Leybourn walked from Westminster Stairs to St Margaret's Church, a heavy, drenching downpour that thundered across the cobblestones and gushed from overflowing gutters and pipes. It enlarged the puddles that already spanned the streets, and Leybourn stepped in one that was knee-deep. Chaloner grabbed his arm to stop him from taking a tumble, although the near-accident did nothing to make the surveyor falter in his detailed description about a new and 'exciting' mathematical instrument.

'I would *love* a Gunter's Quadrant,' he concluded wistfully, 'but it is too expensive for the common man. I offered to borrow one for a few weeks and then write a pamphlet about it – I am well respected in my trade, as you know, and people take my recommendations seriously – but its maker is adamant: no money, no measuring stick. Will you break into his shop and steal it for me?'

Chaloner was not entirely sure he was joking. 'He might be suspicious if you suddenly start producing books and publications demonstrating its use.'

Leybourn nodded thoughtfully. 'I would have to modify

it, pass it off as my own. Incidentally, have you visited St Paul's Cathedral recently? You do not need to be a surveyor to see it is unsound, and I told the King today that he should close it before it falls down and kills someone. Christopher Wren submitted some brilliant plans for its rebuilding, but the clerics baulk.'

'I would baulk, too,' said Chaloner, making a dash for St Margaret's porch as the rain came down even harder. 'Wren's design is nasty – like an Italian mausoleum.'

'Rubbish! It is nothing short of brilliant. In fact, if you had any loyalty to your city, you would break into the old cathedral and set it afire. That would put an end to the clergy's procrastination.'

Chaloner raised his eyebrows. 'First, you encourage me to commit burglary and now arson. Do you want me hanged?'

'Not unless you leave me some money in your will. Then I can buy myself a Gunter's Quadrant.'

A verger conducted the visitors to the crypt, where Maylord was not the only dead citizen to have been granted refuge under its gloomy arches. A total of three bodics lay there, all neatly packed in wooden boxes, their faces decorously covered with clean white cloths. The verger explained that many houses in Westminster were small, and it was not always possible to have a corpse at home until a funeral could be arranged. It was all right twenty years ago, he sighed, because then you dicd one day and were in the ground the next. But in these enlightened times, ceremonies were grander and required more time to arrange. A funeral in London was a statement of earthly achievement, and no one wanted to be shoved underground without first showing off all he had accomplished.

'Maylord,' prompted Chaloner.

The verger removed one of the cloths. 'He used to play the organ here when our regular man was indisposed, and he never charged us for it. He was a good soul.'

'Do you know how he died?' asked Chaloner, gazing at the man who had smiled a lot, even during the dark days of the civil wars. Laughter lines were scored around Maylord's eyes and mouth, and Chaloner thought it a terrible pity that the world was deprived of his gentle humour.

'Cucumbers,' replied the verger. 'Did you not hear? It caused quite a stir.'

'How do you know it was cucumbers?'

'They were on a plate in his room, and he was dead on the floor with a piece in his mouth.' The verger regarded him suspiciously. 'You said you were a friend, so how come you do not know?'

'I have been away,' replied Chaloner truthfully. 'He wrote two days ago, asking me to visit him.'

'Then it is a shame you did not come sooner,' said the verger, rather accusingly. 'You might have been able to help him. You know how he was always happy? Well, these last two weeks he was miserable and bad tempered. He snapped at the choirboys for fidgeting, and he told me to mind my own business when I asked him what was wrong. It was something to do with Court, I imagine. It is an evil place, and Maylord was the only decent one among the lot of them.'

'But you do not *know* it was Court business for certain?' pressed Chaloner. The verger shook his head. 'Did he have any particular friends he might have confided in?'

'He had lots, but the closest was William Smegergill

54

– a Court musician, like him. Do you know Smegergill? He has a ravaged complexion, because of a pox when he was a child.'

The description was not familiar, but Chaloner made a mental note to track Smegergill down. 'Did you ever see Maylord with a solicitor called Newburne?'

The verger was disdainful. 'Of course not! Maylord had more taste than to associate with the likes of him. Why do you ask?'

'Because they both died from eating cucumbers.'

'Coincidence,' replied the verger, so promptly that Chaloner knew it was an observation that had been made before. 'I could cite three other men who have been taken by cucumbers this year alone – namely Valentine Pettis the horse-trader, and a pair of sedan-chairmen. If people *will* eat cucumbers, then they must bear the consequences.'

'You think they are that dangerous?' asked Leybourn.

The verger nodded fervently. 'Oh, yes! They are green, see, and no good will come of feeding on greenery. Have you finished here? Only I need to wash the nave floor. Mud gets tracked everywhere this weather, and this is the Parliament church, so we like to keep it looking nice.'

Chaloner stared at Maylord, and was suddenly seized with the absolute conviction that cucumbers were innocent of causing his death. Physicians, he knew, considered cucumber poison to be insidious – its vapours collected in the veins, and any ill effects tended to occur gradually, not the moment the fruit was taken into the mouth. *Ergo*, either Maylord had suffered the kind of seizure that was relatively common in older people, or someone had done him harm. Moreover, the musician's recent agitation suggested something was sorely amiss, and it was odd that he should so suddenly die. Why anyone would want to hurt him was beyond Chaloner, and he made a silent oath to find out exactly what had happened, and to ensure that whoever was responsible would pay.

He nudged Leybourn, and indicated the door with a nod of his head. He wanted to examine Maylord more closely, but he could hardly do it with the verger watching. Ordinarily, he would have bribed the man to look the other way, but sixpence was unlikely to be enough. It took a moment for Leybourn to understand what he wanted, and when he did, he slapped his hand across his mouth.

'I am going to be sick,' he announced.

The verger gazed at him in horror. 'Not down here!'

'Escort me upstairs, then. My friend can finish paying his respects, and you can take me to fresh—' But the verger did not want a mess, and was already hauling Leybourn away.

Chaloner waited until he could no longer hear their voices, then inspected the musician's hands, head and neck, looking for signs that he had been brained, strangled or had fought an attacker. There was nothing. Then he leaned close to Maylord's mouth and sniffed, but it was an imprecise way to look for poison, and he was not surprised when it told him nothing. He stood back, reluctant to move clothes in a hunt for wounds, because he suspected the verger would not be long and he did not want to be caught doing something sinister. Then he saw an odd discoloration on the face: Maylord's lips were bruised.

Gently, he opened the mouth. An incisor was broken, and when he touched it with his finger, the edge was sharp, suggesting it had happened shortly before death.

Further, teeth marks were etched into Maylord's lower lip. Chaloner had seen such injuries before – when someone had taken a cushion and pressed it hard against a victim's face. It was an unpleasant way to kill, because it involved several minutes of watching a man's losing battle for life at extremely close range. The fact that the culprit had then planted evidence to 'prove' Maylord had died from eating cucumbers suggested a ruthlessness that made Chaloner even more firmly resolved to see him on the gallows.

It was still raining when they emerged from the church, Leybourn resting a hand on Chaloner's shoulder to maintain the pretence of queasiness. Heavy clouds brought an early dusk, and lamps already gleamed in Westminster Hall and the shops around the old clock tower. They set slanting shafts of light gleaming on the wet cobbles, and everywhere people seemed to be in a hurry, wanting to be at home on a night that promised cold and miserable weather.

'Smegergill,' said Chaloner as they walked. 'Do you know him?'

Leybourn shook his head. 'Thurloe might, though.'

Chaloner had wanted to visit Thurloe anyway, to tell him he was home, so he and Leybourn walked up King Street, then along The Strand towards Chancery Lane and Lincoln's Inn. Boys with burning torches offered to light their way, and Leybourn hired one after he skidded and almost fell in some slippery entrails that had been dumped outside a butcher's shop.

'Are you sure you should be doing this?' he asked Chaloner as they went. 'Visiting Thurloe, I mean. He *was* Spymaster General for Cromwell's government, and he is still considered a dangerous enemy of the state, despite having been dismissed from all his posts and living in quiet retirement. You do work for the Lord Chancellor, after all.'

'The Earl does not consider Thurloe a threat, and nor does he object to my continued association with him. It would not matter if he did, anyway. He cannot dictate who my friends should be.'

'Some would say that puts a question-mark over your loyalty to him. Thurloe hired you and trained you, and you remained under his command for nigh on ten years.'

'All of it overseas,' Chaloner pointed out. 'Not once did I spy on the King or his retinue – I only ever gathered intelligence on hostile foreign regimes. And Clarendon knows it.'

Leybourn raised his hands defensively. '*I* do not doubt your allegiance to the Royalist government – I am just telling you what others might say.'

Chaloner made no reply, and Leybourn dropped the subject when they arrived at their destination. Lincoln's Inn, one of four London establishments that licensed lawyers, comprised a range of buildings around two pleasant courtyards. There was a large private garden to the north, and Chaloner was astonished when he saw the change in it. When he had left, there had been an overgrown chaos of elms, beeches and oaks, all shading long-grassed meadows. Now the trees had been pruned or felled, and everything bespoke order and neatness. There were gravelled paths for the benchers – the Inn's ruling body – to stroll around, and little box hedges kept other plants within their allotted spaces. It looked more like an idealised painting than a real garden.

'Does Thurloe mind this?' The ex-Spymaster had

derived much pleasure from his early-morning walks in the wilderness, and Chaloner was not sure the tamed version would be quite the same.

Leybourn smiled. 'He loves it, much to his surprise. The paths mean he can keep his feet dry, and you know what he is like with his health – always fretting about becoming ill.'

They made their way to the smaller and older of the Inn's yards, known as Dial Court. Back in the spring, Dial Court had boasted a sundial – a massively ugly affair of curly iron and oddly placed railings, inexplicably placed so it rarely caught the sun. It had been removed, and in its place was something that looked like a hollow globe.

'It is a device for tracking the movements of the stars,' explained Leybourn, seeing Chaloner look curiously at it. 'The old sundial rusted in the wet weather, and pieces kept falling off, so I recommended this instead. The benchers are very pleased with it, and spend hours out here on clear nights.'

Chaloner doubted there would be many of those – even when it was not raining, London's skies were filled with the smoke from thousands of fires. He followed Leybourn up the stairs to Chamber XIII, where John Thurloe had a suite of rooms that were all wooden panels and leather-bound books. They were warm, comfortable and one of few places where Chaloner felt truly safe.

'Thomas!' exclaimed Thurloe, standing from his fireside chair when they entered. He was a slightly built man, with large blue eyes and a sharp lawyer's mind. 'I expected you home weeks ago and was beginning to worry. What kept you?'

'The situation transpired to be more complex than

I thought,' replied Chaloner vaguely. He did not want to talk about Iberia when he could be soliciting information about Maylord and Newburne.

'Well, I am pleased to see you safe,' said Thurloe, gesturing for his guests to sit near the fire. The room smelled of wood-smoke, wax polish and something pungent and sweet. It put Chaloner in mind of Isabella, and he realised the scent was that of oranges. He glanced at the table, and saw some peel, left from the ex-Spymaster's dinner.

'Vienna is a very dangerous city,' said Leybourn, still fishing. 'The war with the Turks is growing ever more serious, if you can believe the newsbooks.'

'*Can* you believe the newsbooks?' asked Thurloe, deftly diverting the surveyor's attention. He understood his former spy's reluctance to talk about his travels, and would never quiz him about them.

'Not the ones by L'Estrange,' said Leybourn. 'That man would not know the truth if it bit him.'

Chaloner outlined his latest commission from the Earl, while Thurloe listened without interruption. When he had finished, the ex-Spymaster steepled his fingers and looked thoughtful.

'Did William confide details of *his* recent quarrel with L'Estrange?' he asked.

Chaloner regarded Leybourn with a puzzled frown. 'What quarrel?'

'I would rather not discuss it,' replied Leybourn stiffly. 'It is still a sore subject, and will put me in a sour mood for the rest of the day.'

'Thomas knows virtually nothing of London life.' Thurloe silenced Chaloner's indignant objection with a flash of his blue eyes. 'And your experience mirrors that

60

of many other booksellers, William, so you must tell him what the Earl's commission might lead him into. A sour mood is a small price to pay for providing a friend with information that might keep him safe.'

'If you put it like that . . .' Leybourn turned to Chaloner. 'I told you L'Estrange fines booksellers for hawking unlicensed tomes. Well, *I* was one of his victims – to the tune of six pounds.'

It was a lot of money. 'Did you write something seditious?'

'Of course not,' snapped Leybourn angrily. 'The tome in question is the fourth edition of *Gunter's Works*, with diligent amendments and enlargements by me. It is an exciting publication, as you will no doubt be aware, but it is about mathematics and surveying, not politics.'

'Why did he fine you, then?'

'No book can be printed or sold without a licence from L'Estrange. And I made the mistake of selling one of my copies a day – a single, measly *day* – before the license was in force.'

'How did he find that out?'

'Because of Newburne. L'Estrange paid him to spy on the bookshops. I did not even see him lurking behind my shelves when I offered Captain Hammond an advance copy of *Gunter's Works* – not until he emerged with that gloating smile of his. So, *now* do you understand why there are so many men who will be pleased to see Newburne dead? I am just one of hundreds who have been unfairly persecuted.'

'Why did you not tell me sooner?' asked Chaloner, trying not to sound accusing.

'For two reasons. First, because the subject pains me, as I have said. And secondly, because *I* do not want to

61

head your list of suspects. It would not be the first time you have had me in your sights as the perpetrator of a serious crime.'

'That was before I knew you properly.'

The statement coaxed a reluctant smile from the surveyor. 'Well, your confidence is justified, because I did not kill Newburne. However, I might stick a dagger in L'Estrange if the occasion arises, so do not be too ready to see me as a feeble fellow who cowers away from bullies.'

'Let us hope your paths never cross, then,' said Thurloe mildly.

Leybourn glared. 'Let us hope they *do*! Mary says my good nature allows unscrupulous men to take advantage of me, so I have decided to be a bit more ruthless in future. The soft-hearted, gullible Leybourn will be no more, and I shall be a new man.'

'But I like the soft-hearted, gullible Leybourn,' objected Chaloner. 'And I am not so sure about the new man – the one who wants me to burgle instrument-makers and set fire to St Paul's Cathedral.'

'Mary likes me a tad disreputable,' said Leybourn with a lopsided grin. 'And I aim to please her.'

'I am sure she does,' muttered Thurloe disparagingly. He turned to Chaloner before Leybourn could respond. 'I wish the Earl had not given you this particular assignment, Tom. It is too dangerous for a man working alone, and it is Williamson's business, anyway. He will not appreciate you meddling.'

'Especially you,' added Leybourn. 'You have earned his dislike on several occasions.'

'When I first sent you to the Earl, he promised to use you wisely,' Thurloe went on. 'He knows we are friends, and that I will be vexed if anything happens to you. And he did not want me vexed, not when – as Cromwell's spymaster – I know so many secrets about prominent Royalists. Unfortunately, times have changed. It is the gardens, you see. They showed me to be weak.'

'I do not understand,' said Chaloner. 'What do the gardens have to do with anything?'

'I did not want them remodelled, but was unable to stop it – in essence, I lost a very public battle, which allowed everyone to see how my power has waned. People are no longer wary of me.'

Chaloner was alarmed. 'You mean you are not safe? Then you should retire to your estates in Oxfordshire, and—'

Thurloe raised his hand. 'There are plenty of men who want me dead for my faithful service to Cromwell, and nothing has changed there. The current danger is to *you*, Tom. The Earl is no longer afraid of me, which means he may be careless in his use of you.'

'Leave him,' advised Leybourn, 'while you can.'

'And do what?' asked Chaloner. 'I cannot foist myself on my family, because they cannot afford to keep me, and I am not qualified for any other work.'

'I am sure they would prefer a living scavenger to a dead workhorse,' said Leybourn. 'Go home to Buckinghamshire before the Earl's commission lands you in danger. Newburne's killer will not give himself up easily, and you have no idea what you are facing.'

When a bell began to chime, Thurloe said he was due to attend a benchers' meeting in the chapel. Chaloner and Leybourn escorted him across the courtyard, but he was early, so they lingered together in the undercroft – an open crypt that had been designed to allow students to congregate and discuss complex cases, and where lawyers could confer with their clients. It was empty that day, because a rainswept cloister was not a place most men wanted to linger, and the lawyers were keeping to their rooms until the last possible moment.

'Do you know a man called William Smegergill?' Chaloner asked the ex-Spymaster.

Thurloe's expression became thoughtful. 'Smegergill was Maylord's friend. Maylord died of cucumbers, and so did Newburne, so I suspect you are looking for a connection. Am I right?'

'Newburne might have died from ingesting cucumbers, but Maylord certainly did not. He was smothered, and the cucumber left to disguise the fact. It seems to have worked, because no one else seems to be suspicious about his death.'

Leybourn gazed angrily at the spy. 'You told *me* none of this – and you might have done, given that I went to some trouble to cause a diversion for you in St Margaret's Church. What is it with you and secrets? I am getting a bit tired of them, if you want the truth.'

'You did not ask,' said Chaloner, startled by his vehemence.

'Would you have confided, if I had?' demanded Leybourn. 'You will not even tell me where you have been for the past few months, and we are supposed to be friends. In fact, I know very little about you, although you know an inordinate amount about me because *I* am not secretive.'

'I do not know your wife,' hedged Chaloner, amazed that Leybourn should expect him, a professional spy, to be open about his life and his work.

'Mary is *not* his wife – they are living in sin,' said

Thurloe disapprovingly. Chaloner tended to forget the ex-Spymaster was a devout Puritan, and was often taken off-guard when prudish principles bobbed to the surface. 'He should either marry her properly or end the relationship.'

Leybourn glowered at him. 'I am going home. At least there I am respected. Trusted, too.'

He stalked away, leaving Chaloner staring after him in astonishment. He had never seen him so angry, and the provocation had been very slight. He turned to Thurloe. 'What is wrong with him?'

Thurloe's expression was deeply unhappy. 'He has not been himself since that dreadful woman appeared and began to corrupt his mind. I wish they had never met.'

'Mary? But he said she makes him happy.'

'So he claims, but he does not seem happy to me. She is turning him against his friends – she has fabricated all manner of lies about me, and it will only be a matter of time before she begins a campaign of slander against you, too. Further, she encourages him to forget his principles and become something he is not. For example, he is constantly asking me to break the law.'

'In what way?'

'By forging him a marriage certificate or writing letters purporting to be from the Earl of Sandwich, which will see him awarded a lucrative surveying contract. I suspect Mary urges him to resort to dishonest methods, and he does it to please her. I am very worried about him.'

'Who is she? Do you know her family?'

'Her name is Mary Cade, and she claims to hail from Norfolk. I have made enquiries, but have learned nothing so far, although there is certainly something suspect about her. Go to meet her, Tom, and then come back and tell me what you think.'

Chaloner nodded. 'Very well. And while I am there, I shall tell Will what I have been doing in Portugal and Spain. He has a fair point: there is no need to keep secrets from him.'

'From him, no, but I would not confide anything you do not want Mary to know, too. He tells her more than he should about his business, and I do not like the company she keeps.'

'What company?'

'Men with a felonious look about them. I was Spymaster General, so I know a scoundrel when I see one. William has no idea what manner of folk he entertains in his house of an evening. Did he tell you how he and Mary met? She went to buy a book, and he fell in love the moment he saw her. I suspect she spotted a lonely man, and homed in like a snake to its prey. I was delighted at first – he is not successful with ladies and deserves a companion – but then he introduced us and all my instincts told me she is not what he believes her to be. You and I *must* find a way to loosen the claws she has fastened around his heart.'

'Not if he loves her. He will not thank us for that.'

'Wait until you meet her before taking that sort of stance,' advised Thurloe. There was a steely look in his eye that warned Chaloner not to argue. He had not been appointed to one of the most powerful posts in the Commonwealth for nothing, and there was an iron core in him to which wise men deferred. 'And *then* we shall discuss it.'

They were silent for a moment, each wrapped in his own concerns. Absently, Thurloe nodded a greeting to one of his fellow benchers, then turned back to Chaloner.

'You were asking about Smegergill before we became sidetracked with Mary. He is an excellent virginals player – or was, before age stiffened his fingers. He is still very good, but nothing compared to what he was in Cromwell's time. He and Maylord were friends, because both performed for the Commonwealth's court, and then joined the King's after the Restoration. Maylord may well have confided any worries he had to Smegergill. However, before you interview him, I should warn you that he has a reputation for being difficult.'

'Difficult?'

'Eccentric and unpredictable. At times he is charm itself, while on other occasions he is moody and sullen. The artistic temperament, I suppose. You can be rather like that yourself.'

Chaloner had only ever been 'moody and sullen' with Thurloe when he had had good cause, and felt it was an unfair observation. It was not the time to discuss past misunderstandings, though. 'I do not suppose you have heard any rumours about what might have been bothering Maylord?'

'Unfortunately not. However, I met him at White Hall about a week ago, and he asked if I knew where you might be, intimating that there was a matter with which you might be able to help him. I offered him my services, but he declined. So, I have no idea why he was distressed, although I think we can safely assume that it relates to his murder. Of course, he died two days after Newburne, so it is possible that Maylord's killer latched on to cucumbers *because* of Newburne.'

Chaloner nodded slowly. 'You mean no one thought

it odd that Newburne died of eating cucumbers, so the killer assumed – rightly – that no eyebrows would be raised when the same thing happened to Maylord. That means the two deaths are unrelated, that Maylord's killer just heard what happened to Newburne and used it as an excuse.'

'It means he took a cucumber with him when he killed Maylord, which shows a degree of premeditation. Other than that, there is no connection between the two victims that I can see: Newburne was a corrupt and hated lawyer, and Maylord was a popular musician with many friends.'

'The verger at St Margaret's mentioned three other recent cucumber deaths . . .'

'Actually, there have been four.' Thurloe's extensive circle of ex-colleagues, former employees and acquaintances still kept him well supplied with gossip and intelligence. 'A royal equerry named Colonel Beauclair, Valentine Pettis the horse-dealer, and two sedan-chairmen. There was no suggestion of foul play with any of them, although they have all died within the last month.'

'Did they know each other? Or were they acquainted with Newburne or Maylord?'

'Beauclair was interested in riding, the army and virtually nothing else; he would have had nothing in common with a musician and a solicitor. I suppose he might have met Pettis the horse-dealer, though. Meanwhile, Beauclair rode everywhere, Maylord walked, and Newburne had his own carriage, so I doubt any of them knew the sedanmen. What do you plan to do? Look into Maylord's death, as well as Newburne's?'

'Maylord was my father's closest friend, and whoever smothered him with enough force to break teeth deserves to face justice. I *will* hunt down his killer. And I have no choice but to investigate Newburne. The Earl pays me, and I cannot pick and choose from the commissions he dispenses.'

'All I can tell you about Newburne is that a man called Heneage Finch was almost the only person in London prepared to spend any time in his company.'

'Do you know why?'

'Even the most villainous of men have *some* friends, and I think Finch was just that – a fellow able to look beyond Newburne's corrupt, sly manner to see something worthy of companionship. Perhaps he can tell you whether Newburne had a penchant for cucumbers. So, you have two tasks now: interviewing Finch about his friend Newburne, and Smegergill about his friend Maylord.'

'I will start tomorrow.'

'I do not think people will be rushing to help once they learn your aim is to investigate Newburne's death – assuming there is anything to explore, of course. Even rotten lawyers die of natural causes sometimes. Meanwhile, Williamson will object to your interference, and the Earl is angry with you for leaving England for so long. Trust no one – not even Leybourn, I am sorry to say.'

It was good advice, and Chaloner fully intended to follow it.

It was dark when Chaloner left Lincoln's Inn and began to walk to Monkwell Street near Cripplegate, where Leybourn lived. Although the streets were still busy, a different kind of citizen was beginning to emerge for business. Men tried to bump into him as he went, in an attempt to pick his pockets, and youths with dirty faces and oily hands offered to sell him goods at improbably low prices. Chaloner had no money to pay a linksman to light his path, and closed his mind to what he might be treading in as he made his way along the wide thoroughfare called Holborn. Shops were still open, and displays of gloves, spices, wigs, baskets, pots and mirrors could be seen within. Stray dogs had formed a pack near the bridge that spanned the filthy Fleet River, and were feeding on something that lay in the road; they snarled at anyone who went too close.

It took him a long time to reach Leybourn's home, because the streets were so badly flooded. He gave up trying to keep his feet dry, and sloshed through the debris-filled puddles, some of which reached his calves. Thick, sucking mud gripped the wheels of carriages and carts, so their owners had scant control over them, and in some places, they had been abandoned altogether. One lay on its side, and a gang of men were stripping it of anything that could be carried away. Another had caught fire when one of its lamps had been shaken loose by a violent skidding motion; vagrants clustered around, warming their hands in the blaze. Through the flames, Chaloner could see a figure trapped inside, and did not like to imagine what the parish constables would find when they came to clear the wreckage in the morning.

He dived into a doorway when several horsemen cantered recklessly towards him, whooping and cheering as they went. They reeled drunkenly in their saddles, and one had a semi-naked woman perched behind him. A passing leatherworker grimaced in distaste at the spectacle.

'That was the Duke of Buckingham and his cronies.

Do we really want *them* playing ambassador to hostile foreign powers, or directing our country's fiscal policies?'

'Not for me to say.' Because Spymaster Williamson was notorious for hiring spies to goad men into making seditious remarks – it was the sort of activity that gave intelligence officers a bad name – Chaloner never indulged in contentious discussions with people who accosted him on the street.

The man spat. 'Was it for this that we cheered ourselves hoarse at the Restoration three years ago? Perhaps Cromwell was right when he cut off the last monarch's head. Have you heard the talk in the coffee houses? They say there has been a great rebellion in the north.'

He moved away, leaving Chaloner wondering how the Court had managed to squander so much goodwill in such a short space of time. He was thoughtful as he resumed his journey, considering what he would do if the country was plunged into another civil war. His family still regarded the Parliamentarian cause to be a just one, but he had recently come to the realisation that one government was pretty much as bad as another. They all comprised men, after all, with men's weaknesses and faults.

Leybourn owned a pleasant three-storeyed building, with shop, reception rooms and kitchen on the ground floor, and bedrooms and an office above. Chaloner had spent many peaceful hours in the large, steamy kitchen, listening to the surveyor wax lyrical on some incomprehensible aspect of mathematics or geometry. The Leybourn brothers did well at bookselling, although Will was beginning to leave more of the business to Rob, in order to devote time to his own writing.

71

Chaloner knocked on the door. Had Leybourn lived alone, he would have picked the lock and let himself in, but now the house was shared with a lady, breaking and entering was no longer a polite thing to do. There was no reply, so he tapped again. He could see shadows moving under the window shutters, so someone was in, and he wondered whether Leybourn was so angry with him that he was declining to answer. He rapped a third time, and was about to give up when the door was hauled open.

A woman stood there. He supposed she was pretty, although there was something dissipated about her plump body and the sluttish way she leaned against the wall. She wore a low-cut smock that revealed an ample frontage, and her cheeks were flushed in a manner that suggested she had been drinking. When she leaned towards him, squinting in the dim light, he was sure of it.

'What do you want?' she demanded.

He smiled, eager to make a good impression on the person who now shared his friend's life. 'I have come to see Will. You must be Mary.'

'I am *Mrs Leybourn*,' she replied tartly. Her expression was cold and angry. 'I suppose you are Heyden? William said he expected you home any day now.'

'Is he in?' Chaloner asked pleasantly. 'I would like—'

'No,' she snapped in a way that made him question whether she was telling the truth. 'Why? Have you come to borrow money? He told me you never have any of your own.'

'I have just come to spend an hour in his company,' he objected, wondering what else Leybourn had said about him. He struggled to maintain an affable mien,

72

fighting the urge to tell her that the purpose of his visit was none of her damned business. 'It has been a while since we—'

'He is out,' she interrupted coldly. 'You will have to come back another day.'

Chaloner could hear voices in the kitchen, and one definitely belonged to a man. If it was not Leybourn, then who was the surveyor's 'wife' entertaining when he was out? 'I see.'

She moved quickly, blocking his view down the corridor. 'I am busy at the moment, so I cannot invite you inside to wait. The vicar of St Giles is here, asking my opinion about the altar decorations for Christmas. I am sure you understand. Goodbye.'

She closed the door before he could say whether he understood or not. He considered knocking again, and telling her that he had considerable experience with altar decorations and was more than happy to grant her and the vicar the benefit of his expertise. His second notion was to creep around the back of the house and look through the kitchen window. The vicar of St Giles was unlikely to be talking to himself while Mary had gone to answer the door, and he wanted to know whether it was Leybourn with whom he was conversing. But he was cold, wet and not in the mood for what might evolve into a nasty confrontation, so he started to trudge back to his lodgings. He had not taken many steps when he saw a familiar figure – tall, stoop-shouldered and wearing an old-fashioned hat.

'I have been waiting for you at your house,' said Leybourn in a rush. 'I wanted to apologise for snapping at you earlier. I have not been sleeping well, and Thurloe has become like an old woman of late, chastising me for

73

this and that. But I should not have taken my irritation out on you.'

Chaloner was relieved the spat was over. He took a deep breath. 'I have been in Portugal since June. Spain, too, although I went to spy, so the fewer people who know it, the better. I did not intend to be secretive, but it is a difficult habit to break.'

'I understand,' said Leybourn, turning him around and beginning to walk towards his home. 'I should not have tried to pry, although I *am* a scholar, and curiosity comes naturally to me. Did you meet any mathematicians in Portugal? They are famous for their theories pertaining to navigation.'

Chaloner heard the bleakness in his own voice as he spoke. 'No, it was dreadful, Will – one of the worst assignments I have ever been given.' Leybourn looked sympathetic, so he added, 'With the possible exception of a woman called Isabella.'

Leybourn gave him a manly nudge and grinned. 'I knew it! I always envied your luck with ladies. But I have Mary now, and such concerns are a thing of the past. I have told her a lot about you, and she will be delighted to make your acquaintance at last.'

Chaloner held back. 'It is late, and she may be busy.'

'Nonsense,' said Leybourn. 'At least come and share a cup of metheglin with us. Have you ever tried metheglin? It is spiced, fermented honey, and Mary knows where to buy it at its best.' He flung open his door before Chaloner could decline. 'Mary! I am home, and Tom is with me.'

He strode along the corridor, heading for the kitchen. Chaloner heard chair legs rasp on flagstones as someone stood quickly, and then there was a metallic click as the

74

latch on the back door was raised. Leybourn stumbled over a stool that had been left in the unlit hall, long legs becoming hopelessly entangled as he struggled to extricate himself. Chaloner saw it had been placed there deliberately, to give the occupants of the kitchen time to finish whatever it was they were doing before the surveyor walked in on them. Leybourn freed himself eventually, and pushed open the door.

Mary hurled herself forward and clutched his head to her neck, giving him the kind of welcome that he might have expected had he been away months, rather than hours. Wryly, Chaloner noticed that the hug also served to blind him, so he did not spot the door to the garden closing surreptitiously. He wondered why Mary's companions – at least two of them, as there were three empty goblets in the hearth – should be so eager to escape without being seen. When she released Leybourne, leaving him somewhat breathless, the surveyor turned to Chaloner.

'This is Mary,' he said, pride and adoration in every word.

'*Mrs* Leybourn,' said Chaloner, with a bow.

She regarded him coolly, then sat in the surveyor's favourite chair. 'I have been working hard today, and I am exhausted. Fetch me a drink, dear William. Metheglin will do nicely.'

'What happened to the vicar?' asked Chaloner caustically. 'Is he in the garden, exploring its contents with a view to claiming his Christmas decorations early?'

Leybourn gazed at him in confusion. 'Mary has been alone all day, sewing me new shirts. And why would the vicar be in the garden? It is dark.'

Chaloner could see no evidence that shirts or anything

75

else were being sewn, but Mary had risen, and had gone to drape herself around her man. Leybourn smiled fondly as she told him how lonely she had been, with no one for company, and Chaloner saw Thurloe was right: Leybourn was so besotted, he would believe the moon was blue if Mary told him so.

'I will hire you a female companion,' offered Leybourn, going to the hearth and ladling something into three wooden cups. Chaloner recoiled from the strength of the brew, and knew it would make him drunk if he downed it on an empty stomach. 'A maid would be useful, now two of us live here.'

Chaloner agreed, because Leybourn's usually pleasant kitchen was sordid. Unwashed pots were piled on every surface, a bucket of slops had been sitting so long that there was mould growing in the scum across the top, and the floor was sticky, making him feel like wiping his feet on the way out. He was not the most assiduous of housekeepers himself, but at least he usually scoured his dirty pans within a day, and he never left uneaten food on plates for so long that it rotted. The room was a disgrace, and he was surprised his friend could not see it.

'I do not want a companion,' said Mary, rather too quickly. 'You are soaking, poor love! Come and sit by the fire, and warm yourself before you take a chill.'

'I could eat a horse,' declared Leybourn, allowing himself to be cosseted. 'What do we have?'

'Beetroot,' said Mary, waving her hand in a gesture that indicated it might be anywhere.

'I should be going,' said Chaloner, backing away. He was also hungry, but not desperate enough to resort to beetroot.

'Please stay,' said Leybourn, although he spoke absently and most of his attention was on Mary. 'I want to show you Christopher Wren's treatise on weather glasses.'

'Another time,' said Chaloner. He set the metheglin on the table. 'It has been a pleasure, *Mrs* Leybourn.'

Chapter 3

Early the next morning, Chaloner woke thinking about Leybourn's infatuation with Mary. He supposed he should be grateful that their union had not been sanctioned by the Church, because it would be easier to dissolve when – and he was sure it was only a matter of time – Leybourn came to his senses and saw he could do very much better. What was Mary gaining from the arrangement? The answer was obvious: a life of luxury with a man who thought she could do no wrong, gifts, and a home in which to entertain when her lover was out. Chaloner could see exactly why she did not want her victim's friends interfering with her business.

But the spy's first duty that day was not Leybourn, but the investigation into Newburne's death, which he would begin by visiting L'Estrange on Ivy Lane. He found a green front-buttoned coat he had always liked, and a pair of loose breeches. It was not the most fashionable of attires, but it was warm, functional and not too moth- or mouse-ravaged. His boots were sturdy and good for walking, and Isabella's hat would keep both sun and rain from his eyes. Having unimpaired vision was important in his line of work, and although he did not expect the day to bring too many dangers – at least, not like the kind he had recently endured in Spain – he was too experienced to be complacent.

The only thing to eat was a lump of dried meat from the last of his travelling supplies, so he soaked it in water until it was soft. He offered some to the cat, which turned up its nose and went to sit in the window. It began to wash its face, and a gnawed tail near the hearth told him it had acquired itself a fresher meal while he had been sleeping. The dried meat was sadly rancid, and he supposed he should spend his last sixpence to lay in some essential supplies, although it would not buy much and he did not like the notion of being totally penniless. He decided to visit White Hall and claim his back-pay as soon as he had a spare moment.

It had rained heavily during the night, and dawn bathed the streets in a cold, grey light that turned the sodden buildings to shades of brown and beige. It made the city look ugly, and so did the piles of manure, kitchen filth and rubbish that sat at irregular intervals along the sides of the road, each glistening and slick with slime. Dogs and rats scavenged among them, while kites and pigeons perched on the rooftops and waited their turn.

Ivy Lane was a narrow thoroughfare that ran north from St Paul's Cathedral, and Brome's Bookshop, in which L'Estrange had his headquarters, was in the middle, near the junction with Paternoster Row. It was a large, well-appointed building with freshly painted timbers and real glass in the windows. The first floor was L'Estrange's domain – Chaloner could see him pacing back and forth in front of a desk – while the attics comprised living accommodation for the bookseller and his family. The ground floor housed the shop itself, a spacious chamber with neat rows of shelves.

Chaloner pushed open a door that jangled, and entered. The books on sale comprised mostly government-sponsored publications on such diverse subjects as the trees of Bermuda, theology, and various editions of the *Seaman's Kalender*. The floor was clean, the tables dusted, and the entire place gave off an air of quiet efficiency. For all that, Chaloner preferred the chaotic jumble of Leybourn's premises, although he was sure Brome would be able to access any tome in his collection within moments, whereas it sometimes took Leybourn days to locate a specific book. Brome's was a place for busy men who knew what they wanted; Leybourn's was for browsers.

As Chaloner stepped inside, the shopkeeper left the customer he was serving and came to greet the new arrival. He was tall, with thinning ginger hair that was mostly concealed by a brown wig. His eyes were a pleasant shade of green, and he wore spectacles on a chain around his neck. When he smiled, his teeth were white and even. He introduced himself as Henry Brome, and politely asked if Chaloner would mind waiting a few moments until he had finished dealing with Mr Smith. A copy of *The Intelligencer* was provided in the meantime, which Brome said had come directly from the printing presses that morning. It was a refreshing change from being ignored until the first client had left, as happened in most shops.

The spy sat at a table and scanned the newsbook's contents. There were reports from Paris, Denmark and Vienna, and a note about the Queen's health, but most of the eight pages were given over to a tirade about an uprising of phanatiques in York, Richmond and Preston.

Chaloner grinned when he read, *I will not trouble you with hear-says and Reports,* **but** . . .' and the editor then went on to give a great list of unsubstantiated rumours.

'A bright bay mare,' said the customer, when Brome returned to him. 'Twelve hands high, with three white feet and wall-eyes. And you can say there is a reward of twenty shillings for her safe return, on application to Richard Smith at the Bell in Smithfield. That is me.'

Brome finished writing down the instructions and smiled. 'I shall make sure the notice appears in Thursday's *Newes*, Mr Smith. And I hope it brings you luck.'

'I believe it might,' replied Smith. 'When Captain Hammond lost his gelding, one of your advertisements saw it back within *three days*! Making news of horse-thievery means it is more difficult for these villains to operate, and you are doing us a great service.'

'I am delighted to hear it,' said Brome. He looked pained. 'Of course, the real function of our newsbooks is not to help find missing horses, but to keep the public informed of current affairs.'

Smith laughed, long and hard. 'Believe me, Brome, no one buys the newsbooks for their coverage of current affairs! We buy them for the horses, and anyone who tells you otherwise is a liar. And speaking of horses, you can write that mine was stolen by a villain called Edward Treen. One of my servants saw him quite clearly, but he managed to ride off before we could stop him. Make sure you name Treen.'

'We had better not,' said Brome, rather wearily. 'He might sue you for defamation of character, and the courts cannot be relied upon to dispense just verdicts these days. It is safer to leave the notice as it is.'

'Very well,' said Smith, pushing several coins across

the table, which Brome counted carefully before making an entry in a ledger. 'Do you want me to sign anything before I go?'

'Here, to say you have handed me the sum of five shillings,' said Brome, pointing at the book.

'You are wise to keep records, because they will protect you against *allegations*,' said Smith darkly. 'I knew L'Estrange during the wars, and he is a devil for thinking the worst of people. I heard in my coffee house yesterday that he has accused Muddiman of stealing his news.'

Brome regarded him uneasily. 'But Muddiman *does* steal his news – he pre-empted us with a report from Tangier only last week. That *is* theft, just as you losing your bay mare is theft.'

'It is not the same at all,' said Smith dismissively. 'A horse cannot be compared to an item of foreign gossip. I was sorry to hear about Newburne, by the way. You must be very upset.'

'L'Estrange will miss him,' was all Brome said in reply.

When Smith had gone, Brome turned to Chaloner with a smile, apologising for the delay and asking whether he had come to order a book, apply for a publishing license, or buy advertising space.

'I have come to see Roger L'Estrange,' replied Chaloner.

'May I ask why?' Brome shrugged sheepishly when Chaloner raised his eyebrows at the question. 'I mean no disrespect, but it will be better for everyone if you tell me your business first. The last man I allowed in without an appointment transpired to be a phanatique, and the poor fellow was lucky to escape with *one* of his ears still attached.'

From the rabid tone of the newsbooks and what he had witnessed outside the Rainbow Coffee House, Chaloner was not surprised to learn L'Estrange was in the habit of turning violent when confronted with people of whom he disapproved. 'The Lord Chancellor asked me to see him regarding the release of information from Portugal. My name is Thomas Heyden.'

Brome brightened. 'Original news? Excellent! That will put him in a good mood, and it is kind of the Lord Chancellor to think of us. Are you one of his secretaries? A diplomatic emissary, perhaps?'

'Just a clerk.'

Brome regarded him astutely. 'He does not send minions to foreign countries on his behalf, so you must be either relatively senior or trusted. But no matter; I can see from your expression that you would rather not discuss it. We are grateful for any accurate information, regardless of its origin.'

Chaloner changed the subject. Brome's wits were sharp, and he did not want the man guessing he was a spy. 'You said L'Estrange was visited by a phanatique. Do many pay him court, then?'

The bookseller grinned, a little conspiratorially. 'They do, according to him. However, you must be aware that a phanatique is anyone even remotely sympathetic to Puritans, Roundheads or regicides. I am one at the moment, because I said it is time Cromwell's skull was removed from the pole outside Westminster Hall. However, my suggestion has more to do with its nasty habit of blowing down in the wind than with any respect I might have had for its owner. The thing almost brained my wife last week, and most Londoners consider it something of a 'hazard.'

83

Chaloner hoped Thurloe did not venture that way during storms, because he and Cromwell had been friends. 'Is it true that a licence is needed to print any book or pamphlet in London now?' he asked, wanting to learn more about L'Estrange's official business before he met the man.

'In the country,' corrected Brome. 'And not only is it illegal to manufacture a text without a licence from the Surveyor of the Press – L'Estrange – but it is against the law to sell them, too.'

'I understand there are six hundred booksellers in the City alone,' said Chaloner artlessly. 'How does he regulate them all?'

'There are only fifty now,' said Brome. He looked away, and Chaloner was under the impression that he thought it a pity. 'He hires men to visit the bookshops and ensure they only hawk legitimate tomes. Of course, these rules only apply to the printed word. He cannot control manuscripts – handwritten texts – such as the newsletters dictated by Muddiman to his army of scribes.'

'Do you read any newsletters?'

'No, of course not,' said Brome, somewhat cagily. 'That would be disloyal, because they are in direct competition with the official government newsbooks.'

Casually, Chaloner leaned forward and tweaked a sheet of paper from under the ledger, stepping away smartly when Brome tried to snatch it back. Like all newsletters, it was addressed to a specific recipient – something a scribe could do, but that was impractical for a printing press – and the author's name and address were carried banner-like across the top of the first page. In this case, the writer was Henry Muddiman, and his correspondent was Samuel Pepys.

Brome's face was scarlet with mortification. 'That is . . . that is not mine.'

'Pepys is a clerk at the navy office,' said Chaloner, watching him intently. 'I met him once.'

Brome was appalled. 'You know Pepys? Lord!'

Chaloner was amused when he guessed the reason for Brome's agitation. 'Pepys does not subscribe to Muddiman's newsletter, does he? You just borrowed his name, because he is respectable but relatively insignificant, and no one at Muddiman's office would question his desire to purchase such a thing. Meanwhile, Muddiman thinks his missives are being read by a navy clerk, blissfully unaware that it actually goes straight into the hands of his greatest rival.'

Brome coloured even further. 'It sounds sordid when you put it like that. Muddiman sends out a hundred and fifty newsletters each week, so what difference can one more make? Besides, how else are we to monitor the competition?'

Chaloner regarded him thoughtfully. 'This was not your idea, was it? And nor did you elect to pick on Pepys. Whose was it? L'Estrange's?'

Brome put his hands over his face and scrubbed his flushed cheeks. 'He will skin me alive if he finds out I was careless enough to leave that lying around for the Lord Chancellor's man to see. I told him it was stupid to use Pepys, but he would not listen. What if Muddiman meets Pepys, and asks how he likes the newsletters? It was only ever a matter of time before we were found out.'

'So why take the risk?'

'Because we need to know what is in them. Muddiman's sources are invariably better than ours.'

Chaloner was bemused. 'How so? The newsbooks' source of information is the government – and the government knows everything, because it receives a constant stream of information from its spies.' He knew this for a fact, because he was one of those conduits.

Brome swallowed. 'I am afraid you have walked into a war here, Heyden. A news war. You are right: we should have the stories first, but the reality is quite different. Muddiman has contacts and methods – God alone knows who and what they are – which mean he nearly always pre-empts us.'

Chaloner was thoughtful. 'He was the newsbook editor himself until a few weeks ago. That means he knows the government clerks who provide this information. Perhaps he bribes them to speak to him first. It would be a risky thing to do on the clerks' part, because if Spymaster Williamson finds out I doubt he will be very forgiving. But it is not impossible.'

'No,' acknowledged Brome. 'It is not impossible. However, Williamson's spies maintain the clerks are innocent. They watch them all the time, and have observed nothing untoward. So, we do not know how Muddiman always manages to get the news first.'

'What was Newburne's role in all this?'

Brome was startled by the question. 'I suppose you heard Smith consoling me about his death, did you? Poor Newburne! His remit was to spy on the booksellers and keep an eye on Muddiman's dealings. Why do you ask about him particularly?'

'The Lord Chancellor asked me to confirm that his death was a natural one,' said Chaloner, deciding to be honest in the hope of learning more.

'As well as providing us with information about

Portugal?' asked Brome doubtfully. 'You own a strange combination of talents. And why does the Earl think something is amiss anyway?'

'He did not say – he just ordered me to look into the matter.'

Brome regarded him unhappily. 'That will almost certainly prove to be dangerous. Newburne was an unsavoury man who knew a good many unsavoury people. Hectors, no less.'

'The Smithfield gang?'

'The very same. I am not exaggerating: you would be ill-advised to delve into Newburne's affairs. However, if you are under orders from the Lord Chancellor, I suspect you have no choice. So, if you promise to say nothing about our unlawful use of Pepys's name to procure those newsletters, I will tell you what I know of Newburne. Do I have your word, as a gentleman?'

'You do.'

Chaloner was astonished when Brome took a deep breath and began to speak – the man was naively trusting of someone he had only just met. 'Newburne took bribes from some of the booksellers he caught breaking the law. He told them a gift to him would work out cheaper than a fine from L'Estrange.'

'How do you know?' Chaloner was disappointed: he already knew this.

'Because I overheard their discussions, and I witnessed several payments made. I pretended not to notice, because I did not want to end up crushed between him and L'Estrange. He was an associate of Ellis Crisp, you see.'

'Who is Ellis Crisp?'

Brome regarded him incredulously. 'Are you jesting? You *must* have heard of Ellis Crisp.'

87

'I am only recently returned from Portugal.'

'Perhaps you are, but even so . . .' Good manners helped Brome overcome his disbelief at what he clearly regarded as rank ignorance. 'Crisp is the butcher who controls Smithfield – not the legitimate business of selling meat and livestock, but the underworld that thrives in the area. He owns the Hectors, and it is his bidding they do. He is the most dangerous man in London. So now do you see why I urge you to caution as regards Newburne?'

Chaloner nodded, although he had never heard of Crisp, and doubted the man would prove too daunting an opponent. He was grateful for the warning, though. He wondered if the Earl knew a powerful felon might be involved in Newburne's death, which led him yet again to question his master's reasons for ordering the investigation.

'Do you think Crisp killed Newburne, then?'

Brome was startled. 'No, I think Newburne died from eating cucumbers, although I suppose he might have been forced to consume them against his will. I doubt it was by Crisp, though, because Newburne was said to be one of his most valued employees. On the other hand, Crisp *is* the kind of man to kill a wayward minion. There are many tales about the untamed violence of the man they call the Butcher of Smithfield.'

'The Butcher of Smithfield?' echoed Chaloner incredulously. He was tempted to smile, but he did not want to offend someone who was trying to be helpful. He struggled to keep his expression blank. 'Does this title refer to his profession or his penchant for "untamed violence"?'

'Both, I imagine, although I do not think he has much

to do with the meat trade any more. However, I have been told that his pastries offer a convenient repository for his victims' bodies.'

This time Chaloner did not attempt to control his amusement, and laughed openly. 'Then I doubt it is a very lucrative business. There cannot be many cannibals in London, and no one else will be inclined to dine on pies that own that sort of reputation.'

Brome shrugged and looked away, and Chaloner saw the bookseller thought there might well be truth in the rumours. Not wanting to argue, he changed the subject.

'Can I see L'Estrange today, or should I come back later?'

Brome forced a smile. 'I will ask for an interview now. If you are from the Earl of Clarendon, he will probably want to meet you. But be warned – he was not in a friendly frame of mind earlier, so you may have to . . . to speak with caution, so as not to ignite his fragile temper.'

'He will not risk annoying the Earl by slicing the ears off *his* messengers.'

Brome regarded him as though he was mad. 'He does not care who he annoys – which makes for a good editor, I suppose. If you give me a moment, I will present him with Mr Smith's advertisement first. It will put him in a better mood, because it means five shillings in the news-books' coffers.'

Bookshops were always pleasant places in which to while away time, and Chaloner was perfectly content to browse in Brome's while he waited to be summoned to L'Estrange's office. He noticed some of the texts had been penned by L'Estrange himself, most of them virulent attacks on

Catholics, Puritans, science, Dutchmen, Quakers and, of course, phanatiques. Then he saw one that contained speeches made by some of the regicides before their executions. He took it down, and was startled to find a monologue by his uncle, who had neither been executed nor delivered a homily about what he had done. He read it in distaste, supposing L'Estrange had made it up. His uncle had been no saint, but he would never have uttered the viciously sectarian sentiments recorded in the poisonous little pamphlet, either. He replaced it on the shelf, feeling rather soiled for having touched it.

Suddenly, there was an explosive yell from the chamber above. Someone was being dressed down. Chaloner moved towards the stairs, better to hear what was being said.

'*One* advertisement?' Chaloner recognised L'Estrange's voice from the incident outside the Rainbow Coffee House. 'Is that all? It is a Monday, and clients should be flooding through the door.'

'It is early yet,' stammered Brome. 'And I thought you might like to see the first—'

'Do not *think*,' snapped L'Estrange unpleasantly. 'Leave that to me.'

Chaloner heard footsteps coming from a corridor that led to the back of the house and, not wanting to be caught eavesdropping, moved quickly to stand by a pile of tomes about navigation and ocean mapping. He snatched up the top one, and was reading it when a woman entered the room. She closed the door at the base of the stairs, muffling the bad-tempered tirade that thundered from above.

'Are you a sailor, sir?' she asked politely. 'If so, then may I direct you to a specific book? Or have you found what you are looking for?'

Chaloner glanced up from his 'reading' to see a slender, doe-eyed lady, who was pretty in a timid, frightened sort of way. She was tall for a woman – almost as tall as him – although her clothes were sadly unfashionable, and overemphasised her willowy figure. When she smiled, she revealed teeth that were rather long, which, when combined with the eyes, put Chaloner in mind of a startled rabbit. The comparison might not have sprung quite so readily to mind had her hair not been gathered in two brown bunches at the side of her head, and allowed to hang down like floppy ears.

'A sailor?' he asked blankly.

She nodded to the book he was holding. 'Only mathematicians or nautical men are interested in Robert Moray's *Experiment of the Instrument for Sounding Depths*. You do not look eccentric enough to be a man of science, so I conclude you must be a naval gentleman.'

'I developed an interest in soundings on a recent sea voyage,' lied Chaloner. 'But I am just passing the time until I can see L'Estrange.'

She looked alarmed. 'I hope there is no trouble?' Realising it was an odd question to ask, she attempted to smooth it over, digging herself a deeper hole with every word she gabbled. 'That is not to say we are expecting trouble, of course. The newsbook offices are very peaceful most of the time. *Very* peaceful. We never have trouble. Well, not usually. What I mean is '

It seemed cruel to let her go on, so Chaloner interrupted. 'No trouble, just government business.'

'Thank God!' she breathed. Then she shot him a sheepish grin. 'You must think me a goose! All worked up and talking like the clappers over nothing. We lost a colleague recently, you see, and it upset us, even though

91

we did not like him very much. That is to say we did not *dis*like him, but . . .'

She trailed off unhappily, and looked longingly at the door that led to the back of the house, clearly itching to bolt. Chaloner felt sorry for her, thinking she was entirely the wrong sort of person to be employed in the devious business of selling news. He winced when the shouting from upstairs grew louder. 'L'Estrange seems peeved.'

'He is always peeved. Unless a lady happens along. Then he is all smiles and oily charm. If you want his favour, you might consider donning skirts.' She blushed furiously. 'I am not saying you look like the kind of man who likes dressing up in women's clothing, because I am sure you do not, but . . .'

'I never don skirts when I am in need of a shave,' said Chaloner, taking pity on her a second time. 'I find it spoils the effect.'

The comment coaxed a smile from her. 'You should not let that bother you – it will not be your face he is looking at.'

'You are Mrs Brome?'

'Joanna. My husband is Henry. But I expect you already know that. Silly me! Henry is always saying I talk too much, but he is a man, and they do not talk *enough*, generally speaking. Unless they are politicians or lawyers, of course. Then they are difficult to stop.'

Chaloner was relieved when the door at the bottom of the stairs opened, and Brome returned. The bookseller's face was flushed, and his wife rushed to his side with a wail of alarm.

'It is all right, dearest,' said Brome, patting her arm. He turned to Chaloner. 'You have met my wife, I see.

92

She helps me in my business. No one has a head for figures like my Joanna.'

Joanna smiled shyly. 'I do my best. And everything needs to be accounted for, because a single missing penny might result in an accusation of theft. L'Estrange is very particular about money.'

'It does not sound as though he is easy to work with.'

'He is good to us,' said Joanna immediately. 'Well, he is good most of the time, and—'

'It is all right, Joanna,' said Brome quietly. 'Heyden is from White Hall, so I am sure he already knows about L'Estrange's . . . idiosyncrasies.'

Joanna heaved a heartfelt sigh. 'Good! It is difficult to pretend all is well when Mr L'Estrange is in one of his moods, and I dislike closing the door and trying to distract customers with idle conversation in order to drown out his noisy rants. It feels duplicitous, and I am not very good at it anyway.'

'We were delighted when he chose us to help him with the newsbooks,' said Brome, seeming grateful to confide. 'He said our shop suited him better than any other, because it is near all the booksellers at St Paul's, and not far from his home. But he has such a black temper.'

'Actually, he is a bully,' whispered Joanna. She glanced nervously towards the stairs. 'And neither of us were really "delighted" when he said he was going to use our shop from which to run his business. We like the money – he pays rent for his office *and* for our help with his newsbooks – but he is not someone we would befriend, if we had a choice. He is so . . . well, *strong*. And we are not.'

'Yes and no,' countered Brome. 'He does not always get his own way.'

'True,' conceded Joanna. 'We managed to prevent him from publishing that libellous attack on ex-Spymaster Thurloe last month. It took some doing, but he admitted we were right in the end – that there was no truth in the spiteful things he had written.'

'I have no love for Cromwell's ministers, but that editorial was pure fabrication, and would have made us a laughing stock,' said Brome. 'L'Estrange needs our common-sense and sanity.'

Chaloner did not think Joanna would be overly endowed with either, because she seemed rather eccentric to him. Then he reconsidered. Her gauche awkwardness was doubtless due to her shy and nervous nature, and he did not blame anyone for being fearful when the likes of L'Estrange was brooding upstairs. When she smiled at him, and he saw the sweet kindness in her face, he found himself feeling rather sorry for her. He smiled back.

'He is in a foul mood today,' Brome went on. 'Unfortunately, he read that newsletter – the one addressed to Pepys – as soon as it arrived this morning, and it contains some of the stories we had planned to print in Thursday's *Newes*.'

'Again?' asked Joanna, shocked. 'But how? And what are we going to do? This cannot continue, because people will not buy the newsbooks if they are full of old intelligence.'

Chaloner frowned, not sure he fully understood the situation. 'I would have thought printing would confer a significant advantage on you. Surely it is faster to print a hundred sheets than to handwrite them, like Muddiman has to do? How can he disseminate news more quickly than L'Estrange?'

'Printing is a laborious process,' explained Brome. 'It involves hours of typesetting, and then, because compositors make mistakes, everything needs to be checked. Meanwhile, Muddiman employs an army of scribes. As soon as a letter is finished, a boy races off to deliver it, so news can be spread in a matter of minutes. We can flood the city with thousands of newsbooks, given time, but the newsletters are infinitely faster. The advantage is not as great as you might think.'

'If you say the government clerks are not responsible for the leak of information, then what about someone here?' asked Chaloner. He thought about Newburne, and decided 'news-theft' was an excellent motive for murder. Had the solicitor been selling L'Estrange's stories to Muddiman, and been killed for his treachery?

Brome seemed to read his mind. 'It was not Newburne. He was making too much money from L'Estrange to risk losing it.'

'Is that why you are here?' Joanna asked of Chaloner, suddenly displaying the same astuteness as her husband. 'Someone at White Hall thinks Newburne's death was not an accident, but connected to the news? Everyone has assumed the cucumber was responsible, but he did have enemies.'

'He did,' agreed Brome. 'He was corrupt, and I do not think he will be greatly missed by anyone.'

'His family will miss him,' said Chaloner, supposing that even solicitors had them.

Joanna nodded slowly. 'Yes, his wife is upset. However, if someone did kill him, the culprit will not take kindly to questions – and Newburne had some singularly unsavoury acquaintances.'

'I have already told him all this,' said Brome. 'And in

95

reply to your other observation, Heyden, no one here or at the printing-house would give our news to Muddiman. They would not dare, not with L'Estrange watching like a hawk and Spymaster Williamson looming in the background.'

'That is true,' said Joanna ruefully. 'They would be too frightened, and I know how they feel. L'Estrange tends to draw his sword first and ask questions later, and between him and Williamson, our staff are thoroughly cowed into unquestioning obedience. Us included. Well, most of the time. We make a stand if he does something brazenly unwise, like that editorial on Thurloe, and—'

Brome steered Chaloner towards the stairs. 'You had better not keep him waiting. We do not want a repeat of the ear incident.'

At the top of a flight of stairs that creaked, Brome opened the door to a pleasant office. Behind a large oaken desk sat the man Chaloner had seen squabbling with his rival in Fleet Street. His nose appeared even more prominently hooked close up, and the rings in his ears glittered. Because he looked so rakish and disreputable, Chaloner was astonished to see him holding a bass viol and bow.

'You do not mind if I play while we talk, do you?' he asked of Chaloner, waving a hand to indicate Brome was dismissed. The bookseller escaped with palpable relief. 'I am beset by phanatiques on all sides and music is the only thing that gives me the resolve to do battle with them.'

'That is a fine instrument,' said Chaloner, rather more interested in the viol than in pursuing his dangerous assignment for the Earl. 'Is it Spanish?'

'Why, yes,' said L'Estrange, pleasantly surprised. 'How did you know? Do you play?' He went to a cupboard before Chaloner could reply, and the spy saw several more instruments inside it, all equally handsome. 'Let us have a duet, then. It is difficult to find people willing to master the viol these days, because there is a modern preference for the violin. Or the flageolet, God forbid!'

'God forbid, indeed,' murmured Chaloner, running his hands appreciatively over the fingerboard while L'Estrange slapped a sheet of music in front of him.

'One, two,' announced L'Estrange, before launching into the piece with considerable gusto. Chaloner fumbled to catch up, and L'Estrange scowled. 'Count your beats, man!'

Apart from a few occasions when he had used his artistic skills to gain access to the sly Portuguese duke, Chaloner had had no time for music since June, and his lack of practice showed. He played badly, aware of L'Estrange's grimaces when he missed notes or his timing was poor. He would have done better had it been an air he knew, but it was unfamiliar and the notation was cramped and difficult to read. When it was finished, L'Estrange sat back and tapped it with his bow.

'Do you like it?'

'No.'

L'Estrange laughed. 'I composed it, and I am rather proud of it, to be frank. However, at least you were honest. Take it home, and we shall try it again in a few days – when you will make no mistakes, of course. But you did not come here to entertain me. What does the Earl want?'

'Two things. He has asked me to provide you with news about Portugal, and—'

97

'News?' pounced L'Estrange. 'Good! I will pay you double if you sell these reports only to me. Triple, if Muddiman asks for them and you tell him to go to Hell. What was the second thing?'

'He wants me to ascertain whether there was anything odd about the death of Thomas Newburne.'

'Does, he by God! Why? What business is it of his?'

'I wish I knew,' muttered Chaloner.

'Newburne ate a cucumber. I admit it is an odd way to go, but it is not entirely unknown. Colonel Beauclair and a couple of sedan-chair carriers went the same way, just this last month.'

'You think Newburne died of natural causes?'

'Of course he did. Obviously, he encountered a lot of dubious characters when he was working on my behalf – phanatiques, no less. But no one killed him.'

'When you speak of dubious characters, do you mean men like the Butcher of Smithfield?'

'Actually, I was referring to the booksellers he met. His association with Ellis Crisp was his own affair, and none of mine. However, I would have ordered him to consort with the Devil himself, if it meant safeguarding the King and his government. That is why I agreed to become Surveyor of the Press – to serve His Majesty with all the means at my disposal, legitimate or otherwise.'

'Suppressing books on mathematics is serving the King?' Chaloner was thinking of Leybourn.

'Yes, and so is stamping out dishonesty in the publishing trade. I have fined dozens of booksellers for breaking the law, including James Allestry who supplies the Royal Society, and William Nott who counts your master, the Lord Chancellor, among his customers. I mean to root out disobedience wherever I find it, even among those who consider themselves too grand for fines and disgrace.'

Chaloner was inclined to tell him that alienating an entire profession was probably not the best way to make a success of his appointment – and that there was a difference between enforcing the law and gratuitous persecution – but he held his tongue. 'What do you think happened to Newburne?'

'I have already told you: he ate a cucumber.' L'Estrange reflected for a moment. 'Of course, the fruit could have been fed to him by phanatiques. They are always lurking in coffee houses and taverns, waiting to strike.'

Chaloner thought he was being paranoid. 'I doubt they—'

'Are you one of them?' demanded L'Estrange. 'Yes, I imagine you are: your viol finger-work smacks of that old reprobate Maylord – a loyal Parliamentarian first, but then a Royalist when he saw it would serve him better. He had a very distinctive style of playing, and you mimic it.'

'I have never been taught by Maylord,' said Chaloner. But his father had, and he had passed the lessons to his son. He was impressed by L'Estrange's powers of observation, because he had not even been aware that the man had been studying him. 'Did Newburne play the viol with you?'

L'Estrange snorted his derision. 'Hardly! He liked music, but he had no talent for it.'

'I do not suppose *he* had lessons from Maylord, did he?'

The editor snorted a second time. 'Maylord was a good man who would never have subjected himself to Newburne's low company. Why do you ask? Is it because both died from cucumbers and you think there might be a connection between them? If so, then you are wasting your time.'

Chaloner would make up his own mind about that. 'How well did you know Newburne?'

'I did not give him a cucumber, if that is what you are asking. Have you ever heard the saying, "Arise Tom Newburne"?'

Chaloner nodded, although he did not admit that it had only been the previous day.

'It refers to his promotion from common lawyer to a man who worked for *me* – my arrival in London marked a dramatic upsurge in his fortunes. It is a by-word for anything that rises quickly.'

'Is it?' asked Chaloner, bemused. 'I was told it meant something else.'

'Then you were told wrong,' declared L'Estrange. 'Probably by a phanatique, trying to cause mischief. Tell me his name, and I will arrange for him to be visited by some of Newburne's persuasive friends – Hectors. They are useful fellows to know when dealing with dissidents.'

'It was the Earl of Clarendon. Do you want his address, or do you know where he lives?'

L'Estrange glowered at him. 'You should have told me who you were talking about. The Earl and I have known each other for years, and I mean *him* no harm. Indeed, he has always been a good friend to me, and I to him.'

'You hired Newburne to do what, exactly?' asked Chaloner, going back to his investigation.

'Mostly to visit booksellers and assess their stock for unlicensed publications. He was paid a shilling for every one that he discovered, which was a fine incentive for him to succeed. He was good at it, too. He was also in charge of watching Henry Muddiman. Do you know Muddiman?'

'Only by reputation.'

'You mean his reputation as a villainous rogue, who ran a pair of sub-standard newsbooks before Spymaster Williamson arranged for me to be promoted into his place?'

'Something like that.'

'He is a sly devil, and owes allegiance to nothing but money. We all want to be wealthy, but some of us have other interests, too. He does not. Newburne was paid to watch him, to see where he obtains the intelligence for his filthy newsletters. They undermine my newsbooks, you see.'

'Can you not suppress them?' asked Chaloner facetiously. 'As you have the mathematicians?'

Irony was lost on L'Estrange. 'Muddiman does not need one of my licenses, because his reports are hand-written, not printed. And as he does not sell them in shops, they are not within my purvey.'

'They appear in taverns, though,' said Chaloner. 'I have seen them myself.'

'Landlords subscribe to them, because newsletters attract customers eager for information. I do not like it, but it is within the law, and there is nothing I can do to stop it. Unfortunately.'

'Did Newburne ever attempt to steal news from Muddiman? Or try to prevent the newsletters from being written?'

'Yes, but he never succeeded, because Muddiman was far too clever for him. However, much as I would love to see Muddiman swing for murder, I am afraid he did not kill Newburne. No one did – the man died because

101

he ate a cucumber. Do you have anything else to ask me?'

'Not at the moment.'

'Good, because I have had enough of being interrogated. I have answered all your questions, so you can tell the Earl that I co-operated. However, I do not want you prying into Newburne's death any further, because I have appointed a man of my own to do it.'

'Who?' asked Chaloner in surprise. 'And why, if you claim there is nothing odd about—'

'Hodgkinson, the fellow who prints my newsbooks. He was with Newburne when he died, so he is the perfect man for the task. And the reason I asked him to investigate is because I do not want the stink of murder hanging around my office. It is all the fault of people like you, you know.'

'Like me?'

'Suspicious types, who see conspiracy everywhere. Newburne's death was natural, and Hodgkinson will prove it. In fact, he has probably proved it already, so go and speak to him yourself. He lives on Thames Street, although I imagine he will be at Smithfield today; he has a booth on Duck Lane, where he sells printed certificates for meat. Talk to him, then go back to your Earl and tell him there is nothing about Newburne that warrants further investigation.'

'And what of the phanatiques who you say *may* have given Newburne the cucumber?'

L'Estrange shot him a wolfish grin, and his earrings flashed. 'Hodgkinson will ferret those out for me, if they exist. You will not interfere. If you disobey, I promise you *will* be sorry.'

* * *

102

Before Chaloner left Brome's shop, he wrote a brief report about the Portuguese preparations for war with Spain. As he scribbled, he considered his next move. There were now several people he was obliged to interview. First, there was the solicitor's friend Finch. Next, there was Hodgkinson the printer, who, for all Chaloner knew, might already have solved the case. And finally, there were the two prestigious booksellers, Nott and Allestry. Like Leybourn, the pair had endured L'Estrange's persecution, and he wanted to assess whether they felt sufficiently bitter to avenge themselves on his informant. Chaloner knew Nott owned the shop that stood across the road from Brome's, because he had collected books from it for the Earl in the past, so he decided to start there.

When he arrived, Nott was entertaining an important visitor, whose magnificent coach stood outside, selfishly blocking the entire road.

'Heyden,' said the Earl of Clarendon amiably, as the spy entered. 'Nott is rebinding my copy of Rushworth's *Historical Collections*. Shall I have it done in blue-dyed calf-skin or red?'

'Green,' said Chaloner, wondering whether the Earl was there by chance, or whether he was ensuring his spy was doing as he was told. He found himself deeply suspicious. 'Blue is common, and red is favoured by courtesans who cannot read.'

The Earl gaped at him. 'Most of my collection is bound in red or blue.'

'I shall fetch some more samples, sir,' said Nott, beating a prudent retreat. 'In green.'

'I have started looking into Newburne's death,' said Chaloner, when they were alone. 'So far, everyone has

103

either warned me away because Newburne knew a lot of dangerous people, or they say it is quite normal for men to die from eating cucumbers and that I am wasting my time.'

'I saw you go into Brome's shop,' said the Earl. 'Which tale did he spin you? That Newburne's death was natural? Or that you will endanger yourself if you persist with your enquiries?'

'Both. Why *do* you want this case investigated, sir? At White Hall, I was under the impression that L'Estrange had asked for your help in finding out what happened, but he was bemused when I offered my services, and tells me they are not needed. So, what is the real reason? Is it because your own bookseller, Nott, was victimised by Newburne, and you think he might be the culprit?'

Clarendon pursed his lips. 'What a wild imagination you have! I like Nott, and it would be a shame if you learn he is the killer – if there is a killer. He really does produce excellent bindings.'

'You did not tell me that other people have died from ingesting cucumbers, either,' added Chaloner, trying not to sound accusatory. He did not succeed, because he was angry with the Earl for playing games with secrets, and his temper was up.

'I did not tell you, because I did not know,' snapped Clarendon, irritable in his turn. 'If it is true, then perhaps I have sent you on a wild goose chase, and there is nothing to assess. However, Newburne was unpleasant *and* he engaged in sordid dealings – if he was not murdered, I shall be very surprised.'

'But *why* do you want to know? What is Newburne to you? Did you hire him to help you with something? He had a reputation for knowing a good many villains.'

The Earl glared at him. 'Was that an accidental conjunction of two statements, or do you imply that *I* am one of these "villains"?'

It had been an accident: Chaloner was not so foolish as to call his master a villain to his face. All he had meant to say was that Newburne might have known the right people for the unpalatable tasks that often went hand-in-hand with high government office, and that Clarendon might have used Newburne much as he was currently using Chaloner. However, he was not so chagrined by his slip of the tongue that he failed to notice the Earl had used the gaffe to avoid answering his question.

'Did he work for you?' he pressed.

Clarendon grimaced. 'You really are an insolent fellow, Heyden. Were you like this with Thurloe? Accusing him of sordid dealings and then demanding answers to questions that are none of your concern?' He sighed crossly. 'Very well, I shall tell you what you want to know, although I would appreciate discretion.'

'I am always discreet,' said Chaloner, offended by the slur on his professionalism.

'So you say, but there are men with deep pockets who seem able to bribe just about anyone these days, so you will forgive my scepticism. I employed Newburne when I was first appointed Lord Chancellor. He served me well for a while, and I was so pleased with his diligence that I arranged for him to receive a state pension. Then I discovered he was less than honourable, and I dismissed him.'

'Employed him to do what?'

'Petty legal work, although that is irrelevant to what I am trying to tell you. When my secretary, Bulteel, uncovered evidence that Newburne was stealing from me, I sent the man away in disgrace and thought no more about it. After a week or two, he started to work for L'Estrange who, as Surveyor of the Press, is also a government official. The upshot is that, technically speaking, Newburne never left government service, and as with all state pensions, there is a clause stipulating that a sum of money will be paid to the next-of-kin if the holder dies while engaged on official business.'

'And because you organised the award, you – not L'Estrange – are liable to pay it?'

'Precisely! You have it in a nutshell. Newburne's widow came to see me the day after he died and reminded me of my promise – showed me the documents I had signed. Now, I do not mind the expense if he really did die while conducting government business, but I am not so keen on paying if he was murdered because of some corrupt dealing of his own. *That* is what I want you to find out.'

'I see,' said Chaloner. So, he was being commissioned to see whether a widow could be cheated of her due. He began to wish he had stayed in Portugal.

'She is not poor,' said the Earl sharply, reading his mind. 'And all I want is the truth; if you say Newburne died while working for L'Estrange, then I shall happily honour the debt. However, as the pension will come from money raised by taxing the people, I am under a moral obligation to spend it properly, not squander it on tricksters.'

'Right,' said Chaloner noncommittally. 'Why did you not tell me this yesterday?'

'You looked tired, and I did not want to burden you with too much information. Ah, here is Nott. Oh, no! I do not like green bindings at all.'

Chaloner had no idea whether he finally had the truth,

but supposed that cash might well motivate the Earl into wanting to know what had really happened. Clarendon selected blue leather for his books, then was gone in a flurry of noise, horses and lace. Chaloner was left alone with Nott.

'It must be galling for you, living opposite the man who fined you for selling unlicensed texts,' he said, rather baldly. The Earl had annoyed him, and he did not feel like being circumspect.

Nott – a small man with hair tied in an odd bun at the back of his head – grinned. 'It was, but now Newburne will no longer be slinking in and out, life will be much more pleasant. Did the Earl order you to investigate the death? If so, I would be careful, if I were you. There is not a man in London sorry to see him in his coffin.'

'So I have been told,' said Chaloner sourly. 'Several times.'

The sky was overcast when Chaloner left Ivy Lane, and a bitter wind blew in from the north-west. He cut through St Paul's Cathedral, thinking that while it appeared to be magnificent from a distance, Leybourn had been right to voice his concerns about its structural integrity. Cracks snaked up its walls, and fallen clumps of plaster littered the floor inside, along with bird droppings and a thick layer of filth that had been tracked in from the streets and never cleaned up. He left wondering how long it would be before it simply gave up the ghost and crumbled into dust of its own accord, leaving the site free for Wren's monstrosity.

The second bookseller L'Estrange had mentioned was James Allestry, who not only held the grand title of

Stationer to the King, but was also the man who provided books for the Royal Society. Allestry's premises were in a noble Tudor house that stood in the cathedral's yard, but although he answered Chaloner's questions politely enough, he was able to add nothing more than that he had been furious when he had been fined, and that members of the Royal Society had made sure the King had known what had happened. His Majesty was outraged, Allestry declared, although Chaloner suspected the regal annoyance derived from the fact that he had been pestered with such a matter in the first place, rather than the iniquity of the fine itself.

'Do not think *I* murdered Newburne, though,' said the bookseller as Chaloner reached for the door latch to let himself out. 'I would have stabbed him in his black heart, not given him a cucumber.'

'Did you know cucumbers were poisonous?'

'Everyone knows it, although I was always sceptical, to be honest,' replied Allestry. 'I am not sceptical now, though. I wonder if L'Estrange likes them. I may send him a basket if he does. I hear they can be bought in Smithfield *and* Covent Garden these days.'

Chaloner walked to Thames Street, the western end of which stood in the shadow of Baynard Castle, a handsome fifteenth-century palace. The building perched on the banks of the mighty Thames, and twice a day, muddy brown waters lapped around the feet of its elegant buttresses. Chaloner imagined they were currently lapping rather higher than was comfortable for its occupants, given the volume of rainwater that was being discharged into the river upstream.

Richard Hodgkinson's print-shop was a vast, windowless basement, located near the palace's back gate. It was a gloomy place. Its walls dripped moisture and a recent flood had left puddles on the floor, which combined to give the impression that the whole place was below water level.

Printing was a grubby business, and everything in the room was black and sticky with spilled ink. It was noisy, too, with clanking machinery and apprentices yelling to each other as they manipulated heavy plates and sheaves of paper. Nimble-fingered typesetters selected letters from neat rows of boxes, and a listless boy stirred a vat of reeking chemicals. The place stank of hot oil and the thick, sludgy ink that was kept fluid over charcoal fires. There was a greasy mist in the air that did nothing to improve the atmosphere, and Chaloner was able to deduce, from the way the workmen stared curiously at him, that visitors were rare.

Hodgkinson was a smiling, energetic man with an unfashionable beard and hands so deeply stained with the materials of his trade that Chaloner doubted they were ever fully clean.

'You want to purchase cards?' he asked eagerly. 'To advertise your business? I can do some in red, although it costs extra. You wear riding boots, so are you connected with horses? Have you lost one? If you look in Thursday's *Newes*, you will see three separate notices for nags that have been pilfered, and two are returned already.'

'Did Newburne ever advertise a lost horse?'

Hodgkinson was startled. 'Newburne? What does he have to do with anything?'

'The Lord Chancellor has asked me to ascertain how he died. I understand you were with him at the time.'

Hodgkinson gaped at him. 'The Lord Chancellor is

109

interested? Why? Newburne died a natural death – he ate a dangerous fruit.'

'The Earl is interested in many things,' said Chaloner smoothly. 'And L'Estrange tells me he has asked you to look into the matter on his behalf. Will you tell me what you have learned so far? The Earl will be very grateful.'

Hodgkinson nodded keenly. 'I am always willing to help the government, although you must remember that I am a printer, not a constable, and do not possess the skills necessary for looking into sudden deaths. However, I shall tell you what I have gathered to date. As you will be aware, the dead man was responsible for the expression, "Arise, Tom Newburne", but he will not be doing much arising now. He is dead for certain this time.'

Chaloner regarded him blankly. 'He has been dead before?'

'Yes – he died during the Bartholomew Fair. I witnessed the incident myself.'

Chaloner did not know as much about this most famous of London festivals as he should have done. 'In August?' he asked carefully, hoping to elicit more information.

Hodgkinson regarded him oddly. 'Of course in August. That is when it always takes place. It lasts two weeks, when all is flurry, noise and colour, and then Smithfield reverts back to normal.'

'Right,' said Chaloner, wondering how 'normal' Smithfield could be when the likes of Crisp were said to control it. 'So, Newburne went to the Bartholomew Fair in August . . .'

'He, I and several others were watching a rope-dancer, when a stone struck his head. He keeled over and lay as still as a corpse. Then Annie Petwer comes along and

shouts, "arise, Tom Newburne" and up he leaps, like
Lazarus.'

'Who is Annie Petwer?' asked Chaloner.

'A trollop. She charged him five shillings for her services, but I have never seen a man more willing to part
with his money. Newburne was a miserly fellow, despite
the fact that he was rich.'

'I am not sure I understand precisely what happened.
Who threw the stone? Annie Petwer?'

'No one threw it; it was flicked up by a passing carriage.
It happens all the time, as you will know if you have
spent any time in the city.'

'And this woman stepped forward and told him to
stand up?' It did not sound very likely, and Chaloner was
not sure he believed it.

Hodgkinson grinned. 'Exactly! And now you know
where that particular expression comes from.'

'I see. Newburne is famous, then?'

'Locally famous, although he was a rogue, if you want
the truth. He did a lot of business with Ellis Crisp, and
I am sure you do not need me to tell you what *that* says
about a man.' He pursed his lips.

'I do not,' agreed Chaloner, 'but what did Newburne
have to do with Crisp and his gang of Hectors?'

'He gave Crisp's various business ventures a veneer of
legality, and advised him on how to win confrontations
with the law. It was unnecessary really, because people
are so frightened of Crisp that they tend to let him do
what he wants anyway.'

'Are *you* afraid?'

Hodgkinson rubbed his bearded chin. 'I own a small
shop on Duck Lane, which is in Smithfield, so I am
obliged to pay Crisp a sum of money each month. If I

refuse, my stall is subject to thefts and broken windows. I would not say I am afraid exactly, but I own a healthy respect for his authority.'

'So Newburne was involved in this extortion?'

Hodgkinson looked uncomfortable. 'You have a blunt way of putting things! Newburne told Crisp to call it a safety tax, which sounds a lot nicer. Do you really want to know all this? It will see you in danger if you report it to the Lord Chancellor. Crisp has built quite an empire for himself, and he will not appreciate you telling the government about him. Besides, I suspect they already know, and are wisely turning a blind eye.'

'It is wise to ignore bullies who demand money with menaces?'

'*Very* wise. And the fools who told the Butcher they did not want his protection now wish they had kept their mouths shut – those who have not been baked in his pies, of course.'

'Right,' said Chaloner. He turned the discussion back to the solicitor. 'What happened the day Newburne died – not the time at the Bartholomew Fair, but his real death last Wednesday? L'Estrange says you were with him then, too.'

Hodgkinson nodded. 'I had just finished printing the latest edition of *The Newes* when Newburne happened by. He was not a man I would normally have chosen for company, but he offered to buy me a pie at the Smithfield meat market, and I never decline a free meal. Well, who does?'

'I thought Newburne did everything with his close friend Heneage Finch.'

'He did usually, but Finch plays in a consort of trumpets and was busy that evening. If Finch had been available, Newburne would never have asked me to join him.'

'Does Finch ever perform with a musician called Maylord?'

'Maylord the violist? I would not have thought so. Maylord was extremely good, and I doubt he would have bothered with an amateur like Finch. Why do you ask?'

'Idle curiosity. You did not like Newburne, did you, despite him buying you pies?'

'Not much. But I did not kill him.'

'*Was* he killed? You said he died from eating cucumbers.'

Hodgkinson looked flustered. 'I am trying to tell you what happened, but you keep interrupting. So, Newburne and I walked to the market, where we ate pies and drank ale. Then we stopped to watch the dancing monkeys, and he bought a cucumber from the costermongery on Duck Lane. He had some marchpanes, too, and a gingerbread cake. He had been moaning about feeling sick most of the afternoon, but then, without warning, he suddenly gripped his belly and dropped to the ground.'

'Did he complain about feeling sick before or after he ate all this food?'

'Both. He was a heavy drinker, and I assumed too much wine on an empty stomach had made him costive. I encouraged him to eat, because I thought food might ameliorate his sour humours.'

'Did he choke?' asked Chaloner, thinking that if Newburne had swallowed ale, pies, cakes and a cucumber, there would have been ample opportunity for someone to slip him poison – if poisoned he was. If Newburne had been feeling ill anyway, perhaps none of the food was responsible.

113

'He started gasping for breath and clutching his stomach. I thought he was drunk at first – as I said, he enjoyed his wine.'

'And then what?'

'Then he just died. He gasped a few times, shuddered and lay still. When froth poured from his mouth, I realised he was genuinely ill, but by then it was too late – and there was no Annie Petwer to tell him to arise. He lies in St Bartholomew the Less, if you want to inspect his corpse. I have been several times, but he is definitely dead this time.'

'Where can I find Annie Petwer?'

Hodgkinson shrugged. 'God knows. I imagine she lives in London, though. The Fair attracts a lot of folk from the country, but I would say Annie Petwer is local.'

Chaloner shook his head, bemused by the tale. 'What do you think happened to Newburne? A fit? An aversion to cucumbers? Poison?'

'When L'Estrange asked me to investigate, I paid a surgeon to inspect the body. The fellow has written me a certificate saying Newburne really did die from cucumbers.' He extracted a document from a pile on a desk, holding it carefully between thumb and forefinger, so as not to soil it with his inky hands. 'Here. He says cucumbers cause dangerous vapours to collect in the veins, and these eventually result in a fatal imbalance of the humours. I have no reason to doubt his conclusions.'

Chaloner read what was written. The medic had cited the great Greek physician Galen to support his hypothesis, and his own credentials included membership of the Company of Barber-Surgeons, so he was unlikely to be a complete charlatan. Chaloner tapped the letter thoughtfully. 'Unfortunately, this does not tell us whether the

114

cucumber was dosed with some kind of toxin, or whether Newburne just suffered a bad reaction to this type of fruit.'

Hodgkinson scratched his head. 'I suppose not. However, the surgeon said lots of people die from cucumbers, so there is no reason to suspect foul play. Is there anything else I can tell you? If not, I had better be getting back to work, or we will be late with the bills for the play at the Duke's House this evening.'

'One more question: do you know where Henry Muddiman lives?'

Hodgkinson regarded him warily. 'His office is at the sign of the Seven Stars, near the New Exchange on The Strand. Why? Are you not convinced by my explanations? You intend to follow your own investigation, even though there is nothing to look into?'

'I doubt the Lord Chancellor will be satisfied with what I have uncovered so far.'

Hodgkinson's expression was grave. 'You seem a decent man, so here is a friendly warning: walk away from Newburne while you can. It is what I intend to do myself.'

'That sounds like a threat.'

'It is not meant to be. To be frank, it crossed my mind that Newburne might have fallen foul of Crisp somehow – friends turned enemies and all that – and if it was a good man who lay dead, I might press the matter. But we are talking about Newburne here. He is not worth dying for.'

'So you do not believe his death was natural? You are sceptical of your surgeon's conclusions?'

Hodgkinson looked shifty. 'I do believe them – and that is what I shall tell L'Estrange. I am not brave enough to do anything else. Look, I *like* the Lord Chancellor – he

115

is a sober, godly fellow among all those debauched courtiers. Tell him to ignore Newburne, and use his spies to defeat his enemies at White Hall instead. It will be better for all of us that way.'

Unfortunately, Chaloner suspected the Earl would not agree. Pensions cost a good deal of money, and what was the life of an insolent spy when compared to a fortune?

Chapter 4

Chaloner was not very good at ascertaining causes of death from corpses, but he had acquired a certain expertise over the years, and knew he should visit Newburne's in St Bartholomew the Less as soon as possible. Hodgkinson's surgeon had declared there to be no suspicious circumstances, and if Chaloner also saw nothing to suggest the medic had been mistaken – such as broken teeth or bruised lips – then perhaps the commonly accepted tale about Newburne's death was true, and he had indeed died from eating something that had disagreed with him.

Yet there were questions to be answered, even so. Had someone forced him to eat cucumbers, knowing they would do him harm? And did the fact that he was so universally detested really have nothing to do with his death? Chaloner decided he had better speak to Muddiman about the matter regardless, as he was the obvious suspect for any foul play. And there was still Finch's opinion to consider – the only person in the city said to have liked the solicitor. Chaloner supposed he should also interview Newburne's wife, although he would have to tread carefully. He doubted she would be very forthcoming once she learned he worked for the man who was trying to wriggle out of paying her pension. Mulling over all he had learned, he walked to the church.

St Bartholomew the Less was located at the edge of the vast, open, diamond-shaped space that was Smithfield. Livestock lowed and bleated in the semi-permanent stocks, unsettled by the stench of blood and entrails from the nearby butchers' stalls. As he approached the church, Chaloner glanced at the people he passed, wondering whether any were members of the notorious Hector clan. He was disconcerted to note that the area contained more than its share of disreputable types, and he did not like the way loutish-looking men gathered on street corners in small but menacing groups.

The smaller of the two churches dedicated to St Bartholomew had been chapel to the nearby hospital of the same name, and was full of memorials to worthy surgeons and physicians. There were fine stained-glass windows, most depicting scenes from the Bible that involved healing, and the font, screen and pulpit were carved from old, black oak. It smelled of damp prayer-books and the pine cones someone had piled along the windowsills, and its thick, ancient walls muffled the racket from outside. Chaloner was pleased to find it deserted. Ever cautious, he placed a pewter jug by the door, so that if anyone opened it, the receptacle would be knocked over, and the resulting clatter would warn him to stop what he was doing.

He made for the lady chapel, where an elaborately carved coffin was covered by a pall of heavily embroi-dered material. Hurrying, because he was sure he would

118

not be alone for long, he dragged the cloth away, revealing the man underneath. Newburne had been slightly built, with a small, thin moustache, like the King's. Under his rich wig, his pate was bald and shiny, and Chaloner recalled the Earl commenting on Newburne's hairless state. Although Chaloner knew better than to make assumptions about a man's character from the look of his corpse, there was definitely something about Newburne that suggested deceitfulness and villainy.

But it was not the time for leisurely analysis, so Chaloner began his physical examination. First, he opened Newburne's mouth, and looked down his throat. As far as he could tell, it was clear, and he did not think Newburne had choked on his cucumber. His teeth were intact, and there was no indication of bruising around the lips. There was, however, a faint smell of something rank, which made him wonder whether the solicitor had ingested something that had done him no good. There was no sign that he had been struck on the head, although a faint scar on his left temple was evidence of an older injury; Chaloner supposed it had been caused by the stone that had allowed Annie Petwer to order him up from the dead.

He put all to rights, and stared thoughtfully at the corpse. Hodgkinson's description of Newburne's death, along with the smell that lingered around his mouth, suggested poisoning was not out of the question. But was it a natural reaction to eating a fruit generally deemed dangerous, or had someone deliberately ended his life? And if the latter was true, then had the toxin been in the cucumber? Hodgkinson said the solicitor had also partaken of pie, wine, gingerbread and marchpanes, and any one of them could have held something dangerous. Further, Hodgkinson

119

had mentioned Newburne complaining of feeling ill even before he had made a pig of himself. Chaloner considered what he knew about poisons.

Newburne had died quickly, which suggested the substance had been strong. And if it was strong, then it would have left marks – on the innards it had damaged, but also on other parts of Newburne's body it might have touched during the process of ingestion, namely his hands and lips. Chaloner looked in the mouth again, and thought he could detect tiny blisters. Then he turned his attention to the hands. They were cold, limp and unpleasant to the touch, but it was worth the experience, because there were green stains on the fingers, and an underlying redness that looked as though the skin had burned. There was the same unpleasant odour, too, and when Chaloner dipped a corner of the pall into a puddle on a nearby windowsill, and tried to scrub the marks away, they remained. He had his answer: Newburne *had* been provided with a caustic substance that had damaged his fingers and then killed him after he had swallowed it. Such a thing would not occur naturally in a cucumber, which meant someone had probably put it there.

He left the church with a sense of achievement, and went to the stalls that fringed the edge of the Smithfield Meat Market, looking for the costermongery on Duck Lane, where Hodgkinson said Newburne had bought his cucumber. There was only one, because most vendors preferred to sell their wares at Covent Garden or Gracechurch Street, which were famous for their agricultural produce. A sign declared it was the shop at the Lamb – the Lamb being the seedy tavern two doors down – and it sold spices, baskets and pewter plates, as well as a surprisingly varied array of fruit and vegetables. Judging from its neat shelves and well-dressed staff, it was a profitable enterprise. Between it and the Lamb was an odorous establishment that displayed printed cards in its grimy windows. Chaloner wondered whether it was significant that Newburne had purchased his cucumber from the shop that was located next to one of Hodgkinson's two print-works.

'A cucumber?' asked the man who came to serve him. On the side of the counter was a pile of advertisements that claimed he was Samuel Yeo, grocer and merchant. 'They cost threepence – expensive at this time of year, because they need to be grown inside, for warmth. Is it for a lady?'

'No,' asked Chaloner suspiciously, handing over half his worldly wealth. 'Why would it be?'

'Because they use them to obtain beauteous complexions,' explained Yeo.

'Presumably, they can also be eaten?'

Yeo smiled. 'They can indeed, and the seeds are excellent for ulcers in the bladder or expelling an excess of wind, so there are benefits to including them in your diet.'

'Right,' said Chaloner.

Yeo detected his scepticism. 'There is a school of thought that says they are dangerous, but do not believe it. Any fruit is poisonous if taken with greed, and cucumbers are no different. Will there be anything else? We had a consignment of fresh spices this morning – galingale *and* cubebs. Take some galingale – its mild ginger flavour will disguise the taste of any rancid meat you need to use up. If you make a purchase, I shall include a handful of my fine peppery cubebs, too.'

Chaloner parted with another penny in the interests

121

of his investigation. He put the spices in his pocket, hoping it would not be too long before he had an opportunity to buy something to cook them with, and that when he did, galingale would not be needed to disguise its state of decomposition.

'This is an unusual location for a costermonger's shop,' he said conversationally. 'Most are at Covent Garden.'

'We do well here, though. People come to Smithfield for meat, then stop to buy a few carrots or a couple of onions for a stew. We save them a walk.'

'Do you own the shop yourself, Mr Yeo?'

'God bless you, no! The owner is a courtier at White Hall, but he never visits. Mr Newburne managed the business for him, and paid him his quarterly profits. It was an arrangement that suited them both. And me, too – I make a good living without the worry of complex finances.'

Chaloner regarded him in surprise. '*Newburne* managed this shop? And it was here that he bought the cucumber that killed him?'

Yeo became indignant. 'People say he died of cucumbers, but I know for a fact that he swallowed pie, cakes and ale as well. He came to demand a cucumber because he said he had pains in his bladder, but it was not our fine fruit that caused his demise. It was something else.'

'He thought the cucumber would make him feel better? How ill was he?'

'He was experiencing some mild discomfort, probably as a result of all the things he had eaten when he was out walking with Hodgkinson. He was a greedy man – and not a nice one, either.'

'Why do you say that?'

122

'He used his association with Butcher Crisp to bully people. He often came here for food, and he took what he wanted, but never paid for it. When Jones of the Lamb complained that Newburne never paid for his ale, Newburne told Crisp to raise the price of his safety tax. That taught us all to keep our mouths shut.'

'Newburne had that sort of influence over Crisp?'

'He did according to him, although I suspect Crisp pleases himself what he does. There he is.'

He pointed through the open door, and Chaloner saw a man of medium height, swathed in an unfashionable but practical cloak and a tall sugarloaf hat. The Butcher was surrounded by a pack of disreputable-looking henchmen, and he walked with a cat-like arrogance. His people clustered around him in a way that suggested they expected an attack at any moment, and Chaloner supposed constant unease was the lot of a man who made his money by preying on others. He considered going to talk to him about Newburne, but what could he say? That he knew the solicitor had helped with his illegal activities? Crisp's answer was likely to be 'so what?' Reluctantly, because he was getting desperate for concrete clues, Chaloner decided it would be wiser to tackle Crisp only when he had a better idea of what to ask.

Once outside, he slit the cucumber with his dagger and smeared the greenish milk that seeped out across his wrist. He let it dry, but it came off with the most perfunctory of rubs, and it was not the same dark hue as the marks on Newburne, anyway. It confirmed his suspicion that it had not been natural cucumber juice that had caused the damage to the solicitor's hands and mouth. He shoved the fruit in his pocket, but realised the discovery had left him with more questions than answers.

123

He was perturbed that Newburne had been unpopular in quite so many ways. The man had spied on Muddiman. He had persecuted booksellers, even ones with powerful patrons like Nott and Allestry. He worked for L'Estrange, who was also detested. He associated with an underworld king and helped him extort money from people. Almost everyone Chaloner had spoken to admitted disliking the man, and even Newburne's associates – Crisp and the Hectors – were not above suspicion. It was not unknown for criminals to turn on each other with fatal results.

And was there a connection between Newburne's death and Maylord's? It seemed they had not known each other, and they had certainly not moved in the same circles. Had Maylord's killer left a cucumber at the scene of *his* crime because it seemed to be a cause of death that no one would question? Then what about the others who had died from the same thing: Valentine Pettis, Colonel Beauclair and the sedan-men? Had they been murdered, too? They were almost certainly buried, so Chaloner could not inspect their bodies. But what could a military man, a horse-trader, two labourers, a shady solicitor and a musician have in common?

He decided he would ask questions about the other deaths if the opportunity arose, but that he would have his hands full with unveiling Newburne's poisoner and Maylord's smotherer. And he had promised to investigate Mary Cade for Thurloe, too. He would be busy enough without enlarging his investigation to include men who might well have died natural deaths. He sighed, and hoped a visit to Muddiman would provide him with some answers.

* * *

Chaloner walked south along the Old Bailey. It was not raining, although there was an unpleasant chill in the air, and the kind of dampness that suggested the clouds were gathering their strength for future downpours. Although it was barely noon, the day was dark because of the lowering greyness above. Eventually, he reached The Strand, and asked directions to Muddiman's office. He was directed to a tall, respectable house near the New Exchange. Although it was old, it was well-maintained, and there was evidence that recent money had been spent on it – the roof boasted new tiles, the window shutters were freshly painted, and the plaster façade was unusually clean.

He knocked on the door, and was admitted to a comfortable room on the ground floor. It was dominated by a large table that was piled high with papers and pamphlets. He took the opportunity to sift through a few, hoping to find evidence that Muddiman obtained his news from an official government source, but instead he learned that some of the men who subscribed to the newsletters responded in kind by providing Muddiman with information of their own. There was a lot of correspondence about the recent uprising in the north, providing a variety of different opinions. Reading them all would provide the newsmonger with a more balanced view of the situation than just accepting the government's version of events, and Chaloner was not surprised people preferred Muddiman's objectivity to L'Estrange's one-sided rants.

There were also notices in foreign languages, especially French, along with a smattering of scribbled messages from courtiers. None carried news of any great import, and he supposed Muddiman included them to give his readers some light-hearted relief, as a break from the serious political analyses. Also among the chaos was a pamphlet on 'exploding oil' by John Lawrence of Blackfriars, who blithely recommended leaving his compound in places where burglars might find it – the moment a felon tried to use the volatile oil, it would ignite and spare the city the expense of a trial.

After a few moments, a pretty lady in a black wig arrived, smiling and gracious.

'I am afraid my husband has gone out to his favourite coffee house – the Folly on the Thames – with Giles Dury. You have only just missed them. They have been working all morning.'

Chaloner gestured to the table. 'On their newsletters?'

'On *Henry's* newsletters. Giles is just an assistant, and his wife is a seamstress at White Hall.'

'Right,' said Chaloner, thinking it was an odd piece of information to impart. Unless, of course, Mrs Muddiman was trying to tell him that she was a cut above the mere Mrs Dury.

'Roger sees her there occasionally,' she went on disapprovingly. 'That means she has an unfair advantage over me, because he does not like coming here.'

'Roger? You mean L'Estrange?' Joanna Brome had told Chaloner that L'Estrange had a reputation for seducing other men's wives, but surely he would not make a play for Muddiman's and Dury's?

'L'Estrange,' she echoed with a dreamy smile. 'A very handsome man. Do you not think?'

'Too rakish for my taste,' Chaloner replied uneasily. Was she the reason L'Estrange was so willing to draw his sword against Muddiman outside the Rainbow Coffee House? He was hoping to dispatch his rival and so get

126

at his spouse? 'And I prefer men who do not wear earrings.'

'It is the earrings I like,' she said with a conspiratorial grin. 'I bought Henry a set, but he refuses to wear them.'

'I wonder why,' muttered Chaloner.

The Folly, or the Floating Coffee House, was a timber shed on a barge. It was usually anchored midstream, and patrons were obliged to hire skiffs to reach it. That day, however, the Thames was so swollen that the Folly had been moored near the Savoy Palace, and customers could embark directly from the Somerset Stairs. Several men hovered outside it. Some were the drivers of private carriages – which could only just fit down the narrow alley leading from The Strand, and woe betide anyone walking in the opposite direction – and others were idle boatmen whose trade was suspended because of the state of the river. One fellow stood out as not belonging there. He was large, with a face that was the colour and shape of a ripe plum, and he carried a tray of apples that no one seemed very interested in buying.

The Folly was not a large establishment, although it was horrendously crowded, so it was impossible for Chaloner to avoid the coffee-boy who came to see what he wanted to drink. He bought a dish of coffee with his last penny token, and managed to secure a seat at Muddiman's table. The newsmonger was holding forth about the northern rebellion, declaring that the news-books had given it a significance it did not deserve. It was, he claimed, a silly prank devised by a dozen harmless zealots, and not the great, terrifying revolt L'Estrange had described in that day's *Intelligencer*. Men smoked and listened as Muddiman systematically destroyed his rival's arguments. He put his case so well, and with such close attention to detail, that Chaloner found himself doubting the veracity of L'Estrange's reports, too. Eventually, most patrons finished their noonday victuals and went back to work, and Chaloner was able to speak to Muddiman in reasonable privacy.

The newsmonger was dressed in fashionable clothes, and clearly took pride in his appearance. He carried a town sword with a delicately jewelled hilt that looked as though it would be useless in a fight, and perched on his head was the yellow wig he had worn the previous day, when he had argued with L'Estrange. His round face was clean and pink from a recent shaving, and Chaloner felt grubby and disreputable by comparison.

With him was the companion who had protected him from L'Estrange, taller and broader than his friend, but just as handsomely attired. He introduced himself as Giles Dury when Chaloner told them who he was and what he wanted, then crossed his long legs and sat back with an amused grin. His superior, laconic demeanour was an attitude often affected by courtiers, and Chaloner supposed Dury had learned it from them, perhaps when visiting his wife the seamstress.

'So, you are the Earl of Clarendon's man,' said Muddiman, looking Chaloner up and down with thinly masked disdain. 'And you are here to question me about Newburne.'

Dury sniggered. 'Poor Newburne! He will not be arising now, for Annie Petwer or anyone else. Do you know how that saying came about?'

'A stone struck his head—' began Chaloner.

'That is a tale he invented to disguise its real meaning,' said Dury, chuckling. 'He *was* stunned by the stone, but

128

he leapt to his feet in self-defence when he heard Annie Petwer telling him to arise. She was his lover, and "arising" was something he seldom did, according to her.'

'He was impotent,' elaborated Muddiman, obviously thinking Chaloner might not understand the joke unless it was explained. 'Do you know why a grand man like the Earl of Clarendon should be interested in what happened to a devious snake like Newburne?'

'He is interested in the sudden death of anyone connected with the government's newsbooks.'

'How very thorough of him,' drawled Dury. 'But then, he is a tediously thorough man.'

Chaloner sipped his coffee and winced at the flavour: the beans had been over-roasted, and the resulting brew was bitter.

'Well?' demanded Muddiman. 'What do you want to know?'

'Did you have dealings with Newburne?'

Muddiman drank some coffee, sufficiently used to the Folly's habit of bean-burning that no expression of distaste crossed his face. Indeed, he looked as though it was perfectly acceptable, and waved to the coffee boy to bring him more. 'Not directly, although I knew L'Estrange had ordered him to watch me. Both Spymaster Williamson and L'Estrange are jealous of my newsletters – and with good cause. I disseminate information Londoners are pleased to have.'

'The only items of interest in *The Newes* and *The Intelligencer* are the advertisements for lost and stolen horses,' added Dury. He snickered maliciously. 'A man simply cannot *live* without knowing such things.'

Muddiman picked up a copy of *The Intelligencer* from the table, using his thumb and forefinger, as if he considered

129

it unclean. 'A man cannot live without knowing that L'Estrange deems the Norwich Quakers "licentious and incorrigible", either, or that the Danish court plans to hold – of all things – a meeting! I cannot imagine how readers contain their excitement at such tidings.'

'Poor Brome,' said Dury with mock sympathy. 'He had the makings of a decent newsman, but now he debases himself by associating with L'Estrange. The same goes for his frightened mouse of a wife.'

'Rabbit,' corrected Muddiman. 'Joanna is too tall to be a mouse.'

Their spite was beginning to be annoying, and Chaloner felt the sniping attack on Joanna was wholly unnecessary. 'So Newburne spied on you,' he said, forcing himself to be patient. 'Did you meet him in any other capacity?'

'What other capacity?' demanded Dury contemptuously. 'We did not condone his persecution of booksellers, so we had nothing to do with that. Furthermore, we distance ourselves from L'Estrange's newsbooks and the idiots who work on them. And we certainly have nothing to do with Ellis Crisp.'

'Despite all this, Newburne's evil reputation was not entirely justified,' said Muddiman. His eyes gleamed, and Chaloner was not sure if he was being serious. 'He *was* dishonest, but he was not as corrupt as people would have you believe. He was wealthy, as attested by the fact that he owned several houses, but that does not mean he earned his *whole* fortune by cheating, theft and extortion.'

'It was Crisp's doing; he deliberately allowed the rumours to grow to improbable levels,' agreed Dury. 'It is obvious why: Newburne was more useful to him as a disreputable villain who would do anything for the right price. It enhanced Crisp's reputation, too – made people more nervous of him.'

Muddiman chuckled. 'Is that possible? The Butcher of Smithfield does not need anyone *more* nervous of him.'

'The Earl is concerned that Newburne's death may have nothing to do with cucumbers,' said Chaloner, not really interested in their malicious musings. He watched their reactions to his comment closely, but could read nothing in them.

'He certainly ate one before he died,' said Muddiman evenly. 'Hodgkinson is witness to that, and so were several bystanders.'

'Perhaps he ate it knowing it would have fatal consequences,' said Dury with a grin. 'I have heard it said that he was a Roman Catholic, and papists are odd about matters of conscience. I expect his many sins overwhelmed him at last, and he killed himself in a fit of penitence.'

'Remorse led him to commit the even greater sin of self-murder?' asked Chaloner, thinking he had never heard such rubbish. 'That does not sound like the act of a dutiful son of Rome.'

'Then maybe he was drunk.' Dury was resentful that his theory should be so disdainfully dismissed. 'He did not know what he was doing. Do you know for a fact that there is something odd about Newburne's death, or have you allowed the Earl's suspicions to influence you? I heard Hodgkinson hired a surgeon to inspect the body, and he said cucumbers were the cause of death.'

'How do you know about the surgeon?' asked Chaloner.

'We are newsmongers,' Dury sneered. 'Very little

131

happens in the city without it being reported to us. Another example is your own little foray into the world of reporting. You wrote a piece on Portugal for Thursday's *Newes*. L'Estrange is delighted with it.'

'But only because he thinks it will be exclusively his to print,' added Muddiman slyly. 'Of course, you could earn yourself ten shillings, if you were to share it with us.'

Chaloner pretended to consider the offer, his mind working fast. His first assumption was that they had a spy in L'Estrange's office, who was selling secrets. Then he realised that any such spy would have given them the entire piece – it was not very long, and would have taken no more than a moment to copy. *Ergo*, they had learned about his article another way. Ivy Lane was a busy thoroughfare, and loiterers would be difficult to spot by people preoccupied with work. Had Muddiman, or one of his scribes, lurked outside Brome's shop and overheard part of a conversation? It seemed most likely.

'I do not want your money, thank you,' he said, smiling pleasantly at them. 'The Earl would not approve of me accepting bribes. Do *you* believe Newburne died of eating cucumbers? Honestly?'

Muddiman shrugged, clearly disappointed with his response. 'There is no reason to think otherwise. Of course, he had more enemies than stars in the sky, so it would not shock me to learn one of them had elbowed him into his grave.'

'Enemies like you?' asked Chaloner innocently.

'No, not like me. If I had killed him, I would have done it discreetly, and there would be no Lord Chancellor's spy sniffing around the case.'

'You bought three cucumbers from the market in

Covent Garden the day before Newburne died. I do not suppose one of those ended up inside him, did it?'

Muddiman smiled, although there was a glimmer of alarm in his eyes. 'I wondered how long it would be before someone gossiped about that in order to see me in trouble. I use cucumbers in a decoction for wind, but I certainly would never *eat* one. Nor would I expect anyone else to do so.'

'Tell me how you lost control of the newsbooks to L'Estrange,' said Chaloner, abruptly changing the subject in an attempt to unsettle him. 'It happened recently, I understand, forcing you to resort to handwritten news.'

His tactic worked, because Muddiman's expression was decidedly uneasy. 'My newsbooks were popular and lucrative, but success attracts envious eyes. Have you ever met Spymaster Williamson?'

'Once or twice.'

'He was jealous of my financial success, so he lobbied for me to be dismissed and L'Estrange to be appointed in my place – L'Estrange *shares* the newsbooks' profits with Williamson, you see, whereas I kept them all for myself. But Williamson badly misjudged the situation. I have spent years in the business of newsmongering, and it did not take me many days to establish a list of men willing to pay for a weekly letter that contains good, reliable news.'

'How long a list?'

'I sell to about a hundred and fifty customers, each of whom pays a minimum of five pounds per annum. Some give me as much as twenty pounds.' Muddiman's expression was smug. 'I make more than a thousand pounds a year, while the newsbooks manage less than two hundred.'

'Our success has stunned Williamson,' added Dury.

133

'But it should not have done. L'Estrange's publications are rubbish, and our newsletters have flourished, at least in part, *because* of them – people subscribe to us because the newsbooks are so dismally bad. Williamson has lumbered himself with a worthless editor and publications that are a national joke.'

'I imagine he is not pleased,' said Chaloner. It was a gross understatement. Williamson was shockingly greedy, and would be furious to think of a thousand pounds going into Muddiman's pocket.

Muddiman grinned. 'He is livid. Of course, I understand his sense of loss: money is important, and it is certainly all *I* want from life. Yet I have learned that the best way to get rich is by maintaining decent standards in my work. L'Estrange has not understood that lesson, despite Brome's valiant efforts, and his purse and Williamson's are suffering the consequences.'

'We have told you all we know now,' said Dury, standing and stretching languorously. 'And I have a report to write about the northern rebellion – to tell folk what *really* happened up there. You should be wary of pursuing this Newburne business any further, though. There are some things that even the Lord Chancellor's spies should not risk, and tampering with Butcher Crisp is one of them.'

'Why?' asked Chaloner. 'What do you think he might do?'

'Anything he likes,' replied Dury. 'Stay away from the man if you value your life. Just go back to White Hall and tell your Earl that there is nothing about Newburne's death to investigate.'

Chaloner left the Folly feeling that he had learned very little, except that Muddiman and Dury might well have dispatched Newburne, and that the feud over the news-books was more bitter and complex than he had first realised. He was about to visit Newburne's friend Heneage Finch, when he became aware that he was being watched – the plum-faced apple-seller was regarding him with more than a passing interest. He recalled thinking earlier that the man stood out as not belonging, and the feeling intensified when he saw he was making no attempt to hawk his wares.

The trader was a hulking fellow, who wore good riding boots below a scruffy coat. His knuckles were scarred from fighting, but there was a copy of *The Intelligencer* poking from his pocket, suggesting he had acquired a modicum of education. He did not carry a sword, but there was a long dagger at his waist, and a bulge near his knee suggested there was another in his boot. All told, he was a man of strange contradictions – and he was no more an apple-seller than was Chaloner.

'How much?' Chaloner asked, to ascertain whether the man knew the going rate for his goods.

The fellow regarded him appraisingly. 'Good coffee, was it? What did you talk about with those fine gentlemen in there?'

Chaloner was startled by the ingenuous interrogation. 'I do not see that is any of your affair.'

'You want an apple? Then answer some questions.'

Chaloner held out his hand, and was presented with a somewhat wizened specimen. He started to eat it anyway, despite the fact that it was brown in the middle and maggots had been there before him. It had obvi-ously been discarded by a more reputable merchant, and had been retrieved from a refuse pile to provide the man with a cover. Chaloner had done much the same himself

135

in the past, although he hoped his disguises had been rather less transparent.

'What do you want to know?' he asked.

'Who are you?' asked the apple-seller. 'And what did you want with Muddiman?'

The apple-seller was clearly someone's spy, so Chaloner opted for honesty. A number of people already knew who he was and what he was doing, and if he lied and was later found out, it might cause needless trouble. 'The Earl of Clarendon ordered me to investigate the death of Thomas Newburne.'

The apple-seller jerked his head towards the coffee barge. 'I would love to tell you Muddiman or Dury had a hand in it, but I have been watching them for weeks – ever since L'Estrange was given power of the news-books – and I know for a fact that they are innocent.'

'You work for Williamson,' surmised Chaloner. He supposed he should have guessed; the Earl had already told him that the Spymaster would commission his own agents to find out what had happened to the solicitor. 'Are you looking into Newburne's death? What is your name?'

'My name is unimportant. And my remit is to watch Muddiman and Dury – nothing else.'

'Why them?'

The apple-seller sighed impatiently. 'Because the news-books are important. They are the way the government communicates with its people, so they need to be protected from dangerous enemies like Muddiman and Dury. That is what *I* am doing.'

Chaloner was bemused. 'But Newburne was employed to work on the very newsbooks you are paid to safeguard. His death might be a hostile move against them.'

The man stared at him in a way that suggested the idea had not occurred to him before. It did not say much for the efficiency and cunning of Williamson's secret service. 'I suppose it might,' he conceded reluctantly. 'Muddiman and Dury had nothing to do with it, though. I watch them day and night.'

'What happens when you sleep?'

'I only rest when they are in bed. And they rise late, so I am awake before them in the mornings.'

Chaloner was appalled when he saw the man genuinely believed he had them covered twenty-four hours a day – and appalled that Williamson was apparently satisfied with the situation. 'How can you be sure they did not hire someone to do their dirty work? That Newburne was not killed on their orders, while they sipped coffee and you watched them?'

The apple-seller regarded him askance, and Chaloner suspected an astute pair like Muddiman and Dury would run circles around the fellow. One would slip out of a back door while the other sat in plain view, and Williamson's spy would have no idea what was happening.

'They would not do that,' the man declared resentfully. 'They would not dare.'

'What do *you* think happened to Newburne?' Chaloner asked, ignoring the claim. He suspected he was wasting his time in soliciting the opinion of such a fellow, but there was no harm in being thorough.

'He swallowed too much cucumber. He was a glutton for expensive things and they cost threepence. Most people use them in decoctions for wind, but he actually *ate* the one he got from the costermongery in Smithfield. Witnesses said he took real bites, like you are doing with that apple.'

137

'If I were to suggest to you that his cucumber had been poisoned, and invited you to guess who might have tampered with it, what would you say?'

'That neither of us has an hour to spend naming all the possible candidates. However, if I were a betting man, my money would be on L'Estrange.'

Chaloner was taken aback. If the apple-seller was watching Muddiman for Williamson, then it meant he and L'Estrange were on the same side. It was thus an odd choice of suspects. 'Why?'

'Because Newburne had dealings with Ellis Crisp, the Butcher of Smithfield, who operates on the wrong side of the law. Newburne was useful to L'Estrange, but embarrassing, if you take my meaning. It is like hiring Hectors for certain government business. They are good value for money – and efficient at what they do – but you would not want the general populace knowing about it.'

'Are you speaking hypothetically here? Or are you saying Williamson appoints known criminals on the government's behalf?'

The apple-seller gazed at him in puzzlement. 'I thought you said you worked for the Lord Chancellor. Of *course* Williamson makes use of felons! It works out cheaper to hire them as and when they are needed, than to maintain an organised band of louts on a permanent basis. You look shocked. Are you new to government service, then?'

Chaloner was not shocked at all, although he could not help but note that Thurloe had never allowed himself to stoop to such tactics. 'I did not know the Earl—'

'The *Earl* does not run an intelligence service and have a turbulent city to control, so I doubt he is obliged to sully his hands by consorting with villains. But we digress. If you want a suspect for Newburne – assuming he really was murdered – then look to L'Estrange. Hah! Muddiman and Dury are coming off the barge. They are waving to me, damn it! I hate it when they do that. They are not supposed to know I am here.'

Chaloner finished the apple and left the man to his business, thinking Williamson's spy was no proof of guilt, innocence or anything else as far as Dury and Muddiman were concerned.

There was still an hour of daylight left, so Chaloner went to see if he could find Heneage Finch at his home on Ave Maria Lane. It was not difficult to identify the house, because the notes of a trumpet sonata were tumbling through the window of an upper floor. Finch was an enthusiastic but indifferent player, and his performance was not enhanced by the fact that he had chosen a dire composition. It was full of discord, and sounded as though it had been written by someone who could not read music. Or perhaps it was Finch who could not read, and he was butchering a perfectly respectable air.

Chaloner climbed the stairs to the first floor, and found himself in a corridor that had no windows, so was entirely devoid of outside light. A lamp hung on the wall, but it was almost empty of fuel, and illuminated very little. The whole building had a vaguely neglected air and smelled of burned cabbage. He knocked on the door, and a man answered with his trumpet still in one hand. He was tall and thin, with pockmarked skin and the largest ears Chaloner had ever seen.

'Am I disturbing you?' he asked anxiously. 'I assume

you are the fellow who has taken the room next door? My friend Newburne used to rent it, but he . . .'

He trailed off and looked away; someone was distressed by the solicitor's death, at least. Chaloner did not disavow him of the notion that they were neighbours, hoping he might learn more than if Finch thought he was on an errand for the government.

'You play well,' he said, smiling pleasantly. 'Where did you learn?'

'I taught myself,' said Finch, gesturing that Chaloner was to step inside his room. It was poorly furnished and messy, and smelled of wet boots and the mould that was growing up one of its walls. 'I am not very good, although I do play in a consort. My name is Hen Finch, by the way.'

'Tom Heyden. Did you say Newburne rented the room next door? I thought he owned a mansion on Old Jewry.'

'He did, but he kept a room here, too, because it is near the newsbook office, and only a short walk to Hodgkinson's print-house on Thames Street. Sometimes he was obliged to work late at both places, and no man who values his life likes walking too far in the dark.'

'True enough. I was pickpocketed yesterday,' lied Chaloner, to encourage him to talk more.

Finch shot him a sympathetic glance. 'I was robbed once, but Newburne had a word with people, and I got everything back. He was a good friend, and I shall miss him.'

'He knew the thieves who attacked you?'

'Ellis Crisp did. He and Newburne were colleagues.'

Chaloner pretended to be astonished. 'Colleagues? But surely Crisp is a felon?'

Finch stared at his feet. 'I was horrified when Newburne

140

agreed to perform certain legal duties for him – mostly property conveyancing or getting the Hectors out of prison – but he said it was a good career opportunity, and it did make him rich. Besides, he said not all of Crisp's dealings are unethical or against the law. Some of his business is perfectly respectable.'

Chaloner was sure that was true: it would be virtually impossible for a man to do everything on a criminal basis, and there would be times when Crisp had no choice but to revert to legitimate tactics.

'I do not like the sound of his pies, though,' Finch went on in a low, uneasy voice. 'And I shall never eat one, no matter how hungry I might be. They are said to contain the bodies of his enemies.'

'So I have heard,' said Chaloner, trying to keep the scepticism from his voice.

'Working for L'Estrange did not make poor Newburne very popular, either,' continued Finch unhappily. 'But people did not *know* him. If they had taken the time to forge a friendship, as I did, they would have found him charming, witty and kind. He was a great lover of music, and often hired professional consorts to play for him.'

'Did he ever hire a violist called Maylord?'

'Not as far as I know, although he heard Maylord perform at White Hall once. He heard Smegergill on the virginal, too, although I think Smegergill is not as talented as he used to be. It must be because his fingers are stiffening with age, and I suspect his days as a musician are numbered.'

Chaloner smiled his satisfaction. A real connection at last! He had known there had to be one. 'I admired Maylord myself. It is a pity both he and Newburne are dead of cucumbers.'

141

'I heard a surgeon was hired to confirm the nature of Newburne's demise, but I have no faith in leeches. Perhaps he was eating a cucumber when he died – Hodgkinson says so, and he is an honest sort – but can we be sure it actually *caused* his death? Personally, I think someone did away with him.'

'Really? Who do you suspect?'

Finch fiddled with his trumpet. 'A bookseller, perhaps. They broke the law, but acted as though it was Newburne's fault when he caught them. Or L'Estrange, because he did not like the fact that Newburne worked for Crisp, as well as for him. Still, we shall never know, because it is far too dangerous a matter to probe.'

Chaloner pretended to agree, then paused as he was about to leave. 'I do not recognise the sonata you were playing. What was it?'

Finch waved a hand to where the music lay on the windowsill. 'It is a composition I found when Newburne's wife and I cleaned out his room – your room now. She said I could have it as a keepsake, and I have been struggling to master it for his sake. It occurred to me that he might have written it himself, and I thought I might play it at his funeral.'

'Do you think it strikes the right tone for such an occasion?' asked Chaloner, trying to be tactful.

Finch smiled sadly. 'I suppose not. The melody is not pleasant, and there are too many discordant intervals. I have not been asked to perform anyway. I offered, but L'Estrange told me in no uncertain terms that he wanted professional musicians. And no one goes against what L'Estrange wants. He is a bold and powerful man.'

'He certainly likes to think so,' said Chaloner.

* * *

Dusk brought the promised rain, and Chaloner sloshed to White Hall through water that was pouring from the higher parts of the city. When he glimpsed the river between The Strand's mansions, he saw it running swift and brown in the last of the daylight. He wondered whether it would burst its banks.

He needed to do three things at the palace: tell the Earl what he had learned about Newburne, collect his back-pay from the Accompting House, and speak to Smegergill about Maylord. When he arrived, however, he found the accompters already gone home – the Court refused to buy lantern fuel until after the Feast of All Souls, so until then, work finished when it became too dark to see. The same was not true of the Earl's clerk Bulteel, who was bent over his ledgers by the light of a single candle.

'You will spoil your eyes,' said Chaloner, watching him rub them. 'Ask the Earl for a lamp.'

'The Court is not made of money,' snapped the Earl, appearing suddenly at the door to his office. 'And we must all forgo life's little luxuries in the interests of fiscal efficiency. What do you want, Heyden, other than to encourage my clerks to make unreasonable demands? I am busy.'

'I came to tell you that I inspected Newburne's body today, and I am sure he was fed a toxic substance. Not a cucumber, but something else.'

'I am not surprised, given his unpopularity. Who is the culprit? And was it connected to his work for L'Estrange? I spoke to Williamson about *him* paying the pension, since the newsbooks are his remit, but he said I was the one who made the promise, so I should be the one to honour it. It is a highly unsatisfactory

143

state of affairs, and I want you to resolve it as soon as possible.'

Chaloner tried to read his expression in the dim light. Was he being ordered to 'discover' that Newburne's death was unrelated to his government post, to relieve the Earl of an unwelcome expense? He was used to dishonesty, but Thurloe had never asked him to cheat anyone, and he found he did not like the notion that his new master might have different expectations. It occurred to him that it was just as well Williamson did not want him in the government's intelligence services, because he doubted the Spymaster would tolerate squeamish principles among his operatives. He was beginning to suspect that Clarendon might not, either, and decided he had better mask his distaste.

'There are a lot of suspects, sir,' he said vaguely. 'I will continue the investigation tomorrow.'

'Very well, but do not take too long – Newburne's widow wants a decision.' The Earl turned to his secretary, indicating Chaloner was dismissed. 'What did you want me to sign, Bulteel? This? What is it? I cannot see in this light.'

'You could forgo the luxury of reading it in the interests of fiscal efficiency,' retorted Chaloner, before he could stop himself. The Earl's oblique order had unsettled him, and he began to question all over again the man's motive for commissioning the investigation. Was it really to avoid paying a pension, or was there a darker, more sinister reason? He found he did not trust Clarendon to tell him the truth, and it was his wariness of the man's unfathomable games that had prompted the insolent remark.

Anger darkened the Earl's face. 'One day you will push me too far, Heyden. And do not think Thurloe will protect

144

you, because his sun is setting fast. Watch your tongue, or you will regret it.'

'Have you lost your senses?' demanded Bulteel, when Clarendon had stamped away, slamming the door behind him. 'He is the Lord Chancellor of England! Can you not find a lesser mortal to insult?'

Chaloner felt his temper subside. Bulteel was right: nothing would be gained from antagonising the man who paid his wages. And if the Earl was not prepared to be honest, then the investigation was just going to take that much longer and he would have to wait for his answers.

'I do not suppose you know if Smegergill's consort is playing tonight, do you?' he asked, feeling it was time he did something to find out who had smothered Maylord. He had had enough of the Earl and Newburne for one day.

'Yes – at the Charterhouse near Aldersgate Street. However, it is a private soirée, so you will not be admitted. You will have to wait until Thursday if you want to hear him. His group – well, it is Greeting's consort, really – is due to play for Newburne's funeral, which is a public occasion.'

Chaloner was inclined to give up and go home. He had had almost nothing to eat that day – which he suspected might have been partly responsible for his petty remark to the Earl – and he was still tired from his sea-voyage from Portugal. But he was not sure when he would have time to look into Maylord's trouble if he did not act when he had a free evening, so he forced himself past the end of Fetter Lane and the tempting sanctuary of his rooms, and on to where the Charterhouse school comprised the remains of an old Carthusian monastery, set amid pleasant gardens.

145

Bulteel was right in saying he would not be allowed inside, so he did not try. Instead, he found a doorway, and sheltered from the rain as best he could, waiting for the party to be over. Drops pattered on to his hat, and he sent silent thanks to Isabella for making him a gift that would not only protect him from attack, but that was completely waterproof, too.

He was used to standing still for long periods of time, because spying often necessitated that sort of activity, but he was cold and miserable even so. He was not far from Smithfield, and drunken yells and women's shrieks suggested that neither darkness nor inclement weather curtailed the activities that so shocked the Puritan broadsheet writers. He wondered whether it was Butcher Crisp's infamous Hectors who were making such an ungodly racket.

It was some time before the concert came to an end and the entertainers emerged wearily through the back gate. A carriage had been hired to take them to their homes, and Greeting was one of the first to climb in it. Chaloner was careful to stay out of sight: Greeting was a gossip and he did not want the Lord Chancellor to learn he was investigating Maylord's death as well as Newburne's, and risk annoying him even further. Smegergill – described by St Margaret's verger as having a sadly poxed face – was the last to leave; he walked slowly, as if his joints hurt. Chaloner stamped life into his frozen feet before moving to waylay him.

Smegergill was older than Maylord had been. His hair was white, and his face scored with wrinkles. He still possessed an imposing physique, though, despite his age and pain-ridden gait, and the gaze that fell on Chaloner when he emerged from the darkness was imperious. The spy recalled Thurloe saying that the musician could be 'difficult', and hoped he would not decline to answer questions – or suggest he asked them at a more reasonable time of day.

'I am a friend of Maylord's, sir,' Chaloner said, holding his hands in front of him to show he was unarmed. He spoke softly, so Greeting would not hear him and recognise his voice. 'He wrote to me, but I have only just returned to London, and I am afraid I was too late to find out what he wanted.'

'Chaloner?' asked Smegergill, peering at him. 'Nephew of the regicide?'

It was not how he usually identified himself, and Chaloner was immediately alert for trouble, bracing himself to make a run for it when the man yelled that a dangerous rebel was lurking in the shadows. Smegergill sensed his unease and reached out to touch his arm.

'It is all right. I was your father's friend, too – he died during the wars, fighting for the wrong side, like so many good men. You have nothing to fear from me.'

Chaloner did not recall his father ever mentioning Smegergill, but the wars had been a long time ago, and his father had entertained a long succession of men in hooded cloaks during those turbulent years. The musician might well have been one of his clandestine guests.

'Did Maylord tell you what he—'

Smegergill silenced him quickly. 'Maylord said he had written to Frederick Chaloner's son, and you look uncannily like your father. I have been expecting you.

147

Do you remember me? I was at your house in Buckinghamshire many times before and during the wars.'

'I am sorry.'

Smegergill seemed surprised. 'Well, I suppose you were only a child.'

'Hurry up, Smegergill!' shouted Greeting impatiently. 'I am exhausted and want to go home, but the coachman says Hingston and I are to be dropped off last, because we live in Smithfield. The longer you dally, the later we will be in our beds.'

'It is what we always do,' objected the driver, not liking the censure in Greeting's voice. 'We always take the furthest home first, and the nearest last. It is common practice.'

'Go without me,' called Smegergill. 'I am with the son of a friend; he will see me safely home.'

'Be sure he does, then,' ordered Greeting, leaning forward in an attempt to see them. Chaloner moved into the shadows, and Greeting was not curious enough to step out into the rain for a better look. 'Good virginals players are rare these days, and you will be missed if anything happens to you. Keep your hands warm. We are playing for L'Estrange again tomorrow, and you know how critical he can be if our playing does not reach his exacting standards.'

The carriage rattled off. 'My mother played the virginals,' said Chaloner. 'And so do my sisters.'

'All your siblings are talented that way,' said Smegergill fondly. 'Far more so than your regicide uncle, whose only skills were for politics and intrigue. But we should not talk about him; he is best forgotten in this current climate. Is that oak tree still at the gate to your father's manor?

148

Each May-day, he had it decorated with ribbons, and there was music from dawn to dusk.'

'It blew down.' It was a pity, because the spring celebrations under the Chaloners' oak were famous across the whole county, and they had continued even when the Puritans had declared such festivities illegal. Maylord had been a regular guest, and had declared it his favourite event of the year.

Smegergill shook his head sadly. 'Everything is changing, and not for the better. What can I do for you, Chaloner? Or may I call you Frederick?'

'Frederick was my father, sir. I am Thomas.'

'Quite so, quite so. Maylord said he wrote to you because he wanted your help. He discovered something, and he did not know what to do about it. Documents.'

Chaloner's pulse quickened. 'Documents? Do you know what was in them?'

Smegergill sighed. 'He would not let me read them, because he said it would be dangerous, and I am too old and wise to have pressed him. We play music in the homes of wealthy, powerful men, and I suppose he discovered something amiss in one of them. He was agitated over the last two weeks – he even left his pleasant cottage on Thames Street, and refused to tell anyone where he was going.'

'The Rhenish Wine House in Westminster,' supplied Chaloner. He took a breath, deciding a blunt approach would be the best one. 'He was murdered. Suffocated.'

Smegergill's hands flew to his face in horror. 'No! He said he feared assassins, but I thought he was overreacting. Are you sure about this? Everyone else said he died of cucumbers.'

'I inspected his body, so yes, I am sure.'

149

Smegergill looked away, and Chaloner saw a tear course down his leathery cheek. It was some time before he spoke. 'I should have guessed, but the truth is that I did not want to see the truth. He hated cucumbers – he avoided all green fruits, because he said touching them gave him itching skin and boils. He would *never* have eaten one. Damn my foolish blindness!'

'Do you have any idea who might have meant him harm?'

'None at all – everyone loved him. Why? I hope you do not intend to investigate. It might prove to be dangerous.'

'I would like to see his killer face the justice of the law-courts.'

Smegergill regarded him unhappily. 'I do not know about this. I was fond of your father, and I do not want to see his son in peril.'

'Do not worry about that, sir. Smothering an old man and harming me do not represent the same sort of challenge, and the killer may decide there are limits to the risks he is willing to take. But we will not know unless we see these documents. Do you know where they might be?'

Smegergill smiled sadly. 'It was my friendship with your father that prompted me to warn you against investigating, but I am glad you are not a coward. Maylord was my closest friend, and I do not want his murderer to go free. I shall help you find out what really happened. What shall we do first? You say he lived in the Rhenish Wine House?'

Chaloner did not like the notion of embroiling Smegergill in whatever Maylord had discovered, but did not want to alienate him by excluding him too soon. 'We

150

should read these documents before deciding on a course of action.'

Smegergill gripped his arm. 'You are a good boy, Frederick. I shall tell your father when I see him.'

'I am Thomas, sir, and my father died years ago.'

'So he did. During the wars, fighting for the wrong side, like me. I am a Royalist now.'

'So am I,' said Chaloner, beginning to have serious reservations about Smegergill's potential as an ally. 'Do you think Maylord's documents will be in his room?'

'He would not tell me where he had put them – for my own safety, apparently. It will take a cunning lad like you to discover where he hid these papers, though; I doubt a silly old man like me will have any luck. Where is the carriage that will carry me home? We can ask the driver to take us to Maylord's lodgings first.'

'It has already gone. We shall have to hire another.'

'Of course. But it is no good waiting here for one to come along, not at this time of night. We shall have to walk to Long Lane. There are always hackneys in Long Lane, ready to take people home from the Smithfield taverns.'

Chaloner assumed he meant the brothels. 'What about your hands? Greeting told you to keep them warm. Perhaps you should go home, and leave me to—'

'I am seventy years old,' said Smegergill sharply. 'And during that time I have learned how to look after myself. I may be forgetful, but I am not stupid.'

Chaloner was startled by the sudden curtness, and supposed it was what Thurloe had meant when he had described Smegergill as difficult. He mumbled an apology, then hastened to grab the musician's arm when he started to stalk off in entirely the wrong direction. He turned

151

him around gently, and began to ask questions, knowing it would be unwise to place too much trust in the old man's memory, but desperate enough to take intelligence from any source available, no matter how addled.

'Was anything else worrying Maylord? Other than the contents of these documents?'

'He thought he was being cheated,' replied Smegergill as they walked. The streets were dimly lit by lanterns placed outside some houses, but the rain-clouds blotted out any light there might have been from the moon. 'Do you know Cromwell? He has a discerning ear for music.'

'How did Maylord think he was being cheated?'

'He owned some property, although I forget what, exactly. He told me it was not making the sort of returns it should, and was quite upset about it. Do you play the viol, Frederick? No! You said you play the virginals, like your mother. You see? I am not as senile as you think!'

Long Lane was wholly devoid of hackney carriages, so they turned south, taking a short-cut to Duck Lane, which Smegergill insisted would be teeming with coaches. They had just reached St Bartholomew the Great and its dark, leafy graveyard, when the hairs on Chaloner's neck stood on end, the way they always did when something was amiss. He stopped dead in his tracks and listened hard.

'Perhaps you should find the man who cheated Maylord over his property,' chattered Smegergill, 'They might have argued and come to blows. Perhaps *he* stabbed poor Maylord.'

Chaloner drew his sword and pushed the musician behind him. Something was definitely wrong.

'What is the matter?' asked Smegergill. Alarm flashed in his eyes. 'Is it the Bedlam men?'

152

Chaloner had no idea what he was talking about, and was more concerned about the danger lurking in the shadows, anyway. 'The what?'

'The wardens from St Mary's Bethlehem – the lunatic house,' Smegergill gabbled. 'Two Court musicians have been locked away there recently, and I might be their next victim.'

'Why?' asked Chaloner, most of his attention on the churchyard, because he was certain someone was hiding there. 'You are not insane.'

'Neither were they. You will not let them take me, will you? The others were snatched on dark nights, just like this one.'

Chaloner silenced him with an urgent wave of his hand and took a step towards the trees. Then something struck him hard on the jaw and his senses reeled. He fell to his knees and saw a stone at his feet; someone had lobbed it with considerable strength and accuracy. He was vaguely aware of footsteps behind him and of Smegergill speaking, but the words were a meaningless buzz. He tried to stand, but his movements were sluggish and uncoordinated, and he was powerless to prevent the sword being pulled from his fingers.

Then he was dragged off the road and into the churchyard. He struggled, but too many hands were holding him, and he was dizzy and disorientated. A kick to his stomach effectively quashed any further attempts to extricate himself, leaving him gasping for breath. When someone started to go through his pockets, he supposed he was the latest victim of Smithfield's infamous Hectors. He was disgusted with himself, furious that common thieves had so easily bested a man of his experience.

'Nothing,' came one voice. Chaloner supposed his

purse had been found, and for once he was glad it was empty. 'Except a cucumber.'

'A poisonous one?' asked someone else. He laughed nasally, as though he had a cold. 'Make him eat it.'

'Where is the old man?' said a third man. His lilting accent said he was from north of the border. 'He was here a moment ago.'

Chaloner made a mammoth effort to break free, and the dagger he kept in his sleeve slipped into the palm of his hand. One man tried to grab it, but reeled back with a badly sliced finger for his pains. Chaloner had just staggered to his feet when someone dealt him a powerful blow with a cudgel. It was hard enough that it would certainly have killed him, had he not been wearing Isabella's metal-lined hat. Even so, it knocked him flat, and he could not have moved to save his life. He heard more voices, then there was a soft crack, as if a blow had fallen. Moments later, someone kicked him in the side, although not very hard. It was followed by more footsteps and silence.

Chapter 5

Chaloner climbed to his feet, wincing at the sharp ache in his head as he moved. It was pitch black in the church-yard, but when he removed his hat, his probing fingers detected a substantial dent in the protective metal. The robbers would be astonished to learn he had survived such a solid clout. He stood still for a few moments, willing the dizziness to recede, then began to search for Smegergill.

It did not take him long to locate the old man. He tripped over him in the dark, where he was lying face-down in a puddle. He hauled him up quickly, but Smegergill was already dead. Chaloner felt sick with self-recrimination. It was his fault the musician had embarked on a futile search for a carriage in the dead of night, and then he had failed to protect him. He closed his eyes, disgusted with himself. St Bartholomew's was in Smithfield, and he had been listening to tales about the dangers of that place all day. How could he have been so stupid? Furthermore, a man with his skills and experience should never have allowed a gang of common louts to best him. He pulled the body into a faint shaft of light from the road, and saw a cut on Smegergill's lip. Had someone lobbed a stone at him, too, then pressed his face into water until he had stopped struggling?

Recalling how he had been searched for valuables, he tried to locate Smegergill's purse, and was surprised when he found it still attached to his belt. It was empty except for a key. The thieves had also missed a heavy – and doubtless valuable – ring that Smegergill had been wearing on his index finger. Chaloner did not intend to remove it, but it slid off into his hand when he tried to inspect it. As he gazed numbly at it, he tried to work out what had happened. Sensibly, the robbers had dealt with their younger, stronger victim first, so it was no surprise that Chaloner had been stripped of his possessions immediately – or would have been, had he owned anything worth taking – before they had turned to Smegergill. So why had Smegergill been left with his ring and purse? Had the felons been disturbed before they could finish? Chaloner had not heard a third party arrive, but that was not surprising, given that he had been barely conscious at the time.

Nearby voices made him jump in alarm. Should he shout for help, or were the robbers returning to end what they had started? His head pounded, and he doubted he would emerge triumphant from another skirmish. Of course, the voices could belong to people who would help him carry Smegergill to a church and send for the parish constable. Unfortunately, though, he suspected they were more likely to draw entirely the wrong conclusion from a man kneeling next to a corpse, and accuse *him* of the murder instead. He scrambled to his feet when a man and a woman stepped into the churchyard with a lantern, apparently intent on finding a dry spot for a romp.

156

The man stopped dead in his tracks when he saw Chaloner, and his eyes were drawn to the still figure on the ground. 'What have you done?' he cried, beginning to back away.

Instinctively, Chaloner donned his hat. It was partly to stop the light from lancing into his eyes, but also to conceal his face. He could predict from the tone of the question how the encounter was likely to end, and did not want the fellow or his lady to be able to identify him later. He had enough to do, without being obliged to prove his innocence for a crime he had not committed.

'He has a ring,' shouted the woman. The fact that she had noticed such a detail in the dim lamplight indicated she was the kind of person who would be more interested in what happened to Smegergill's belongings than his earthly remains. 'He is going to steal it. Robbery!'

'Murder!' yelled her friend. 'Call the Hectors! They will not like this!'

There was no point in Chaloner trying to tell his own side of the story, and the fact that the Hectors were going to be summoned before the official forces of law and order did not bode well. People were beginning to rally to their howls – he could see torches bobbing on the street. There was really only one thing to do. Chaloner turned and ran.

He blundered through the dark trees, branches clawing at him as he went. He tried to move faster, but was unsteady on his feet and could not make the kind of speed he needed to escape. Meanwhile, his pursuers knew the lie of the land, and they had lamps to guide them. They were gaining, and it was only a matter of time before they would have him. And then they would kill him, because they would be inflamed by the thrill of the

157

chase, and he doubted they would be interested in listening to reason.

He was on the verge of turning to face them – he still had a dagger, and would not go without a fight – when he lost his footing on the slippery ground. He started to slide downwards, wincing when he twisted his left leg, which had not been right since it had been injured in the Battle of Naseby almost twenty years before. He landed with a splash in a deep ditch. He imagined it usually ran dry, but that night it was swollen from the rain and a powerful current began to tug him towards a culvert. He could have extricated himself without too much difficulty, but that would have put him in the hands of his pursuers, so he let the water sweep him into a low tunnel. He stopped it from taking him too far into the darkness, because he did not know where it went, and he had no wish to share Smegergill's fate and drown. At the entrance, he saw torches bobbing as people searched for him.

He held his breath when he heard dogs barking, but the rain and the stream meant tracking him was impossible, and it was not long before the hunters' determination to catch him wavered before the prospect of a fire and a jug of hot ale. He waded to the entrance, checked the coast was clear, and scrambled up a bank that was thick with brambles. When he reached the road, he turned up his collar and began to walk. He was cold, wet, his head and leg hurt, and he did not feel up to trudging all the way home to Fetter Lane, so he headed for a haven that was considerably closer: Leybourn's house in Monkwell Street.

He tapped on the door and leaned against the wall, feeling exhaustion wash over him. There was no reply and the house was in darkness. He supposed Leybourn had gone to bed, and was on the verge of picking the lock to let himself in when he recalled that the surveyor now had a wife who might not appreciate an uninvited guest at such an hour. He knocked again, and eventually the door opened.

'What do *you* want?' came Mary's disapproving voice. 'It is close to ten o'clock, and decent folk are in bed. Have you no consideration?'

'Who is it?' called Leybourn, from the stairs. 'Lord, help us, Mary! Have you actually opened the door? How many times have I warned you against that? You will have us both slaughtered in our beds, because no honest men call at this hour of the night.'

'That is true,' said Mary, a note of triumph in her voice. 'It is your friend, Heyden. He is drunk, and I do not think we should let him in.'

'Why?' asked Chaloner. His voice sounded hoarse and slurred to his own ears, so he did not like to imagine what Mary would make of it. 'Is the vicar of St Giles's here again, fretting about his Christmas decorations?' He winced when a lamp was thrust towards him.

'Christ, Tom!' Leybourn sounded shocked. 'What happened to you?'

'Smegergill is dead,' said Chaloner, aware that relief and tiredness were making him incoherent, but not really caring.

'What is he talking about? Who is Smegergill?' demanded Mary. She released a low screech of alarm when Chaloner pushed his way past her into the house. 'He is covered in blood! He must have killed someone. Perhaps he will kill us, too!'

Leybourn half-dragged, half-carried Chaloner through

159

the dark bookshop, clamouring for answers as he settled him next to the embers of the kitchen fire. Chaloner was simply too weary to reply. He closed his eyes.

When Chaloner regained his senses, he was in Leybourn's favourite chair. He looked around, noting that the kitchen was no cleaner than the last time he had seen it, and that there was an unpleasant smell of burning. He jumped up in alarm when he saw someone had covered him with a blanket and stoked up the fire – and that he was gently smouldering. He quickly patted out the flames, wondering whether Mary had done it on purpose, to put him off making inconvenient visits in the future. It was a draconian measure, but she struck him as a woman who did not do things by halves.

He squinted against the light of the lamp and wondered how long he had been asleep. Leybourn was dozing in the chair opposite, while Mary was sitting at the kitchen table with a sour expression on her face. Chaloner supposed her displeasure derived from the fact that he had woken up before he had been incinerated. His movements disturbed the surveyor, who opened his eyes and took a deep, noisy breath. When Chaloner looked back at Mary, the sulky glare was gone and she was smiling sweetly.

'How are you feeling?' she asked Chaloner politely. He was not deceived by her concern, but was determined he would not be the one to start an argument.

'Better, thank you. What is the time?'

'I heard the watchmen call four o'clock not long ago,' she replied, in the same pleasant tone. 'Will you be leaving soon, while it is still dark? I imagine you will not want anyone to see you.'

160

'What do you mean?' asked Leybourn, looking from one to the other uncertainly.

'The murder,' said Mary, all quiet reason. 'There is blood on him, and none of it is his own.'

Chaloner rubbed his head and tried to remember what had happened, but found his memory was hazy. 'Smegergill is dead. He drowned when he was held face-down in a puddle.'

'Who is Smegergill?' asked Leybourn uneasily. 'Who did this to you?'

'Do not ask,' advised Mary. 'It is better we do not know, because knowledge of his crimes puts us at risk, and I have no wish to be hanged as his accomplice. Make him leave, William. You are not a carefree bachelor now. You have a responsibility to your dependents: me.'

Leybourn regarded her in anguish, and Chaloner saw the surveyor was hard-pressed to make the choice. Eventually, he swallowed hard. 'You had better go to my brother, Mary. Rob will make sure none of this reflects on you.'

'You choose him over me?' she asked, aghast.

'No,' said Chaloner, standing up. 'I should not have come. I was not thinking properly.'

'You were not thinking at all,' said Leybourn kindly. 'You were dazed. But you are safe now, and we will ask no awkward questions – what we do not know, we cannot tell. Best say nothing, Tom.'

Chaloner regarded him in surprise. 'I have done nothing wrong,' he objected, astonished to think Leybourn might imagine he had.

'You killed someone,' reiterated Mary. Her voice was harsh now she had won Leybourn to her way of thinking, and she was making no attempt to mask her dislike. 'There is blood on your hands.'

Chaloner had a sudden, vivid recollection of almost severing a man's finger, and gradually, the events of the night began to trickle back to him. 'Smegergill and I were going to take a carriage to the Rhenish Wine House, but we were attacked outside St Bartholomew's Church. I should have been able to repel them, but I failed. And Smegergill paid the price for my ineptitude.'

'Smegergill was killed by robbers?' asked Leybourn. He sounded relieved, and glanced at Mary, to make sure she had heard. 'They must have been Hectors, since St Bartholomew's is their domain.'

'He knew my father,' said Chaloner, realising he was not relating the tale in a logical order but unable to do much about it; his wits were still not functioning properly. 'He was afraid the thieves were actually wardens, come to take him to Bedlam.'

'Perhaps it was you they were after,' muttered Mary.

Leybourn frowned a gentle admonishment at her, but the scowl dissolved when she treated him to a loving smile. The moment he turned back to Chaloner, she shot the spy a look of such blazing dislike that he recoiled. He was aware of similar feelings towards her, which surprised him, because it usually took longer for people to generate such strong emotions in him. He was sorry, because their antipathy towards each other was likely to end up causing Leybourn pain.

'Why should Smegergill think he was bound for Bedlam?' asked Leybourn. Mary made the kind of noise that said she was not going to listen to more lies, and went to the pantry. A few moments later came the sound of wine being decanted into a goblet. She did not come back, and Chaloner was relieved to speak to Leybourn alone.

'He did not seem insane, but I am no judge of such matters.' He rubbed his head again and sighed. 'What am I saying? Of course he was not insane: he was one of His Majesty's musicians, and the Court does not appoint lunatics to such posts. He was just forgetful, as the elderly are sometimes. He was telling me about some documents Maylord had found. Maylord was being cheated by someone.'

Leybourn frowned. 'I think I follow you, although this is a garbled explanation, to put it mildly. Shall I send for a surgeon? Their hall is just across the road.'

'No, thank you.' Chaloner did not like surgeons. 'But I cannot think properly, Will. It is all a blur, and I am not sure what really happened. There was a cut on Smegergill's lip and he certainly drowned, but his purse was not stolen, and neither was his ring.'

'Perhaps the robbers were disturbed before they could finish.'

'That is what I thought, but no one came until later. And his empty purse is odd. We were going to hire a carriage, but he had no money.'

'Maybe he thought you were going to pay,' suggested Leybourn. 'Or he forgot to fill it before he left home. Or the thieves took the coins and left the pouch. Or this was their first robbery, and they did not know what they were doing, although that is difficult to believe – the Hectors are usually very good at thievery. Did you see any of them? Could you identify them, if you saw them again?'

Chaloner touched the bruise on his jaw. 'No. They threw a stone first, which slowed me down. That is not something inexperienced felons do. It meant I could not fight properly.'

'Some of the Hectors carry slingshots, so I imagine that is what hit you. You are lucky to be alive, because it is not unknown for men to die after being struck by Smithfield-hurled missiles.'

Chaloner wondered whether that was what had happened to Smegergill. 'I suppose someone took exception to my questions about Newburne, and decided they should end. Poor Smegergill made a fatal mistake when he agreed to catch a carriage with me. Mary is right: I *did* kill him.'

'Easy,' said Leybourn gently. 'Do not jump to wild conclusions.'

But Chaloner was feeling wretched, sure the old man would still be alive if he had not been careless. It would not be an easy burden to bear for the rest of his life.

'Williamson's agent told me the government hires Hectors on occasion,' he said, trying to pull himself together. The least he could do was ensure that Smegergill's killers faced justice; brooding about his ineptitude could come later. 'Perhaps Williamson wanted to stop me from investigating.'

'Him and half of London. I am not keen on you unveiling the culprit myself – not for a snake like Newburne. You think it was you they wanted, then? You do not think it was a random attack?'

Chaloner thought about the interviews he had conducted that day. He had been warned away from the investigation by every person he had spoken to: L'Estrange, Brome and Joanna at the newsbook offices; Hodgkinson the printer; Hen Finch; Muddiman and

164

Dury; and even Williamson's man. Meanwhile, Crisp's name had cropped up rather a lot, too.

'I am sure Smegergill was about to tell me something important,' he said bitterly. 'I *know* he was. If only I had protected him properly.'

'You are a good spy,' said Leybourn soothingly. 'You will discover whatever it was another way.'

It was not much of a consolation, especially for Smegergill. 'I should be going,' he said, when Mary returned with a cup of wine clasped in her plump fingers.

'No,' said Leybourn firmly. 'You are still not right, and—'

'Leave through the back door, please,' said Mary. 'It will be safer for us if you are not seen.'

'Mary!' cried Leybourn, distressed. 'He must stay until daybreak. Supposing the Hectors are still looking for him? Supposing they try again?'

'It would be a tragedy,' said Mary flatly.

Leybourn shot her an agonised look, then turned to Chaloner, who was inspecting his dented hat. 'She is jesting with you,' he said with an unconvincing smile. 'She is a great one for jokes, and we are always laughing together.'

Chaloner wondered how much Leybourn would laugh when he discovered her true character, because it was only a matter of time before the bedazzlement faded and the surveyor was exposed to what really lay beneath. He opened the door and stepped into the garden. The rain had stopped, and the early hour meant the air smelled of wet earth and damp leaves, coal fires and the reek of industry being doused for the night. He heard Leybourn and Mary exchanging low, angry words behind him, and was sorry he had brought discord to his friend's

165

house. When he turned, the surveyor had gone, and Mary was waiting, hands on hips, to make sure he really left. He moved towards her, making her flinch back in alarm.

'Most people would summon a constable if they thought a killer was on their doorstep, but you only clamour for me to be gone. Now, why would you do that? Are you hiding from the law?'

She gaped at him. 'How dare you! I am just trying to protect my husband.'

'You are a liar, *Mrs* Leybourn. The truth is that you do not want a brush with the forces of law and order, not even to help the victim of an assault.'

She regarded him with a glittering hatred, and when she spoke her voice was a low, menacing hiss. 'If you meddle in my affairs, I will see you dead. Now go, and do not come back. Not ever.'

Chaloner had never appreciated being threatened. 'And what will you do if I refuse?'

She leaned towards him. 'Ellis Crisp owes me a favour, and his Hectors will be more than willing to teach you a lesson. All I have to do is ask.'

The remark was more revealing than alarming, and Chaloner regarded her thoughtfully. 'An underworld king is an odd acquaintance for a respectable woman, I would have thought. Perhaps I will ask questions in Smithfield, and see what I can learn about you.'

Mary's face became ugly with rage. 'If you try to interfere with my business, I will ensure you destroy your friend in the process. He is happy with me and I am content with him. But if you harm me, I will ruin him – financially and emotionally. And then Crisp will see you pay in ways you cannot possibly imagine.'

166

'You would hurt the man you profess to love?' Chaloner was disgusted.

'If the alternative is losing a nice house, plenty of money and a life of leisure? What do you think?'

'Tom!' called Leybourn, appearing behind her, slightly breathless. He carried his second-best cloak. 'This will keep you dry until you reach home. And here is a crown for a carriage, since your own money was stolen.'

Chaloner accepted the cloak but not the coin. Leybourn had one person who only wanted him for his wealth, and he did not need another like it. Without a word, he started to make his way home.

When he arrived in Fetter Lane, Chaloner lay on his bed and thought about Leybourn. Although the surveyor was clearly delighted to have secured himself a lady at last, it was not a happy union. There had been the uncharacteristic spat of temper when Leybourn had stormed out of Lincoln's Inn, and he had also mentioned an inability to sleep. Chaloner wondered if he sensed that Mary was not as enamoured of him as he was of her – or even that her attachment was really to his money – but stubborn desperation prevented him from seeing the truth.

Should Chaloner do as he had threatened, and ask questions about Mary until he discovered her secrets? Thurloe would certainly encourage him to do so. Or should he stand back and wait for Leybourn to learn the truth himself? Leybourn was a grown man, so well able to make his own decisions. Or was he? Perhaps she had bewitched him, and he was no longer responsible for himself. Besides, interfering in matters that were none of his concern was how Chaloner made his living, and it

167

was difficult to stand by and watch a friend make a terrible mistake. He decided he *would* add Mary Cade to his list of enquiries, and discover as much about her as he could. That made three investigations. He considered them in turn, aware that all had connections to the mysterious Crisp.

First, Mary claimed to know Ellis Crisp, bragging that she was in a position to order a repeat attack of the one that had almost killed Chaloner that night. Or was she just trying to unnerve him? He was not sure how to proceed with her, although a visit to Newgate was as good a place as any to start. He would make a sketch of her and show it to the guards, to see if they recognised her as a criminal. He had recently discovered a talent for drawing, and knew he could produce a reasonable likeness. He would need money to bribe them for information, though, so he would have to visit White Hall first, to collect his back-pay.

Secondly, there was his enquiry into Newburne's death. Why had so many people advised him to abandon the investigation? They could not *all* have sinister reasons for doing so. He sensed the warnings of Brome, Joanna and Hodgkinson had been kindly meant, and so was Leybourn's, but what about those issued by Muddiman, Dury, the booksellers and L'Estrange? Even Finch, Newburne's friend, declared himself unwilling to look into the matter. Could Crisp, who was only a felon when all was said and done, really terrify so many people? Chaloner decided to ask Thurloe the following day. The ex-Spymaster was sure to have heard of such an infamous villain.

And finally, there was the smothering of Maylord. Maylord was linked to Crisp – albeit tangentially – because

Chaloner had been attacked by Hectors while walking in Smithfield with Maylord's friend. The villains had been quietly proficient, and had hauled him and Smegergill off the road and into the privacy of the churchyard with a minimum of commotion. He imagined it was exactly the kind of activity at which the legendary Hectors would excel. Was Crisp responsible, because he did not want Newburne's death investigated? Or was it coincidence that the attack had occurred in Crisp's domain? As soon as it was light, Chaloner decided to visit the Rhenish Wine House and find the documents Smegergill had mentioned – assuming they existed, and were not the product of a confused mind.

He went to the jug on the table and drank some water. His head ached and so did the bruise on his chin where the stone had struck him, and he knew his wits were still not properly clear. He thought about the attack, still sickened by his failure to protect Smegergill. What had the old man been going to tell him about Maylord being cheated? Had a vital clue about Maylord's death been lost because of his own carelessness? He removed the ring and the key from his pocket, and stared at them. He knew he should not have taken them, because he now had the added responsibility of returning them to Smegergill's next of kin – hopefully without being accused of the murder himself.

He went back to his bed, and jumped in alarm when the cat suddenly joined him there. He spent several minutes trying to oust it, but each time he shoved it away, it came back. In the end, he gave up, and allowed it to nestle in a warm ball at his side. It began to purr, and he supposed there was something comforting in the close presence of another living creature. Perhaps that was

169

what Leybourn craved, and was why he was prepared to overlook Mary's all too obvious failings. He wondered what the surveyor would say if his friends suggested replacing Mary with a cat.

Chaloner had not meant to sleep and was startled when he awoke to hear the church bells chiming eleven o'clock, horrified that so much of the day had been lost. It meant he would not be able to visit White Hall and claim his back-pay, because there were other duties that had to come first. His head ached when he sat up, but not as badly as it had done the night before. The pain made him irritable, though, and he swore under his breath when the cat jumped up on to the bed again. He grimaced in revulsion when he saw a mouse in its jaws, and tried to push it away. It deposited the corpse on the bedclothes and mewed in expectation of reward. It did not receive one, because Chaloner's larder was bare, and he had nothing to give it.

His temper flared again when he went to fetch his sword from the pantry, and the animal tripped him by winding around his ankles. The stumble jarred his lame leg, which was still stiff from his slide into the ditch. All in all, it was not a good start to the day.

The clothes he had worn the previous night were wet, muddy and ripped, which was a problem, because they were the best he had. He picked through the others help-lessly, eventually choosing a shirt that was yellow with age, and a pair of breeches he recalled wearing during the wars. His jaw was purple from its encounter with the stone, and it made him distinctive, which was always something he tried to avoid. So he darkened his stubble with soot from the chimney, then found a leather cap that hung low

170

over his forehead and cheeks. Once he put Isabella's dented hat on top, very little of his face was visible. He felt slovenly and disreputable, and the presence of a dead mouse in his pocket – ready to be tossed into the nearest gutter – did not help, but he supposed the garb would do for Newgate and the Rhenish Wine House, the latter of which he intended to enter without being seen.

In Fleet Street, he saw the Earl's clerk, Bulteel, who shrieked in alarm when a scruffy man seized his shoulder and bade him good-day. He stopped abruptly when he recognised Chaloner's grey eyes.

'We should pay you more,' he said shakily. 'You look terrible.'

'You *should* pay me more,' Chaloner agreed. 'My disguise is good, then?'

'I did not recognise you. You have even changed the way you walk – you were limping. Did you hear about Smegergill the musician? He was killed in Smithfield last night, for his purse and a valuable ring. Some bystanders saw the culprit and gave chase, but the devil eluded them.'

'One of the Hectors?' asked Chaloner, thinking of the ring and key in his pocket. He had considered leaving them at home, but there was nowhere good to hide them, and he had decided they would be safer on his person.

'Apparently not, and they are said to be furious that someone dared to commit murder on their territory. I suspect they are telling the truth, because usually they brag about such crimes – it shows they do what they like and no one can stop them. The killer must be terrified, because Butcher Crisp has vowed to catch him and put him in a pie.'

'Did these witnesses give a good description of the culprit?' asked Chaloner uneasily.

'He kept his face concealed, but they say he was injured as Smegergill battled for his life, because he was unsteady on his feet. Personally, I hope Crisp roasts him alive. What kind of monster would harm a helpless old fellow like Smegergill?'

'Is anything being done? Legally, I mean – not whatever the Hectors are about.'

'Nothing *can* be done. It is their domain, and Crisp is the one who will be asking questions.'

Chaloner was aghast. 'But what about the constables? Murder is a capital crime. Surely, they will want it investigated themselves, not leave a band of felons to do it?'

'Not if they have any sense. And you had better not interfere, either. The Earl told me today that you must discover what happened to Newburne as a matter of urgency. The widow paid him another visit this morning, and he will not want you pursuing other enquiries as long as she is on the warpath.'

Trying not to limp, Chaloner walked to Westminster. Eventually, he reached the Rhenish Wine House, entering its smoky, humid interior with a sigh of relief – it had been a long walk for a man not in the best of health. His heart sank when he saw a porter at the foot of the stairs that led to the private rooms above. He had no money to bribe his way past, and doubted he would be allowed by wearing his current outfit, anyway. He needed a distraction.

It did not take him long to devise one. The dead mouse was still in his pocket, because he had forgotten to dispose of it. He waited until Landlord Genew placed a bowl of stew in front of a patron whose attention was fixed on one of the serving women, and dropped the small body into the food as he passed the man's table.

172

Then he perused the newsbooks while he waited for a reaction.

The Intelligencer was the only thing on offer, because Muddiman's newsletters had already been claimed by other patrons. He read a frenzied editorial about the rebellion in York that made him wonder whether its writer was in his right mind, and learned that Mistress Atwood's house at Havering had been broken open and the good lady relieved of two silver cups. Meanwhile, Mr Benjamin Farrow of Eltham, Kent had lost a 'broad bay mare' while he was out at his coffee house, and the Queen was suffering from a distemper, which Chaloner thought made her sound like a dog.

He glanced at the ogler, and wished the man would tear his longing gaze away from the maid and pay attention to his stew. He was beginning to think he might have to consider another way to distract the porter, when a spoon was finally dipped into the bowl. The results were well worth the wait. The ogler suddenly found himself with a mouthful of fur; he spat the offending object across the table, and began to gag. The porter and Genew rushed towards him, and Chaloner darted up the stairs unseen.

The attic, where Genew had said Maylord had lived, was five storeys up, and Chaloner was breathing hard by the time he reached the top. He found himself faced with three doors, any one of which might be Maylord's room. He listened intently at the first, trying to ascertain whether it was occupied, then took a small metal probe from his pocket and inserted it into the lock when he thought it was not.

It did not take him many moments to pick his way

inside. The room was tiny, sparsely furnished, and not very clean. The absence of any kind of musical instrument told him it was not Maylord's, and he was about to close the door and try the next chamber when something caught his eye. There was a small table in the window, placed to catch the light, and on it was one of L'Estrange's newsbooks. It had been smothered in red ink. Intrigued, he slipped into the room and closed the door behind him.

The newsbook's typeface was fuzzy, and whoever had been reading it had marked all the typographical errors that had been found. There were also notes in the margin, which Chaloner recognised as instructions to a printer. The date on the front page said Thursday 5 November, and he realised he was looking at a future issue of *The Newes*, not one already in circulation. Someone had obviously been given the task of checking the text, and was in the process of correcting it. Puzzled, Chaloner turned his attention to the pile of documents that sat next to it. The first sheet comprised a summary of the second item in the newsbook, which described a recent earthquake in Quebec. Other articles had been paraphrased, too, and hidden underneath them was a small book in which every précis had been carefully logged. A sum of money was entered in the margin against each, as if denoting its value. More lists appeared on previous pages, but these had initials next to them.

When Chaloner flicked through the book, he saw the accumulation of small amounts of cash amounted to a considerable whole – someone had made a lot of money by copying L'Estrange's news. He studied the ledger more closely. There were several sets of initials, but the most common was HM. Chaloner could only assume it referred

174

to Henry Muddiman. No wonder people claimed L'Estrange provided old news, and that Muddiman always told it first!

But who would betray the government's official news-books, something that would almost certainly be deemed an act of treason? Hodgkinson the printer? Chaloner immediately discounted him on the grounds that he was unlikely to be entrusted with checking the text he himself had set. What about Brome or Joanna? Would they have the courage for such a dangerous activity? Somehow, Chaloner did not think so. He supposed he would have to find out who proof-read L'Estrange's early drafts, and investigate them accordingly.

He began a systematic search of the room, looking for clues as to the traitor's identity. Several law books lay on a shelf, along with a copy of a tome in Latin. When he picked it up, it fell open to a page that had a red cross at the top; the reader had wanted to highlight something. The title showed it to be a text by Galen, which Chaloner translated as *On the Powers of Foods*. The marked section contained the heading *Cucumeris*, and went on to say that eating these particular fruits caused cold, thick juice to accumulate in the veins, which could not be converted to good blood without problems.

Chaloner rubbed his head. Someone had been reading about the toxic effects of cucumbers – or the theory according to the ancients, at least. It was a person with a connection to L'Estrange's newsbooks, who also had an interest in law. The obvious conclusion was that it was Newburne, because he was a solicitor associated with cucumbers, but he had lived in Old Jewry, and would not have needed a garret in the Rhenish Wine House. Then Chaloner recalled what Finch had said: that

Newburne had rented a room in Ivy Lane, because it was near L'Estrange and the print-house. The solicitor had been rich, so perhaps he had leased other places across the city, too, to facilitate his various duties for L'Estrange, and perhaps Crisp, as well.

Aware that time was passing, Chaloner abandoned his musing, and returned to his search. There was a sheet of music on the windowsill, although there was no instrument to go with it. He transposed the written notes into a tune in his head. It was not an attractive jig, and he wondered why the composer had bothered. He put it back where he had found it, and dropped to his knees to look under the bed. In the deepest shadows, hidden among the balls of fluff and a greasy layer of dust, was a scrap of paper. He retrieved it with his dagger, but was disappointed to find it was just a receipt for the rent. Then he saw the payee's name on the back: Nobert Wenum. So, the occupant was not Newburne after all, but someone Chaloner had never heard of.

There was no more to be learned from the dismal little chamber, so he headed for the door. He was about to open it when his eye fell on the small book that still lay on the table. At some point, he was going to have to tell L'Estrange that an employee called Wenum was betraying his trust, and the ledger offered solid proof of it. He slid it and the annotated *Newes* into his pocket, then left. There was still a commotion coming from downstairs, suggesting the ogler was making the kind of fuss that went before a claim for compensation.

He put his ear to the door of the second room, but someone was snoring inside, so he went to the third. The lock was more obstinate than Wenum's, newer and stronger. Had Maylord installed it himself, and it was testament to the fact that he knew he was in mortal danger? Picking it took too long, and Chaloner was sweating by the time he had it open.

He stepped inside and closed the door behind him. He knew he was in the right place when he saw two viols and a table that was covered in music. Some was in Maylord's hand, and Chaloner hoped someone would play it one day. He picked up a page, and the haunting melody that sailed through his head made him want to grab one of the viols and bow it immediately. Reluctantly, he set it down.

It occurred to him that Maylord had died in that very room, and that his body had been found there with the cucumber nearby. There was no cucumber now, although a plate adorned with dried green smudges showed how the killer had almost succeeded in masking his crime. Warily, Chaloner inspected a cushion that lay on the bed, and dropped it in distaste when he saw a pinkish stain and a small tear: Maylord's blood-tinged saliva and a rip caused by a broken tooth. He turned his attention to his search and the documents Smegergill thought were hidden there.

As an intelligencer, Chaloner knew most of the tricks people used when they wanted to conceal things. He tested the floor for loose boards, assessed walls and ceiling for hidden compartments, and ran his hands along the undersides of beds and chests. Finally, he inspected the chimney. It was brick, and he almost missed the fact that one stone stood very slightly proud of the others. He was impressed, and doubted it would have been noticeable to anyone but a professional spy. He jiggled it until he was able to draw it out. Behind it was a tiny recess containing a bundle of papers and a key. The key was identical to the one he had taken from Smegergill. However, there was nothing in Maylord's room for either of them to open.

He stuffed documents and key in his pocket, intending to examine them later, certain they would shed light on why Maylord had been murdered. Perhaps they would also explain why the old man had thought he was being cheated, and why he had spent the last two weeks of his life in nervous agitation. Chaloner was just replacing the brick when he heard voices in the corridor outside. He leapt to his feet and glanced around quickly. There was nowhere to hide: the bed was solid with drawers at the bottom, and the chest by the window was too small for him to climb inside. There was a scraping sound as a key was inserted in the lock.

'Thank you, Genew,' came a voice Chaloner had heard before. He flattened himself against the wall as the door opened. 'You are dismissed. Go downstairs and placate your mouse-eating patron.'

The landlord's footsteps retreated along the corridor, and two men entered the room. The one at the front was tall and lean, with an impossibly large nose. Chaloner deduced quickly that he was in charge, while the thickset, pugilistic fellow behind was his henchman. When they started to talk to each other, he knew they were two of the three who had attacked him the previous night – the henchman's Scottish burr was unmistakeable, while the leader spoke nasally, as though he had a cold. Chaloner stayed stock still, although at least this time he had surprise on his side.

The leader, whom Chaloner had dubbed Nose, looked quickly around the room, and his eyes lit on the soot that had been dislodged when Chaloner had removed the stone from the chimney. He swung round fast, reaching for his sword as he did so. Wasting no time, Chaloner felled the Scot with a clip to the chin, then raced through the door and shot along the corridor. Unfortunately, he had not expected a third man to be keeping guard at the top of the stairs. He cursed his stupidity. Of course there would be three, just as there had been three the previous night. The man's hand was tucked inside his coat, and Chaloner realised he was the one who had all but lost a finger during their previous fracas.

The injured man braced himself as Chaloner thundered towards him, and the spy only just avoided the lead piping that flashed towards his skull. It struck the wall and punched a hole in the plaster. He hit the man's jaw when he was still off balance, and followed it with a sharp jab to the neck. There was a howl of fury from Nose and the sound of running footsteps. Chaloner took the stairs too fast, wincing when his weak knee twisted in a way that he knew would slow him down. He reached the second floor, but sensed they would catch him before he gained the front door. And if not, then he could never outrun them on the streets while he was limping.

Just when he was beginning to think he might have to stand and fight, a door opened and a well-dressed man stepped out, key in hand. Chaloner darted towards him, shoving him back inside the chamber and closing the door behind them. The man opened his mouth to object, but snapped it shut when he saw the dagger. Chaloner put his finger to his lips, and the man nodded, terrified. The spy understood his fear, knowing how he must look with his unshaven face, old clothes and wild appearance. Feet clattered on the stairs outside, and then there was silence.

179

Chaloner hobbled to the bed and indicated his prisoner was to sit next to him. The man complied, shaking almost uncontrollably.

'I mean you no harm,' said Chaloner softly. 'May I wait here until the commotion is over?'

He held a knife, so his captive knew there was really no choice, but the polite request served to reassure nonetheless. 'They are Hectors,' he whispered, desperate to appear helpful. 'They used to visit Wenum, who was probably one, too.'

'*Used* to visit?' queried Chaloner.

'He is recently dead, according to Landlord Genew. I am not sure how, but it was probably unnatural – Wenum was a sly man, and he doubtless met a sly end. I never did like him. The skin rotted on his chin, which made him look like a leper. Oh, Lord! He was not your friend, was he?'

Chaloner laughed at the fellow's horrified embarrassment. 'No. What else can you tell me about him?'

Relieved, the man hastened to oblige. 'He spent very little time here, and used his room mostly for business, which is why Hectors and other devious types were always queuing up to get in.'

'So, Wenum is dead and Maylord is dead,' said Chaloner thoughtfully. 'It seems to me that the Rhenish Wine House is a dangerous place to live.'

The man's eyes went wide. 'Perhaps I had better move, then, because I do not want trouble. Why do you think I always turned a blind eye to Wenum and his dealings? When I realised he did business with Hectors, I went out of my way to avoid him, as any sane man would have done. What have you done to incur their wrath?'

'We had a disagreement about some property. Did Wenum know Ellis Crisp, then?'

'Wenum knew *Hectors*; I have no idea if he knew Crisp. I almost met Crisp myself once, at a dinner for the Company of Butchers, of which I am a member, but he cancelled last minute. I cannot say I was sorry. We did not really want him to join our ranks.'

Chaloner was confused. 'You mean Crisp practises his trade without a licence from the relevant guild? I thought that was impossible – and illegal.'

'Normally, it is, but he just arrived in Smithfield and started work, and by the time we decided to take action against him, he had accrued too much power to be stopped. He gives us meat merchants a bad name, especially regarding the alleged contents of his pies. We asked him to attend our dinner, because some of our members thought he might mend his ways if we let him into the fold. Personally, I am sceptical, and would rather keep my distance from the fellow.'

Chaloner suspected he was right to be wary, and thought the Company was naïve to imagine they could tame Crisp's antics with an offer of membership. 'What about Maylord? Did you ever see Crisp visiting him? You were neighbours these last two weeks.'

The man's face softened. 'Poor Maylord. Something upset him badly before he died, which is probably why he moved here. It did not save him though. Cucumbers got him regardless.'

'Did you ask him what was the matter?'

'He declined to confide. I cannot say why, but I was under the impression that someone owed him money and he was having trouble getting it back.'

'Did you ever see Wenum and Maylord together?'

'No, but they must have passed the time of day when they met in the corridor. It would have been rude otherwise, and Maylord had beautiful manners. I would be surprised if he had anything more to do with Wenum, though. Are you going to rob me? I do not own much money, but you can have it.'

Chaloner stood. 'All I want is your silence. You tell no one you saw me, and I tell no one we hid together. Then we will both be safe.'

'Agreed,' said the man with palpable relief.

The Hectors were still searching for Chaloner, so he was obliged to leave the Rhenish Wine House carefully. He turned his coat inside out to make it a different colour, and exchanged skullcap and hat for an old wig he discovered in his pocket. It reeked of horse, and he could not for the life of him remember where it had come from, but he was glad it was there. He scanned the street in both directions, then escaped by jumping on to the back of a cart filled with dirty straw. The driver did not notice him until they reached St Giles-in-the-Fields, at which point he grabbed a pitchfork and threatened to use it unless his passenger made himself scarce. Chaloner limped away, then made a tortuous journey that involved not only doubling back on himself, but making use of one or two private gardens. Only when he was certain he had not been followed did he enter Lincoln's Inn and head for Chamber XIII.

'Tom!' exclaimed Thurloe, opening the door to let him in. 'William told me you have had some trouble. Come and sit by the fire, and share my dinner.'

Chaloner could not remember when he had last eaten, and took more of the ex-Spymaster's victuals than was polite, although Thurloe was too courteous to draw attention to the fact. While they dined, he gave a brief account of all that had happened.

'The city was never this dangerous when *I* was Spymaster,' declared Thurloe, shaking his head disparagingly. 'Safe streets, low crime rates and a marked absence of gangs are just a few of the advantages conferred by a military dictatorship, such as the one we enjoyed under Oliver Cromwell.'

At first, Chaloner thought he was joking, but saw from his wistful expression that he was not. He changed the subject before they argued. 'I am not sure what to think about Wenum's notebook,' he said, handing it over for Thurloe's inspection.

'You will have to tell L'Estrange,' said Thurloe, raising his eyebrows as he flicked through it and saw the extent of the betrayal. 'Wenum is undermining the government by his actions. People say the newsbooks contain stale news, which means there is a very real danger that they will founder – and from this ledger, I would say Wenum is largely responsible. You are duty-bound to expose it.'

Chaloner was uneasy with that. 'There are six sets of initials in Wenum's book, one of which is probably Muddiman's. What will happen to him once Williamson learns what has been happening?'

'I doubt L'Estrange will tell Williamson that one of his carefully vetted workers has been betraying him, so I imagine nothing will happen to Muddiman. Wenum will be discreetly dismissed and the whole embarrassing business quietly forgotten. Government officials dislike this sort of scandal.'

'Have you ever come across Wenum?'

'No. Muddiman ran the newsbooks for me during the

183

Commonwealth – and then until he was ousted in favour of L'Estrange a few weeks ago – but there was no Wenum on his staff. L'Estrange must have appointed the fellow, as he appointed Brome. It is fortunate Brome accepted because he keeps L'Estrange in check to a certain extent. He and Joanna may appear to be meek, but their quiet common sense acts as a brake to some of L'Estrange's wilder follies.'

Chaloner was more interested in the traitor. 'My first assumption was that Newburne was the culprit, because of the law books and Galen's views on cucumbers. And from what I have been told, he was the kind of man to sell secrets to the highest bidder. But instead it was Wenum.'

Thurloe was quiet for a moment. 'Have you heard the rumour that says Newburne owned a small box filled with precious jewels, and that he hid it before he died?'

Chaloner regarded him in concern. 'No! Is it true?'

Thurloe shook his head. 'I sincerely doubt it. The story began to circulate shortly after his death, but those sorts of tales always proliferate when rich men die. Everyone loves hidden treasure.'

'Well, *I* do not,' said Chaloner vehemently. 'Secret hoards nearly always bring trouble.'

'I doubt Newburne's will bother you unduly. I am fairly sure its existence is a myth, and I only mention it so you can consider it as a motive for his murder.'

'You just said it does not exist.'

Thurloe frowned. 'But others may think it does, and be beguiled by the prospect of easy riches. You are slow today, Thomas. It must be all that food you have just eaten.'

Chaloner was overfull, but his mind was clearer than

it had been when he was hungry. He turned his attention to another matter. 'Do you have any paper? I would like to make a likeness of Mary.'

Thurloe's blue eyes gleamed. 'Since you have more sense than to be dazzled by the woman, I assume you concur with me: that there is something unpleasant about her, and you have a plan to prise her claws from William's heart.'

Chaloner detailed Mary's hostility towards him, especially their last conversation, as he sat at the table and drew what he remembered of her face. 'She made no effort to hide her real intentions,' he concluded. 'I will take her picture to Newgate today, to see if the wardens are familiar with her.'

Thurloe watched the picture take shape, as Chaloner sketched first with charcoal and then with a pen. Proudly, he lent the spy his Fountain Inkhorn, a newfangled device that carried its own supply of ink, but it had a tendency to blot, and Chaloner soon reverted to a quill.

'There is certainly something felonious about her,' the ex-Spymaster said, going back to his fireside chair. 'But I doubt you will learn much at Newgate. She is cunning, and will have effected a disguise when she homed in on William. The guards will not recognise her now.'

'We will not know unless we try, and her unease of the law suggests something is amiss.'

'What if you do prove she has a criminal past? She will deny it, and William might decide it is unimportant anyway. He is utterly besotted by her. Did I tell you he claimed she was as fair as Aphrodite when he first introduced us? I do not think his eyesight is very good. And she probably keeps the lamps low at night, to ensure he cannot see her properly.'

Chaloner laughed as he held up the finished drawing. 'Have I captured her well enough?'

Thurloe inspected the work critically. 'You should make her eyes smaller, and her mouth thinner. And how about putting a pitchfork in her hands, and the devil whispering in her ear?'

Chaloner stood when he heard the clock chime three. 'I should visit Newgate before dark. You say it will do no good, but I cannot think of any other way forward.'

But Thurloe took the picture and placed it in his own pocket. 'I still have a few contacts from the old days. Leave this to me – and my heavy purse. Do not look dubious, Thomas. I was Spymaster General, if you do not mind. I can do this sort of thing in my sleep.'

Chaloner was not so sure. Thurloe was excellent at theory, but fared less well at practical matters. However, he was right in that bribery would be the most effective method of gaining information, and Chaloner supposed he should let him try.

Thurloe came to rest a solicitous hand on his shoulder. 'You have hated prisons ever since that episode in France a few years back. Why put yourself through the ordeal of a visit, when I can do it?'

He had a point. Chaloner did own a deep-rooted aversion to gaols, and was willing to go to considerable lengths to avoid them. He nodded his thanks, and went to sit next to the fire.

'We will prevail against this vixen, Tom. However, I am more concerned about you than William this afternoon. You are clearly not thinking straight, because you have not once asked why the men who almost killed you last night should be searching Maylord's room today. What did they want? The documents? The key? Money?

186

Maylord was comparatively wealthy, unlike Smegergill, whose unpredictable temper meant *he* had no rich pupils – with the possible exception of that big-nosed lutanist whom no one liked.'

Chaloner had thought of little else all the way from the Rhenish Wine House, but had no idea why the three men should be in the same two places. 'Perhaps they went to lay claim to Maylord's key, because I took the identical one from Smegergill.'

'That makes no sense. If they had wanted that, they would have removed it from Smegergill's body when they had the chance. What is it for, do you think? It is too small for a door of any substance.'

'A cupboard? A box?'

Thurloe examined them both. 'They could be chain-lock keys – devices that secure things to walls. Musical instruments, perhaps. Now, tell me, in detail this time, what happened in Smithfield last night.'

Chaloner did not want to relive his failure yet again. 'I cannot: it is still blurred. Why do you want to know anyway? I am painfully aware that it is my fault Smegergill died. I should not have let him walk around Smithfield at such a late hour, and I should not have let a gaggle of Hectors best me.'

'Do not underestimate them, Tom. They are no mere louts like their rival gangs, the Muns or the Tityre Tus. Many were soldiers, and some are even professional men – such as Newburne and Wenum, it would seem. So, tell me what you recall. Leave nothing out.'

With a sigh, Chaloner obliged, although it was an uncomfortable process. Thurloe listened without inter-rupting, then sat back thoughtfully.

'I disliked Smegergill. He was secretive about his origins

187

when I tried to vet him for Cromwell's court, and you never knew when he was going to turn on you with a caustic remark.'

'He was not caustic last night. He barely remembered our conversation from one sentence to the next, and at points he thought I was my father.'

Thurloe steepled his fingers. 'It seems to me that his role in the attack was ambiguous. No, do not argue, Tom. Hear me out. He could not have *organised* the ambush, because you went to see him out of the blue, and he had no time to make such arrangements. Yet he was not surprised by it, either.'

Chaloner was astonished by the line the ex-Spymaster's thinking had taken, and disagreed strongly with his interpretation. 'How do you know he was not surprised?' he demanded bitterly. 'He never had the chance to discuss it with me, because he was dead before it was over.'

'Think, Thomas, and analyse the evidence objectively, as I have taught you to do. You heard Smegergill talking to the attackers before you were dragged into the church-yard – *talking*, not yelling for help, as most men would have been doing.'

'He was probably frightened. He was old, frail and not in his right wits. And if he believed the attackers were Bedlam men coming for him, then it is not surprising that he failed to raise the alarm.'

'We are not talking about his failure to raise the alarm – although I find it odd that he did not at least cry out when armed rogues appeared – we are discussing the fact that he *spoke* to them. And he cannot have been overly witless, or Greeting would not have hired him to play in his consort. Greeting is fiercely ambitious, and is

188

highly selective about the musicians he allows to join him.'

Greeting was ambitious, Chaloner knew, and certainly would not tolerate a consort member who might do something to damage his reputation. 'But this does not mean Smegergill—'

'Then what about the fact that Smegergill suggested a specific location from which to take a carriage, but had no money with which to pay? Perhaps he had no intention of riding with you to Maylord's room, and his real purpose was to keep you away from it at all costs. Everyone knows Smithfield is dangerous at night. Have you considered the possibility that he led you there deliberately, knowing what would happen?'

'What happened was that he was killed and I escaped.'

'And I am sure that was not the outcome he was anticipating. Besides, you *would* have died had you not been wearing your metal hat. They came closer than I like to think.'

Chaloner still did not believe he was right. 'There are all manner of explanations for his lack of money, including the fact that he was forgetful and may have overlooked filling his purse—'

'Then why were you searched and he was not? He kept his ring and his key, despite the fact that the men who attacked you sound like professional thieves who would be unlikely to pass over such items. And you say his only injury was a small cut to his mouth?'

'I heard a blow falling when I was lying on the ground. They did hit him.'

Thurloe raised his hands defensively. 'Then perhaps he is a victim after all. I am not saying there is anything odd about Smegergill, Tom, just that you should bear

189

the possibility in mind. And you should not wallow too deeply in remorse until you are absolutely sure it is justified.'

Chaloner was unconvinced. 'What do you know about Crisp?' he asked, to change the subject.

'He is associated with everything illegal in the Smithfield area, but only for the last two years or so. I would not have tolerated him when *I* was in government – as I said, a military dictatorship confers all manner of advantages, and an absence of underworld kings is one of them.'

'Have you heard his name associated with Newburne's?'

'No, but it does not surprise me that they knew each other: a felon and a corrupt lawyer make for comfortable bedfellows.'

'Where does Crisp live? Who are his associates?'

Thurloe scratched his head. 'He must live in Smithfield, because that is his realm of influence. He is often seen there, surrounded by Hectors, but tends to shy away from appointments outside the area. Because he is rich, powerful and influential, some of the Guilds have tried to establish a connection with him – for business purposes – but he declines to make major public appearances.'

'Maylord was smothered and Newburne was poisoned. Crisp knew them both.'

'Crisp knew Newburne,' corrected Thurloe. 'We cannot be sure that he knew Maylord.'

'He must have done – it was probably his men who visited Maylord's room. Why would they have been there, if there was no connection? And do not say because of Smegergill – I do not believe he deliberately tried to have me killed by Hectors. Perhaps they met through Wenum.

190

He was a Hector *and* he was Maylord's neighbour at the Rhenish Wine House.'

'But that neighbour said Maylord would have had nothing to do with Wenum, other than exchanging pleasantries in the hallway,' pounced Thurloe. He hesitated. 'I do not mean to tell you your business, Tom, but I have been wondering whether you ever intend to examine the documents you retrieved from Maylord. They might provide you with answers, and render some of our discussion obsolete.'

'Christ!' muttered Chaloner, removing them from his pocket. 'I had forgotten all about them.'

'I thought as much,' said Thurloe. 'You are not yourself today, or you would have had them open the moment you arrived.'

Chaloner untied the dirty ribbon that bound them together and unfolded the first sheet. Then he examined the second and the third. 'Music,' he said in astonishment. 'It is just music.'

Thurloe sat back, disappointed. 'Well, I suppose Maylord was a composer.'

'He did not compose these, though,' said Chaloner. 'This is not his writing.'

Chapter 6

Thurloe wanted Chaloner to stay in his chambers while he went to speak to his informants about Mary Cade, and Chaloner did not object, because they were warm, comfortable and the pantry was well-stocked with food. He sat by the fire intending to study the music from Maylord's chimney, write another article about Portugal as an excuse to re-visit L'Estrange, and think about his investigation. He dashed off the article quickly enough, but the music was difficult to understand and his investigation had him confounded, so he spent most of the time asleep. Hours later, Thurloe returned to say he had met with no success. Worse, he had failed to gain access to Newgate, because he had arrived too late, which meant Chaloner would have to go after all. The prospect did not fill the spy with enthusiasm.

'No one knows Mary, except as a lady newly arrived in Cripplegate,' Thurloe said, as he returned the drawing. He was tired and dispirited. 'It is almost as if she never existed before she bewitched William.'

'She existed,' said Chaloner grimly. 'The way she threatened me suggested I am not the first man she has tried to intimidate, and all we have to do is encourage her other victims to talk to us.'

'We shall have to find them first. Perhaps they are all in the provinces. Will you travel the length and breadth of the country in an attempt to unveil her?'

'If that is what it takes to save Will, then yes.'

Chaloner left Lincoln's Inn at ten o'clock, when the streets were quiet, and most fires were doused. He walked to his lodgings, and slept until the bellman announced that it was five o'clock on a cold, rainy morning. He washed in the bucket of water his landlord had left for him, shaved, and rummaged in his clothes chest for something respectable to wear.

His choices were even more limited than they had been the previous day, and he was obliged to settle for a shirt that was too small for him, and a purple coat he had been lent three months ago, but that he had forgotten to return. He bundled up the insect-ravaged remainder of his clothes and tossed them over his shoulder, intending to spend his last two pennies on matching thread as soon as the markets opened. He was perfectly capable of making basic repairs, and a lack of suitable attire would start to impede his work soon, by barring him from the places he needed to visit. Dick Whittington style, with the cat at his heels, he crept down the stairs and let himself out through the front door. When it saw drizzle falling steadily, the cat promptly turned around and stalked back inside again.

It was still pitch black, although London was beginning to stir. Lamps and fires were lit in Fetter Lane, and the smell of burning wood mingled with the scent of bread from a nearby cook-shop. The aroma reminded Chaloner that he needed to acquire some money before he starved.

193

He cursed under his breath when his first step ended in a splash, and freezing water seeped into his boots. He recalled Thurloe mentioning the previous day that the Houses of Parliament were flooded, and that prayers were being said all over the city for a break in the weather.

He crossed Fleet Street, and aimed for Hercules' Pillars Alley, a narrow lane named for the famous tavern that stood on its corner. Lights gleamed inside the inn, and muted cheers suggested a gambling session was in play. Since the Restoration, taverns had reverted to the age-old tradition of staying open for as long as their patrons demanded, and Londoners were proud of the fact that ale and wine were available in their city twenty-four hours a day.

About halfway down the road was a tall, three-storey building separated from the traffic by a line of metal railings and an attractive courtyard. Its window shutters, firmly closed against the foul weather, were newly painted, and everything about the place bespoke quality and affluence. It belonged to Temperance North, who had once been Chaloner's neighbour. She had invested her entire inheritance in the house, then stunned her friends by opening an elegant bordello that was very popular among wealthy courtiers. Chaloner loved Temperance like a sister, but had not yet been to tell her he was back from his latest travels. She would be hurt if he left it too long, so a visit was already overdue.

He tapped on the door and waited, shivering as the wind blew rain into his face. Eventually, he heard a bar being removed, and the door was opened warily by a man called Preacher Hill. Hill was a nonconformist fanatic, who worked as a night-porter for Temperance, so his days could be free to stand in public places and

194

spout inflammatory sermons. It was men like Hill who fanned the flames of religious dissent, and he and Chaloner had never seen eye to eye.

'What do you want at this hour of the morning?' demanded Hill. He glanced up at the sky. 'It is still dark.'

'Is Temperance ill?' asked Chaloner, suddenly aware that had the 'gentleman's club' been operating as normal, Hill would have been outside, helping patrons into carriages or on to horses. Lights would have been blazing from windows, and there would have been some sort of sound – soft music or the murmur of voices. He wondered if she had been attacked during the time he had been away, and forced to close.

'She is well,' replied Hill. He sighed, knowing better than to annoy his employer by dismissing her friends. 'Come in and I will fetch her, although I cannot imagine she will be pleased to see you.'

He stamped off down the hallway, and Chaloner waited uncertainly, noting that the chamber where the revelries usually took place was empty. It was also clean and tidy, and had clearly not been used for any sort of entertainment the night before.

'Thomas!' came Temperance's voice from the stairs. She was wearing an elegant velvet mantua, a robe-like garment usually worn over night-clothes. 'Where have you been these last four months? Mr Thurloe said you had gone abroad, but you could have left me a note, too, so I would not worry.'

'There was no time.' Chaloner was sorry to hear the reproach in her voice. He had very few friends in London – he would have fewer still if Mary Cade had her way over Leybourn – and he did not want to alienate any of them.

195

She inspected his face, raising her hand to touch the bruise on his jaw. 'You have been fighting, I see. You have not changed!'

'You have,' said Chaloner. She had grown plumper, and her glossy chestnut hair was set in the style favoured by Lady Castlemaine. There were expensive rings on her fingers, and she had somehow acquired the casual, mocking smile that was currently the vogue at White Hall. In all, they were not pleasant developments, and he wondered what was happening to her.

'It has rained almost constantly since you left,' she said, when he did not elaborate. 'The old folk say it was the worst summer ever. Special prayers were said for the harvest, but they did scant good.'

'It is the wrath of God,' said Preacher Hill in a voice that was far too loud for the early hour. 'He disapproves of debauchery, and sends a scourge of rain to lead us back to the path of righteousness.'

Chaloner wanted to point out that this was rank hypocrisy from a man who earned his daily bread in a brothel, but he did not want to offend Temperance, so he held his tongue. He followed her along the hallway to the large, warm kitchen, while Hill disappeared on business of his own. Normally, the room was busy, as scullions prepared for the new day by scouring pans and fetching water. That morning, however, the hearth was a mass of dead, white ashes, and the room was still and silent. Temperance began to lay the fire, while Chaloner looked around him.

'Where are your people? The cooks and the maids.' And the prostitutes, he was tempted to add, but was still not quite sure how to refer to them without causing offence.

196

'In bed,' she replied. She glanced up at him. 'Yesterday was All Saints and today is All Souls.'

He regarded her blankly. 'I do not understand.'

She raised her eyebrows indignantly. 'The club does not operate on religious high days, Thomas. That would be immoral.'

Temperance was eager to tell Chaloner all that had happened in London during his absence. He did not ask whether she had heard about the deaths of Newburne and Maylord, but they were included in her summary anyway. It was not long before she was joined by her matronly assistant Maude, and the discussion became even more detailed. Although listening to gossip was not something he particularly enjoyed, it was a necessary part of being a spy, and he was good at asking questions that prompted a decent flow of information.

He discovered that the bishops had successfully vetoed a Bill that granted indulgences to Catholics, and the King – unfashionably tolerant of 'popery' – was furious about it. The old Archbishop of Canterbury had died, and was succeeded by a man who was unlikely to soothe troubled waters. The Devil was making regular appearances in a house in Wiltshire, obliging the Queen to send agents to investigate – Chaloner was grateful he had not been given *that* commission – and the King had hesitated to acknowledge Lady Castlemaine's latest baby as his own; she was said to be livid at what amounted to a slur on her fidelity.

'How do you know all this?' he asked when they had finished. Their chatter had saved him the bother of reading back-issues of the newsbooks, and knowing Court gossip and a smattering of current affairs made him feel less of an alien in his own country.

197

'Our customers often bring newsletters for us to read,' explained Temperance. 'After all, everyone is interested in intelligence these days. It is the latest fashion.'

'We buy the news*books*,' elaborated Maude, 'but they are a waste of money. The news*letters* are better, especially Muddiman's. L'Estrange's rags contain a lot of rubbish that the government wants us to believe, but that must be taken with a fistful of salt. Take Monday's *Intelligencer*, for example. Were phanatiques really intent on seizing York? Or does L'Estrange exaggerate?'

'Muddiman says the rebellion was confined to a few misguided lunatics,' said Temperance. 'So, I think we can ignore L'Estrange's attempts to make us think we are on the brink of another civil war.'

Chaloner was sure their opinion of the newsbooks echoed that of most Londoners, and thought Williamson had better do something to improve them before they slipped so far into disrepute that they would never recover.

'Have you met L'Estrange's assistant, Tom?' asked Maude. Her expression could best be described as lecherous. 'Henry Brome is a *lovely* man, and it is a pity he is married.'

'I do not think much of Joanna,' said Temperance immediately. 'Far too thin. And she reminds me of a rabbit – all teeth, ears and eyes. I cannot abide skinny women.'

Chaloner regarded her in surprise. Temperance was not usually catty, and he supposed her own expanding waistline made her jealous of those who had theirs under control. 'I rather like her.'

'Everyone *likes* her,' drawled Temperance acidly. 'She is so *sweet*. Personally, I usually feel like grabbing her by the throat and shaking some backbone into her. Timid little mouse!'

Chaloner laughed at her vehemence. 'I prefer her to some of the people I have met since arriving back in London. And speaking of unpleasant men, you mentioned the death of a solicitor called Newburne earlier. Did you ever meet him?'

'He came here once,' said Temperance, not seeming to think there was anything odd in the question. 'He was a small, bald fellow with the kind of moustache that made him look debauched – like the King's. I did not like him. He pawed the girls, then left without paying.'

'Actually,' countered Maude, 'he told Preacher Hill that he would send payment with Ellis Crisp. Of course, it amounts to the same thing. Who would dare ask Crisp for money?'

'It is curious that Newburne died of cucumbers,' mused Temperance. 'There has been a lot of it about of late. First, there was that charming Colonel Beauclair, equerry to the Master of Horse. Then there was Valentine Pettis, the pony-dealer—'

'Two men associated with nags,' said Chaloner, wondering if it was significant.

'And finally two sedan-chairmen,' finished Temperance, 'who had nothing to do with nags, because they are effectively mules themselves. I expect it is just a bad year for cucumbers, probably because of the rain. Perhaps the dismal weather produced a crop with unusually evil vapours.'

'Do not forget Maylord,' added Maude. 'He died of cucumbers, too, although he once told me he never ate anything green. He said it made him break out in boils.'

199

'I miss Maylord,' said Temperance sadly. 'He came here to play for us sometimes. He told me he taught your father the viol, Tom. Is it true?'

Chaloner nodded. 'Did he perform for you during the last two weeks or so? Someone told me he was upset about something, and I would like to know what.'

'Money,' supplied Maude helpfully. 'He thought someone had cheated him of some, and was very angry about it – not like him at all. He did not say how much he was owed or the name of the debtor, but it was obviously a substantial sum or he would not have been so agitated. Did you hear his close friend Smegergill was murdered on Sunday? At Smithfield.'

'Was he?' asked Temperance, startled. 'That is a pity. I cannot say I took to Smegergill, because he was odd, but I am sorry to hear he met a violent end.'

'How was he odd?' asked Chaloner.

'He was losing his memory, and was convinced he was about to be committed to Bedlam,' replied Temperance. 'He often made peculiar remarks about it – the kind that make a person uncomfortable.'

'That was his idea of a joke,' argued Maude. 'He did not really believe there was anything wrong with him. It was just something he liked to claim, perhaps so people would contradict him and say he was as sane as the rest of us. Which he was.'

Temperance was thoughtful. 'Do you really think so? I was under the impression that it was a genuine fear, and he *was* becoming more forgetful.'

Maude remained firm. 'It was clear he was just amusing himself by pretending to be addled. I saw him laughing fit to burst once when he told the Duke of Buckingham he was turning into an elephant, and the Duke responded by providing him with a large handkerchief for blowing his trunk.'

'Well, he once told me that his name was Caesar, and so he should be allowed to rule White Hall,' said Temperance, unconvinced. 'That is not normal behaviour by anyone's standards. But we should discuss something else before we quarrel. Have you seen William since you returned, Tom? He has fallen in with a very devious person.'

'He brought her to meet us,' said Maude. 'She was more interested in our silverware than our company, and then she said she knew plenty of ladies who would like to work for us.'

'They will not be *ladies*,' said Temperance disapprovingly. 'And we are very selective about who we hire. We have our reputation to consider, and I doubt she knows any respectable girls.'

Chaloner doubted the whores who worked for Temperance would be deemed 'respectable girls' by most Londoners, either. He showed them his drawing. 'I am going to take this to Newgate today, to see if anyone recognises her.'

Maude regarded the picture critically. 'You need to make her eyes colder and harder, and add more weight to her jowls. I am glad you intend to separate her from Mr Leybourn. If you do not, she will have every penny from him, and crush his heart, too. We will help you.'

'How?'

'My sister lives in Smithfield, and her cakes are just as popular with villains as with law-abiding men. Leave your picture with me, and I will ask her about Mary Cade.'

'She told me she was a friend of Ellis Crisp,' said Chaloner.

201

Maude immediately shoved the drawing back across the table. 'Well, in that case, I shall mind my own business. And so should you. No one should put himself on the wrong side of Butcher Crisp.'

Temperance was appalled. 'Are you saying William is in the clutches of the Hectors? But that is terrible! We must do something to save him, even if it does mean coming to blows with Crisp.'

'No,' said Chaloner firmly. 'It is too dangerous. Leave it to me.'

'For once, I agree,' said Maude fervently. 'I shall do as you say, and so will Temperance. I am no coward, but there is no point in asking for trouble, and I would hate to see the club in flames.'

Chaloner gazed at her. 'It is that bad?'

'Worse,' declared Maude. 'Mr Leybourn will just have to take his chances – and hope he lives to learn his lesson about women like Mary Cade.'

'There is one thing we can do, though,' said Temperance. 'William once told me he keeps all his money in a sack under a floorboard, because he does not trust bankers. You must persuade him to take it elsewhere, Tom. Mary and her cronies might lose interest in him once it is no longer available.'

Chaloner had known about Leybourn's careless attitude towards his life-savings, but it had slipped his mind. He supposed he should steal it, to keep it safe until his friend had come to his senses. 'I will devise a way to stop them getting it,' he said, deliberately vague. He did not want to involve Temperance and Maude in a plan that would almost certainly involve burglary.

'Good,' said Temperance, 'but do it discreetly. Do not

give the Hectors reason to suspect you are responsible, or you may end up in one of the Butcher's pies.'

'Where are you taking that bundle of clothes?' asked Maude in the silence that followed Temperance's unsettling remark. 'To the rag-pickers? They are in a sorry state, so I doubt you will get much for them.'

'They only need to be mended,' objected Chaloner, rather offended. 'I was going to buy thread——'

Maude inspected them critically. 'Only a seamstress of the highest calibre will be able to salvage these! You had better leave them with me.'

'They are all I have,' said Chaloner, hoping she would not decide they were beyond repair and throw them away. He could not afford to replace them.

'Do not worry. You can trust me – with a needle at least.' Maude winked disconcertingly at him.

'Meanwhile, we shall lend you something that does not make you look like a Parliamentarian fallen on hard times,' said Temperance, businesslike and practical. 'Our customers often leave garments behind, so we actually possess an impressive wardrobe.'

'I cannot visit White Hall wearing clothes abandoned in a brothel,' objected Chaloner, thinking about what might happen if an owner recognised them.

'We will pick you something bland,' replied Maude, rather coolly.

She heaved her ample rump out of her chair and returned a few moments later with a green long-coat and breeches. The coat had buttons up the front, on the pockets, and along the sleeves. She insisted that he also wear boot hose – leggings with lace around the knees that hid the top of his boots – on the grounds that not to do so would look peculiar. The ensemble was finished

203

with a clean white 'falling band', a bib-like accessory that went around the neck and lay flat on the chest.

Maude regarded him appreciatively. 'What a difference a few decent clothes can make to a fellow! You have gone from impecunious servant to a man of some standing.'

'You look nice,' agreed Temperance, smiling. 'I might even make a play for you myself.'

Chaloner glanced sharply at her, but saw she was teasing him. She had been enamoured of him once, but had since learned that she did not want a husband or a protector telling her what to do. And he certainly had no intention of dallying with a brothel-mistress.

When Chaloner left the bordello, the rain had stopped, although dark clouds suggested there was more to come. Everything dripped – houses, churches, trees, the scruffy food stalls in Fleet Street, carts and even horses. The usual clatter of hoofs on cobbles was replaced by splattering water and sloshing sounds as people made their way through lakes of mud. Even the pigeons roosting in the eaves looked bedraggled, and the black rats in the shadows had coats that were a mess of spiky wet fur.

When he passed a cook-shop, delicious smells reminded him that he was hungry, so he decided to visit White Hall to claim his back-pay first. He was horrified to learn from the clerks in the Accompting House that he had not been on their records since June. Sure there had been a mistake, he went to the Stone Gallery, and found the Lord Chancellor in earnest conversation with a dark, brooding man who wore the robes of a high-ranking churchman. Chaloner waited until the cleric had gone before approaching the Earl.

'Sheldon agrees with me,' confided the Earl gleefully, rubbing his hands together. 'That will show Parliament who is right!'

Chaloner had no idea what he was talking about, and supposed he would have to read the old newsbooks after all. 'I am pleased to hear it, sir,' he replied.

Unfortunately, the Earl knew a noncommittal answer when he heard one. 'You do not know him, do you! You *must* settle down and learn something about your own country, not race off to foreign parts at the drop of a hat. Sheldon is the new Archbishop of Canterbury. He has just promised to make a stand against religious dissenters with me. It is good news.'

'Is it?' Chaloner did not think so. There were a lot of people who did not want to conform to the Anglican Church's narrow protocols, and he felt it was unwise to alienate such a large segment of the population. He was sure such a rigid stance would come back to haunt the Earl in the future.

Clarendon's expression hardened. 'Yes, it is. There are far too many radical sects, and their false religion is an excuse for sedition and treason. The fires of fanaticism burn hot and wild if left unchecked, and we must douse them while we can. And if you disagree with me, you are a fool.'

'Yes, sir.' It was always safer not to argue with anyone where religion was concerned.

Clarendon eyed him coldly. 'Well? What do you want? Have you come to tell me the name of Newburne's killer?'

'I think it may be more complex—'

The Earl held up a plump hand. 'Do not make excuses. I am tired of being treated with disrespect by all and sundry. Buckingham and his young blades mock me; the King's mistress flaunts her latest bastard in my face; and you insult me whenever we meet. I have had enough of it.'

'Perhaps I should stay in White Hall, then, to learn about your enemies' plans to—'

'No!' snapped the Earl. 'You will assist L'Estrange, as I ordered. I need his goodwill, because he controls the newsbooks, which means he also controls the hearts and minds of London. *Ergo*, discovering Newburne's killer is important.'

Chaloner suspected Muddiman controlled a lot more hearts and minds than L'Estrange. 'He does not want my help, sir. He said to thank you for your kind offer, but to decline it politely.'

The Earl's eyes narrowed. 'That means he has something to hide. You will look into this.'

'I will try my—'

'No!' shouted Clarendon, loudly enough to startle several passing nobles. 'You will not *try*, you will succeed. And to add an incentive, I shall not put you back on my payroll until you do. I deleted you when you abandoned me for the Queen – why should I pay a man working for another master? – and you will only be reinstated when you have proved your loyalty by exposing Newburne's killer.'

'You doubt me, sir?' Chaloner asked, stunned that the Earl should be suspicious of him after he had risked his life on several occasions to further the man's cause.

'I doubt everyone these days. I know you have helped me in the past, but that was then and this is now. If you want to work for me again, you must prove yourself in the matter of Newburne.'

Chaloner was tempted to tell him to go to Hell, but

206

then what would he do? The Earl offered the only opportunity for intelligence work – at least, until the Queen recovered from her illness. And even then it was possible that Chaloner's foray to the Iberian Peninsula had been a single commission, and she would have her own people for more routine business. Besides, he suspected Her Majesty's main concern would be the King's mistresses, and he had no wish to spy on *them*. Some were infinitely more deadly than the Butcher of Smithfield.

The Earl saw he was cornered, and began to gloat. 'It was your own decision to dash off to Portugal. I asked you not to accept the Queen's commission.'

'Only after you had ordered me to go, when it was too late to change my mind,' objected Chaloner. 'If you had made your position clear sooner, I might have been able to think of an excuse.'

'So, it was my fault, was it?' demanded the Earl. 'How dare you! I am the only man in London willing to hire you – and that means you are not in a position to be insolent. I am sick of impudence and I am putting my foot down. I mean to show everyone what I am made of.'

And what he was made of was a lot of petty spite, thought Chaloner. He could not best his peers, so he was venting his spleen on someone who could not fight back. His instinct was to tell the man he was a mean-spirited bigot, but while that would be satisfying, it would do him no good. He swallowed his pride and nodded acceptance of the Earl's terms.

Clarendon smirked, savouring the victory, then reached out to pull him into the light of one of the windows, peering into his face. 'Have you been fighting?'

'Working for you is dangerous,' retorted Chaloner,

ignoring the fact that he did not know for certain whether the ambush was related to his investigation into Newburne. 'I was attacked trying to question suspects for you.'

'Well, you seem to have survived,' said the Earl unfeelingly. 'What did you learn?'

'That someone called Wenum has been selling L'Estrange's news to Muddiman. It is possible that Newburne discovered this, and was killed to ensure his silence. However, it is also possible that he was murdered because of his association with Ellis Crisp—'

'Spymaster Williamson is investigating Crisp, so he and his nasty Hectors will soon be a thing of the past. He has his best man – a fellow called Hickes – on the case.'

'Do I know Hickes?' asked Chaloner. It could not be the apple-seller for two reasons. First, because the man had been ordered to watch Muddiman, not Crisp. And secondly, because the country was in deep trouble if that slow-witted specimen represented the secret service's 'best man'.

'I have no idea who you might have encountered in the sordid world of espionage,' replied Clarendon haughtily. 'So, you think Newburne's death might be related to the newsbooks, do you? That is unfortunate, because it means I shall be obliged to pay the widow's pension after all.'

'All I can do is hunt out the facts, sir. What you do with them is your business.'

The Earl regarded him thoughtfully, and Chaloner braced himself for another dressing down. Instead, Clarendon turned to gaze out of the window. 'Your discovery about Wenum is interesting. Do you think L'Estrange knows he is being betrayed, and is trying to keep it from the government? Williamson will be furious when he finds out. No wonder the newsletters are always so much better to read than the government-run newsbooks.'

'L'Estrange is aware that someone is selling his news to a third party, but he does not know the identity of the culprit.'

'Then tell him,' ordered the Earl. 'And make sure he knows the information comes courtesy of me. I warrant Williamson's agent has not been so assiduous.'

'Yes, sir,' said Chaloner with a sinking heart. The last thing he needed was to be used as a pawn in a battle between the Earl and Williamson. 'Is there anything else?'

'Yes. You have five days to unmask Newburne's killer. It is Wednesday today, so you have until Monday. If you have not solved the matter by then, you can find yourself another master.'

Chaloner left the Stone Gallery feeling his life had just taken a dramatic and unnerving plunge towards disaster – and that the Earl's own situation was probably not much better. The man was wise to distrust his peers, but there was no need to alienate his staff, too, not unless he wanted to find himself with no allies – and in a place like White Hall, to be friendless was dangerous. He was assailed with a sense of misgiving, not sure he could trust the Earl to reinstate him even if he did provide answers – assuming Crisp or some henchman did not kill him first, of course. And how was he supposed to manage for five days with no money? He was so engrossed in his concerns that he did not hear Bulteel calling him, and the secretary was obliged to tug his sleeve to claim his attention.

'He is in a foul mood today,' Bulteel said, jumping back when he saw a dagger appear in the spy's hand, as if by magic. 'If I had seen you first, I would have recommended that you communicate in writing. Did he dismiss you? If so, you will be the third today.'

'What is the matter with him?'

Bulteel gestured with his hand, encompassing everything. 'He hates politics and intrigue, and would far sooner be at home with his family. Yet when he is home he worries about what might be happening behind his back. That spat with the Earl of Bristol last spring hurt him deeply, and although he emerged victorious, he knows it is only a matter of time before another enemy rises against him.'

'They will rise a lot sooner if he drives away the people who are willing to help him.'

Bulteel gave one of his shy smiles. 'He will be sorry tomorrow for what he said to you. Are you still helping him with this Newburne business? He badly needs loyal men, and this is important.'

'Why is it important? I am still not sure he is telling the truth about why he wants the matter investigated. Is it really because he does not want to pay the widow's pension?'

Bulteel looked furtive. 'If I tell you, will you promise never to reveal where you heard it?' Chaloner nodded cautiously. 'It is because Newburne was *his* spy.'

Chaloner was not surprised, because it had already occurred to him. 'He said Newburne was hired for legal work, but of course I drew my own conclusions – the Lord Chancellor of England will have access to far better solicitors than poor Newburne. And then he was dismissed for stealing.'

210

'That was a ruse. Newburne was never dismissed – he was the Earl's man for more than a decade.'

Now Chaloner *was* surprised. From what he had learned of Newburne, the solicitor was not the kind of man with whom any upright noble would want to associate long term. And the Earl was upright, despite his faults. 'Are you sure?'

'He sent us information about Cromwell during the Commonwealth. It was more gossip than genuine intelligence, if the truth be told, but the Earl was grateful anyway. Then he kept us appraised of what was happening in Smithfield as Crisp began to rise in power. And latterly, he reported to us about L'Estrange's running of the newsbooks.'

Chaloner was thoughtful. 'Then perhaps L'Estrange killed Newburne because he objected to being watched. It would explain why he ordered me not to look into the matter.'

'Assuming he knew what Newburne was up to. Our sly solicitor was very careful.'

'Could Newburne have sold L'Estrange's stories to the newsletters, then?' Chaloner was asking himself more than Bulteel. 'With Wenum's help? If the Earl was his real master, why not betray L'Estrange?'

Bulteel shrugged. 'All I can tell you is that he was loyal to us, and the Earl appreciates trustworthiness. He knew Newburne was no angel, and that he dabbled in devious business, but he will miss his reports. I hope you uncover his killer, although you must take care.'

'I always take care.'

'I am sure you do. However, remember that Williamson may have guessed what Newburne was doing, and he has a way of ridding himself of people who cross him.

211

He will not want you exposing *him* as a killer. Meanwhile, L'Estrange is a hothead, who would think nothing of running you through for an imprudent remark, and you do have an insolent tongue. Also, the booksellers would prefer Newburne to be quietly buried and forgotten. Meanwhile, Crisp's power is on the increase, and he might well have dispensed with a man who knew too many sensitive details about his business—'

'Is there anyone in London not on your list of suspects?'

Bulteel thought carefully. 'The Queen. She had a distemper at the time of Newburne's death, and was in bed, surrounded by physicians. But I had better deliver these letters, or you will not be the only one to suffer the Earl's sour temper.'

Chaloner watched him scurry away, all frayed gown and flapping sleeves. Was he telling the truth? Was the Earl's determination to catch Newburne's killer explained at last? And did it really matter, given that Chaloner was obliged to solve the case anyway, if he wanted a job at the end of the week? He was about to leave White Hall when he saw Greeting hurrying towards the Privy Gardens with a violin under his arm. He knew he should go to Ivy Lane and tell L'Estrange about Wenum, but Smegergill's death was preying on his mind, and he wanted answers.

'The Queen is still ill, and her surgeon says music might help,' said Greeting rather breathlessly when Chaloner waylaid him. 'He has chosen me to play, so I cannot talk to you for long.'

'I thought she was getting better.'

'She is, which some courtiers attribute to a rather lovely air I composed and played to her myself. She actually smiled when I finished it, and told me I was an angel.'

'Was she delirious?'

Greeting winced. 'I suppose that remark pertains to my shabby clothes. Where did you buy that coat? I wish my Court appointment provided *me* with a decent income. I can never make ends meet, no matter how hard I try. Will you put in a word for me with the Lord Chancellor? I understand you clerk for him, when your duties at the Victualling Office allow. I could clerk, too, in my spare time.'

'I was sorry to hear about Smegergill. I understand he was a member of your consort.'

'I could hardly believe it, especially so soon after Maylord. I live in Smithfield, and Hingston – the organist – is staying with me, because his house is flooded. It might have been *we* who were attacked.'

Chaloner was surprised he should think so. 'I thought a coach was provided, to deliver you all safely home. You were never in any danger.'

Greeting pulled a disagreeable face. 'You obviously do not hire many hackneys. When only Hingston and I were left, the driver demanded a higher fare than we had agreed, and when we refused, he ordered us out. We walked past the very place where Smegergill was murdered. Indeed, we saw Crisp arrive to inspect the scene of the crime, but we never dreamed Smegergill was the victim. We should not have let him go with that stranger; I blame myself for not demanding the villain's identity.'

'Would Smegergill not have resented the interference? I was told he could be difficult.'

Greeting gave a wan smile. 'That is putting it mildly – he was downright contumacious at times.'

'He told me he was afraid he might be taken to Bedlam.'

213

'He often talked about that, but I am not sure if it was a genuine concern or a bizarre way of fishing for compliments – his mind could be very sharp at times. Two of our colleagues were taken to Bedlam recently, although not for insanity. There is a rumour that they were spies, and that Williamson caught them red-handed. It sent a clear message to all would-be informers: dabble in espionage at your peril.'

'You are wet,' said Chaloner, indicating Greeting's sodden clothes. 'What have you been doing?'

'I have just come from the Rhenish Wine House, where Maylord's will was read. He left everything to Smegergill, and it is a pity the old man did not survive to enjoy any of it.'

'Did Maylord own a lot of property, then?'

'A fair amount – two houses, a large collection of books and musical instruments, a shop of some kind, money invested with bankers. Oh, and there was a fine nag, too.'

'Nag?' Chaloner was thinking about the other cucumber victims – the equerry and the horse-trader.

'A racing beast. He kept it at Newmarket, although I do not think he was very interested in the sport. It was an investment, for when he could no longer earn a living by music. There is a lesson for us, Heyden. There is no point in worrying about the future, because there may not be one.'

'I have been told that someone owed him money, or that he was being cheated.'

'Very possibly. It would explain why he was angry and nervous in the two weeks before he died. The Court is infested with vultures, and his good nature would have made him easy prey.'

214

'Poor Smegergill,' said Chaloner sadly. 'Maylord's money would have kept him from Bedlam.'

'He knew he was Maylord's beneficiary – we all did. There are those who say *he* gave Maylord the cucumber, because he wanted his inheritance.'

Chaloner did not believe for an instant that Smegergill had hastened Maylord's end. The old man's distress when told his friend had been murdered was genuine. 'What do you think?'

Greeting raised his eyebrows. 'That this is White Hall, and people would gossip about the saints themselves, should they be unfortunate enough to find themselves here.'

Chaloner walked to Ivy Lane, thinking about the best way to tell L'Estrange about Wenum. He did not want to accuse someone who might have been a much-loved friend, and risk L'Estrange brandishing a sword at him. Chaloner would probably win the encounter, but he did not want to be arrested for wounding a government official – or worse.

When he arrived, Brome's shop was full. The bookseller and Joanna were dealing with a healthy queue of customers, while L'Estrange was grumbling about the length of time it took for his papers to be printed. Hodgkinson was explaining that ink took a while to dry, and that rushing the process resulted in smudged and unreadable text.

'Alcohol of sulphur,' said Chaloner. L'Estrange and the printer stared at him. 'In Holland, printers add alcohol of sulphur to ink, because they say it promotes faster drying. I have no idea if it works—'

'Buy some,' ordered L'Estrange, turning back to

215

Hodgkinson. 'We must do something to give us an edge over Muddiman. But why are you here, Heyden? I told you I do not want you investigating Newburne's demise. He died of cucumbers, so let that mark the end of the matter.'

'I came to give you more intelligence about Portugal,' replied Chaloner. He handed over the notice he had written in Thurloe's room the previous evening.

L'Estrange read aloud. '"About the beginning of October, the Earl of San Juao, with 5500 foot, 1300 horse and 8 field pieces entered into old Castile, out of the province Tras os Montes, and passed far into the country without opposition, where he sacked a matter of 60 towns and places, but burnt none, for His Majesty had forbidden it". Is this true?'

Chaloner regarded him askance. 'Of course it is true!'

'Have you sold this to Muddiman, too?' demanded L'Estrange. His earrings glittered as walked to the window to read the rest of the report, and Chaloner thought he moved like a tiger, all compact muscles and soft-footed tread. 'You hope to be paid twice for the same piece?'

Chaloner half-wished he had thought of it. 'Is that what your other sources do?'

L'Estrange finished reading and shoved the paper in his pocket. 'They would not dare. The government news-books are Spymaster Williamson's domain, and only a fool crosses him.'

Was Wenum a fool, then, wondered Chaloner. Did betraying the Spymaster account for his death, and perhaps Newburne's, too? Was this what the Lord Chancellor wanted his spy to discover – that a powerful minister was responsible for a series of murders? And if so, was it to bring Williamson down with the disgrace, to acquire a way of controlling the Spymaster for his own ends, or to pit Chaloner against a deadly adversary to avenge himself for what he saw as a lack of loyalty?

'If people are so frightened of Williamson, then why are Muddiman's newsletters so often ahead of the newsbooks?' Chaloner asked. 'Obviously someone is not afraid to sell secrets.'

L'Estrange's eyes narrowed, and his hand dropped to the hilt of his sword. 'You have a blunt tongue, and I am tempted to cut it out. The Lord Chancellor will not mind – he has complained about your insolence on several occasions.'

'Do not stoop to violence, Roger,' said a chubby woman, edging forward to rest her hand on his arm. She was pretty after a fashion, with pale blue eyes. 'It will make a mess on the floor.'

L'Estrange's expression immediately softened. 'Mrs Hickes, my dear,' he crooned, bending to kiss her cheek; she simpered at him. 'You know I would do nothing to offend *you*.'

'Mrs Hickes is the spouse of Williamson's best spy,' whispered Hodgkinson in Chaloner's ear. 'Hickes is also supposed to be investigating Newburne's death, although I am told he has had scant success so far.'

'His mind is probably on what L'Estrange is doing to his wife,' murmured Chaloner, thinking of Mrs Muddiman and wondering whether any woman was safe from the man's advances.

Hodgkinson chuckled. 'I wish I knew his secret. They all seem to melt at his feet, even the ones devoted to their husbands. Like Mrs Newburne.'

'Christ!' muttered Chaloner. Was this yet another motive for murder? 'Did they actually—'

'They enjoyed each other's company when Newburne was out. Beyond that, I know nothing.'

'Did Newburne know nothing, too?'

'I cannot say, although it is no secret that L'Estrange has a penchant for married ladies. However, even if Newburne did *not* know about the visits, he certainly would have been aware that L'Estrange would go a-calling sooner or later.'

Chaloner watched Mrs Hickes leave the bookshop with the other customers, and was astonished to note that she was not the only one who flung L'Estrange a longing glance as she walked through the door. So did the wife of Mr Smith of the Bell Inn, who had apparently come to make sure the advertisement for his stolen horse was going to appear in *The Newes* the following day.

'We were talking about betrayal, Heyden,' said L'Estrange, dropping his courtly leer as soon as the ladies had gone, and only he, Hodgkinson, Brome and Joanna were left. Chaloner noticed that L'Estrange's liking for married women did not extend to Joanna, whom he all but ignored. 'You want to know why Muddiman always has the news before me? It is because of phanatiques.'

Joanna stepped forward, her eyes great frightened orbs. 'It is not phanatiques,' she said in a trembling voice, clearly uneasy at contradicting the great man. 'Someone *is* sending our intelligence to rivals, but not for sinister political reasons. The traitor is being paid for them. It is all about money.'

'Nobert Wenum,' said Chaloner. 'Does he work for you?'

All four looked blankly at each other. 'I have never heard of him,' said Brome. 'He is nothing to do with the bookshop.'

'And there is no one at my print-houses by that name, either,' added Hodgkinson. 'Who is he?'

'The man who has been selling your secrets.' Chaloner handed over the annotated copy of *The Newes* and the ledger, with a brief explanation of what each logged entry meant.

Hodgkinson snatched the paper from the startled L'Estrange. His jaw dropped and he turned to Chaloner in horror. 'But this is not due to be made public until tomorrow! How did you come by it?'

'And this book?' asked Joanna, peering over L'Estrange's shoulder. 'Where did you find it? It *proves* something is amiss – just as Henry and I have suspected for weeks. Oh, dear!'

Brome's face was filled with dismay. 'So, it is true, after all? I was hoping we were mistaken, because betraying the official newsbooks is such a monstrous thing. Treason, in fact.'

'I found both in a room rented by Wenum,' explained Chaloner. 'Apparently, he has a rash on his jaw and is probably a Hector.'

'That describes you,' said Hodgkinson. 'There is a mark on *your* jaw, and *you* might be a Hector. You work for a government minister, and they are not averse to hiring felons for certain business.'

'Do not confuse Heyden's Earl with Williamson,' said Joanna quietly. 'They are not the same.'

Chaloner was not so sure. 'Can you think of anyone else who matches that description?' he asked, looking at each one in turn.

Hodgkinson shook his head, L'Estrange continued to glare at the ledger, and Joanna's expression was one of appalled disbelief. Her mouth hung open slightly, so her teeth seemed longer than usual.

'Can you tell us anything else about him?' asked Brome. 'The colour of his hair? His height?'

'I have never seen him,' said Chaloner. He pointed to the paper Hodgkinson still held. 'However, it looks as though he was proof-reading *The Newes* in his lodgings. If you give me a list of the people you employ in such a capacity, I can investigate them for you.'

Brome and Joanna exchanged an acutely uncomfortable glance. 'Perhaps you had better tell him, Mr L'Estrange,' said Joanna unhappily. She cringed when the editor glared at her, but she stood her ground. 'Tell him their names. Please.'

'My proof-readers are not traitors,' declared L'Estrange, lobbing the ledger at Chaloner to express his contempt for the evidence it provided. 'I do not employ *men* for that task, and especially not Hectors with rashes. I hire *women*. So, you can take your damned accusations elsewhere.'

Chaloner tried to be patient. 'Then perhaps one of these women passed the proofs to Wenum—'

'No!' snapped L'Estrange. 'There are a dozen ladies who work as my proof-readers, and I can vouch for the loyalty of every one. I call them my Army of Angels, and they make a pleasant change from dealing with damned phanatiques.' He glared around, suggesting he thought there were several damned phanatiques in the room with him at that precise moment.

'Tell me who they are,' pressed Chaloner. 'If they have done nothing wrong, it will—'

'I most certainly shall not. This is none of your affair – and none of the Lord Chancellor's either. They are good ladies, and I will not let you loose on them.'

'But we need this matter resolved,' said Brome, making

no effort to hide his frustration. He turned to Chaloner. 'They are the wives of wealthy citizens who have time for the careful, painstaking work of checking type for errors. It is not difficult, but it is exacting, and not everyone has an eye for it.'

'Ladies are better than men,' said L'Estrange, on the defensive now. 'Men are careless, and you never know when one might transpire to be a phanatique.'

Brome appealed to the editor's sense of self-preservation. 'If Williamson sees that annotated paper, he will draw the same conclusion Heyden did – that a proof-reader is responsible. We do not want him thinking we are protecting the culprit, because it will mean us losing our shop, and you losing your government appointments.'

L'Estrange scowled. 'I worked hard for these posts. I will not let anyone take them from me.'

'Then let us make sure no one does.' Brome turned to Chaloner. 'Our proof-readers include Mrs Smith and Mrs Hickes, both of whom were here just now. Also, Mrs Newburne, Mrs Muddiman . . .'

'The wife of your rival?' asked Chaloner, shocked. 'And she does this proof-reading at home?'

'Of course not!' shouted L'Estrange, shooting Brome and then Chaloner furious glares. 'She does it here. They all do. We go upstairs together, and I supervise them very closely. No draft newsbook ever leaves the premises. I am inordinately fond of Mrs Muddiman, but I am not such a fool as to let her take a pre-published journal to her husband's lair.'

But he was fool enough to let her see them in the first place, thought Chaloner, and if she had a good memory, she might even be able to quote them verbatim to her grateful spouse. Then he recalled the way she had spoken about L'Estrange and wondered whether the editor's piratical charm *was* sufficient to keep a still tongue in her head. He was bemused. Surely not every woman L'Estrange encountered fell for him, especially if she knew she was only one of dozens so favoured? Chaloner could see nothing remotely attractive in the dark, glittering features, the swinging earrings and the gap-toothed grin, but supposed there was no accounting for taste.

'Is there a Mrs Hodgkinson?' he asked, of the printer. 'Is she a member of this Army of Angels?'

'She lives in the country,' said the printer. He shot a defiant look at L'Estrange, making Chaloner wonder whether she had been sent there for a reason.

'Other Angels include Mrs Allestry and Mrs Nott,' continued Brome, ignoring L'Estrange's furious sigh at his continued revelations. 'And then there is—'

'The wives of the booksellers?' interrupted Chaloner, his mind reeling. 'The booksellers L'Estrange fined in his capacity as Surveyor of the Press?'

'Their unfortunate marriages make no difference to their ability to highlight printing errors,' said L'Estrange haughtily. 'And they are pleased to help me, because I reduced their husbands' fines substantially, out of the goodness of my heart. They are indebted to me.'

'Apart from the Army of Angels, security is very tight,' said Joanna, trying to be helpful. 'All unpublished proofs are locked in a chest in Mr L'Estrange's office. They only leave the building when they go to Mr Hodgkinson for printing.'

'The government contract is important to me,' added Hodgkinson, when Chaloner turned towards him. 'I am not so rash as to risk losing it by selling news to Muddiman. My compositors produce *one* copy – for proof-reading – in advance of the main print-run, and I bring it to L'Estrange myself.'

'We have a little ritual,' said L'Estrange scathingly. 'I lock it in my chest, and he watches.'

It was Hodgkinson's turn to become defensive. 'Damn right I do! I do not want to be accused of letting news escape to our rivals. I cannot imagine a worse fate than to fall foul of the Spymaster.'

'Who has the key to this chest?' asked Chaloner.

'I do,' said L'Estrange, holding it up. 'And Newburne had the only other in existence. But this is none of your business, and I resent the implication that we are lax—'

'Where is Newburne's key now?'

'I would like the answer to that question, too,' said Brome. He flinched when L'Estrange whipped around to scowl at him.

'It is not just your livelihood, but ours, too,' said Joanna, going to stand next to her spouse. She swallowed uneasily when L'Estrange fixed her with his glittering eyes, and her fingers tightened around her husband's arm. But she took a deep breath and finished what she wanted to say. 'Henry and I have worked hard for this shop, and we love it dearly. Please answer Mr Heyden's questions, or run the risk of Williamson asking them instead.'

'Williamson!' jeered L'Estrange unpleasantly. 'How will he find out about any of this?'

'Because *I* shall tell him,' said Joanna defiantly. 'I would rather you were cross with me than have Williamson thinking Henry and I are traitors. I will tell him about this Wenum fellow.'

Chaloner watched L'Estrange seethe with impotent rage, and was impressed that such a timid woman had

223

mustered the courage to defy him. He suspected, however, that she had fired all her cannon with the threat, and that a serious counter-attack from L'Estrange would see her crumble. Fortunately for Joanna, L'Estrange was less adept at reading people.

'You would not dare,' he breathed, but there was uncertainty in his voice.

'Would she not?' asked Brome, putting his arm around her. His voice dripped pride. 'There is strength in my Joanna, so you had better do as she says.'

'I do not know where Newburne kept his key,' L'Estrange snapped. 'But his funeral is tomorrow, so I shall ask his widow.'

'Good,' said Joanna. 'But be sure you do not forget, or I *will* pay a visit to White Hall.'

In the absence of anyone else to pick on, L'Estrange homed in on Chaloner. 'Here is a shilling. I do not usually pay for news in advance of publication, but I want you gone from my office – permanently. I resent your accusations and the way you have turned my staff against me.'

'I shall take my article about the pirates of Alicante to Muddiman, then,' said Chaloner.

L'Estrange had been in the process of stalking from the room, but he stopped dead in his tracks, and his hand dropped to the hilt of his sword. With a weary sigh, Brome stepped forward.

'What Heyden meant to say was that he will be obliged to come to your office for as long as he has information to sell you,' he said quietly. 'He did not intend to sound insolent.'

'You had better pay him double, though,' said Joanna. She was buoyed up by her victory, and the rabbit face

224

wore a small smirk of triumph when the editor turned to gape at her. 'I have it on good authority that Muddiman pays *two* shillings for decent intelligence. And tales about pirates from Alicante come into the category of "decent", I would say.'

L'Estrange seemed about to give her a piece of his mind, but she met his glower with a steady gaze, and it was he who backed down. He tossed a second shilling at Chaloner.

'Here,' he snarled, before rounding on the Bromes. Both flinched, and Joanna's bravado began to slip. 'But this is as far as your nasty rebellion goes. Any further insurgence and I shall take my business to another bookseller. I will not tolerate phanatiques in the ranks.'

He stamped from the room.

'You were magnificent,' said Hodgkinson to Joanna. 'I always said L'Estrange would be lost were it not for your common sense, and today you proved it yet again. Forcing him to cooperate with the Lord Chancellor is good for us all, and you did the right thing by standing up to him. Both of you.'

Brome rubbed his eyes with shaking hands. 'My nerves are frayed, and I need the medicinal effects of a dish of coffee. We shall go to Haye's Coffee House and Heyden can write about the pirates there.'

'Good,' said Joanna. 'Mr L'Estrange will be back to collect the advertisements soon, and we do not want him to find Mr Heyden still here. I have had enough turmoil for one day, thank you!'

While Brome went to fetch his coat, Chaloner smiled his thanks at Joanna for getting him the extra shilling. She beamed back at him, all teeth and gums. He found himself

225

beginning to like her, appreciating how difficult it must have been for such a timid woman to oppose a charismatic bully like L'Estrange. Hodgkinson was doubtless right in that the Bromes kept L'Estrange from doing too much damage to the newsbooks – and to himself – but Chaloner doubted it was easy. He was glad he was not obliged to keep the man in check, sure it would tax his diplomatic abilities – such as they were – to the limit. The shop door rattled suddenly, and a fat, red-faced merchant waddled in.

'May I help you?' asked Joanna. She patted the rabbit-ear braids at the side of her head, and smoothed down her apron as she walked towards him. 'We at the newsbooks are always ready to—'

'I want to place an advertisement,' declared the man. 'I lost a grey gelding from the Queen's Arms, Feversham, and everyone should know there is a reward for information leading to its safe return.'

Joanna began to write. 'Your name, sir? And where do you—'

'James Bradnox of Vintners' Hall. Mr Wright told me he placed a notice in *The Newes*, and his nag was home within a week.' Bradnox addressed Hodgkinson and Chaloner, assuming them to be customers, too. 'These advertisements mean it is difficult for stolen animals to be sold on the open market – traders know what is currently missing, see. Newsbook notices are five shillings well spent.'

'Yes,' agreed Joanna. 'I have been told several times that our most important function is to facilitate honesty in the horse trade. Of course, we have other functions, as well, and we—'

'It *is* important,' insisted Bradnox. 'Far more valuable

than that rubbish about phanatiques. Who cares about them? Yet we all care about horses.'

'The newsbooks were founded to keep the people informed of current events,' said Chaloner when Bradnox had gone. 'Yet they are loaded with notices about missing livestock. It seems they—'

'I know,' cried Joanna, wringing her hands unhappily. 'Mr L'Estrange does not mind, because they cost five shillings each and they take up space. I know it is wrong, and that people would rather have real news, but what can we do? If we did not sell advertisements, we would be limited to whatever *he* wants to write about phanatiques. And the occasional piece about Spanish pirates.'

'It is just as well I am going out,' said Brome, as he returned wearing a coat that was buttoned to his chin, as if he thought he might catch cold otherwise. 'Mrs Chiffinch's carriage has just pulled up outside. She looks upset, and I imagine her husband has been unfaithful again. She will not appreciate me being here, when all she wants is another woman's ear.'

L'Estrange had also seen the coach, and was thundering down the stairs from his office, eyes and earrings gleaming. Chaloner supposed the feckless Chiffinch was about to learn that wives could be unfaithful as well as husbands – or that the Army of Angels was about to receive another recruit. He, Brome and Hodgkinson left the editor fawning over the new arrival, while Joanna hovered uncertainly in the background. Before he closed the door behind him, Chaloner saw Mrs Chiffinch looking rather pleased with the editor's attentions, and wondered yet again what women saw in the fellow.

'L'Estrange has a fiery temper,' he said, as the three of them walked along Ivy Lane.

227

Brome nodded. 'His sword is in and out of its scabbard like nobody's business these days. The death of Newburne has unnerved him more than he likes to admit.'

'And yet he does not want it investigated?' said Chaloner.

'Some stones are better left unturned, and Newburne really did emerge from under a particularly slimy one. I would not want the responsibility of determining what happened to him – assuming anything untoward did, of course.'

'That surgeon's report relieved me of the responsibility of probing further, thank God,' said Hodgkinson fervently. 'I wish to know no more about the affair, and neither does L'Estrange.'

'Muddiman's newsletters make for interesting reading,' said Brome, off on a tangent. 'They contain so much *domestic* information. I do not wish to be rude, Heyden, because I am sure Alicante is a fascinating place, but I would much rather read about events in London.'

'Ask Williamson for some, then,' said Chaloner. 'He is Spymaster General, so should be awash with intelligence, not to mention political reports. If anyone can supply you with home news, it is he.'

'And there lies the problem,' said Brome glumly. 'He does not like to part with it. He thinks telling the public too much about what the government does will encourage them to disagree with it.'

Chaloner laughed. 'He is almost certainly right.'

A beggar was singing a ballad in a pitiful, wavering voice, and Brome stopped to give him a penny. It took a long time for him to unbutton his coat, locate his purse and refasten the garment again. Chaloner might have been moved to pity, too, had he not seen the fellow in

228

the window of a nearby cook-shop earlier, enjoying a sumptuous meal. The man was a trickster, who preyed on the kind-hearted. They were about to move on when Brome happened to glance back up the road.

'Oh, no!' he breathed in horror.

'Butcher Crisp!' exclaimed Hodgkinson, equally alarmed. Chaloner saw a man in a wide-brimmed hat and a long cloak striding purposefully along the street. 'Is he going inside your shop?'

'Joanna!' gasped Brome in a strangled voice. He ran a few steps, then stopped in relief. 'No, he is passing by. Lord save us! I thought for a moment that he might have come to register a complaint about L'Estrange's rant on criminals last week. Felons can be sensitive, and Crisp might think some of the comments were directed against him personally.'

'They were,' said Hodgkinson. 'L'Estrange all but said his empire should be crushed.'

'You should have seen the article before I edited it,' said Brome. 'It was full of names and unfounded accusations. I deleted them, because there is no point in asking for trouble. And thank God I did! I do not like the notion of Crisp invading our shop and venting his spleen on my Joanna.'

Nor did Chaloner. A willingness to oppose L'Estrange occasionally did not equate with being able to cope with the notorious Butcher of Smithfield. Joanna would have been out of her league.

'Crisp often uses Ivy Lane when he travels between Smithfield and St Paul's,' said Hodgkinson. 'The Hectors run a lottery in the cathedral, you see, and he likes to keep an eye on it. He is turning the corner now, Brome. You need not race home to protect your wife.'

229

Brome shot the printer a rueful smile. 'Good! I am not built for dealing with rough men. Even Joanna is better at it than me. She has great courage. Not every woman could work in the same building as L'Estrange and have the strength and ingenuity to dodge his advances. I am not sure if our business would have succeeded, if it were not for her. But I do hate that man.'

'L'Estrange?' asked Chaloner.

Brome grimaced. 'Actually, I admire L'Estrange, because he follows his conscience. His morality does not always coincide with my own principles, but he has the courage to do what he thinks is right, no matter what the consequences.'

'So do fanatics,' said Chaloner acidly. 'That is what they are: people who think they know better than anyone else.'

Brome declined to argue. 'When I said I hated that man, I was referring to Crisp. I am not ashamed to admit that he terrifies me.'

'There are his Hectors,' said Hodgkinson, pointing to several unsavoury-looking characters. 'I did not think they would be far away. He seldom leaves his domain without them these days, although they keep their distance, to maintain the illusion that he is a normal citizen.'

'He is not normal,' said Brome with a shudder.

Haye's Coffee House was another smoky, busy place, located in an alley so narrow that carts could not access it. It meant pedestrians could, though, and were not obliged to be constantly on the look-out for wheeled vehicles that did not care what they hit. A large dog sat outside, chewing what appeared to be a wad of tobacco. Inside, the owner Robert Haye had let his beans roast too long, and the air was thick with the reek of burning. The mishap did not stop him from grinding them up and seething them in boiling water, though, and the resulting beverage was far from pleasant. There were complaints galore, but Haye pointed out that coffee tasted nasty even when prepared properly, and if his patrons wanted the benefits of the aromatic herb, they should drink what they were given. Chaloner was astonished when everyone did, thinking that customers in Portugal would not have been so meekly compliant.

'What news?' called Brome to the throng, as he, Hodgkinson and Chaloner squeezed on to a bench where there was not really enough room for them.

'You are the newsmonger, so you tell us,' quipped Nott, the Lord Chancellor's bun-haired bookseller. His companions laughed.

'And if you have none, Nott will tell you about the vicar of Wollaston,' said a fat man in an apothecary's hat.

Brome exchanged an uneasy glance with Hodgkinson. 'We are carrying that story in tomorrow's *Newes*, so how do you know it already?'

Nott held up a handwritten newsletter. 'The vicar's Book of Common Prayer was so besmeared with tar and grease that he was obliged to use another one to conduct the divine service. I warrant L'Estrange will blame phanatiques.'

There was more laughter, and Brome looked dismayed. 'Damn this Wenum and his treachery! I am not a violent man, but I would like to punch him for what he is doing to us. Will you stop him, Heyden? I know L'Estrange told you not to meddle, but this cannot go on.'

'Wenum is dead,' replied Chaloner. 'But he may have

231

had connections to Newburne. And I am obliged to investigate *him*, because the Lord Chancellor ordered me to do so.'

'Good,' said Brome. 'However, I recommend you do not tell L'Estrange. It would be a pity to lose you to his ready sword.'

Hodgkinson pulled a face when he tasted Haye's beverage. 'Try a pipe, Heyden. It takes away the taste of coffee, which is the only reason men smoke. If there was no coffee, there would be no need for tobacco.'

'I disagree,' said Brome, tearing his thoughts away from dead men and stolen news. 'Tobacco has its own virtues, and its popularity is quite independent of coffee. Joanna likes a pipe on occasion, but she would never touch coffee.'

'I bought a notice in *The Newes* last month,' announced the fat apothecary. 'I lost a bay gelding from near the pump in Chancery Lane, and was hoping an advertisement might see it home. Tom Wright got his beast back when he bought a notice, and so did Captain Hammond. But I am still waiting for mine to appear.'

'You are just unlucky, Reeves,' said Nott. 'Not everyone who advertises is fortunate enough to have his property returned. The thieves must have taken it into the country, away from the influence of the newsbooks. Not everyone reads them once you get past Islington.'

'We were talking about the relative virtues of coffee and tobacco, Reeves,' said Brome, not wanting to discuss business when he could be relaxing. 'Which do you prefer?'

'Tobacco, of course,' replied Reeves. 'But *we* were talking about horses, which is far more interesting. Unless you have news to impart? And I do not mean foreign stuff, either. How is the Queen? The last I heard, she had distemper. My dog had that, and it was not pretty.'

'You had better call it an "indisposition" next time,' whispered Hodgkinson to Brome. 'Reeves is not the first one to question your use of "distemper". I know it is what the Court physicians told you, but they obviously do not know how to communicate with the general public, and you do not want to be responsible for the rumour that the Queen is a hound.'

'She is a good lady,' said Chaloner coolly, thinking of the small woman with the dark, unhappy eyes who had asked him to go to Portugal. 'You should never write anything disparaging about her.'

'William Smegergill is murdered,' said Nott, addressing the room in general. 'His brains dashed out, and then his head forced into a puddle until he drowned.'

'Oddsfish!' exclaimed Reeves. 'That is an unpleasant way to go! I heard he had taken to playing strange music of late, and that Maylord did the same. On one occasion, they bowed a discordant harmony at Court, and the King was obliged to order them to stop.'

Nott tamped more tobacco into his pipe. 'What an odd coincidence! L'Estrange has been doing the same thing. My shop is opposite, as you know, and I often hear him playing. For the last three weeks, he has been practising some very nasty tunes.'

'Foreign jigs,' elaborated Reeves darkly. 'They are probably designed to bewitch us, so Dutchmen can steal our horses while we listen. Why do you think they have built themselves a navy?'

'To develop trade routes to Africa, America and the Far East,' replied Chaloner. He knew a lot about the

233

Dutch, and their navy was an interesting subject to him. 'They are expanding their—'

'Rubbish,' said Reeves, evidently not of a mind for erudite discussion. 'They want our horses, and anyone who disagrees with me does not deserve to own one.'

Thurloe and Temperance had been right when they said no one at Newgate would know Mary Cade, and even the two shillings Chaloner had earned from L'Estrange did not buy him the information he had hoped for. It was not easy to part with funds that could have been spent on food, but he reminded himself that a few lean days were a small price to pay for his friend's welfare. One warden, more helpful than the others, suggested he try the Fleet Prison, because it held mostly debtors, and the woman in the picture looked too well fed to be the common kind of criminal. Chaloner supposed it was worth a try, although he was loath to set foot in another gaol that day. Visiting Newgate had left him nauseous, and he wondered whether he would ever be able to enter a prison without the uncomfortable sense that he might never come out.

That evening, he played his viol, then sat at the table, studying the music he had taken from Maylord's chimney. It made no more sense to him than the rest of his investigation, and when he attempted to play it, his landlord hammered on the wall to make him stop. He wondered why the old musician had kept such dismal compositions when the best place for them was on the fire. Chaloner might have put them there, had he been able to afford the fuel to light one.

He was too restless to sleep, mostly because he was hungry and there was nothing to eat. When he saw it

234

had stopped raining, he went out, not with any specific destination in mind, but just to prowl around the city that was now his home. He glanced at the lamp-lit windows of the Golden Lion before he left, and was bemused to see Giles Dury there. The assistant news-monger was gazing absently into the street, and although Chaloner could think of no earthly reason why Dury should be watching him, he still slipped back inside his house and exited through the back door instead.

He wandered aimlessly, alert to the sounds of the night: the rumble of drunken voices from alehouses, the shriller babble of an argument in a coffee house, the distant howling of a pack of dogs, and the ever-present roar of water rushing under London Bridge. He went all the way to Cripplegate without anyone giving him more than a passing glance. When he arrived at Monkwell Street, he took refuge in the gate to Chyrurgeons' Hall, standing so still that he was invisible to all but those with the very sharpest eyes. Leybourn's house was lit in two places. The attic on the top floor had a lamp, and Chaloner could see his friend working there, snatching books from the shelves around him with a fierce concentration that said he was deep in one of his incomprehensible theories.

The second light was at the back, so Chaloner scaled a wall and dropped silently into the garden. He walked stealthily towards the kitchen and looked through the window. Mary sat by the hearth, and three men were with her, all drinking from Leybourn's best silver goblets. Chaloner regarded them thoughtfully. They were the same three who had attacked him and Smegergill, and then who had chased him at the Rhenish Wine House: Nose, the leader, and his henchmen, the Scot and Fingerless. Mary had obviously not been boasting when

235

she claimed to know dangerous people. Yet surely *she* could not have set her cronies after him that night? They had exchanged a few cool words by that point, but nothing to warrant murder. Or had she already identified Chaloner as a threat to her plans, and had decided to act promptly?

He could not hear what the foursome were saying to each other, and suspected they were keeping their voices low so as not to be heard upstairs. He looked at the door that led to the hallway and saw a piece of twine emerging from under it. He did not understand its significance until he heard the faint jangle of a bell. Immediately, the men rose and made for the back door. As they left, the Scot and Fingerless shoved Leybourn's goblets in their pockets, although Nose left his on the table. None of them noticed Chaloner in the shadows. A few moments later, Leybourn appeared, yawning and rubbing his eyes. Mary insinuated herself into her arms, and he bent to kiss her.

Chaloner turned away and made his way home.

Chapter 7

For the first time since Chaloner had returned from Portugal, the sun was shining when he woke. It caught the brown leaves in the churchyard of St Dunstan-in-the-West, and turned them to a deep, glowing orange that shimmered in the breeze. Yet even the glories of a bright autumn day did not distract him from his worries.

He was deeply disturbed by what he had witnessed at Leybourn's house the previous evening, and his inclination was to visit the Fleet Prison in a concerted effort to see what could be learned about Mary. But Newburne was due to be buried at noon, and there was a chance that Chaloner might overhear something important as the mourners talked together. He would be no good to Leybourn if he was obliged to leave London because of a lack of employment, so he decided to dedicate the morning to the solicitor's murder.

Newburne had lived on Old Jewry, an affluent thoroughfare that ran between Cheapside and the London Wall, which boasted two churches and the kind of houses that were owned by the upper mercantile classes. It did not take him long to identify Newburne's home. It was one of the largest, and a lot of money had recently been spent on it. He recalled the tales of Newburne's wealth, and saw they had been true – and so they should be, he thought. The man had earned a wage from L'Estrange, had business dealings with Crisp, *and* had been in the Lord Chancellor's pay.

It was too early for anything to be happening, but Robin's Coffee House was opposite, and provided a comfortable refuge in which to watch and wait. He found a seat in the window, and handed over a large leather token worth threepence to the coffee-boy; his cat had knocked a jar from the mantelpiece that morning, and he had recovered the token from among the shards. It was enough to buy him three dishes of a thick black sludge that felt as though it was doing harm when he swallowed it, and free access to a fire and *The Newes*, published that morning. Men came to drink before they started work, all thrusting through the door with the cry, 'What news?' Most received the reply that there had been an outrage perpetrated on Mr Cobb. Curious to know what outrage, Chaloner read:

> *It came to me this day, from a very sure hand, that one Mr Cobb, the Vicar of Wollaston, Northamptonshire, applying himself according to his duty to God and the lawes of the land to the Reading of the Divine Service, found the Common Prayerbook so bedaubed with tar and grease upon the services for the day that he was obliged to borrow another. Something I should add to this, of what I myself know for a certain truth. But first, it is too **early** to mention it; and secondly, it is too **foule** for the Honour of the Nation to be made publique.*

It sounded intriguing, and Chaloner wondered whether L'Estrange really did have a 'foule' secret to impart to

238

his readers, or whether it was just a device to make them buy the next issue. He glanced across the road, but Newburne's house was still closed, so he read that Rowland Pepin, famous for his Cure of the Rupture and Broken Belly, also made 'easy truffles of all kinds', and that Theophilus Buckworth's lozenges still worked against coughs, catarrhs and strongness of breath. He also learned that in Vienna, there was news of the Turks 'up and down', which was vague enough to mean nothing at all. His own piece was there, too, although it had been edited to make it more sensational than it should have been.

Eventually, when he started thinking he should have gone to the Fleet Prison after all, the door to Newburne's mansion opened, and people began to arrive to pay their respects. First in was a man in a cloak and a large hat, surrounded by a mob of heavily armed henchmen. The Butcher of Smithfield was obviously intent on dispatching his obligations early, although Chaloner did not imagine there would be much of a queue, given Newburne's unpopularity. He was surprised to see he was wrong: the funeral was not due to take place for another three hours, but a huge number of folk followed Crisp's example. Chaloner could only assume they were making obligatory appearances, so as not to offend one of Newburne's three powerful and generally nasty masters. After a while, when the initial rush was over and Crisp and his henchmen had gone, the spy attached himself to a party of law-clerks and followed them inside.

The front parlour contained Newburne and his coffin, reclaimed from St Bartholomew the Less for the occasion, and Dorcus Newburne. She was prettier than he

239

expected, and her face was kind. She sat in a chair at the foot of the casket, clothed in black from head to toe. L'Estrange was at her side, hand resting solicitously on her shoulder, while Brome and Joanna hovered uncertainly nearby.

Brome looked uncomfortable in his dark mourning gear. The sword he wore was thin and new, and Chaloner was under the impression that it had never been drawn. Joanna was equally awkward in a boned waistcoat that over-accentuated her skinny figure. She eschewed the current fashion for wigs, and her brown hair still fell in the ridiculous rabbit-ear style he had come to associate with her. She was pale and sad, and her large brown eyes looked bigger than usual that day. When Dorcus began to cry, she knelt next to her and held her hand. L'Estrange leaned down to murmur something encouraging, and the widow reached up to touch his cheek. He shot her one of his grins, all flashing teeth, gleaming eyes and glinting earrings, but the smile faded when he spotted Chaloner. Ignoring Dorcus's squeal of distress, he abandoned his post and came to grab the spy's wrist, shunting him into an antechamber where they could speak privately.

'I told you: I do not want the Earl meddling in Newburne's death,' he hissed. 'Why are you here?'

'The Lord Chancellor sent me to represent him,' said Chaloner, freeing himself with rather more vigour than was necessary. He disliked being manhandled.

L'Estrange folded his arms and looked resentful. 'I am sorry for you. Funerals are grim affairs, and I would give a good deal to be elsewhere today. However, Dorcus has need of me, so here I am.'

'I am sure she does,' muttered Chaloner.

'These occasions invariably attract phanatiques,' grumbled L'Estrange, waving a disparaging hand towards the mourning chamber. 'The types who daub tar on prayer-books.'

Chaloner could not see any obvious religious bigots. 'Where are they?'

L'Estrange flapped another vigorous hand, so his earrings swung. 'The booksellers for a start. Why do you think I want to fine them all into oblivion? Then there is Muddiman – a *brazen* phanatique. Even Brome and Joanna display disconcerting signs of treachery on occasion – I heard them playing music composed by Locke last night, and he was a damned Roundhead!'

'Did you retrieve Newburne's key?' asked Chaloner, changing the subject. L'Estrange was deranged, and should not be allowed to control the government's sole means of disseminating information. He might use it to start another civil war. 'You said you—'

'I cannot bring myself to do it,' interrupted L'Estrange. 'Not today. I will ask tomorrow, when her husband is not in the coffin next to us. I plan to pay her a little private visit in the morning.'

He waggled his eyebrows, and Chaloner regarded him askance, astonished that he should baulk at asking for a key, but think nothing of foisting romantic attentions on her. Or was it Chaloner who had no understanding of such matters? It was, after all, L'Estrange who had the harem.

'Someone is stealing your stories,' he pointed out. 'And anything that damages your newsbooks also harms the government. You cannot afford to have a vital key missing.'

L'Estrange glowered at him. 'How does the Earl put

241

up with your impudence? He is not a tolerant man, by any stretch of the imagination. I thought about what you said yesterday, incidentally – your conclusions about the annotated *Newes* and that ledger – and I have decided your theory is irrelevant. Someone must have broken into my office and stolen that one set of proofs, but it was a random event, not a regular occurrence. And the ledger can be interpreted in a number of ways.'

Chaloner gaped at him, scarcely believing his ears. Was the man really so blind? 'But—'

'The leak is *not* at my office. My Angels are beyond reproach, and I forbid you to speak to them. So, the matter is closed, just like the death of Newburne. You will forget both incidents.'

Chaloner saw there was no point in arguing. L'Estrange's mind was made up and, as with most ignorant men, it would be virtually impossible to change. Instead, he thought about the enigmatic comment at the end of the prayer-book article.

'Do you really have a foul secret to impart to the nation, when the time is right?'

'You have been reading *The Newes*,' said L'Estrange, pleased. 'I hope it will pique your interest enough to purchase *The Intelligencer* on Monday. And yes, I know *lots* of foul secrets about all manner of dreadful phanatiques.'

Chaloner was disappointed. 'I thought that might be the case.'

'Phanatiques are a danger to us all,' ranted L'Estrange. 'And that is why you must leave my newsbooks alone. Tell the Earl there is nothing to investigate – about Newburne *or* these so-called leaks. If you disobey, you will be sorry. You look very well, by the way.'

Chaloner did not like the juxtaposition of the two comments. 'Is there any reason I should not?'

L'Estrange shrugged. 'None at all. Let us hope you stay that way.'

Chaloner returned to the mourning room. He was about to introduce himself to Dorcus Newburne as a clerk from the Victualling Office, but L'Estrange reached her first.

'This is Heyden, the Lord Chancellor's man,' he said with a sneer. 'Come to pay his respects.'

'Why would the Earl send a representative here?' Dorcus asked tearfully. 'He promised me a pension, but now he is trying to wriggle out of honouring it.'

Chaloner winced. 'He sends his deepest sympathy, ma'am,' he said gently.

She looked away, touched by the kindness in his voice. 'My husband *was* on official business when he died, you know. In fact, you can tell the Earl that I believe he was murdered in the course of his duties.'

'He died of cucumbers, Dorcus,' said L'Estrange, a little impatiently. 'It is horrible, I know, but it could happen to anyone.'

'But he did not like cucumbers,' protested Dorcus, beginning to cry. 'And who can blame him? He said he was unwell before he left for work last Wednesday, so perhaps he was already ill then.'

'Did he eat breakfast that day?' asked Chaloner, ignoring L'Estrange's furious glare for disobeying his orders and pursuing the investigation.

Dorcus shook her head. 'And no dinner the night before, either, because he was too late home. All he had were some lozenges – the ones he usually took for pains in his stomach. And we all know why he had to purchase

243

so many of *those*: because he was anxious about working for so many powerful men.'

'But he did eat a cucumber, my dear,' said L'Estrange, trying hard to mask his irritation, but not succeeding very well. 'Hodgkinson was with him when he devoured it, and there are other witnesses, too. He did not dislike them as much as you think.'

Dorcus wiped her eyes. 'He might have swallowed some of the seeds to ease his wind, I suppose, but they should not have killed him. There is something odd going on, and I want my pension.'

'Leave it to me, pretty lady,' crooned L'Estrange; his voice was soft, but he still glared at the spy. '*I* shall make sure you are awarded your pension. You certainly do not want Heyden prying into your husband's private life.'

'Arise, Tom Newburne,' said Dorcus bitterly, clutching Joanna's fingers hard enough to make her wince. 'Will I never be allowed to forget the shame of that nickname? I should not have let him drink so much last Christmas, and then he would not have tried to knight the Archbishop of Canterbury with that wooden sword.'

'Did he?' asked L'Estrange, startled. 'Here is a tale I have never heard before.'

'Nor I,' said Joanna, equally taken aback. 'We were aware that he liked a drink, but he was always quiet in his cups. Of course, I am not saying he was a drunkard, only that he—'

'Christmas was different,' interrupted Dorcus shortly. 'He was in a good mood then, because Butcher Crisp had offered him a share in his pie enterprise.'

'Oh, dear!' whispered Joanna. 'Did he accept? Only they are said to contain . . . well, they are . . .'

'Pork?' asked Dorcus, apparently unaware of the

rumours that surrounded Crisp's baked goods. 'I like pork, especially when cooked with sage and onion.'

'Did your husband know a musician called Maylord?' asked Chaloner, before the conversation could veer too far into uncharted waters. 'He is said to have died of cucumbers, too.'

L'Estrange's eyebrows drew together in a scowl, but Dorcus answered before he could stop her. 'Thomas did not fraternise with artisans. He liked music, but not as supplied by that dissolute Court.'

Chaloner had more questions to ask, because he was not sure what to think about Dorcus. Was she really the grieving, dignified widow she appeared, or did she know more about her husband's devious activities than she was prepared to admit? Her determination to have the pension, even though she was already rich, was testament to a certain greed, and he was keen to gauge her measure. He was not to be granted the opportunity, however, because L'Estrange declared she was looking pale. Before she could demur, he had gathered her into his arms and swept her upstairs. They were followed by astonished stares from the assembled mourners.

'Heavens!' said Brome, watching them go. 'That is bold, even by his standards.'

'She did look wan, though,' said Joanna. 'And even he will refrain from seduction on this of all days.'

Brome struggled to be as charitable as his wife. 'Perhaps he just wanted to separate her from Heyden. He has said all along that he does not want the Earl prying into his business.'

'Has he?' asked Chaloner. 'Does he have a lot to hide, then?'

'I expect so,' said Joanna guilelessly. 'He does work for

the government, after all. Yet, for all his faults, he is gentle with women, and Dorcus is in kind hands now.'

Brome sighed his relief. 'Good. I am more than happy to comfort a distressed widow, but I suspect everyone thinks we are hypocrites for it. We disliked Newburne as much as the next man.'

'Let them think what they like,' declared Joanna spiritedly. 'We are doing what is right. Dorcus needs friends, and it is common decency to help her. I am surprised to see so many people here, though. Crisp was the first to arrive, and I think he brought every last Hector with him. I had no idea he was master of such an enormous body of men. They marched in like the Parliamentarians' New Model Army, all cudgels, guns and glittering swords.'

'I was afraid they might burgle the house while they were here,' said Brome. 'There is a rumour that Newburne owned a box of valuable jewels, you see, and I thought they might decide to have a look for it. But they behaved like perfect gentlemen.'

'They will not burgle in broad daylight,' said Joanna. 'And there is nothing to say the hoard is here anyway. It might be in one of his other houses – his Thames Street cottage, or the attic he hired on Ave Maria Lane, for example. Of course, that is assuming the box actually exists. I doubt it does.'

'Did he rent rooms at the Rhenish Wine House, too?' asked Chaloner, wondering if he could establish a connection between the solicitor and the mysterious Wenum.

Brome and Joanna looked blankly at each other. 'Not as far as we know,' replied Brome. 'Why? Have you discovered otherwise? If so, then it means you have ignored our advice and are continuing to probe.' There was concern in his eyes, an emotion that was reflected in Joanna's face, too.

'A friend of mine died of cucumbers in the Rhenish Wine House, just two days after Newburne,' Chaloner explained, touched by the fact that they seemed anxious for him.

'You mean Maylord?' asked Joanna. She rested her hand on his arm in a shy gesture of sympathy. 'I had no idea you were acquainted. I am so sorry. We heard him play several times in White Hall.'

'L'Estrange invited us there, because he knows we like music,' explained Brome. 'But do not try to change the subject, Heyden. Our warnings about Newburne were not delivered lightly. In fact, we heard just moments ago that the case may have claimed another casualty. Newburne's friend Finch has been found dead in his room.'

Chaloner gazed at them in shock. 'How did he die?'

Brome was unhappy. 'I do not want to tell you. It may encourage you to dive even deeper into these murky waters, laying your life on the line for men who are not worth the risk.'

Joanna agreed. 'Your Earl may be the most upright man at Court, but that does not make him an angel, while Crisp . . . well, suffice to say you are best not attracting his attention, if you can help it.'

Brome seemed to sense they were wasting their breath, and switched to something less contentious. 'Joanna wants to hear more about the pirates of Alicante, so will you dine with us tomorrow? We may even have some music after, but do not tell L'Estrange, or he will want to come, too.'

'And then he will do all the talking, and we shall hear nothing about privateers,' said Joanna. She took

Chaloner's hand, rabbit-eyes pleading. 'Please come. We would both like to know you better.'

'Thank you,' said Chaloner, supposing he was about to make new friends. It was about time, especially as Leybourn was all but lost to Mary and Temperance's brothel was turning her into a stranger. He was used to being alone, but that did not mean he was never lonely.

'Finch,' said Brome unhappily. 'I said I would not tell you how he died, but perhaps if I do, you will understand the folly of pursuing your investigation further. L'Estrange told us the news when we arrived here: Finch died of eating cucumbers.'

Finch's house was not far from Old Jewry, and Chaloner had more than an hour before the funeral. He walked briskly, and arrived to find, unlike last time, that there was a bright lamp burning in the corridor on the first floor; he supposed the death of a tenant had forced the landlord to make his building more hospitable to the friends and relatives who might visit. He put his ear to Finch's door, but it was silent within. He tried the handle. It was locked, but it did not take him long to pick it open. He slipped inside and secured the door behind him.

He was not sure what he had expected to find, but it was not Finch's body sprawled on the bed; he had assumed someone would have moved it, or at least straightened the contorted limbs, as a sign of respect.

He went to inspect it. Finch had been playing his trumpet when he had been overcome, because it was lying on the floor at his side. Since no one who loved music would drop an instrument without good cause,

248

Chaloner supposed it had slipped from his fingers as he had breathed his last. He examined it closely, then put it back where he had found it. He glanced at the table, where a cucumber – or most of one – lay on a plate. There was a knife next to it, as though Finch had been chopping off pieces to eat. There was also a box of Theophilus Buckworth's lozenges.

He was about to leave when he heard heavy feet ascending the stairs. Unlike at the Rhenish Wine House, this time he was not caught with nowhere to hide. He stepped smartly into the adjoining pantry, which had its own door that led to the hallway. He opened it a crack and peered out, just as the person reached the bedchamber and began to examine the door. He frowned thoughtfully when he recognised the hulking form of the apple-seller.

What was Williamson's spy doing there, when he should have been watching Muddiman and Dury? Had he been relieved of that duty and given a different assignment, perhaps because it was obvious that his quarry knew he was there? Curiously, Chaloner crept down the corridor as the apple-seller – declining to waste time on picking the lock – smashed the door by hurling his burly frame at it. It shattered into pieces, which meant he could not close it behind him. Thus Chaloner was able to watch exactly what he was doing inside.

The apple-seller looked slowly around the room. His eyes lingered briefly on the body and, like Chaloner, he knelt to examine the trumpet. Then he stood and walked to the windowsill, on which lay a sheet of music and a half-eaten pie. He grabbed the music and stuffed it in his pocket. Chaloner was mystified. The fellow's scarred knuckles suggested he would not be manually dextrous

249

enough to manage an instrument – unless it was a drum. Or had Williamson ordered him to collect documents, and he had taken the music because he did not know the difference between letters and notes?

'—funeral at noon,' came a familiar drawl from the stairs. 'Are you going? It might be fun.'

Chaloner had been so intent on watching the apple-seller that he had not noticed the soft-footed approach of other people. The apple-seller also spun around at the noise, and Chaloner found himself trapped between him and the advancing newcomers. He punched the lamp with his fist, plunging the hallway into darkness. The men on the stairs yelled their indignation.

The apple-seller was rushing towards the corridor, determined to lay hands on whoever was spying on him, so Chaloner darted back to Finch's pantry and aimed for the window. There was a grunt of surprise when the apple-seller found the hallway empty, and Chaloner began to wrestle with the casement catch. It was rusty, and would not move. He pulled harder, and it squeaked open just as the apple-seller realised Finch had more than one room. Chaloner scrambled on to the sill and launched himself out, sliding down a roof that was slick with slime. He reached the edge, put a hand down to steady himself, and jumped into a gloomy little yard. It was not a huge leap, but landing jolted his lame leg, and he felt the familiar twinge that meant he would limp for the rest of the day.

He ducked when tiles began to smash around him. At first, he assumed the apple-seller was throwing them, but he glanced up to see the big man trying to claw his way across the roof. It was unequal to his weight, and he released a howl of alarm when he began to slide off.

Chaloner hobbled towards the gate. As he did so, he glanced up and saw two heads at Finch's open window. They belonged to Muddiman and Dury, and he realised it had been Dury's drawl he had heard on the stairs.

He was confused. Were the newsmongers following the apple-seller now? And why were any of them visiting Finch? He sensed he could not afford to be identified until he understood what was happening, so he kept his head low, Isabella's hat shielding his face, as he wrenched open the gate and hurried into the alley on the other side. He heard a thump and several more crashes as the apple-seller finally lost his battle with gravity and hit the ground. Moments later, Chaloner was walking along Cheapside with his hands in his pockets. He was fairly sure none of the three had gained a good look at him in the shadowy yard, but he bundled his coat under his arm and exchanged his hat for a black cap anyway. There was no point in taking unnecessary chances.

He tried to work out what had happened. Had the apple-seller been sent by Williamson, to look for documents on the government's behalf? But why were Muddiman and Dury there – and why had Dury been lurking in the Golden Lion the previous night? Was it because *Finch* was actually the mysterious Nobert Wenum, and they wanted to dispose of any evidence that might prove it? Finch was Newburne's friend, after all, and Newburne might well have passed him the newsbooks' secrets. Yet Finch had been poor, living in a room that verged on the squalid, and there was nothing to suggest he had earned the fortune detailed in the ledger.

The bells of St Olave's Church were already tolling for Newburne's funeral, and Chaloner walked faster when they stopped. He was going to be late. As he went, he turned his thoughts to what his brief foray to Ave Maria Lane had told him about Finch's death.

There had been green stains on the man's fingers, and blisters in his mouth. Like Newburne, he had been poisoned. However, Chaloner was sure the cucumber had not been responsible for two reasons. First, not enough had been eaten to do a man serious harm, even if Finch had suffered from an aversion to them. And secondly, no wind-player ever ate while he practised, because fragments of food might become lodged in an instrument's innards. Chaloner was sure the cucumber had been left as a diversion, to ensure no one looked deeper into Finch's demise. He smiled grimly. But the killer was out of luck, because Chaloner *would* look deeper, and he *would* discover who had murdered the hapless trumpeter.

Chaloner was late for the funeral. He opened a door that clanked, so people turned to look at him. A few minutes later, the door rattled a second time, and Dury and Muddiman entered. Chaloner nodded a greeting to them, and the offhand way they responded confirmed that they had not identified him with the disturbance at Finch's house.

Deciding to take the bull by the horns, he sauntered towards them. They were looking especially foppish that day, with more lace than a courtesan's boudoir and a good deal more perfume. He glanced at their feet and saw both wore clean shoes with long toes and gleaming silver buckles. They had not walked to the church from Ave Maria Lane, but had been transported.

'Sedan-chairs,' explained Muddiman, seeing where he was looking. 'It is the only way to travel these days.

252

Carriages are too big for alleys, and hackneys are unpredictable – you never know when they might stop and order you out. Sedans are small, manoeuvrable and, if you pay them well, fast.'

'I keep my own,' added Dury. 'Do you?'

Chaloner shook his head. Apart from the fact that he seldom had the money for such extravagance, sedans had an unpleasant jerking motion that took some getting used to. 'What business makes you late for the requiem of the man who sold you L'Estrange's news?' he asked bluntly.

Muddiman's eyebrows shot up, and Chaloner suspected he would have issued a jeering laugh had he not been in a church. 'I produce high-quality work from impeccable sources, and I would *never* deign to accept anything from Newburne – or any other of L'Estrange's minions.'

'A man named Wenum kept a ledger that suggests otherwise,' said Chaloner, wishing he had brought it with him. 'It details payments made for specific items of news over the last six months. I am sure Williamson will be very interested to learn how you are undermining the government.'

'He will not believe you,' said Dury. 'He has had us followed for weeks, hoping to catch us out, but we have nothing to hide. Besides, Wenum is dead – he fell in the Thames about a week ago – so there is no one to corroborate your accusations.'

'And do not think this ledger will prove anything, either,' added Muddiman, grinning. 'It will be a forgery. L'Estrange is not the only newsmonger with powerful patrons, and ours will not see us in trouble over some book of dubious origin.'

Chaloner wondered how they came to know the manner of Wenum's death, when no one at the Rhenish

253

Wine House had been able to enlighten him. Did it mean Muddiman and Dury had decided Wenum had become too much of a risk, so they had killed him before he could expose them?

'There was a commotion at Hen Finch's house on Ave Maria Lane not long ago,' he said, abruptly changing the subject. 'I saw you two leaving it.'

'We went to arrange his funeral with the landlord,' said Dury slyly. 'His friend Newburne is obviously not in a position to do it. Poor Finch. Another victim of the wicked curse of the cucumber.'

Muddiman chuckled softly when he understood Chaloner's interest in the trumpeter. 'You think Finch is Wenum! Well, it is an intriguing theory, but bear in mind that Wenum was swept to his death by the swollen river a week ago, and Finch was still alive last night.'

'At least a dozen people have died in the floods so far,' said Dury, regarding the spy in amusement. 'They like to watch the Thames race by, but they stand too close to the edge and lose their footing. It could happen to anyone. Even you.' The grin faded, leaving an expression that was far from amiable.

'So, have we answered all your questions now?' asked Muddiman, inspecting his fingernails. 'Do you have enough to satisfy your Earl's curiosity about matters that are none of his concern?'

'Not yet,' replied Chaloner. 'But I shall.'

Muddiman's expression hardened. 'How we get our news is our affair, and it is not something we shall reveal to the Lord Chancellor's creature. Be warned: stay away from us.'

Chaloner treated the remark with the contempt it deserved by ignoring it. 'Why are you here? You say you did not buy news from Newburne, but I cannot imagine you were friends with him.'

'Everyone in the publishing trade is here,' replied Dury, gesturing around him with a shrug. 'It would look odd if we stayed away, and such occasions are wonderful opportunities for business.'

Chaloner moved away from them. Their clumsy attempts at intimidation did not bother him, but they were the kind of men who gave the Court a bad name – selfish, avaricious, deceitful and superior. Perhaps Williamson had been right to remove Muddiman from the newsbooks, because Chaloner certainly would not trust him to be a loyal servant of the Crown.

At the end of the service, the vicar announced that L'Estrange had organised some music, as a mark of affection for a lost friend. There were a number of bemused glances at L'Estrange's claim that he and Newburne had been close, and even Dorcus looked startled. Brome kept his face admirably blank, although Chaloner could see Joanna gaping at his side. The consort hired for the task was Greeting's, and the playing was excellent, despite the fact that they had lost Maylord and Smegergill within a few days of each other. Chaloner recalled Maylord's urgent note with a pang of guilt, a feeling that intensified when he thought about his failure to protect Smegergill. He leaned against a pillar full of dark thoughts, and took no pleasure in music that would normally have delighted him.

L'Estrange enjoyed it, though. The church was perfect for both the style of consort and the airs that had been selected, and Chaloner could tell from the editor's satisfied expression that he had expected no less. The violists

255

were inspired by the way the acoustics complemented their playing, and it was clear to everyone that L'Estrange had taken advantage of the situation to perform a musical experiment to please himself. It had nothing to do with paying tribute to his 'dear friend Newburne'.

When the performance was over, the musicians were treated to some unexpected and wholly inappropriate applause, so the vicar was obliged to clear his throat to bring the proceedings back to sombre order. Greeting muttered something about another commission, and slipped out through a side door. Chaloner followed, and waylaid him by an ornate tombstone bearing the name of Sir Robert Large, a former Lord Mayor of London. It was looking like rain again, and the sky was dark, even though it was barely noon.

Greeting gave a jubilant grin when he saw Chaloner. 'Did you hear us? It was not just the building that rendered the conditions perfect for that particular combination of instruments, it was the fact that the church was full of people. They absorbed some of the echo you get in these old places – but not too much. L'Estrange knew what he was doing when he commissioned us to play those particular pieces.'

'Have you heard any more rumours about the deaths of Maylord or Smegergill?'

Greeting became sombre at the mention of his dead colleagues. 'Only that the Hectors are determined to catch Smegergill's killer. Apparently, one of them – a fellow called Ireton – knew Smegergill, although I find that hard to believe.'

'Knew him in what capacity?'

Greeting shrugged. 'I have no idea. Perhaps they were

neighbours or frequented the same coffee house. Or perhaps Ireton was learning a musical instrument. Personally, I prefer to confine myself to respectable patrons, but not everyone has that luxury.'

Chaloner recalled being told that some of the Hectors were professional men, not mere louts, so supposed it was not impossible that one had purchased music lessons. A connection scratched at the back of his mind, and he struggled to make sense of it. It was to do with noses. Thurloe had talked about Maylord's plethora of wealthy students and Smegergill's lack of them – with the exception of 'a long-nosed lutanist whom no one liked'. One of the Hectors who had attacked Chaloner owned a sizeable nose. Had Smegergill been giving *him* lessons? Could that explain why Chaloner had heard Smegergill talking to the Hectors after the initial attack – they knew each other? But if they were acquainted, then why had Smegergill been killed? Or were the Hectors innocent, as they claimed, and someone else had come along and dispatched the old man for reasons of his own?

'Of course,' Greeting was saying, 'this Ireton fellow could be lying. Incidentally, have you heard that Hen Finch is dead of cucumbers? The news is all over White Hall.'

'Who told you?'

'My colleague Hingston, who is sharing my room at the moment because his house is flooded. But he had it from Muddiman, so it must be right. The news is only a couple of hours old, which shows Muddiman has an excellent intelligence-gathering network. No wonder Williamson is jealous of it.'

Muddiman again, thought Chaloner, wondering

whether the newsmonger had the information first because he had perpetrated the crime. But then surely he would have maintained his distance, and let others do the gossiping?

'Did you know Finch played the trumpet?' he asked.

'Yes, but he was not very good. I shall have to inspect his body this afternoon, and poke around in his rooms. You were not surprised when I told you about Finch's death, which means you already knew. Have you heard any interesting rumours about it? I have been charged to investigate, you see.'

Chaloner raised his eyebrows. '*You* have? By whom?'

'My consort performs for Spymaster Williamson on occasion, and I happened to be with him, discussing the music for a dinner he is hosting, when his spy Hickes came to say that Muddiman was spreading the word about Finch. Williamson ordered him to look into it, but then confided that the fellow would be unlikely to turn up any sensible answers. So I offered to find him a few instead.'

'Why did you do that?' asked Chaloner, mystified. 'You are a musician, not a spy.'

'A musician whose outgoings exceed his income,' explained Greeting ruefully. 'I told you: I can no longer make ends meet. No one hires a tatty consort for his soirées, but looking the part is expensive, as you will know. Those clothes must have cost you a pretty penny.'

'You *volunteered* to work for Williamson?'

Greeting pulled a face. 'I had no choice. I moved to cheaper rooms, and I still cannot afford the damned rent. You seem to do well from espionage – do not deny it, because Williamson told me you are no victualling clerk, and that you spy for the Earl of Clarendon. So, we are

258

colleagues, and if you tell me what you know about Finch, I will tell you something about Maylord in return.'

'What makes you think I am interested in Maylord?' Chaloner was not pleased that Williamson had been talking about him – a spymaster should know better. Of course, this particular spymaster detested Chaloner, and would doubtless be delighted to see him and his investigation compromised.

'You quizzed me about him the other day, and I know he was a friend of your father's, because he told me so himself. Of course you want to find out why he was so upset before he died.'

There was no point in denying it, so Chaloner inclined his head. 'Go on, then.'

Greeting looked sly. 'You first.'

Chaloner folded his arms. 'Would you eat a cucumber while you played a trumpet?'

Greeting was bemused by the question. 'Of course not. I would not eat anything – a crumb might get lodged somewhere, and cause a blockage at an inconvenient moment. Why?'

'Because I heard there was a piece of food lodged inside Finch's instrument. Someone wanted an investigator – you – to think Finch was eating a cucumber, and so died of natural causes.'

What Chaloner did not mention was that the piece he had found when he examined the instrument had been planted in a place it could not have reached, had it been in a player's mouth – whoever put it there knew nothing about trumpets. It was not much of a clue, but it was better than nothing. Chaloner frowned as something else occurred to him. He had reasoned that Finch would not have been munching a cucumber as he played,

259

but what about the half-devoured pie in the window? The same applied, which suggested Finch had been performing and someone else had been eating while he listened. Who? The killer? Or someone quite innocent of the whole affair?

'Who told you this?' demanded Greeting.

'One of Finch's neighbours,' lied Chaloner. 'No names. We do not want him murdered, too.'

Greeting nodded acquiescence. 'Very well. Thank you. I shall tell Williamson that Finch's death is certainly suspicious, and Hickes can do the rest. He is supposed to be Williamson's top agent, after all, no matter how much Williamson grumbles about him behind his back. I agreed to ask a few questions, but my consort will never be hired if my clients think I am a spy.'

'Who is Hickes? What does he look like?'

'Yes, you would do well to avoid him. I am sure he is a Hector – he certainly behaves like one. He is over there, look, gasping for breath like a pair of bellows. He is supposed to be following Muddiman and Dury, but he finds it hard to keep up with them, especially when they send their private carriage in one direction, then leap into sedan-chairs that take them in another.'

Chaloner gaped. 'The apple-seller? Surely not! *He* is the best Williamson can muster?'

'Apple-seller? I suppose you have seen him in one of his disguises. They are never very good.'

Chaloner rubbed his chin, lost in thought. The Earl had told him that Hickes was investigating Newburne's murder, but Hickes had declared Muddiman and Dury innocent. So why was he still following them, and not concentrating on other suspects? Had he lied, perhaps to throw a rival investigator off the scent? And what about Greeting? Had he really offered to spy for Williamson in such a casual manner? And had Williamson really been willing to accept the musician's services under such conditions? It did not seem likely, and Chaloner supposed Greeting was just another person of whom to be wary at White Hall – a liar who undertook dubious assignments.

'What are you going to tell me in return?' he asked. 'About Maylord.'

Greeting smiled amiably. 'Two things. First, there are descriptions circulating about Smegergill's killer – medium height, stocky build and very fast on his feet. He sounds rather like you, and I know for a fact that you wanted to talk to him. I am making an assumption—'

'I never harmed Smegergill,' said Chaloner, alarmed. He was horrified that Greeting had associated him with the description, because it suggested the musician was more clever – or better informed – than he let on, and if he told the Hectors, it would be a nuisance. Chaloner could not find Newburne's killer in the time allotted to him, and dodge murderous henchmen at the same time.

'He went off with some rogue after our Monday night performance, although the villain took care to hide his face when I tried to look at it. It was not you, though – I glimpsed his general shape before he stepped into the shadows and he was too short to be you.'

'And the second thing?'

'Both Maylord and Smegergill branched out into other kinds of music before they died, but it was not good music. I cannot help wondering whether they had commissions from someone who wanted a particular kind of sound, although it was not one real art-lovers would favour . . .'

261

Chaloner thought about the discordant music he had found in Maylord's chimney. 'What of it?'

'Ellis Crisp has an eclectic taste in music. I am told he favours tunes from the East.'

Chaloner stared at him. 'Maylord and Smegergill were playing melodies for Crisp?'

Greeting raised his hands. 'I am combining two points of information and drawing a conclusion, not repeating a fact. Perhaps it has a bearing on Maylord's death – or Smegergill's – and perhaps it does not. But I should be off: Ireton is inside, and I want to be gone before he comes out.'

'Why?'

'Because *I* am medium height, stocky build, and very fast on my feet, and I was in Smithfield the evening Smegergill was killed, because I live there. I do not want Ireton thinking I am the culprit.'

The funeral procession was moving out of the church and towards the hole in the churchyard by the time Greeting left. Chaloner lagged at the end, watching. At the front was Dorcus, held up by L'Estrange on one side and Joanna on the other. Brome was a solid, re-assuring presence behind. He placed his cloak solici-tously around Dorcus's shoulders when she shivered in the drizzle.

'A sorry sight.'

Chaloner turned to see Hodgkinson standing behind him. The printer was clad entirely in black as a mark of respect for the deceased, and his face was suitably sombre. His beard looked darker than usual, too, and Chaloner wondered if he had put soot in it for the occasion. The current mourning fashion at Court was not only to wear dowdy clothes, but to eradicate anything shiny, too – buckles, jewellery and even weapons. It seemed that Hodgkinson had thoughtfully extended the prohibition to his facial hair.

'Very sorry,' agreed Chaloner. 'I was told Ellis Crisp is here. Which one is he?'

Hodgkinson scanned the faces. 'I cannot see him at the moment. There is his father, though: Sir Nicholas.' He pointed to a heavily built man in his sixties who moved with an arrogant swagger. Four liveried servants held a canopy above his head, to ensure he was not dripped on, and Chaloner was not surprised he had sired a son who had carved a small kingdom for himself in Smithfield.

'I do not think I will linger if the Butcher is here,' said Hodgkinson uneasily. 'I owe him October's safety tax for my shop in Duck Lane, but I do not have it with me. I would rather deliver it myself this afternoon, than have his men ask for it now. I do not like the way they make requests.'

He hurried away, leaving Chaloner inspecting the crowds for the sort of man who could inspire such fear among law-abiding citizens. No one stood out as particularly menacing, although he spotted his three attackers – Nose, the Scot, and Fingerless. At some point they would pay for what had happened to Smegergill. Nose glanced in his direction, and Chaloner tensed, wondering whether he would be recognised. But none of his clothes were the same as the ones he had worn during the attack – even Isabella's hat had been replaced by another, albeit reluctantly – and the churchyard had been dark. He relaxed when the man's gaze passed him by.

He was surprised to see Leybourn among the mourners,

although the surveyor's coat was a rather bright blue and the buckles on his shoes gleamed defiantly. Mary was at his side, clinging to his arm. Chaloner was tempted to ask why she had been entertaining three felons the night before – and whether Leybourn had noticed the absence of his best goblets – but it was neither the time nor the place for such a discussion. He would do better to delay the interrogation until he could demand production of the silverware and actually show Leybourn the bell that warned her when he was coming.

Leybourn was pleased to see him. 'Tom! Are you better?'

'Why are you here, Will? I thought you did not like Newburne – his spying saw you fined.'

'I detested the man, but every bookseller in London is here, and Dorcus has invited us all to a funeral party afterwards. It will be an excellent opportunity to meet colleagues I have not seen in ages. And do not think me a hypocrite for accepting the hospitality of his widow, because *everyone* feels the way I do. Besides, if Dorcus provides some decent victuals, I may even warm to her husband's memory.'

'Why are you here, Mr Heyden?' asked Mary sweetly. 'I thought you did not know Newburne. Or are you hoping to make the acquaintance of Ellis Crisp? I am told he is here today.'

'No, he is not hoping to meet the Butcher,' said Leybourn firmly. 'He knows too many devious people as it is. And so do you, if the truth be told, Mary. I do not like the look of some of the men with whom you have exchanged greetings today.'

'You mean Hectors?' asked Chaloner, with a sweetly innocent smile of his own.

'Hectors?' echoed Leybourn, shocked. 'Do not be

264

ridiculous, Tom! She may have nodded to one or two disreputable types, but they were certainly not Hectors.'

Mary's expression was martyred. 'They are men from whom I buy victuals at the market, no more. It would have been rude to ignore their polite good-days. Your friend is having some mischievous sport at my expense, William. Tell him to stop.'

'Yes, stop it, Tom,' said Leybourn sternly. 'A funeral is no place for japes.'

'If you want to meet Ellis Crisp, you must hurry, Mr Heyden,' said Mary, with another false smile. 'He is just getting into a carriage with his father.'

'No,' said Leybourn in alarm, gripping his shoulder when Chaloner stepped away. 'Tom, don't.'

But Chaloner was only moving to get a better look at the man; he still preferred to delay accosting him until he had a clearer understanding of his role in the various deaths he was investigating. As the carriage rattled away, he caught the briefest glimpse of a face. It was round, pink and smiling.

'It is odd that a respectable merchant should have a son who is a butcher-cum-underworld king,' he mused, when the coach had gone. 'I understand Sir Nicholas is a member of the Council for Trade.'

Leybourn gave a bark of mirthless laughter. 'Do not be too impressed by titles. Sir Nicholas is a powerful advocate for the African slave trade, which does not make him respectable at all. I would say both make their fortunes in dirty business. And look at the Hectors, moving around the mourners with their ears flapping. They are listening to disparaging comments, so Crisp will know his enemies. It is a bit like Newburne, spying on the booksellers.'

265

'Be careful,' warned Chaloner sharply, suspecting Mary might do likewise.

But Leybourn was not listening. 'Look, there is Allestry, and Nott is with him!' he exclaimed with pleasure. 'I have not seen them in weeks. They were also victimised by Newburne.'

The two booksellers were with their wives. The men were talking together, but the women were lagging behind, watching L'Estrange. When the editor happened to glance in their direction, both waved coquettishly at him. Chaloner was amused to note that L'Estrange was the subject of admiring glances from a number of ladies among the crowd, which led him to suppose that the Army of Angels was rather larger than he had been led to believe.

When he turned to mention it to Leybourn, he found him gone to greet his colleagues, leaving Mary behind. Chaloner expected her to follow, sure she would not want the company of a man she so openly despised, but she lingered uncertainly. He glanced to one side and saw the Scottish Hector standing not far away. He was not looking at Mary, but it was clear he intended to approach her as soon as she was alone. Meanwhile, Mary seemed to draw confidence from his proximity.

'You are a murderer, Heyden,' she said coldly. Fortunately, a gust of wind took her words, and the Scot did not hear them. 'There is a description circulating about the man who dispatched the elderly musician, and it matches yours. I have not forgotten the blood on your hands when you arrived later that very same night, and I am drawing my own conclusions.'

'Then they will be wrong,' said Chaloner, more calmly than he felt. 'Smegergill was a friend of my father's, and

I had no reason to harm him. Indeed, his death is a source of great sadness to me.'

'I do not believe you.'

Chaloner shrugged, effecting carelessness. 'Then ask Will about me. He will tell you I am not the sort of man who goes around killing old people.'

'He said you work for the government – that men of power give you unusual commissions. He believes these duties account for your condition that night. He also said you are fiercely loyal to the King, and would do anything for him. Perhaps that includes murdering old musicians.'

Chaloner knew Leybourn had offered the explanation because he had not wanted her to think badly of him. However, confiding such details carried its own dangers, and Chaloner heartily wished Leybourn had said nothing at all. He was about to reply when she gave a sudden frown, and he turned to see Thurloe walking towards them.

'Another of William's faithful friends,' she sneered. 'He is happier with me than when he just had you two for company. Why can you not accept that, and leave us alone?'

'He means a great deal to me, madam,' said Thurloe. He shot her one of his unreadable smiles. 'I love him as a brother, and would sacrifice anything to see him content.'

Mary was momentarily disconcerted, not quite sure what he was saying. Nor was Chaloner, although he doubted the ex-Spymaster was merely making pleasant conversation. If Mary had any sense, she would take pains to ensure she did nothing to annoy Thurloe.

'I do not want William associating with murderers,' she said loudly, resuming her attack on Chaloner, who was easier to read. 'You killed Smegergill, which probably means you killed Maylord, too. They were friends, and the death of one almost drove the other insane before you dispatched him. I heard Smegergill went around telling people that he was Caesar.'

'Thomas has not killed anyone, madam,' said Thurloe. He leaned closer to her, and his voice was smooth and softly menacing. Even Chaloner, who had known him for years, was slightly unsettled by it. 'At least, not yet. He was out of the country when Maylord died, and this can be proven by a dozen witnesses in a court of law. You would be wise to drop your accusations.'

She was unnerved, but not such a novice in the world of deception that she was ready to back away without some bluster. 'You think you can prise me away from William, but you are wrong. He loves me, and I shall stay with him for as long as I choose. And I meant what I said the other night, Heyden: you will be sorry if you cross me – and so will William.'

She stamped away, and the Scottish Hector moved to intercept her. She took a breath, and Chaloner sensed she was about to tell him what had transpired. Then she glanced back, and there was something in Thurloe's expression that stopped her. She swallowed hard and reconsidered; from her gestures, Chaloner could tell she was making innocuous observations about the funeral.

'She is just a bag of wind,' said Thurloe, watching. 'She cannot harm you.'

'Yes, she can. She is talking to one of the men who attacked me in Smithfield. He visited her late last night, and when he left he stole Will's silver goblets – the ones from the Royal Society.'

Thurloe was horrified. 'That particular man is a Hector – a fellow called Kirby. I arrested him on suspicion of conspiring to murder Cromwell once, but was forced to release him for lack of evidence. I have always assumed the Hectors' loyalty to the Cavalier cause during the Commonwealth is why the government has turned a blind eye to their felonious activities ever since the Restoration.'

'And perhaps why Williamson hires them when he needs dirty work done.'

'Very possibly. So, it seems Mary Cade is dangerous after all.'

Chaloner nodded, but made no other reply. He was beginning to feel overwhelmed by the three investigations that confronted him, and he was afraid for Leybourn.

Thurloe patted his arm consolingly. 'You will find answers, do not fear. But do not allow yourself to be blinded by guilt over Smegergill. I have told you before that there may be more to his death than a harmless old man hit over the head and left to drown.'

'I am running out of time,' said Chaloner gloomily. 'The Earl wants Newburne's killer named by Monday, and I will be dismissed if I fail. And I have a thousand questions but no answers.'

Thurloe gave one of his small smiles. 'I have an answer for you. Nobert Wenum. I was mulling it over last night, and it is an anagram. Rearrange the letters, and what do you get?'

Chaloner stared at him, his mind working fast. 'Tom Newburne!'

Thurloe inclined his head. 'Precisely. So, the man with the annotated copy of *The Newes*, who kept a careful record of the sales he made to L'Estrange's rivals, was none other than your devious solicitor. You should not be surprised – you already knew he was corrupt.'

Chaloner was not happy with the explanation. 'I also know he was clever, so why would he choose such an obvious alias?'

'It was not obvious, Thomas. You had not worked it out.'

But Chaloner was still not convinced. 'The landlord of the Rhenish Wine House made disparaging remarks about Newburne. I doubt he would have let him rent one of his attics.'

'Newburne disguised his name, so perhaps he disguised his face, too. What did the neighbour say about Wenum? That he had a jaw that looked leprous? One of the first things I taught you about disguises is that if you give yourself an outstanding characteristic – a scarlet nose, a big moustache, lousy hair – people will see that and nothing else. Perhaps Newburne devised himself a disfiguring rash knowing that no one would remember anything more about him.'

Chaloner supposed it made sense. And if it had been Newburne renting the room next to Maylord, it made for another connection between the two deaths. Had Maylord heard or seen something about the lawyer's dubious activities that had frightened him into trying to solicit Chaloner's help?

'Only two men have made positive comments about Newburne,' he mused. 'His friend Finch, who was not objective. And Muddiman, who said Newburne was not as corrupt as everyone claimed.'

Thurloe saw where his analysis was going. 'The ledger is proof that Wenum – Newburne – was selling secrets to L'Estrange's rivals, including Muddiman. Muddiman's assertion that Newburne was not as bad as he appeared may have been him protecting an ally. You still look doubtful. Don't be. Sometimes things really are just what they seem.'

Late that night, Chaloner revisited Hen Finch's home. The body had been removed, and so had various other items, including anything written. As no house was ever completely devoid of documents – all men had a letter from a friend, a deed of ownership, or even a bill of sale tucked away somewhere – he assumed they had been removed *en masse*. He had no idea whether Finch was associated with Newburne's corrupt dealings, but someone was obviously taking no chances.

Next, he went to Newburne's house on Old Jewry, watching it from the garden until he was sure everyone was in bed and all lights doused. A window on the first floor had been left open, and he scaled the wall and climbed inside with a confidence born of experience. He listened carefully, but the household was exhausted by the strains of the day, and everyone was sound asleep.

He had paid careful attention to Dorcus's tearful eulogies during the post-funeral gathering, and had concluded she had had scant idea about the real nature of her husband's businesses. She had also expressed surprise when Hodgkinson had mentioned late nights kept when the newsbooks were being printed, leading Chaloner to deduce that she and Newburne had occupied separate bedrooms. There were several chambers on the upper floor, but only one with a door left open. Chaloner stepped inside it, and knew from its lingering aroma of sweat and tobacco that it had been used by a man.

He closed the door and lit the lamp, and it did not

271

take him long to locate what he had come to find. There was a tiny box on a shelf near the window, with a piece of paper glued to the lid that identified its contents as Theophilus Buckworth's Personal Lozenges. He assumed they were the pills Dorcus said her husband had swallowed the day he had died.

Wearing gloves, he picked one up and sniffed it, but could not tell whether its unpleasant aroma was medicinal or something sinister. He rubbed it on the inside of his wrist, under the lace of his cuff, and it left a greenish smear. Nothing happened, so he searched the rest of the room, disappointed when it yielded nothing to help his investigation. He supposed the solicitor had kept his sensitive papers in his various lairs across the city. Then he became aware of an unpleasant burning on his arm. He pulled up his sleeve and saw blisters. He rinsed them with water from a pitcher in the closet, but they continued to sting for some time, even so.

He now had an explanation for two deaths. The lozenges had killed Newburne, although not instantly, and he had lived long enough for the cucumber to bear the blame – perhaps the burning had induced him to swallow something he thought would cool his innards. Lozenges had also killed Finch, because Chaloner had seen an identical box on the table by the cucumber. However, like Finch's papers, the lozenges had been removed by the time Chaloner had returned. So who had taken them?

He himself had seen three people in the room: Hickes, then Dury and Muddiman. Had the newsletter men gone to remove the evidence of their crime, only to find Chaloner and Hickes were there before them? Had Hickes committed the murder, perhaps on Williamson's orders, and had gone to collect poison and papers once he was sure Finch was dead? Or was someone else responsible? Greeting's sudden decision to serve Williamson had left Chaloner uneasy, for example.

Or did the lozenges actually serve to absolve Muddiman? He had bought cucumbers from Covent Garden the day before Newburne's death, allegedly for medicinal purposes. Now Chaloner knew lozenges were responsible, it meant cucumbers were irrelevant. Or were they? Someone was still leaving them at the scenes of his crimes, to confuse any investigation that might take place. Chaloner scratched his itching wrist, and heartily wished he could find a clue that would provide him with answers, not just more questions.

Chapter 8

The following day, Chaloner was disconcerted to wake to the realisation that he had been dreaming about Joanna. He could not imagine why, as he usually preferred women with more spirit, and he sat up feeling vaguely ashamed of himself. He recalled her invitation to dine at noon, and found he was looking forward to it. His occupation played havoc with any social life he might have had, so such occasions were rare for him. The notion of pleasant company, good food – or any food, for that matter – and perhaps some music was an attractive proposition for a man who knew so few people in the great, seething metropolis that was London.

The streets were bathed in the kind of dull, grey light that presaged more rain, and his cat was sodden when it nudged open the window and made its way inside. It had a rat in its mouth, which it left by the hearth. Chaloner hoped it would restrict itself to rodents, and not graduate to birds, because he liked birds. He was going to toss the rat out of the window, but there was already too much traffic, and he did not want a fight to ensue because it hit someone. As it was too large to fit comfortably in his pocket, he placed it on the mantelpiece, intending to throw it out when he returned that night.

A sixth sense warned him that someone was lurking in the shadows near the door when he started to leave the house, and his landlord was lucky not to find himself slammed against the wall with a dagger at his throat. Chaloner had warned Ellis before about loitering in the dark, but as the man did not know what Chaloner did for a living, he had no way of knowing that ignoring the advice might have potentially fatal consequences.

'The rent,' said Ellis, rubbing his hands together like a fly. Surreptitiously, Chaloner returned his knife to its customary hiding place. 'It is overdue. And you owe me for August and September, too.'

'I know,' said Chaloner apologetically. 'There has been an administrative hiccup at the Victualling Office, but it should be resolved by Monday.'

That was the Earl's deadline, and by then, Chaloner would either be able to request an advance on his salary, or would have to acquire the money by some other means. Of course, if Mary and the Hectors had their way, he might also be dead, which would be a pity for Ellis; the man had been remarkably patient with his impecunious tenant, and Chaloner hated being in debt to him.

Ellis continued to rub his hands. 'I shall have to charge extra for the tench your cat had yesterday. I left it on my kitchen table, and she made off with it when my back was turned. Then she had the gall to sit on the roof and devour it before my very eyes, bold as brass.'

'Christ!' muttered Chaloner, hoping the animal would not transpire to be expensive. 'She brought me a rat this

275

morning. I do not suppose you would consider accepting that as a replacement?'

He was joking, but Ellis considered the offer carefully. 'Rat is a good winter dish, but I do prefer tench. Besides, rats are ten a penny these days, with all this rising water.'

Chaloner regarded him uneasily. 'You eat rats?'

'Of course. Do not tell me you have never tried them?'

'Only during the wars, when there was nothing else.'

'Then you will know they are a sadly underrated meat. There is nothing like rat stew on a cold night, especially when flavoured with plenty of sage and an onion.'

Chaloner walked to the Fleet Prison, a grim edifice with its sturdy gate, thick walls and tiny barred windows. It crouched on the eastern bank of the river for which it was named, adding its own reek to the stinking industries that surrounded it – bone boilers, makers of glue and paint, and the dye-works. There were always people outside the Fleet, mostly kin of the inmates, who had the pinched, hopeless look of extreme poverty about them. Chaloner was sure *they* would not turn up their noses at rat stew.

Because of his past experiences in gaols, it took considerable willpower to walk up to the door and start a conversation with the guards. As he had no money to buy information, he was subjected to insults, threats and even a physical assault before he found a warden willing to talk to him. Unfortunately, the man did not seem entirely sane, and confided to Chaloner that he worked in the prison because it was the only place where he felt safe from an attack by sparrows.

'Look,' he whispered, gesturing to the surrounding rooftops. 'They just sit there, biding their time. Then,

276

when your attention strays, they swoop down and peck out your eyes. You must have read about phanatiques in the newsbooks? Well, the writer actually refers to sparrows. It is code, see.'

'Right,' said Chaloner. He showed the sketch he had made of Mary. 'Do you know if she has ever been in the Fleet Prison?'

'Yes, but not for debt, though, like most of them. She was in for thievery, but her husband came and greased the right hands, if you know what I mean. Her name is Annabel Reade.'

'She is married?

'To a man,' supplied the guard helpfully. 'She stole from Richard Bridges, the Cornhill linen-draper. He sells calico to the navy, although the sparrows get most of it for their nests. She was his cook-maid, and had his silver off him when he dismissed her for not doing what she was hired for.'

Chaloner recalled Leybourn saying that he and Mary were obliged to send for food from cook-shops, because she lacked any culinary skills herself, and his kitchen had been rendered a pigsty. So, Leybourn was not the first man to discover Mary possessed no real domestic abilities.

'Richard Bridges lives on Cornhill?' he asked, deciding to talk to the man that morning. Now he knew Mary was linked to the Hectors, and by extension to Newburne, he did not feel he was wasting time by investigating her past. All three enquiries – Newburne, Maylord and Smegergill, and Mary – had merged to a certain extent, and exploring one might well yield answers to the others.

The guard nodded. 'He accused her of theft, but then he came here with Reade's husband and said there had been a misunderstanding. Can you see that bird looking at us? See its beady eyes?'

'Buy a cat,' suggested Chaloner. 'Sparrows will not attack if there is a cat about.'

'I had one,' said the porter gloomily, 'but the sparrows ate it. Every last morsel.'

The Stocks Market was at the junction of Cornhill and Cheapside, and Friday was one of its busiest days. Cows, sheep, geese, chickens, goats and pigs were driven down the road to feed London's growling stomach, and Cheapside was a chaos of noise and movement. One drover had decided the best way to get his cattle to market was to stampede them there, and they cut a bloody swathe through anything that stood in their way. Carts were overturned, animals broke away from their owners, and horses bucked and pranced. Feathers were thick in the air as birds squawked their panic, and stray dogs added to the confusion by barking and worrying at the hapless beasts.

Chaloner was trying to hurry, aware that he had a lot to do before dining at noon, but was forced to slow down when, within the space of a few moments, he narrowly avoided being crushed by an escaped bull, pecked by a frightened swan and run over by a driverless cart. Other pedestrians were less fortunate, and the cries of the injured and furious added to the general cacophony.

When he eventually reached Cornhill, he was directed to a handsome mansion. Temperance's good clothes and his confident manner bought him access to the linendraper's front parlour without being obliged to state his business first. He stood with his hands clasped behind

278

his back, fretting about Leybourn. It was not long before someone coughed behind him, and he turned to see a man unremarkable in every way, except for two very rosy cheeks. Bridges smiled nervously when Chaloner took the liberty of informing him that he was with the Lord Chancellor's office.

'We are investigating Annabel Reade,' he said, producing her picture.

Bridges's anxiety intensified. 'That is her, although the artist should make her jowls bigger.'

'I understand she was employed by you, and that she stole some silver.'

Bridges shook his head vehemently. 'There was a mistake. I found the items I thought she had taken, and her husband and I immediately went to the prison, where I paid for her release.'

Chaloner regarded the man sympathetically. He was terrified. 'Did someone force you to—'

'No!' cried Bridges, in what amounted to a squawk. 'She was innocent! She took nothing, and I should have been more careful when I laid charges against an upright, honest woman. And now you must excuse me. I leave for Tangier in a few days, and there is a great deal to do.'

'Who is doing this?' Chaloner asked gently. 'Making you abandon your home and sail for a—'

'No one!' shouted Bridges. His red cheeks had turned a ghastly grey. 'I am going to inspect calico for the navy. No one is driving me away. You must leave – and please do not tell anyone you have been here. I will make it worth your while.'

Chaloner stopped him when he started to reach for his purse. 'No one will know, I promise, but I need your help. Annabel Reade is now preying on another man. His name is Leybourn, and he—'

'Will Leybourn?' interrupted Bridges. 'He designed the astrological ring-dial I keep in my garden. I shall miss it when I go to Tangier. Poor Leybourn. If Reade has her claws in him, then . . .'

'I would like to prise them out,' said Chaloner. 'But I need solid evidence.'

'I cannot help you.' Bridges was close to tears. 'Not even for Leybourn. You will have to find someone else. God knows, there must be more of us who were deceived by the woman.'

'Then tell me about her husband. Who is he?'

'He called himself Mr Reade, although I have no way of knowing if it was his real name. He is a fierce fellow with a number of fierce friends. I do not want to attract his attention again. Not ever.'

'Hectors?' asked Chaloner.

Bridges looked out of the window, and did not reply.

'If you are leaving, what do you have to lose?' asked Chaloner, suppressing the urge to grab the man and shake the information out of him. 'Even Hectors cannot touch you in Tangier.'

'I am not gone yet, and I shall be leaving a house and valued servants to mind it. I am sorry, but I must protect my interests. Leybourn is clever; he will devise his own way out of his predicament.'

Only if he knew he was in one, thought Chaloner. He tried to press Bridges further, but the draper stubbornly refused to say more, and eventually called for his retainers, threatening to remove Chaloner by force if he did not leave of his own volition. Chaloner turned after he had stepped outside.

'If you have second thoughts, my name is Heyden, and I can be reached through the Golden Lion.'

'I will not have second thoughts,' said Bridges firmly. 'Not for anyone.'

It was ten o'clock, and Chaloner still had two hours before he was due to dine with Brome and Joanna. He walked inside the Royal Exchange, to think about what to do next. The Royal Exchange had been built a hundred years before, as a place where merchants could meet to do business. It comprised a rectangle of tiered shops around a cloister-like piazza, and was always busy. Finding a spot where he would not be jostled or asked to buy something was not easy, but he managed eventually, and stood staring across the rain-swept square, considering what he had learned.

What was Crisp's – and his Hectors' – role in the murders Chaloner was investigating? The Butcher had employed Newburne; he may have commissioned music from Maylord and Smegergill; and the unhappy Finch had been playing tunes that were similar to the discordant harmonies found in Maylord's chimney. Mary Cade also claimed to know him, and given that she entertained Hectors in Leybourn's home, it was possible that her artful deception on Leybourn was being conducted with Crisp's blessing and help. They had certainly rallied when Bridges had exposed her felonious activities. Yet the connections between Crisp and the murders were like cobwebs; they appeared to be substantial, but they were not – and Chaloner could not *prove* Crisp was involved in any of the deaths.

Reluctantly, he supposed he would have to make the Butcher's acquaintance after all. He was not really ready to tackle a man whom everyone said was powerful and dangerous, but with only three days to go before he lost his last chance of intelligence work – and probably even less time before Mary told her cronies that he was the man they were hunting for the Smegergill incident – he was out of options. Resigned to what he was sure would be a difficult interview, he made his way to Smithfield.

The meat market was hectic. The pens in the great open space were full of bleating sheep and lowing cattle, and men yelled and bartered, oblivious to the eye-watering stench of old urine, manure and rotting entrails from the nearby slaughterhouses. Hectors moved in small, confident bands, exchanging nods and sums of money with drovers and merchants, and a baker's-boy was doing a roaring trade with his tray of fruit pastries. Two sharp-featured youths jostled a clerk Chaloner knew from White Hall; when the fellow whipped around to face them, a third thief cut his purse strings from behind. When something similar started to happen to the spy, one reeled away with a bleeding nose, while the other found himself flat on his back with Chaloner's foot across his throat.

'Where can I find Ellis Crisp?' Chaloner asked quietly.

'I do not know,' squeaked the pickpocket in alarm. 'No one does. You have to arrange a meeting through one of his Hectors. Jonas Kirby is the best. That is him, over there.'

He pointed, and Chaloner recognised the Scot. He released the lad, and regarded Kirby thoughtfully. Perhaps an early confrontation with the Butcher could be avoided after all. Kirby had attacked Chaloner the night Smegergill had died; he had been with Nose in Wenum's room; and he had stolen one of Leybourn's silver goblets. He could answer some questions in his master's stead.

Chaloner's coat had a hood, and he used it to conceal his face as he lurked in an ally near Duck Lane. Kirby was selling Leybourn's goblet to a fat cleric, who should have known better than to buy it. The Scot was well dressed for a henchman, although Chaloner imagined the clothes were stolen, perhaps from someone who had been stripped when he had been robbed in a dark church-yard. He supposed he was lucky he and Smegergill had not been subjected to that indignity at least.

Eventually, Kirby completed his business and moved towards a dim thoroughfare that was home to a number of seedy taverns. Chaloner accosted him as he was about to enter a particularly dingy one; the sign above its door advertised it as the Bear. A smell of cooking pies wafted from it, although the aroma was rank and meaty, and not in the least bit appetising.

'Jonas Kirby,' said Chaloner softly. 'I want to talk to you.'

Kirby struggled to mask his surprise that someone had managed to creep so close behind him without being heard. 'You were at Newburne's funeral,' he gabbled. 'Leybourn's friend. What do you want?'

From that response, Chaloner surmised that Mary had not yet shared her suspicions about his role in Smegergill's death. 'I thought we could talk about the Rhenish Wine House. You were there with a long-nosed man whom I believe is called Ireton.'

Kirby's eyes narrowed. 'So, it was you we almost caught, was it? Ireton will want to meet you – he objected to someone searching Maylord's place before us, and removing valuable documents.'

'There were no documents. Perhaps someone else was there before both of us.'

Kirby looked sceptical, then took a sudden step forward. A knife appeared in his hand, but Chaloner was faster. He had knocked the weapon away and had his own blade under Kirby's chin before the henchman realised what was happening.

'Easy!' squawked Kirby, when Chaloner's blade nicked his neck. 'There is no need for rough manners. Let me buy you a pie. The Bear does good pies – Crisp's best.'

He smiled weakly, but then there was a second dagger in his hand. Chaloner had been anticipating such a move, and hooked Kirby's feet from under him, causing him to fall flat on his back, while the weapon skittered into the nearest drain. The noise brought several patrons to the tavern door, and at least two sniggered when they saw Kirby sprawled on the filthy ground. Kirby glowered at Chaloner as he waved them away, and the spy saw he would not forget his humiliation in a hurry.

'What do you want from me?' he growled.

'The answers to some questions. Shall we go and sit down, like civilised men?'

Kirby climbed slowly to his feet, then led the way inside the Bear. Chaloner looked around quickly. A back door led to an unsavoury little yard that reeked of urine, and there was a gate that would open into Duck Lane. He took the seat by the wall, leaving Kirby the one that would bear the brunt of any attack from the main entrance. As they sat, a dirty pot-boy slapped two pies on a rickety table, and mumbled something about them coming compliments of the owner.

'You killed Smegergill,' said Chaloner, pushing the pie away from him. Despite his nagging hunger, its oily scent was making him queasy and he found he was loath to

284

touch anything that might contain parts of Crisp's enemies.

'I never touched him,' declared Kirby vehemently. 'None of us did. I hit his friend hard enough to scramble his brains, but he somehow survived, and must have vented his spleen on the old man when he came to. He was younger – medium height, sturdy build. A bit like you, now I think about it.'

'It was not me. Why do you think he killed Smegergill?'

'Because no one else was there, and Smegergill was alive when we left him. Ireton had talked to him, and told him that if he kept quiet, he could escape unscathed.'

Had Ireton killed him, then, Chaloner wondered, while his accomplices were under the illusion the old man was being offered his life? 'What was the purpose of the attack?'

'We were following orders. Find the Court musicians; kill the younger one; let the old man go. We only found out later that it was Smegergill. We all know him – by sight at least – because he always plays the organ at the Bartholomew Fair.'

'Orders from whom?'

Kirby looked as though he might refuse to answer, so Chaloner drew his dagger. 'I do not know! We had written instructions. They said we were to get letters from the young one's purse, but it was empty and there *were* no letters. They were early, too, so we were not quite ready for them. We had to improvise, which is why I forgot to make sure he was really dead.'

'How do you know you attacked the right people?'

'Because Smegergill was wearing the uniform of the King's Music. It is distinctive, so of course they were the right ones.'

Several facts settled into a sensible pattern in Chaloner's mind at last, and the germ of a solution began to take shape. He saw his unplanned waylaying of Smegergill had set in motion a chain of events that no one could have predicted.

'Greeting,' he murmured to himself. 'His elderly friend Hingston is staying at his Smithfield lodgings, because his home is flooded. They were expected to walk past the churchyard later that night, because the driver of their carriage demanded extra money to take them all the way home, and ousted them when they could not pay. It was deliberate. And they were both wearing uniforms.'

Kirby ate his pie while Chaloner continued to analyse his conclusions in silence. So, no one had wanted to kill him or Smegergill. The intended victim had been Greeting, who probably *did* have letters with him, given that he, by his own admission, worked for Williamson. Chaloner supposed he would have to talk to Greeting and ascertain what he had been carrying that night.

So what had happened to Smegergill? Kirby, Ireton and Fingerless had followed their orders – or thought they had – and Ireton had gone to demand Smegergill's silence, while Kirby and Fingerless searched Chaloner. Had Ireton killed Smegergill when he realised the wrong men had been attacked? Yet Kirby did not seem to think a mistake had been made, and so perhaps Ireton did not, either. So, why had Smegergill ended up dead?

Chaloner thought about the elderly musician. Thurloe had distrusted him, while Temperance and Maude had conflicting opinions: one thought he was coolly rational, amusing himself at the expense of gullible sympathisers, while the other believed he was losing his wits. Which was true? And what of Greeting's information – that Smegergill had enjoyed an association with Hectors? Had playing the organ for the Bartholomew Fair led to other things? But if Smegergill was friends with the Hectors, then why had he been killed? Surely, he would have been spared? Or had he annoyed Crisp by being 'difficult', and Ireton had taken the opportunity to dispatch him?

A flicker of movement interrupted his reflections. Someone was outside: the Hectors were finally ready to rescue their crony. Chaloner indicated with a flick of his dagger that Kirby was to stand, then shoved him hard before he was properly balanced, so he went sprawling through the entranceway. The timing was perfect. Kirby became hopelessly entangled with his friends, which gave Chaloner vital seconds to escape. The spy opened the back door and shot into the yard. The gate was locked, forcing him to scramble over the wall, thus losing the small advantage of time he had gained.

The lock did not slow Kirby down. He kicked it once, and the gate flew into pieces. With half a dozen Hectors at his heels, he thundered after Chaloner, screaming for someone to stop him. A few passers-by made half-hearted lunges, but most looked the other way, unwilling to become involved. The spy tore along Duck Lane, grabbing an apple cart as he went, and spinning it to spill its contents across the road. Two of his pursuers took tumbles. Then a ponderous meat wagon moved to block the road in front of him. Without breaking speed, he aimed for the space between the moving wheels, curled into a ball and rolled under the thing to shoot out the other side. Frustrated howls indicated the pursuing Hectors were unwilling to duplicate the manoeuvre, and they bellowed at the driver to get out of their way. The

287

sudden clamour panicked the horses, making them difficult to control.

Chaloner raced on, and found himself near the costermongery where he had purchased the cucumber. Loath to run further than necessary, he considered taking refuge in it, but it was closed and shuttered. Then he remembered that Hodgkinson owned the shop next door. He slipped through the door and saw the printer talking to a customer. Unseen, he ducked under a table and peered into the street through a crack in the wall. Kirby lumbered by, backed by a dozen men, all yelling and waving cudgels.

Chaloner stayed where he was, feeling his heartbeat slow to a more normal rate after his exertions. In the grime under the counter, his fingers encountered something hard. With most of his attention still on the street, he retrieved the object and glanced at it. It was a Fountain Inkhorn, like the one Thurloe had lent him when he had been sketching Mary. This pen was silver, and looked valuable.

'Well,' came a laconic voice that made him jump. 'The Lord Chancellor's spy under a table? Whatever next?'

Chaloner climbed quickly to his feet to find himself facing Muddiman. The newsmonger was looking particularly elegant that day, in a suit of lemon satin and tiny white shoes. Chaloner thought it was the most impractical outfit he could possibly have chosen, given the unpredictable weather and the state of the roads. He glanced towards Hodgkinson, but the printer's attention was still focussed on his client, and he had not noticed what was happening by his counter.

'I found this,' said Chaloner, holding up the Fountain

Inkhorn in an attempt to explain away his curious behaviour. 'Someone must have dropped it.'

'I see,' replied Muddiman, and his grin suggested he did not believe a word of it. 'Look at the state of you! I hope you do not plan on going anywhere nice for dinner.'

'Christ!' Chaloner regarded his clothes in dismay. The dive under the cart had left him filthy.

'Allow me,' said Muddiman, dabbing at the mess with his handkerchief. 'No, that is no good. You need a woman with a cloth. I shall pay for one if you tell me something novel about Portugal. You did a splendid piece for L'Estrange – the best thing in the entire issue – so now you can help me.'

'L'Estrange forbade it,' said Chaloner, aware that it would unwise to accept Muddiman's offer when the newsbooks' printer was within earshot. It would cause trouble for certain.

'I am sure he did,' said Muddiman, amused. 'And are you going to obey him? I suppose you are afraid of what Spymaster Williamson might have to say if you assert your independence, are you?'

'Spymaster Williamson does not deign to speak to the likes of me.'

'You are lucky – he will not leave *me* alone. He set Hickes after me, which is fast becoming tiresome, while his creature L'Estrange makes constant accusations about me stealing his news.'

Chaloner showed him the ledger he had recovered from the Rhenish Wine House – the one Muddiman had denied existing when he had last mentioned it. 'I would say L'Estrange has good cause to think his news is being stolen.'

Muddiman took it. 'A forgery, as I said yesterday.

Besides, Wenum is dead, and without his testimony, this nasty little document means nothing.'

'It still proves you paid for news you should not have had. And if you are talking about corroborative testimony, you are obviously anticipating that you will be charged in a court of law, where specific proceedings are followed. I do not think Williamson confines himself to that sort of trial.'

Muddiman regarded him thoughtfully. 'Even he would be playing with fire if he attempted that sort of tactic on an influential newsman. It would be asking for editorials to be written about suppression and corruption. Still, I take your point. How much do you want for your silence?'

Chaloner replaced the ledger in his pocket. 'I am not for sale.'

Muddiman raised startled eyebrows. 'No wonder you have the look of poverty about you! Why do you not take what is freely offered? Everyone else does, for which I daily thank God. My newsletters would not be nearly as good if men in positions of power declined to do business with me.'

'Was Wenum in a position of power, then? I know he did not work at the newsbook offices or at Hodgkinson's print-houses.'

Muddiman's smug smile was back in place. 'I understand he drowned in the Thames; he fell in near White Hall, where all the politicians and clerks lurk, if you take my meaning. Unfortunately, his corpse was never recovered, so who knows how he really died?'

A missing corpse was very convenient, thought Chaloner. 'I think Nobert Wenum was actually Tom Newburne – the names contain the same letters, which seems too coincidental to overlook. Perhaps *that* explains why no body was recovered.'

Muddiman chuckled. 'I wondered how long it would be before you worked out the Newburne–Wenum connection. However, I can tell you from my long experience as a newsmonger that things are seldom what they seem, and that "facts" are multi-faceted. People say there are two sides to every story, but I would contest that there are usually a good many more.'

'You are no doubt right. So, are you telling me that Newburne and Wenum were *not* the same?'

'We always met in the dark, so I cannot say with certainty, although he did have the most awful rash on his jaw. I could scarcely take my eyes off it, and spent most of our encounters praying that it was not contagious. However, I also know such things can be achieved with powders and paints. So, perhaps it was Newburne, but I suspect it was not.'

'Do you ever take Theophilus Buckworth's lozenges?' asked Chaloner, trying a different tack.

'Why?' Muddiman shot back. 'Do they guard against death by cucumber?'

'Why are you here?' asked Chaloner, seeing he was not going to get very far with questions about Newburne, Wenum or Finch. 'Hodgkinson is L'Estrange's printer – and thus L'Estrange's ally.'

'Why should that prevent me from using his services?' Muddiman showed Chaloner a printed bill, which advertised his handwritten newspapers, delivered promptly each week and containing domestic news no man of business or affairs would want to miss. He laughed at Chaloner's astonishment. 'It was Dury's idea – it allows us to flick a thumb at Williamson, as well as L'Estrange.

Ah, Hodgkinson, you are free at last. Heyden has been admiring your work on my notices.'

Hodgkinson looked sheepish. 'He made me a very good offer, Heyden, and L'Estrange's newsbooks will not run for ever. I may need Mr Muddiman's patronage when they collapse.'

'*When* they collapse?' queried Chaloner sharply.

Muddiman nodded with great confidence. 'It is only a matter of time. Who wants to read that the vicar of Wollaston found himself with a dirty prayer-book? Or reports confiding that Turks are "up and down", whatever that means? Besides, once the government realises that the newsbooks' only real function is to facilitate the return of lost horses, it will withdraw its investment. Eh, Hodgkinson?'

Hodgkinson nodded uncomfortably. 'I am afraid you may be right.'

'Have you shared these concerns with Spymaster Williamson?' asked Chaloner of the printer.

Hodgkinson looked horrified. 'No! Why? Will you tell him? If you do, please do not say you heard it from me. I am just a man trying to make a living. Besides, I would not be forced to do business with Mr Muddiman if Williamson did his job and kept the city in order. The safety tax imposed by the Butcher of Smithfield is crippling, and this is the only way I can make ends meet.'

'A valid point,' said Muddiman, not seeming to care that Hodgkinson had all but admitted their association to be an unsavoury one. 'But I doubt Heyden will be talking to Williamson. Our dear Spymaster has a nasty habit of shooting messengers who bring bad news, which is why his spies seldom tell him much of import. Especially stupid old Hickes.'

'Did I hear you say you need a woman with a cloth?' asked Hodgkinson, keen to change the subject. 'Brome said you are dining with him today, and Joanna will not think much if you arrive looking like that. I will fetch Mother Sales.' He was gone before Chaloner could stop him.

'Poor Hodgkinson,' said Muddiman with a sigh. 'He wants to be loyal to L'Estrange, but he can see the portents of doom. It is a pity Brome cannot. I have offered him an alliance, but he declines, misguided fool. But you are not so foolish, I think.'

'No, I am not. So I will not give you intelligence about Portugal, because L'Estrange will know exactly where it came from.'

Muddiman's expression was crafty. 'True, but perhaps you heard chatter about the *Spanish* court while you were there. L'Estrange will not associate that with you. And you really do need the services of a cloth if you want to impress Joanna. The rabbit will not appreciate mud all over her nice burrow. Yet how will you pay this venerable old crone? I can tell from here that your purse is empty.'

Chaloner supposed there was no harm in repeating some Spanish gossip to Muddiman, and he did not want to make a direct enemy of a man whose role and motives in the murders he did not understand. And nor was there time to go home and change. 'There is to be a marriage contract drawn up between the Infanta Margarita and the Emperor. The political ramifications of such an alliance—'

'I know what the repercussions will be, and they are far-reaching,' interrupted Muddiman. 'Do not concern yourself with analysis: leave that to the experts, like me.

You are sure about this contract? If you feed me dross, I shall certainly find out.'

Chaloner shrugged, not blaming him for being cautious. 'I overheard it, but it is true.'

Muddiman grinned. 'You have made a wise decision, my friend. I shall pay Mother Sales on your behalf, and you have acceded to the polite request of a powerful man. And I am a powerful man, Heyden. People want very much to stay on the right side of me.'

Chaloner was not sure if he was being threatened or cajoled. 'Do they?'

'They do. Now what do you say to another arrangement? If you agree to look no further into this Newburne and Wenum business, I will add you to my list of subscribers. As my newsletters cost a minimum of five pounds a year, this is a generous offer.'

'It is indeed. Generous enough to lead me to surmise that you must have a strong reason for wanting the matter quietly forgotten, and that Newburne – Wenum – was indeed your informant at L'Estrange's office.'

'You can assume what you like. It is a free world, although it will not stay that way if L'Estrange succeeds in censoring everything that is printed.'

'Is that what drives you?' asked Chaloner. 'Freedom to write what you like?'

Muddiman laughed. The foppish image was suddenly gone, and Chaloner had a glimpse of something else entirely. 'Lord, no! That would be tediously moral, would it not? My sole aim in life is to make money. And why not? The pursuit of wealth is an honourable goal, and honest after a fashion.'

'Mother Sales will be here shortly,' said Hodgkinson, returning rather breathlessly. He patted his beard, as if

294

he was afraid his exertions might have ruffled it. 'She is just finishing Kirby's breeches. They are covered in blood again – not his, though, more is the pity.'

Chaloner handed him the Fountain Inkhorn he had found. 'Is this yours?'

Hodgkinson almost snatched it from him. 'Where did you find it? I thought it was gone for good! The King sent it to me when I agreed to print L'Estrange's newsbooks. It is silver, but it is more valuable to me than the weight of its precious metal.'

'The King gave me a clock,' said Muddiman boastfully. 'A big gold one.'

'You must be very proud of it,' said Hodgkinson, upstaged.

Muddiman shrugged. 'I sold it for twenty pounds. I would *much* rather have the money.'

Mother Sales's cloth managed its duties better than Chaloner anticipated. He was quite wet by the time she had finished, and some stains remained, but at least he did not look as though he had been fighting. He walked quickly to Ivy Lane, and knocked on the door just as the bells chimed twelve.

The Brome residence was larger than he had first thought. Besides the spacious chamber that was used as the bookshop, and the office above that was occupied by L'Estrange, there was a pleasant sitting room overlooking a garden at the back. A narrow corridor led to a kitchen, and there were bedrooms on the floors above. It was not grand, but it was warm, welcoming and full of the signs of a contented life – plenty of books on the shelves, a virginals in the corner and mewling kittens in a box near the hearth. He was pleasantly surprised to find Leybourn there, too, and his spirits rose even further when he learned that Mary had had a prior engagement, so could not come.

'It is good of you to invite me, Brome,' said Leybourn, settling more comfortably on a bench and stretching his hands towards the fire. 'It has been ages since we enjoyed a meal together.'

'Far too long,' agreed Joanna, beaming at him. 'However, we asked you to join us several times in the last few months, but you are always too busy.' She blushed furiously. 'That is not a criticism, of course. I just meant to say that Mary must be occupying a lot of your time.'

'Oh, she is,' said Leybourn with one of his guileless grins. 'We are always doing something or other. I cannot recall a time in my life when I have been to more plays and fashionable soirées. It is expensive, but no cost is too high to see my sweet Mary happy.'

Chaloner managed to mask his concern at the comment, but Joanna's rabbit-like features creased into an expression of open dismay. He was not the only one with reservations about Mary Cade.

'Two of my silver goblets have disappeared, Tom,' said Leybourn unhappily, when she and Brome had gone to fetch the food from the kitchen. 'The ones from the Royal Society. Mary reminds me that the last time we saw them was before you visited, but I know you have no interest in baubles.'

Chaloner was not surprised she had taken the chance to malign him, and wondered what other poisonous things she had said. 'I saw some that looked remarkably similar in the hands of a man called Jonas Kirby recently. Ask Mary if she knows him.'

Leybourn shot him a puzzled frown. 'She will not know Kirby – he is a Hector. But how did *he* come by my cups? I suppose he must have broken in when we were out. Mary forgets to lock up sometimes.'

'Is that so?' murmured Chaloner flatly.

'Here we are,' announced Brome from the door, carrying a large tureen. Joanna was behind him with a basket of bread. 'Rabbit stew.'

'Lord!' muttered Leybourn, disconcerted. 'I do not think I can eat it, not with Joanna . . . I mean . . .'

Chaloner was not so squeamish, and as it was one of few decent meals he had had in weeks, his appreciation was genuine. Afterwards, slightly queasy from gluttony, he sat by the fire and listened to Brome and Leybourn debate the merits of Gunter's Quadrant, while Joanna played with the kittens. It was a pleasant, happy scene, and he did not want it to end. It was the first time he had felt so relaxed and contented since the love of his life, Metje, had died the previous year.

'Have you met Mary, Mr Heyden?' asked Joanna in a low voice, once Brome and Leybourn were so engrossed in their debate that neither would have noticed anything short of an earthquake.

'I am afraid so.'

She regarded him sombrely. 'William is a very dear friend, and he deserves better than her. If you can find a way to prise them apart, and you need my help, you only need ask.'

'Thank you,' said Chaloner. 'But I cannot think of anything that will not see him hurt.'

She frowned. 'Then perhaps we can think of something together. The thought of that horrible woman using poor William for her own selfish ends makes me want to . . . to knock out all her teeth!'

'I *know*,' said Brome loudly, in response to some point

297

the surveyor was making. 'I have all your publications, do not forget. *And* I have read them.'

'Have you?' asked Chaloner, impressed. 'There are dozens of them, all equally incomprehensible.'

'How is Dorcus Newburne?' asked Leybourn, changing the subject. He was used to Chaloner's lack of appreciation for his chosen art, but that did not mean he liked it. 'Still missing her vile husband?'

'She loved him, William,' said Joanna reproachfully. 'And he had some virtues.'

'Such as fining good men and spying,' said Leybourn acidly. 'I am sorry if she is unhappy, but I disliked him intensely. And I refuse to say nice things about him just because he is dead.'

'He loved music,' said Joanna stubbornly. 'That is a virtue. I recall seeing him with Maylord only last week, planning a concert for her birthday.'

'Do you think they kept it a secret from her?' asked Chaloner, recalling how Dorcus had denied an acquaintance between her husband and Maylord when he had asked her about it.

'They tried, but she knew anyway,' said Brome. 'She was looking forward to it, although with husband and musician gone, I suppose she will have to find some other way to celebrate.'

There was a short silence, during which Chaloner experienced a sharp pang of grief for his old friend. 'Do you like working for L'Estrange?' he asked, keen to talk about something else for a while.

Brome glanced towards the door, to ensure it was closed. 'He is not an easy master, but my association with him has certainly allowed my business to expand – we sell almost all the government's publications now.

I suppose I could object when he treats me like an errant schoolboy, but I do not want to lose everything over a minor spat. The bookshop is important to me – to us.'

'Hush!' said Joanna in an urgent whisper. 'I think he is coming.'

'I saw you arrive an hour ago,' said L'Estrange to Chaloner, marching in when Brome opened the door to his impatient rap, 'but I thought I would let you eat your rabbit before we had some music.'

'You mean to play now?' asked Chaloner, startled by the presumption. 'Here?'

'Why not?' L'Estrange snapped imperious fingers, and two servants entered, carrying viols. 'I am in the mood, and no one can have anything better to do. What do you play, Leybourn?'

'I sing,' declared Leybourn loftily. Chaloner's heart sank. Leybourn did not have a good voice, which L'Estrange was sure to comment on, and the surveyor was sensitive about it.

'Very well, then,' said L'Estrange. 'You can trill to us, and we shall have some proper consort playing when you have finished. Did you practise those airs I gave you, Heyden?'

'No,' said Chaloner shortly, resenting the intrusion. He saw Joanna and Brome did not appear very keen, either, and hastened to stand up for them. 'And I do not feel like music now. It is not—'

'What was in this rabbit stew?' demanded L'Estrange of Brome. 'A lot of suet, to make his brains muddy? Come on, come on. It is only for a few minutes. Joanna can play the virginals to our viols. She is not very good, but we shall choose a piece where she does not have to do much.'

Chaloner might have laughed, had the man not been insulting people whose hospitality he was enjoying. He was about to tell him to go to Hell when Brome began to set chairs into consort formation and Joanna sat at the virginals, shooting the spy a glance that begged him not to make a fuss. Chaloner nodded acquiescence, although he objected to being bullied, and thought Brome a fool for not drawing the line at being ordered about in his own home. L'Estrange tapped the chairs with his bow, to indicate where he wanted people to sit, and then he was ready.

Unfortunately, so was Leybourn. He began to sing in a key entirely of his own devising, impossible to match, and the resulting harmony was far from pleasant. L'Estrange's jaw dropped at the caterwauling and he struggled to find the right notes. Chaloner smiled encouragingly at the surveyor, maliciously gratified to note that L'Estrange was not enjoying it at all.

Stop!' shouted Leybourn, breaking off and glaring at L'Estrange. 'You are hopelessly out of tune. Just be quiet, and let Tom play. *He* knows what he is doing with a viol.'

Joanna's eyes were bright with suppressed laughter, and the spy wondered if she had known what was going to happen – that she and Brome had allowed L'Estrange to prevail because they had heard Leybourn sing before. The surveyor warbled his way through two more ballads, while L'Estrange's face contorted in agony, like a man sucking lemons. When he had finished, Leybourn picked up his coat.

'I am afraid I cannot entertain you any longer, because

Mary will be waiting for me. Thank you for your hospitality, Joanna. I hope you visit us soon. Mary does not cook, but our local tavern makes an excellent game pie, and Chyrurgeons' Hall opposite has an ice-house, which means sherbets.'

'I thought they used the ice for keeping corpses fresh,' said Chaloner uneasily.

Leybourn waved an airy hand. 'They wash everything off.' Leaving his friends wondering exactly what was meant by 'everything', he sailed out.

'I am glad he has gone,' declared L'Estrange. 'I do not think I could have endured much more of that, but was loath to tell him he sounded like a scalded cat lest he subjected me to more of his repertoire to prove me wrong.'

He launched into a well-known piece without giving them time to find the right music from the sheaf he had thrust at them, but they quickly fell in, and the sound of three viols and virginals was pleasing, although there was something muted and flat about the virginals, as though the damp had got at it. L'Estrange was not happy with the result, though.

'Perhaps it should be played on the trumpet,' he mused.

'No,' said Brome, uncharacteristically firm. 'Trumpets are vulgar, raucous instruments, and four of them would make for a racket. What else do you have?'

'This,' said L'Estrange, passing out more sheets. 'I would like to hear it played as a quartet.'

The music was written by someone with a cramped hand that was not easy to decipher, but although the poor quality of the manuscript might have resulted in a few wrong notes, it could not account for all the discord. Chaloner glanced at Brome's page after a particularly

301

jarring interval, sure the bookseller must have lost his place, but the fault lay in the music, not the player.

'Enough!' cried Joanna, putting her hands over her ears. 'I do not mind humouring you with pleasant tunes, Mr L'Estrange, but this is horrible.'

L'Estrange grimaced. 'My apologies. I just wanted to hear the piece aloud. It pains me to admit it, but I am not good at anticipating how an air will sound, just by looking at notes. My playing is excellent, of course, and the fault lies in the fact that I was not taught to read as well.'

While Brome replaced the chairs and L'Estrange lectured Joanna on her posture, Chaloner studied all four scores together. Unlike the newsbook editor, he *was* good at reading music on paper, but could tell that whoever had composed this particular arrangement had done so with scant regard to melody or mode. The timing fitted, so everyone started and finished together, but that was about all. He recalled the other odd music he had encountered recently – the 'documents' he had recovered from Maylord's chimney. Surreptitiously, he pulled one of the sheets from his pocket and compared it to L'Estrange's. What he saw made his thoughts whirl in confusion.

Both were penned by the same hand, because there were identical eccentricities of notation. But why would Maylord and L'Estrange own pieces by the same composer – especially as that composer was one whose 'tunes' would never be popular, not even with the tone-deaf? Then it occurred to him that he had come across two more examples. First, there had been sheet music in Wenum's room, although all he could recall about that was that it was an unattractive jig. And secondly, Finch had been playing a discordant melody the first time

302

Chaloner had visited; he had probably been practising it before he had been poisoned, too, because it had been lying on the windowsill. Then Hickes had come along and stuffed it in his pocket. Chaloner had assumed Hickes could not read and had just taken something with writing on it, but what if he was wrong? What if the music *was* significant?

And that was not all. Greeting had said that Maylord and Smegergill had been heard playing odd tunes of late, and had made the assumption that they had been commissioned to perform for someone with eclectic tastes – namely Crisp. Was Greeting right? Chaloner was not at all sure, because he had not heard anyone else say the Butcher of Smithfield was artistically inclined, and 'tunes of the Orient' seemed rather an exotic interest for a meat merchant with a penchant for putting his enemies in pies.

He reviewed what he knew, trying to be objective. Four sets of the odd music had been in possession of four different men: Maylord, who had been smothered; Finch and Newburne–Wenum, who had been poisoned; and now L'Estrange. Chaloner shoved Maylord's 'document' out of sight when L'Estrange came towards him.

'May I keep this?' he asked, waving the score they had just played. 'To practise?'

L'Estrange raised his eyebrows. 'If you must, but you will be wasting your time. I do not think greater familiarity will make it sound any better.'

'How did you come by it?' Chaloner asked curiously.

L'Estrange looked oddly furtive. He shrugged, so his earrings glinted. 'Oh, here and there,' he replied vaguely. 'And now, unless you have practised the air I wrote and are ready and willing to play it to perfection, I have more important things to do than dally with amateurs.'

303

'Have you, indeed?' murmured Chaloner, watching the editor stalk out.

L'Estrange wanted another news item about Portugal, so Chaloner sat in the editor's office and penned a description of the preparations that were taking place in Lisbon for the predicted war with Spain. Even as he wrote, he was sure the newsbook readers would prefer a report on the Queen's health.

'Nonsense,' declared L'Estrange, when Chaloner said so. 'However, I suppose I can include a sentence about Monsieur de Harcourt, who had a dangerous fit of apoplexy in Paris last week.'

'Who is Monsieur de Harcourt?' asked Chaloner.

'Damned if I know,' replied L'Estrange. 'But the news should satisfy any ghoulish cravings among my readership for tales of sickness.'

Chaloner left when Mrs Nott arrived for a proof-reading session, although her careful face-paints and immaculate dress suggested she intended to do more than just look for typographical errors. He heard the office door lock behind him when he stepped out, although L'Estrange called out that it was only a precaution against phanatiques. Chaloner was tempted to ask why it had not been secured when *he* had been working there, but there was no point in deliberately antagonising the man. He walked down the stairs, treading softly out of habit, rather than with any serious desire to move unseen. He had almost reached the bottom, when he heard voices in what he assumed was the kitchen. He glanced towards it, and saw a familiar figure framed in the doorway, standing with his back to him. It was Hickes, the apple-seller, commonly thought to be Williamson's 'best spy'.

Chaloner ducked into a coat-cupboard when he heard the faint clink of coins. A purse was changing hands.

'Leave through the rear door,' said Brome in a low voice. 'I do not want L'Estrange to see you.'

'I can well imagine,' said Hickes dryly. 'Until next time, then.'

Chaloner was in a quandary. Why was Hickes giving money to Brome? Was it to provide the Spymaster with inside information about L'Estrange? Chaloner had assumed that, because Williamson and L'Estrange were on the same side, one would have no need to monitor the other. Yet the world of the newsmongers was opaque and confusing, and he was not sure who owed allegiance to whom. He already had proof that Hodgkinson had developed an understanding with Muddiman, and Newburne had been betraying the newsbooks on a regular basis, if the ledger was to be believed. Chaloner scratched his head, not sure what to think. He liked Brome, and sincerely hoped there would be an innocent explanation for what he had just witnessed.

His instinctive dive into a hiding place had left him in an awkward position. Brome was now in the kitchen, and Chaloner could not leave as long as he was there, because he would be seen – and he did not want Brome to think he had enjoyed his hospitality and then immediately resorted to clandestine activities in his home. So, as there was no way he could escape from the coats until the coast was clear, he was obliged to wait. Joanna was in the shop, serving a customer.

'Read it back to me,' the man was demanding. He sounded excited. 'I want to hear it, to make sure you have it right. This is very important, and we cannot afford a single mistake.'

'"Mr Turner's dentifrices, which clean the teeth, making them white as ivory,"' intoned Joanna. '"Prevents toothache, makes the breath sweet and preserves the gums from canker and impostumes."'

The man rubbed his hands together gleefully. 'You have it perfectly! That is just what Mr Turner's dentifrices do, and your words will have folk clamouring at my door for them. Read on, read on!'

'"They are sold by Mr Rokkes at the Lamb and Ink Bottle, at the east end of St Paul's Church."'

'Yes, yes!' cried Rokkes. 'And it will appear just like that? My own name on the line below the praise for Mr Turner's dentifrice?'

'Just like that, Mr Rokkes,' said Joanna, beaming at him. 'I imagine you will recoup your five shillings in a matter of days. Will you sign the ledger, to say you have given us the fee?'

Rokkes left the shop singing to himself, but Joanna had done no more than scatter sand on the wet ink before a figure materialised from where it had been lurking on the stairs. Uneasily, Chaloner wondered just how long it had been there, and what else it had seen.

'We should not accept notices from men like him,' said L'Estrange softly. 'It is a waste of space.'

'He paid his five shillings,' objected Joanna. He had made her jump with his sudden appearance. 'And people might prefer to read about teeth than horses, for a change. Of course, I am not saying dentifrices are more interesting than livestock in the overall scheme of things—'

'Horses raise the tone of a publication,' argued L'Estrange. 'On the other hand, Mr Turner's dentifrices will make us a laughing stock. Can you imagine what Muddiman will say, when he reads that this concoction acts against impostumes? I do not even know what impostumes are. Do you?'

'Abscesses,' replied Joanna promptly. 'Or persons with dubious morals, when used figuratively. Where is Mrs Nott? Not that I think *she* has dubious morals, of course, but—'

'Proof-reading.' L'Estrange glanced down the corridor, saw Brome silhouetted in the kitchen, and moved briskly out of his line of sight to catch Joanna's hand. He held it to his lips, and treated her to one of his wolfish, gap-toothed grins. She did not seem outraged by the unsolicited gesture, but her smile did not seem overly encouraging, either. Chaloner watched in confusion, wondering what sort of man flirted with his employee's wife while another woman eagerly awaited his attentions upstairs.

'I had better take these notices to Hodgkinson,' said Joanna, heading for the coat-cupboard. 'We do not want *The Intelligencer* to be printed late again.'

Chaloner braced himself for discovery, but rescue came from an unexpected quarter. Without taking his eyes off Joanna, L'Estrange reached back and snagged her cloak, tweaking it off the peg and whisking it around her shoulders in a single suave manoeuvre. Surreptitiously, Chaloner eased deeper into the remaining garments, thinking it fortunate that Brome owned so many of them. When Joanna staggered slightly, L'Estrange put both hands on her waist in a move that was unmistakeably intimate.

'Steady,' he breathed, his mouth close to her ear. 'We do not want you to fall.'

It was some time before Chaloner was able to escape, and his mind was full of questions, not just about the

307

significance of the music, but about Brome and Joanna, too. What was the meaning of Hickes's visit, and had L'Estrange really made a play for Joanna? Chaloner liked her, but failed to see her as someone to be seduced. Then it occurred to him that L'Estrange might not be so fussy. However, he was left with an uncomfortable, sordid feeling about the entire situation, and wished he had not witnessed it.

He had not gone far when he saw Hickes emerge from a cook-shop with a pie in his hand. Thinking it was a good opportunity to question him about Brome, he moved to intercept the man, but changed his mind at the last minute. He began to follow him instead, finding comfort in the familiar business of trailing someone. He was not sure what he hoped to achieve, but Hickes was moving with purpose, and Chaloner had the sense that it would be helpful to know where he was going. He kept his distance as Hickes trudged along, but he need not have bothered. Hickes was more interested in evading the spray from carts than in making sure he was not being pursued, and tracking him was absurdly easy.

It was not long before Williamson's master spy reached the Fleet bridge at Ludgate. Crossing it was easier said than done, though, because the normally sluggish stream had become a raging torrent, and the structure was awash. The water was only calf-deep, but it flowed wickedly fast, and Chaloner saw two men take a tumble, only saved from being swept away by clutching the balustrades. Hickes was too heavy to be toppled, and splashed carelessly through the hazard. Chaloner was more wary; he skidded twice and almost fell, and knew it would not be long before the authorities deemed the bridge too dangerous to keep open. Eventually, Hickes

308

arrived at Muddiman's office on The Strand, where he took up station opposite, and began to eat his pie. With nothing better to do, Chaloner approached him.

'You should be wary of those things,' he said in a low voice that made the man jump. 'I have heard they are not very wholesome.'

'Ellis Crisp's are not,' agreed Hickes, regaining his composure quickly. 'I do not eat my friends – and anyone who opposes the Butcher of Smithfield can consider himself a friend of mine.'

'I know. You are Mr Hickes, ostensibly Clerk of the Letter Office, but actually Williamson's spy.'

Hickes grimaced his annoyance. 'Who told you that? Muddiman? Well, I suppose it does not matter. Are you going to tell me who *you* are? You fibbed last time. You said you worked for the Earl of Clarendon, but I looked on his payroll and you are not listed.'

'So I have discovered,' replied Chaloner ruefully. 'Are Muddiman and Dury in?'

'Muddiman went to Smithfield this morning, but he came back, and the pair of them have been at their writing ever since. Can you see them, sitting at the table?'

Chaloner wondered whether it was words or music they were poring over so intently. 'And they have been there all afternoon? Are you sure? You have not gone off on an errand of your own?'

'I have not moved,' said Hickes firmly. He nodded towards Muddiman's house. 'You can ask them if you do not believe me. They look up every so often and wave.'

'Do you know Henry Brome?' asked Chaloner, bemused by the brazen lie.

'We have never met. Why? Do you want to know when

he goes out, so you can visit Joanna? She is a sweet lady, and I might tip a hat at her myself, but Mrs Hickes would not like it.'

Chaloner supposed he had no idea Mrs Hickes was a member of the Army of Angels, and all that entailed. 'Do many men visit Joanna, then?'

'No, she is a respectable soul. It was your motives I was questioning. Why do you ask about her husband? Because there must be something suspect about a man who can put up with L'Estrange?'

'Is there something suspect about him?' asked Chaloner. 'Does he accept bribes or—'

'I have no idea,' replied Hickes firmly. 'I have never met him, as I said.'

'Did you know Hen Finch?' asked Chaloner, to see if Hickes dissembled about everything.

'You are full of questions today. Why do you want to know about him?'

'Because a man matching your description ransacked his chambers yesterday.'

Hickes glared at him. 'It is rude to ask a question if you already know the answer. And I did not *ransack* his chambers – I was very respectful. Williamson ordered me to take a look around, but I was too late, because someone else was there before me. The thief was after documents.'

'How do you know what he wanted?'

Hickes regarded him patronisingly. 'Because Finch was poor. He owned nothing of value, so what other reason could a burglar have had for being there? He was a trumpeter, but I dislike music, personally, except when it is used to heal the sick. Did you know Greeting played his violin to cure the Queen of distemper?'

'I understand Finch and Newburne shared a fondness for music – for pleasure, not medicine.'

'There is a lot of it about,' said Hickes distastefully. 'Finch once trumpeted to Maylord's viol, and Newburne was among the listeners. I was forced to sit through it, too, because Muddiman and Dury were there.'

Chaloner regarded him thoughtfully. Could Hickes be trusted to tell the truth about an association between Maylord and the unsavoury solicitor? Of course, this was really a link between Maylord and *Finch*, and Newburne had just happened to be there. Yet if Hickes was right, then music was a connection between three men who had been murdered.

'What did Williamson expect you to find in Finch's room?' he asked.

'Jewels.'

'Jewels?' pressed Chaloner, when no further explanation was forthcoming. 'What sort of jewels?'

'All sorts. Surely, you have heard the rumour that Newburne owned a box of them? Well, Williamson wanted me to see if Finch had it, given that his widow denies all knowledge. Personally, I do not believe it exists, but he told me to look anyway.'

'Is that all? Williamson did not tell you to collect letters? Or music? Or evidence that Finch – with Newburne's help – might have been selling items of news to L'Estrange's rivals?'

Hickes glared at Chaloner and while his attention was taken, Dury slipped out of the house he was supposed to be watching. Hickes did not notice. 'You have a suspicious mind! If you must know, he also told me to collect anything written, so he could decide whether it was significant. Unfortunately, the thief had

311

got it all, and virtually nothing was left. Williamson was vexed, I can tell you!'

Chaloner assumed the killer was responsible – he had eaten his pie while Finch had suffered the effects of the deadly lozenges, then he had grabbed all the documents he could find, set the cucumber and fled. Later, after Hickes and Chaloner had been, he had returned to the scene of his crime and removed the pills and any remaining papers – Chaloner doubted Hickes had mounted a very thorough search, and he himself had not had time before he had been interrupted.

'Finch did not die of cucumbers, though,' said Hickes, somewhat out of the blue. Chaloner raised his eyebrows questioningly. 'I know there was one on a plate near his body, but there were some green tablets, too, and I think *they* killed him. I saw boxes of Theophilus Buckworth's Personal Lozenges when Colonel Beauclair and Valentine Pettis perished, you see.'

Chaloner frowned. 'You refer to two of the other men who died after eating cucumbers?'

Hickes nodded. 'But Beauclair had a box of these lozenges in addition to the cucumber by his bed. I saw both when I inspected his body.'

'What led you to do that?'

'Protocol. Beauclair died in White Hall, and Williamson's secret service is obliged to look into all deaths that occur there, even natural ones.'

'And Pettis? He was a horse-trader, I believe.'

'He died in Hyde Park, showing off some nags, but because the King happened to be there, his death had to be probed, too. Pettis was allegedly eating cucumber before he died, but he also had a pot of these Personal Lozenges in his pocket. They were wrapped nice, and

312

I thought they might have been given to him as a gift. They made my fingers itch when I picked one up.'

Chaloner was surprised Hickes had looked past the obvious, when it must have been tempting to opt for the easy solution and put the blame on cucumbers. He saw he would be wise not to underestimate James Hickes, tempting though it was to see him as a dull-witted lout barely capable of following his Spymaster's instructions. Hickes continued with his explanation.

'My wife eats cucumbers all the time – for wind – but they never harm her. And Pettis and Beauclair were strong, healthy men, so I do not believe a mere cucumber could have felled them. Maylord was also said to have died of cucumbers, although I know for a fact that anything green brought him out in hives. He would never had touched one, not unless someone forced him. It is patently obvious that someone poisoned all these men, although Williamson refuses to believe me.'

'You have told him your theory?'

'He just laughed at me,' said Hickes resentfully. 'He said it was the sort of rubbish he would expect from a man whose salary amounts to less than ten pounds a year.'

'You should have demanded an increase, then, so he will take you more seriously in the future.'

Hickes chuckled. 'I wish I had thought of that. Mrs Hickes has been on at me to get a rise, because she wants to buy herself some new clothes. She likes dressing up and going out.'

Chaloner was sure she did, especially if it involved a trip to the newsbook offices. He took his leave of Hickes, walking briskly to catch up with Dury. He followed him

313

to the Rainbow Coffee House on Fleet Street, where Dury chose a table in the window. Within moments, he was joined by someone who was already inside. It was long-nosed Ireton, the Hector with the penchant for attacking people in dark churchyards. Chaloner watched them talk together until hunger and weariness drove him home.

Chapter 9

Time was running out for Chaloner, but he had reached a dead end with Newburne's death. He smiled wryly as he sat in his room with the cat for company. He had never particularly liked working for the Earl, but now there was a very real danger of dismissal, he was determined to make sure it did not happen. It was a ridiculous situation, and he wished Cromwell had not died, the Commonwealth had not collapsed, Thurloe was still Spymaster, and he was still a regularly paid intelligence officer working overseas. His life had been a good deal less complicated – and less impoverished – when he had been under Thurloe's orders.

He dragged his mind away from his own predicament, and began to consider his investigations, beginning with Theophilus Buckworth's lozenges. The advertisement in *The Intelligencer* meant a lot of them were being sold, so it was clear they were not all deadly. *Ergo*, someone had devised a way of doctoring them, and chose who they would kill – namely Newburne, Finch, Colonel Beauclair and Valentine Pettis. And perhaps others, too, whose names Chaloner did not know. Then cucumbers were left at the scene of the crime, and rumour allowed to take over. Yet there had been a cucumber with Maylord's body, too, although Chaloner knew for a fact that he had not been poisoned. Did that mean there were two killers? Or was Maylord smothered because he refused to eat the green pills? Several people had mentioned Maylord's aversion to green food.

Chaloner reviewed the victims in more detail. Beauclair was an equerry in His Majesty's Horse, and Pettis had been a horse-dealer. Maylord had owned a racing horse. Newburne had no equine connection, as far Chaloner he knew, and Finch had been too poor to dabble in the exclusive world of expensive nags. And the two sedan-chairmen had connections to cucumbers, but not to horses. He wracked his brain for a clearer connection, but gave up when no answers were forthcoming.

Restlessly, he went to his viol and began to play. Of course, there was also a musical connection between some of the victims and suspects. Finch had been trumpeting one of the tuneless compositions when he had died. Maylord had kept a bundle of them in his chimney. Greeting thought Smegergill and Maylord had been commissioned to perform peculiar music for Crisp. L'Estrange had insisted that Chaloner, Brome and Joanna play one of the pieces, so he could hear how it sounded. Newburne had shared an interest in music with Finch and Maylord, although Dorcus Newburne had denied that her husband had owned an acquaintance with the violist.

When he heard the night-watch shout that it was ten o'clock on a cold, wet night, Chaloner stood and stretched. He had no desire to go out, but Leybourn was his friend, and it was his duty to protect him from Mary.

Thus he had to acquire the surveyor's hidden money before it was either stolen or she demanded so many gifts that it dwindled to nothing. Chaloner was sure she would leave Leybourn the moment his fortune was gone, and a timely burglary might encourage her to relinquish her prey sooner rather than later. He recalled Joanna's offer to help him prise Mary away from Leybourn, and smiled. He was sure breaking and entering was not what she had in mind, but equally sure her affection for Leybourn would compel her to rise to the challenge – or try to rise, at any rate. He doubted she would be much of an asset, though, and he had always preferred working alone.

The cat unearthed something from a dark corner and began to eat, which reminded him of the rat on the mantelpiece. Unfortunately, his landlord was saying goodbye to a friend on the doorstep below, and Chaloner could not lob the thing out of the window as long as they were there; nor did he fancy carrying it downstairs in his hand, so it stayed where it was. He donned dark, shabby clothes and Isabella's hat, then walked down the stairs, letting himself out through the back door to avoid questions from Ellis.

He padded through the sodden streets, sure London could not absorb much more rain, and wishing it would stop. The Ludgate bridge was closed, so he was obliged to use the Holborn crossing over the Fleet instead. The diversion meant he would have to approach Cripplegate via the edge of Smithfield, but he was not overly concerned. His scruffy attire would render him an unattractive target for Hectors, and as long as he stayed out of trouble, he would not be recognised – either as the man who had humiliated Kirby that day, or as the 'musician' they thought they had been paid to kill the previous Sunday.

317

Smithfield never slept. The legal meat trade started very early in the morning, which meant some butchers began work in the middle of the night. Already, apprentices were cleaning and scrubbing by the flickering light of lamps. And for other businesses, the hours of darkness were their prime time. Taverns, bowling alleys, brothels and gambling dens were in full swing, while prostitutes flaunted their wares and sly men emerged from nowhere to sell blankets, wine, and their sisters – and brothers – at suspiciously low prices.

There was a large canvas-rigged structure near Duck Lane, and Chaloner could tell from the bouncing shadows within that it was full of people. He slipped inside, curious to know what had attracted such a huge audience. It was crammed to the gills with men, all swaggering and cheering. Among them were greasy-headed whores, revealing rotten teeth in boisterous laughter. The atmosphere was moist and warm, thick with the stench of sweat, cheap perfume and tobacco. Money was changing hands around a bloody little arena, and two proud birds were killing each other in a flurry of feathers and claws. Chaloner left in disgust; he had never understood the appeal of cock-fighting. He was almost outside, when he spotted a familiar dark-cloaked figure surrounded by Hectors. Crisp was evidently not so squeamish, and was settling himself down to enjoy the spectacle.

The city gates were always closed at night, but Chaloner needed to go through Aldersgate in order to reach Monkwell Street. He was just debating whether to charm his way past the guards or scale the famously ruinous wall to the north, when two burly figures moved out of the shadows to intercept him. The scene was illuminated by a lamp that hung from the gate itself, a flickering, unsteady

318

light that swayed in the breeze. Of the official guards there was no sign.

'Friend or foe?' asked the larger of the pair. Chaloner recognised him immediately, although he hoped it was not mutual. It was Fingerless, the third member of the trio that included Kirby and Ireton. His left hand was still bandaged, and it was tucked inside his coat.

'They are all friends at this time of night, Treen,' quipped his crony with a snigger.

Treen, thought Chaloner, coldly dispassionate. Now he had all their names, and they would pay the price for what they had done to Smegergill, no matter how vehemently they denied harming him.

'Anyone who gives us sixpence is a friend,' laughed Treen. 'Of course, anyone who refuses is a foe, but no one is that stupid.'

Chaloner wished he had given Smithfield a wider berth, because he did not want to enjoin a skirmish that would draw attention to himself – especially on an empty stomach and when he was already tired. If he had had sixpence, he would have handed it over, just to be rid of the nuisance Treen represented.

'You do not want trouble with me,' he said quietly. 'Stand aside.'

His voice carried enough conviction that Treen's friend did as he was told, melting away as though he had never been there. Unfortunately, Treen had been a bully far too long, and could not tell when it was wiser to step away. Fury crossed his face and he drew his sword.

Chaloner sighed and did likewise. 'You will regret this,' he warned.

'No,' came another voice, this one sibilant and more educated than Treen's. '*You* will regret it, because I

319

know who you are. You are the villain who murdered Smegergill.'

Ireton's nose was visible even in the dim light, and so was the sword he carried with the easy grace of the seasoned warrior. Uneasily, Chaloner peered into the shadows, hoping there were not more Hectors lurking there. While he was more than a match for Treen, being outnumbered by skilled swordsmen like Ireton was a different proposition entirely.

Treen turned towards his friend in astonishment. 'He is the murderer? Are you sure?'

'Oh, yes,' replied Ireton. 'I recognise his hat. And if you want more proof, look at his chin, at the bruise where my stone struck it. You should learn to be more observant, Treen.'

Treen shot him an unpleasant look. 'Kirby and I did not waste time inspecting hats, because we were hunting for documents, like we were told. And then he almost severed my finger. He will pay for that – but not tonight. First, the Butcher will want to ask why he killed Smegergill, and then Kirby will want to talk to him about a certain rough interview that was conducted earlier today.'

Ireton shook his head firmly. 'He dies now, by my hand. I do not approve of men who murder harmless old musicians.' He began to advance, and Chaloner prepared to defend himself.

'Wait!' snapped Treen, rashly making a grab for Ireton's sword arm. 'Crisp will be furious if you kill him before he is interrogated. And if *you* cannot see that annoying the Butcher is unwise, then you should go back to strumming your lute and leave this sort of business to me.'

Ireton's expression was dangerous. 'How dare you countermand me! You are just a lout, a hireling Crisp uses for his dirty work. And you cannot even do that properly! If you had killed this man on Sunday, as you were ordered, we would not be in this situation now.'

They began to quarrel, leaving Chaloner somewhat nonplussed. He took a few steps away, aiming to leave while they were preoccupied. But Ireton saw what he was doing and came at him in a rush of flailing steel. The Hector was good, better than Chaloner had anticipated, and he saw they were fairly evenly matched. Then Treen lumbered forward and tried to pull Ireton away. Ireton's expression was murderous, and Chaloner half expected him to skewer his comrade there and then.

'Drop your weapons,' came a voice that was far from steady. A figure stepped out of the shadows by the gate, holding a large, old-fashioned gun. It trembled in his hand. 'Do it now, or I will kill you.'

Treen needed no second warning. His sword clattered to the ground, and he slunk away quickly, apparently one of those men who appreciated the deadly power of firearms, even ancient ones gripped by hands that shook. Ireton was not so easily intimidated, however, and his temper was up.

'Go on, then,' he sneered. 'Shoot me.'

Chaloner felt Ireton's assessment of the situation was accurate: the gunman was far too frightened to pull the trigger. Thus, when the still night air was shattered by a booming crack, it took everyone by surprise.

Chaloner leapt forward to disarm the astonished Ireton, who aimed a quick punch that forced the spy to duck, then tore away when he was off balance. Chaloner did

321

not care, and made no attempt to stop him. When the running footsteps had been swallowed by the night, he turned to face his rescuer.

'Christ!' breathed Greeting unsteadily. He flopped down on a nearby wall, dag dangling limply from his fingers. 'All I did was twitch and the damned thing went off. Did I hit anyone?'

Chaloner shook his head. 'You can come out now, Hodgkinson. They have gone.'

The printer emerged cautiously from behind a water butt. He clutched a scarf, and had evidently intended to disguise himself before joining the affray. Greeting held a similar garment, but had forgotten to put it on. Amateurs, thought Chaloner in some disgust.

'How did you know I was there?' asked Hodgkinson uncomfortably.

'I saw you.' Chaloner pulled the shocked Greeting to his feet. 'We cannot stay here. They will be back with reinforcements, because they will not appreciate you making fools of them. Come with me.'

He led the way to the crumbling section of the old city wall, although both printer and musician complained that it was too difficult a climb and made heavy work of the exercise. Eventually, he managed to pull, cajole and threaten them over the top, then took them to the churchyard of St Giles Cripplegate, where they hid among the trees until he was sure they were safe.

'You have some very odd skills,' grumbled Greeting. 'Bandying swords with felons, scaling walls, knowing your way around dark cemeteries. Is this where part-time spying for the Lord Chancellor leads? What are you doing here at this time of night, anyway? I thought you lived on Fetter Lane.'

322

'I could ask you the same question,' said Chaloner, still alert for any sign of pursuit.

'Hodgkinson owns a print-shop on Duck Lane and I rent the attic above it. We *live* here – you do not. And what were you thinking of, taking on Hectors? Are you insane?'

'Are *you* insane?' countered Chaloner. 'I cannot see Hectors being very happy about heavy-fingered gunmen taking up residence in their domain, either.'

'He is right,' said Hodgkinson sternly to the agitated musician. 'I told you to point it and wait for me to sneak up behind them, not merrily blast away at whatever took your fancy. The sound of a gun discharging might have brought the entire gang down on us.'

Chaloner regarded them uncertainly, not sure what to make of their timely appearance. 'You are working together?'

'Williamson wants to know what really happened to Smegergill – he investigates all White Hall deaths.' Greeting was shaking almost uncontrollably now the danger was over. 'So he told me to come to the place where he was murdered, to see what kind of villains lurk. He believes such men are creatures of habit, and rarely stray far from the scenes of their crimes. I think he normally hires Hectors for this sort of thing, but as one of *them* might be the killer, he ordered me here instead.'

'It is brave of you to do it, though,' said Chaloner, thinking the man was a fool to accept such a commission when his ability to protect himself was dubious, to say the least.

Greeting seemed close to tears. 'I had no choice! He said my consort would never play again if I did not do as he asked. If I had known that offering my services *once* would amount to me selling my soul, I would never have done it. I am not cut out for this sort of thing. I am an artist, not some lout who wanders around in filthy clothing and knows how to fight and climb walls.'

'And you?' Chaloner asked Hodgkinson, overlooking the insult on the grounds that Greeting probably did not realise what he had said. 'Are you blackmailed into helping Williamson, too?'

'Greeting and I are friends – I publish his music, and he rents my attic. When he told me what he had been compelled to do, I offered to help, because I did not think he should do it alone.'

'Luckily for you, Heyden,' added Greeting shakily. 'I am no Sir Galahad, and would never have tackled Ireton and his friends had Hodgkinson not told me what to do.'

'Why did you risk yourselves?' asked Chaloner, declining to mention that he had never been in any real danger. Ireton had represented a challenge, but not with Treen getting in the way and grabbing his arms. And unfortunately for Greeting and Hodgkinson, their act of bravado was likely to have grave consequences for their future in the area.

'Because Treen said you were the man who attacked Kirby today,' replied Hodgkinson sheepishly. 'That makes you a hero to anyone who resents the Hectors and their safety taxes, and we wanted to save you from them. However, our rescue did not go quite as planned. Greeting forgot to put on his mask, and then he fired his dag before I was in position.'

'Mask?' Greeting looked at the material in his hand, then groaned. 'Oh, Christ! That means they saw my face! What have I done? Damn Williamson and his unreasonable demands! And damn you, too, Heyden. I told

Hodgkinson we should not interfere, regardless of your courage in pressing a knife to Kirby's throat. And speaking of murderous attacks, Ireton seemed to think you might know more about Smegergill's demise than you have led me to believe. Is it true?'

'I did not kill Smegergill,' said Chaloner quietly.

'So you have said before. However, you were with him when he was attacked, because Ireton recognised you, and he is not stupid. And you do match the description given by the witnesses.'

'Heyden is not the killer,' said Hodgkinson with considerable conviction. Greeting looked at him in surprise, and so did Chaloner. The printer hastened to explain himself. 'Whoever killed Smegergill also stole his ring, and Heyden is no thief. He found a valuable pen this morning – he could have kept it, but he returned it to me without a moment's hesitation. A man who kills for money does not blithely relinquish a silver Fountain Inkhorn.'

Chaloner sincerely hoped they would not ask to see the contents of his pockets, because Smegergill's ring was in one of them. 'I was with Smegergill that night,' he admitted. 'And I failed to protect him, to my eternal shame.'

Greeting nodded his satisfaction. 'I knew you were involved somehow. But if you say you did not harm Smegergill, then I shall believe you. Maylord always said nice things about you, and that is good enough for me. How much longer do we have to stay here? I am wet through and want to go home.'

'You cannot go home,' said Hodgkinson. 'You do not have anything to tell Williamson yet – other than that Treen and his cronies charge an unofficial toll for using

Aldersgate, and he probably knows that already. You will have to go back, and see who else comes crawling along.'

'Ireton, Kirby and Treen attacked the wrong two men the night Smegergill died,' Chaloner said to Greeting, when Hodgkinson had gone to see if the coast was clear. 'They were ordered to ambush an old musician and his younger companion, and be sure to kill the latter. But their victims arrived early, and they made a mess of the attack. I believe the real target was you. Not me, and not Smegergill.'

Greeting gazed at him. 'Me? I do not believe you.'

'Your coachman was probably bribed to make you get out of his carriage early, forcing you to walk the rest of the way. And Smegergill's unanticipated decision to forgo your consort's official transport led to a case of mistaken identity. You were carrying documents that night, and Ireton was charged to steal them. What were they? Something you were commissioned to deliver to Williamson?'

Greeting's face was white. 'This cannot be true,' he said shakily.

'Spying is a dangerous game, Greeting. People die all the time, especially those who work for Williamson – he considers them a readily disposable asset. You can keep his confidence if you like, but bear in mind that he will not be equally loyal to you.'

'It was music,' said Greeting in a low, frightened voice. 'Just music. I tried to tell you.'

Chaloner frowned. 'You mean the strange tunes you said Smegergill and Maylord had been practising? It was their music you were carrying?'

'I think so. L'Estrange was at the Charterhouse concert that night, and Williamson told me to collect papers from

326

him and take them to White Hall the following day. L'Estrange gave me a pouch, and I peeped inside when I got home. It was just music.'

Chaloner was confused. Had L'Estrange exchanged letters for tunes, because he knew the courier was going to be intercepted in St Bartholomew's churchyard? 'Presumably, you delivered the pouch to Williamson the next day. Was he surprised to see you? What did he say when he opened it?'

Greeting gazed at him, then raised an unsteady hand to rub his eyes. 'What have I embroiled myself in? I have no idea whether he was surprised to see me, because his face is always impassive and impossible to read. He took the package, inspected it briefly, then threw the whole lot on the fire.'

Leybourn's house was in darkness, so Chaloner let himself in through the back door. The surveyor kept his worldly wealth under a floorboard in the attic he used as a study, but before Chaloner could start up the stairs, he heard someone coming down them. Not wanting to be caught, he slid into a cupboard, taking refuge among brooms, rags and a brimming bucket of slops that someone had shoved out of sight and forgotten about. The stench in the confined space almost took his breath away.

He was expecting to see Leybourn or Mary, heading to the kitchen for a drink. But it was neither, and he frowned when he recognised Kirby. Over the Hector's shoulder was Leybourn's money sack.

Chaloner was tempted to make a commotion, so Kirby would be caught red-handed, but he was not sure what excuse *he* could give for being in his friend's house in the depths of the night. Mary would certainly make hay with the fact that he had broken in, and he did not want to put Leybourn in a position where he was forced to choose between them again. He followed Kirby outside, and accosted him as he cut through the graveyard of St Giles without Cripplegate, careful to keep his face in shadow and his voice soft enough to be anonymous. He had reloaded the gun he had confiscated from Greeting – the musician was a danger to himself with it – and he pointed it at Kirby as he called through the trees.

'Put the bag on the ground and raise your hands above your head.'

Kirby leapt in alarm. There was enough light from the street for him to see his assailant was armed, but he quickly regained his composure. He was braver than Treen. 'What if I refuse?'

Chaloner cocked the gun. 'The sack goes on the ground with or without your cooperation.'

Slowly, Kirby set it down. 'Come to a tavern with me,' he said wheedlingly. 'There is no need for rough tactics. We can share the contents over an ale, and both be happy.'

'Walk away,' ordered Chaloner. 'And do not look back.'

But Kirby was not ready to relinquish such a large fortune without making some sort of stand. 'You will not shoot me,' he blustered. 'If you want the sack, you will have to come and get it.'

Chaloner was tempted to make an end of him, but he had never enjoyed killing, even during the wars, and was loath to shoot a man in cold blood. On the other hand, he had no intention of fighting for Leybourn's treasure. He aimed at a spot just above Kirby's shoulder and squeezed the trigger. The henchman gasped his alarm at the sudden report, covering his head with his hands as twigs and leaves fell around him.

'The next ball will be between your eyes,' whispered Chaloner. 'Walk away or die.'

When Kirby had gone, Chaloner grabbed the bag and hid behind a tomb, waiting for Kirby to double back and try to catch him. The man was predictable, and came from precisely the direction Chaloner had anticipated. He watched him pass by on his futile errand, then headed south, where he kept to the smaller alleys, and the sight of the gun meant no one was reckless enough to stop him and ask what was in the sack.

Because he was being careful, it took an age to reach home, and by the time he did, he was heartily sick of wind-blown rain. He was about to go through his front door, when he saw several people sitting in the tavern opposite. It was outrageously late, even for the Golden Lion, and instinct warned him to be wary. He crouched behind an abandoned hand-cart and waited. Eventually, one of the patrons stood and stretched. It was Giles Dury – again.

Dury did not seem to be watching Chaloner's house – at least not obviously so – and the Golden Lion was the kind of inn that conducted all manner of clandestine business, so the newsman's presence might have nothing to do with the spy. But Chaloner was now respon-sible for Leybourn's entire personal fortune, and could not put it at risk by returning to his own rooms to sleep. So he went to Lincoln's Inn instead. Sinister shadows lurked there, too, although Chaloner was sure they had nothing to do with him. The Inn was home to several controversial lawyers and some of the country's most rabid religious fanatics, so was often under survcillance.

He did not feel inclined to walk through the front gate even so, and scaled the wall at the back instead. Then it was a tortuous journey through the wet gardens, and a forced entry through a ground-floor window. By the time he reached Chamber XIII and tapped softly on the door, he was exhausted. So, when Thurloe answered wearing a comical night-cap, Chaloner was too tired to stop himself from laughing. The ex-Spymaster regarded him coolly.

'You are filthy and soaked through. What have you been doing? Robbing houses?'

Chaloner nodded as he set the sack on the table. 'Hopefully, Mary will leave Will when she learns he is destitute – and that it is not her friends who have the proceeds.'

Thurloe's eyebrows shot upwards. 'Is this how you use the skills I taught you? To burgle your friends? Should I put my valuables under lock and key when you are visiting?'

'When I am *not* visiting,' recommended Chaloner. 'If I am here, you can keep an eye on me.'

'What do you intend to do with it? He will be distressed when he finds it gone.'

'Mary will almost certainly order my room searched by Hectors, so we cannot leave it there. Will you put it somewhere safe? He can have it back when he comes to his senses. Or when he is too far under Mary's spell for redemption, and we are obliged to give up on him.'

Thurloe regarded him soberly. 'Let us pray for the former. I will conceal it in—'

Chaloner held up his hand. 'What I do not know, I cannot be forced to tell.'

Thurloe's face creased in worry. 'Do you think it might

come to that? Perhaps you should just give it back. William will not think his savings worth your life.'

'Then convince him – and Mary – that I had nothing to do with its theft. You will not be lying, because I really did not steal it. I intended to, but Kirby was there first.' Chaloner laid the gun on the table, next to the sack. 'You had better keep this, too. No one followed me here, but I want you to have the means to protect yourself, even so.'

Thurloe's expression became pained as he told him how he had thwarted Kirby's burglary.

'You were with me all night,' said Thurloe. 'We have been discussing Newburne's death and its various twists and turns, and then, since the weather is foul, I insisted you sleep here. You were never out tonight, so how can you have anything to do with the disappearance of William's sack?'

Chaloner woke on Saturday with the sense that time was of the essence, and that he only had two days left before the Earl dismissed him. It was a foul morning, with splattering rain carried on a gusting wind. Although it was still dark, Thurloe was already up, writing at the table in his bedchamber. He shared some thinly sliced bread and watery ale – old man's food, though he was not yet fifty – which did little to alleviate Chaloner's hunger.

It was the day of Maylord's funeral, and Chaloner could hardly attend wearing his housebreaking gear, so he went home first. Remembering who he had seen in the Golden Lion the previous evening, he climbed into a neighbour's garden to avoid using his own front door, and slipped up the stairs to his room without being seen. The tiny fibre that rested on the door handle was still in place, and so were the hairs in the hinges of his cupboard and chest, which would have told him if anyone had searched

331

them. The cat was out, although a second dead rat by the side of the bed told him it had been around. He placed the new corpse next to the first one, thinking he would get rid of them later.

The clothes he had worn the previous day were almost dry, so he donned them again, then looked in his pantry. There was no reason to suppose anyone had left him a gift of food, and there were so many people who wanted him dead that he would not have eaten it anyway, but Thurloe's meagre breakfast had done more to whet his appetite than relieve it, and he was ravenous. The cupboard was bare except for the cucumber and spices – galingale and cubebs. They released a mouth-watering aroma, and served to make him hungrier than ever. He was not, however, desperate enough to resort to the cucumber.

He knew he should report to the Lord Chancellor first, to let him know he was still on the case. He did not want to be dismissed because the Earl was under the impression that he was lying at home all day, waiting for answers to appear. Of course, he thought ruefully, as he jumped across a puddle that contained a drowned pigeon, answers were not coming at all, despite his best efforts, and he had more questions now than when he had started.

When he passed the Rainbow Coffee House, he met Joseph Thompson, the rector of his parish church, who invited him inside to share a dish of chocolate. Chaloner accepted, although chocolate was a foul, oily, bitter beverage that few men could swallow without wincing. He and Thompson began a lively discussion about the political implications of the Infanta Margarita's marriage contract to the Emperor, which had featured in Muddiman's latest newsletter, although most other patrons said they did not care about foreign weddings. However, they all said they were looking forward to the next *Intelligencer,* because they had been told there was to be an especially large missing-horse section.

'Perhaps it will mention the Queen's distemper, too,' said Thompson eagerly. 'And more news about that dreadful earthquake in Quebec.'

The men at his table scoffed derisively. 'It will hold forth about phanatiques,' said one.

'It was probably phanatiques who caused the earthquake,' said another, making his cronies laugh.

It was raining hard when Chaloner left the Rainbow, and he thought about his investigations as he walked to White Hall. As far as Mary was concerned, his enquiries were complete. He had satisfied himself that she was definitely a felon – Bridges' reluctant testimony proved that, and so did Kirby's theft of the sack – and she only wanted Leybourn for his money. Now the surveyor did not have any, she would leave him and move to greener pastures. Of course, Leybourn also owned a pleasant house, a thriving business and a stock of books and valuable mathematical implements, but Chaloner did not think they would be enough to hold her. He was sorry his friend was about to have his heart broken, but knew it would have happened anyway, with or without his interference.

Less satisfactory was his investigation into the murder of Newburne. What could he tell the Earl about it? That he was uncovering more information with every passing day, but that it made no sense? That he had started off with Muddiman as his prime suspect, because the newsletter-man had bought cucumbers at Covent Garden the day before Newburne had died, but that now his list of potential culprits included virtually everyone he had met and some folk he had not? For example, Joanna and

333

L'Estrange were more intimate than was respectable, and Newburne might have tried to blackmail them. Meanwhile, Brome was an enigma, and Chaloner had no idea whose side he was on. Then there were hundreds of booksellers who wanted Newburne dead, and even the Army of Angels might have exchanged innocent lozenges for ones that were deadly. So might Newburne's wife, or Crisp. The cucumbers or poison connected Newburne to Colonel Beauclair, Valentine Pettis, the sedan-chairmen and Maylord. And there was the music.

And Maylord? Chaloner had no clue as to who might have smothered him, and nor did he understand the strands that linked the musician to the other cucumber deaths. The same went for Smegergill, although he was beginning to question his previous certainty that Ireton, Kirby and Treen were responsible.

He arrived at White Hall, and found it in chaos. Servants rushed everywhere, staggering under the weight of furniture, heaps of paper, kitchen equipment, armfuls of clothes and the contents of the King's scientific laboratory. The last time Chaloner had witnessed such alarm was during the first civil war, when the Royalists had won a number of battles and Parliament-loyal settlements had packed all they could carry in the face of imminent invasion. Then Cromwell had trained the New Model Army, and it had been Cavalier households that had faced the humiliation of enemy occupation.

'What is happening?' he asked a passing soldier, a rough fellow called Sergeant Picard.

'The tide is coming in,' explained Picard tersely.

Chaloner prevented him from dashing off. 'It does that most days. Twice, usually.'

'Well, this time it is worse,' said Picard, freeing himself

334

impatiently. 'It is predicted to be an unusually high one, and the river has already breached its banks around Deptford.'

'Is the palace being evacuated?' But Picard was gone, and Chaloner was left to make what he would of the situation.

The frenzy reached new heights when it was discovered that one of the kitchens was on fire, too. Because White Hall comprised mostly timber-framed buildings, Chaloner ran towards the smoke to see what could be done to prevent an inferno. He and a competent military man, who said he was John Bayspoole, Surveyor of Stables, grabbed buckets and doused the flames between them, while scullions watched but could not be induced to help in any significant way. The blaze was not a serious one, so it was not long before they had it under control.

Bayspoole wiped the sweat from his face with his sleeve. 'Everyone is so obsessed by the notion of flood that they forget fire is a far more serious hazard. And look at those cooks! They are racing to save their precious cakes, but there are *horses* waiting to be evacuated. Has the world gone mad, when a pastry is considered more important than a palfrey?'

Chaloner watched the bakers dodge around them, bearing trays of tarts. They were still warm from the ovens, and their scent was enough to make a hungry man dizzy. 'Did you know Colonel Beauclair?' he asked, to take his mind off his empty stomach.

'Owned a fine black stallion and a sweet bay mare. Died of eating cucumbers, apparently, although I suspect the real culprit was those green lozenges he was sent. The spy Hickes showed them to me.'

'Sent by whom?'

'Some acquaintance from his coffee house, probably. His horses went missing after his death, which was a damned shame, because I would have bought the black stallion from his heirs.'

Chaloner frowned. 'You think he was killed because someone wanted his horses?'

Bayspoole nodded. 'Of course. Horses are the only thing worth stealing, as far as I am concerned. You can keep your jewels and your fine gold, but horses . . . speaking of which, I had better go and make sure the King's beasts are taken to St James's Park, because no one else will bother.'

He hurried away, and Chaloner resumed his walk to the Earl's offices, deep in thought. Horses were a theme in the murders – Maylord had owned one, Beauclair was an equerry and Pettis was a horse-trader. Had Maylord been killed for his nag, too? But what about Newburne and Finch? They had nothing to do with horses. Or did they? Both had lived near Smithfield, which was famous for its livestock. And Crisp was the Butcher of Smithfield.

Chaloner reached the Privy Gardens, and climbed the stairs to the Earl's offices, but they were abandoned by everyone except Bulteel, who was working with the air of a wounded martyr.

'Has the Earl threatened to dismiss you again?' asked Chaloner, wondering why the clerk was always at his desk. He knew Bulteel was married, because the happy day had been the previous January, and Bulteel had given him a piece of cake. It had been very good cake, too, better than anything he had had since. He rubbed his stomach, and wished he could stop thinking about food.

Bulteel sighed. 'He says if I cannot find a more efficient

336

way of managing his business, he will hire another secretary. But this *is* the most efficient system, and there is no way I can make it better.'

'And I am a good spy,' said Chaloner ruefully, 'but he makes me feel as though I am more of a nuisance than an asset.'

Bulteel regarded him thoughtfully. 'Perhaps you and I should join forces.'

Chaloner smiled, always ready to forge new alliances. He was wary of trusting anyone at White Hall, but there was no reason why he and Bulteel should not assist each other from time to time. 'All right. Do you know anything that will help me with Newburne?'

Bulteel nodded eagerly, pleased with his ready acquiescence. 'I know the Earl is determined not to pay Dorcus Newburne's pension – he says he would rather spend a night with the King's mistress, so that should tell you the extent of his resolution. And I know he wants you to prove Muddiman is responsible for Newburne's death, because then he can pass the burden of the pension to him.'

Chaloner regarded him in distaste. 'Really?'

Bulteel nodded again. 'So, if you expose Muddiman as the culprit, you will be reinstated. However, if you discover the killer is some pauper, or that Newburne died in the course of his government duties, he will not be so generous.'

'I cannot tell him it was Muddiman if I find evidence to the contrary. I am no lapdog, uncovering "evidence" to orders.'

Bulteel regarded him appraisingly, then gave his shy smile. 'I knew you would say that – I am a good judge of men, and I know an honest one when I see him.'

Chaloner shot him a searching look of his own. 'I suspect, from your reaction, that you have devised a way to resolve my dilemma.'

'You are astute, and the Earl is a fool not to cultivate your loyalty. What you need is a plan that will please him no matter what you discover, and I have been mulling one over for some time. Newburne was wealthy – he owned a mansion on Old Jewry, one on Thames Street and two in Smithfield.'

'Do you happen to know if he rented rooms in the Rhenish Wine House, too?'

Bulteel was puzzled. 'He hired a garret on Ave Maria Lane, but his other places were proper houses which he owned himself.' He looked wistful. 'The Thames Street property is the nicest, in my opinion. It is not very big, but it has a lovely view of Baynard Castle.'

Chaloner rubbed his chin. 'I do not suppose it is next to Hodgkinson's business, is it?'

'Oh, no,' said Bulteel in distaste. 'Print-works smell, and he had more genteel neighbours than that. In fact, one was Maylord the musician.'

'Is that so? Maylord abandoned his Thames Street home shortly before his death, perhaps because he heard or saw something that frightened him. I wonder whether it was anything to do with Newburne? I have struggled to find connections between them, but being neighbours would certainly count.'

'I inspected Newburne's accounts for a government survey once, and a lot of courtiers hired his legal services. Perhaps Maylord was one of them, and their relationship was that of lawyer–client.'

'You do not remember for certain?'

Bulteel shook his head. 'I kept notes, though, so I can

338

check for you. However, what really stuck in my mind were the inconsistencies in Newburne's accounts. He was swindling the government quite openly – not the Lord Chancellor, but other departments.'

'Did you report him?'

Bulteel winced. 'I do not possess your moral courage, and Newburne was in high favour at the time. I overlooked them, as I was expected to do. That is where the saying "Arise, Tom Newburne" comes from – success despite ethical shortcomings.'

'Is it, indeed?' murmured Chaloner. How many more alternative meanings would he be given for the curious phrase?

'But we digress. What I want to tell you is that he owned a box of jewels. He invested his legitimate income with bankers, but could hardly do the same with the profits from his shady business, so he stored those in a little chest.'

'I was told his hoard was a popular folktale, that it has no basis in fact.'

'Then you were told wrong,' said Bulteel with great conviction. 'It does exist. I have seen it.'

Chaloner was not sure whether to believe him. 'Where?'

'He kept it buried in the cellar of his Old Jewry house. He dug it up in front of me once, when we needed to lend the Earl some ready cash.'

'The Earl owed Newburne money?' asked Chaloner with a sinking feeling in the pit of his stomach. If there was ever a good motive for murder, then an unsavoury debt was among the best.

'It was repaid in full ages ago,' said Bulteel, seeing what he was thinking. 'The Earl did not kill Newburne.

339

However, if you can lay hold of this treasure, you can present it to him and it will serve two purposes: it will pay Dorcus's pension, regardless of what you learn about her husband's manner of death; and it will ensure you keep the Earl's favour.'

'But that means Dorcus's pension will be paid from her own money – her lawful inheritance.'

'Not so. Newburne earned those jewels by cheating the government, so they are *not* hers.'

'That is contorted logic. Devious logic, too.'

'The chest belongs to the government,' insisted Bulteel stubbornly. 'And I would rather our Earl had it than anyone else, because he may use it to pay his servants – you and me. However, you should present it to him only *after* you have identified your suspect, to soften the blow. Unless the culprit is Muddiman, of course, in which case you should leave it where it is. Then you will have it in reserve, for when you need to prove your loyalty the next time.'

'And what do you gain from this arrangement?'

'You will tell the Earl that we solved the case together, so we can both claim credit for the victory. Then he will see us as indispensable, and we will be safe until the next crisis comes along.' Bulteel looked uncomfortable. 'I know you will be taking all the risks, but I really cannot help you with a burglary, because I would not know what to do. However, it is *my* information.'

Chaloner had heard worse offers. 'How do you know you can trust me?'

'I trust you,' said Bulteel with surprising conviction. 'You have had several opportunities to feather your nest from your work, but you never have, despite being in desperate straits. You are honest.'

'I am a spy,' countered Chaloner. 'We lie without thinking about it.'

Bulteel grinned, revealing his bad teeth. 'And I am a lawyer, so there is little I do not know about deception, either. I am not asking for your hand in marriage here, Heyden – just a temporary alliance. As soon as we are back on the payroll, we can revert to our usual antipathy, if you like. But my wife is expecting our first child soon, and I need regular employment.'

'Very well,' said Chaloner, holding out his hand.

Bulteel clasped it. 'Thank you. You will not regret trusting me, I promise.'

Chaloner hoped he was right. 'The chest is buried in Newburne's cellar?' he asked, supposing it would be no great trouble to break into the house and take a look. He had done it before, after all.

'There is a single barred window, and the treasure is just below it. He may have covered the spot with an old box or a heap of rags.' Bulteel stood. 'Meanwhile, the Lord Chancellor is in the Shield Gallery, watching the river through the window. I will escort you there, if you like.'

The flooded Thames was an unsettling sight. It was brown and swift, and in it were whole trees, the shattered pieces of wooden buildings, clothing and even a woman's body, face-down and undulating among the waves. Sand-filled sacks had been placed in front of the palace's water-gates, but they were a futile measure against such a powerful force, like trying to kill a pig with a pin.

'The tide will turn in an hour,' said the Earl, watching it from the comfort of the gallery. All the windows had

341

been thrown open, and courtiers jostled for vantage points. The King was among them, and his mistress, Lady Castlemaine, clung to his arm, declaring in a penetrating voice that it would do no harm for some of the capital's hovels to be washed away, because they were ugly.

'They are people's homes, my love,' said the King, although there was no real sting in his words.

'Then this is their chance to build prettier ones,' she retorted petulantly. 'I am weary of squalor – it is so tiresome. Lord, I am bored! Will no one play billiards with me?'

There was an immediate flurry of raised hands, although most were hastily lowered again when the King cast a laconic eye over them. He snapped his fingers for wine, although half the Court looked as though it had imbibed far too much already, despite the early hour. Chaloner looked away, thinking it might not be a bad thing if the river also took White Hall and its dissipated occupants when it swept away the slums that so offended Lady Castlemaine's sensitivities.

'How is the Queen?' asked Chaloner, standing at the Earl's side. Although the Lord Chancellor had clawed back some of the power he had lost during his recent spat with the Earl of Bristol, he remained an unpopular man – the other windows were crowded, but the Earl had one all to himself, because no one wanted to be with him.

Clarendon regarded him sharply. 'She is better, but certainly not well enough to see you. She was pleased with your reports, as I said, but she can have no need of a spy in White Hall. Your only hope is to please me over this Newburne business. What have you learned?'

342

Chaloner shrugged apologetically. 'The more information I uncover, the more questions it poses. I have uncovered a lot of information about Newburne, but at the same time I seem to know less.'

Clarendon gave him a wan smile. 'It sounds like a paradox, but I know what you mean. I feel the same way about my enemies at Court. Dorcus Newburne was here again yesterday, by the way, demanding her pension. Wretched woman! Her husband left her well provided for, so I do not see why she should expect me to impoverish myself to give her more.'

'No, sir,' said Chaloner.

He was about to outline what he had reasoned about the music, but the Earl clearly had better things to do than listen to the vague theories of his spy. He started to walk towards one of his few courtly allies, then glared pointedly when Chaloner made no move to leave.

'Is there anything else, Heyden? If not, you had better go and find me some sensible answers, because you only have two more days, and I *will* dismiss you if you do not tell me what I want to know.'

Chaloner did not think he would be very impressed with the few facts he had gathered, so decided it was better to say nothing. He bowed and left without another word.

Maylord's funeral was not until noon, and the day was still young, so Chaloner decided to visit Dorcus. On his way, he stopped to see Temperance; she was still in bed, but rose when told the identity of her visitor. Maude was already bustling about the kitchen, making some of her poisonous coffee. She offered Chaloner a dish, but he declined. Preacher Hill had once told him Maude's brew was so potent that her first husband had sipped some and died on the spot. Chaloner had no idea whether the story was true, although he did know that even a few mouthfuls invariably resulted in a rapidly pounding heart and an unpleasant burning in the stomach.

'I am sorry,' he said as Temperance joined him at her kitchen table. He looked around surreptitiously to see if there was anything to eat. 'I am used to you being up at dawn for chapel, and I never expect you to be in bed this late.'

'Eight o'clock is hardly late,' objected Temperance with a yawn. 'And my days of rising at ungodly hours for church were a long time ago. I only go on Sundays now, because I have abandoned the Puritan fancies my parents taught me. And you *do* have a nasty habit of arriving overly early, Thomas. Come later in future because I seldom retire before four.'

'Four in the *morning*?'

'Well, I do not mean four in the afternoon.' She grimaced. 'The Puritans are wrong to insist on dawn devotions. The King should do something about them.'

'You think they should be suppressed?' Chaloner tried not to sound shocked.

'Yes, I do. You cannot reason with fanatics, and allowing them to express their bigoted opinions encourages them to shout all the more loudly. It is only a small step from yelling hate to putting it into practice with guns and swords, and outlawing their gatherings will make the country far more safe.'

Chaloner struggled to conceal his unease. He had never expected to hear such sentiments from a woman whose family had endured a good deal of suffering for its religious beliefs. Yet his dismay at her changing political views

344

was nothing compared to his astonishment when she produced a pipe and began to tamp it with tobacco.

'Christ, Temperance!' he exclaimed. He supposed he should hold his tongue, but he could not help feeling some responsibility for her well-being. 'You are full of surprises this morning.'

She examined the pipe fondly. 'I have been developing a fancy for it. We are told smoking is for men, but why should they have all the fun? Besides, I do not do it in public, only with friends. Would you care to join me? I have several spares.'

He shook his head, hoping she might offer him some breakfast instead. She did not, although Maude handed him a pile of mended and cleaned clothes. He offered to return the ones he had borrowed, but the women waved him away.

'You look nice in them,' said Temperance, puffing contentedly. 'And you probably need to go to Maylord's funeral today, so you should dress properly for the occasion. Our boy will deliver these others to your house, so there is no need to take them with you now.'

'They are saying in the coffee houses that the river has burst its banks at Deptford,' said Maude conversationally, when the spy had lavished a suitable amount of praise on her handiwork.

'Did they read that in Muddiman's newsletter or *The Newes*?' asked Chaloner, wondering how Maude was party to coffee-house chat. Such establishments were supposed to be exclusively for men, although he did not imagine many would have the courage to ask her to leave if she did decide to avail herself of one.

Maude pulled a disparaging face. 'All *The Newes* contained was a lot of rubbish about a dirty prayer-book

345

and the Turks being "up and down" in Vienna. And the Queen is recovered from distemper, but now she is said to have an indisposition, which is probably worse.'

'The note about Sherard Lorinston's bay mare was interesting, though,' said Temperance. 'Someone read his advertisement in the newsbooks, and saw the animal being sold in Limehouse. The good Samaritan has a reward, Lorinston has his mare back, and the thief has nothing. I shall ask him about it when he comes tonight.'

'Ask the thief?' queried Chaloner.

Temperance pulled a face at him. 'Ask Lorinston. We do not entertain criminals here, Thomas. It is a *gentlemen's* club, and we are very selective about our members.'

'I thought the Duke of Buckingham was among your clientele. You cannot be that selective.'

'Now, now,' tutted Maude. 'There is no need to malign the duke; he cannot help being a rake.' She changed the subject in the interests of avoiding a spat, because Temperance was looking irritated. 'When I was coming back from buying eggs just now, I heard that Smegergill's will was read in the Inner Temple this morning.'

'Before eight o'clock?' asked Chaloner. 'At such an ungodly hour?'

'You are sharp today,' said Temperance coolly. 'Besides, wills are read by lawyers, who love ungodly things. Did you once say you studied law at Cambridge, Thomas, and that you were at Lincoln's Inn with a view to becoming a clerk before Thurloe recruited you to an even more devious occupation?'

'Greeting is the sole beneficiary,' said Maude before Chaloner could reply. 'He is said to be astounded, although Smegergill had no family, so obviously he was going to favour a friend.'

346

Chaloner thought about the ring and the key he had taken from the old man, and supposed he could now pass them to their rightful owner. It would be good to be rid of the responsibility, although he hoped he would be able to do it without being accused of murder.

'Greeting told me Smegergill kept visiting the costermongery in Smithfield after Maylord died,' said Temperance. 'But Greeting is an odd fellow, and I never know when he is telling the truth. I do not suppose *he* studied law, did he, Thomas?'

Chaloner held his hands in the air. 'I surrender! I am sorry if I offended you. Can we call a truce before one of us says something he will later regret?'

'I enquired about Mary Cade for you,' said Maude, when Temperance inclined her head stiffly but said nothing. 'Her real name is Annabel Reade, and she is well known around Smithfield.'

'I thought you decided against asking questions when you learned she might be associated with Crisp,' said Chaloner.

'I just mentioned Mary in passing, and my sister started to talk. There is no harm in listening, is there? Anyway, Annabel Reade went to work for a man called Bridges, but there was a disagreement over silverware. Word is that her beau, Jonas Kirby, went to visit Bridges, and Bridges withdrew the charges the very next day. She had actually been sentenced to hang, so it was not just a case of Bridges saying he was mistaken, either. I heard a *lot* of his money went into buying that reprieve.'

'Kirby is Mary's lover?' asked Chaloner, supposing it explained why he visited her while Leybourn was otherwise engaged, and why he had been the one to steal the money sack.

'So it would seem,' said Temperance. 'However I made a few enquiries, too, and the boy who delivers our flour told me her real name is Annie Petwer, and she was *Newburne's* whore.'

Chaloner gazed at her, thoughts reeling. 'Annie Petwer and Mary Cade are one and the same?'

Temperance nodded. 'Her description of Newburne's performances in the bedchamber gave rise to some vulgar expression about his manhood, apparently.'

She shot Chaloner a challenging glance, apparently to see if she had shocked him. He did not react, so she and Maude began a debate on which of the three names was the original. Chaloner half-listened, thinking about the implications of Mary's association with the man whose murder he had been charged to solve. Did that mean the Hectors were responsible for the deadly lozenges? How had Mary managed being Newburne's mistress as well as Leybourn's 'wife' and Kirby's beau? Then it occurred to him that Leybourn was busy with his shop and his writing, so she probably had a lot of time on her hands. No wonder she was determined to keep him. Not only did he provide her with a comfortable home and forgive her laziness regarding household chores, but his own unique lifestyle gave her the freedom to do whatever she liked, too.

Temperance smiled thinly as he stood to leave. 'Are you sure you would not like a dish of coffee or a pipe before you go? How about some pickled rhubarb? That is said to soothe sharp tempers.'

Chaloner left feeling less than manly, a sensation that was becoming stronger and more frequent as Temperance's real personality began to flower. He could not drink her coffee, tobacco was an expensive habit he could not afford

348

to acquire, and he was squeamish about her political opinions. Perhaps she knew she unsettled him, and did it on purpose, to amuse herself. He had seen more of the world than she ever would, and had met people with far more radical views than the ones she propounded, but she was his gentle Temperance, and the change in her was disconcerting. He wondered how long it would be before they no longer had anything in common, and their friendship began to flounder.

Maude's information about Annie Petwer was the first real clue he had had about Newburne for some time, so Chaloner decided a visit to Leybourn was in order, but when he emerged from Hercules' Pillars Alley, everyone appeared to be heading for the river. He listened to snippets of conversation as people passed, and learned that the tide was still rising, and they were hurrying to see if it would breach its banks. He joined the throng moving towards Temple Stairs – he did not want to be the only person in London walking in a different direction.

When he reached the river, he thought there were far too many folk standing on the wooden platform that formed the Temple Stairs; water was lapping across its slick surface, and there was a very real danger of someone being swept off. He stayed well back, looking away when a cow floated past, lowing its distress. A boatman set out after it, determined to have the prize, and the crowd watched in stunned silence when the bobbing craft capsized the moment it approached the struggling animal. The boat was swept on, but there was no sign of its owner.

Then Chaloner saw a familiar face. Leybourn bought the paper he used for writing his books from a stationer at Temple Stairs, and often visited the area; he had a ream of it under his arm. Chaloner went to stand next to him, looking around for Mary. He could not see her, and supposed Leybourn must have made the journey alone. He wondered what sort of gathering was taking place in the surveyor's house when he was out, and was tempted to run to Monkwell Street to find out.

'Hello, Tom. This is a grim business. Did you see that poor fellow? Drowned, just like that.'

'White Hall is preparing for the worst, too – bakers are ferrying cakes to the Banqueting House.'

Leybourn stifled a gulp of laughter. 'Do not make jokes at such a time; it is not seemly. Thames Street is suffering. Hodgkinson told me he has had to suspend all his paper from the ceiling beams. He cannot take it else-where, because the streets are so foul with mud that carts cannot get through.'

'This weather cannot last much longer.'

'It will if the prophets of doom are right, and God is producing another Flood to relieve the world of wicked-ness.' Leybourn's voice became pained. 'And London *is* wicked – I was burgled last night.'

'Were you?' asked Chaloner, experiencing a sharp pang of guilt when he saw the distress on his friend's face. He had been going to tell Leybourn what he knew about the missing silver goblets, but saw it would not be a good time.

'My money sack is gone.' Leybourn glanced behind him. 'Mary says you took it.'

'Why would she think that?' Chaloner's indignation was genuine, given the circumstances.

'Because the thief knew exactly where to look, and she thinks you are the only one who knows where I keep

350

it. I dare not mention that Temperance knows, too, lest Mary takes against her as well. She says you are jealous of my new-found happiness.'

'I am not jealous of what you have with Mary,' said Chaloner ambiguously.

Leybourn was too lost in his own misery to pick up subtle nuances. 'She detests Thurloe, too, although I cannot imagine why. He has never been anything but courteous to her, although perhaps a little cold. Her disapproval of you I understand – you can be downright rude. She says I should no longer have anything to do with either of you.'

'She is still with you, then?' asked Chaloner, disappointed she had not packed her bags the moment she learned Kirby's mission had failed.

Leybourn gaped at him. 'What a vile thing to say! Of course she is still with me! Do you think she only wants me for my money? She loves *me*, not my wealth.'

'He is right,' said Mary. Her voice close behind Leybourn made the surveyor jump, although Chaloner had seen her coming. 'The theft of this sack means nothing, and I shall stay with him for as long as I choose . . . I mean as long as he will have me.'

'I will have you for ever,' vowed Leybourn passionately. 'And I will marry you—'

'Yes, we do not doubt each other,' interrupted Mary, patting his cheek in a way Chaloner thought patronising. She turned to the spy, and her expression changed from condescention to naked hostility. 'But the same cannot be said for you. William trusts you, but I have reservations, so I shall give you a chance to prove yourself to him. He was saving up to buy a Gunter's Quadrant and there is such an instrument in a shop in Moorfield. Will you get it for him?'

351

'I do not have that sort of money,' said Chaloner, surprised she should think he did. Or perhaps she thought he should use Leybourn's hoard for the purpose.

'It would be a wonderful thing to own,' said Leybourn wistfully. 'I *almost* had enough before . . .'

'If he had one, he would be able to survey St James's Park, and earn himself a fortune,' interrupted Mary. 'He has already been offered the commission, but he cannot accept without owning the necessary implements. I repeat: will you get it for him?'

'You mean *steal* it?' asked Chaloner, finally understanding what she was telling him to do.

'I mean *borrow* it,' corrected Mary slyly. 'You will do it if you are his friend.'

'But if he is seen using this quadrant, it will be obvious where it came from,' Chaloner pointed out, aware of Leybourn looking uncomfortable – although not uncomfortable enough to tell her to stop. 'People will assume he stole it.'

Mary gave one of her nasty smiles. 'Then you will have to step forward and take the blame. But I doubt you need worry. William tells me you are adept at worming your way out of difficult situations, and that you have practical experience of thievery. Incidentally, where were you last night?'

Chaloner answered with an observation of his own. 'I understand your friend Kirby was lurking in the area at the time when Will was burgled. Ask him the identity of the culprit. Or should we see what Annie Petwer or Annabel Reade have to say?'

'Tom,' said Leybourn sharply. 'I do not like your tone.'

'You have been asking questions about me?' asked Mary, not sounding as alarmed or shocked as Chaloner thought she should have done. 'That is ungentlemanly. But do not hope to drive a wedge between me and William over my past, because he already knows about the false charges laid at my door by that horrible Richard Bridges.'

'Does he know you were Tom Newburne's lover, too?'

'Tom!' cried Leybourn, appalled. 'Enough! That is my wife you insult.'

'I did know Newburne,' said Mary coldly. 'But I most certainly was not his lover, and if you claim otherwise, I will make you very sorry.'

Chaloner left Temple Stairs with a sense that he had underestimated Mary, and that she was winning the battle for Leybourn. He also did not like the challenge she had laid at his feet regarding the quadrant. Obviously, her intention was that he should be caught committing a crime. Was she hoping Leybourn would be implicated, too, and that when they were both hanged for theft, she would be left with house, shop and what remained of his money? But that would not happen, because Leybourn's brother would inherit – Chaloner had witnessed the will himself. He supposed she must have some other plan in mind, and knew he should learn what it was before it swung into action.

And what should he think about her denial that she had been Newburne's lover? He had accepted Temperance's story without question, because it made sense in the light of the other things he knew about Mary Cade, Annie Petwer and Annabel Reade. But could Temperance have been wrong? She listened to gossip, and it would not be the first time she had repeated a tale that had no basis in fact.

353

He put Mary from his mind – with difficulty – and walked to Old Jewry, intending to do two things: ask Dorcus Newburne if her husband had kept a mistress, and locate the solicitor's mythical hoard. As he walked, he tried to stay in the lee of the wind that swept in from the river. It was verging on a gale, and rattled loose tiles on the housetops. Birds struggled against the confused air currents, trees roared and swayed, and dead brown leaves swirled in fierce little eddies.

He reached Old Jewry eventually, and knocked on the door to Newburne's house. A servant showed him into a pleasant chamber at the front. He had not been waiting many moments before the door opened, and Dorcus swept in. She wore black, to indicate mourning, but the cloth was of the finest quality, and she looked elegant and prosperous. She had recovered from the funeral's ordeal, and her face was no longer pale; she did not look happy, but neither was she prostrate with grief.

'Have you come to bring me news about my pension?'

'Only to say that the matter has gone to the relevant committee for discussion,' he lied. It would explain the delay, and he could hardly tell her the truth if he wanted her cooperation.

She sighed. 'Good. It was promised to me, and I intend to make the government keep its word.'

'Do you need it urgently, ma'am? Shall I ask the Earl to expedite the matter?'

She smiled faintly. 'It is kind of you to offer, but I do not need the money at all, because my husband was very rich. In fact, I intend to donate it all to St Olave's Church when it comes.'

Chaloner was puzzled. 'If you intend to give it away, why petition for it with such fervour?'

'It is a matter of principle. My husband was your master's eyes and ears for years, and most recently in the newsbook business. Williamson would have killed him if he had found out, but the Earl promised to protect him. Then my husband died, allegedly of cucumbers, but we all know it was poison.'

'You think Williamson murdered your husband?' It was possible; the Spymaster was ruthless.

She nodded slowly. 'He might have done, although there were others who disliked Thomas, too. But that is not the point. The real issue is that your Earl vowed to look after him, and he failed. I want the government to pay for its broken promise, and this is the only way I can think of to do it. I want to hit the Earl where it most hurts – in the coffers.'

It was certainly having the desired effect, thought Chaloner: the Earl hated the notion of being out of pocket. 'Your husband's funeral was well attended. I do not suppose Annie Petwer was—'

Dorcus's eyes narrowed. 'I suppose someone told you "Arise, Tom Newburne" was to do with a mistress, but I explained how that expression came about – his antics with a wooden sword.'

'You seem very sure.'

'I am sure. Thomas had a pox ten years ago, and it left him with no interest in women. Hence it is impossible that he could have had a lover. And his rising from the dead was another silly tale, too.'

'Hodgkinson says otherwise, and he was there.'

'Hodgkinson is an impressionable fool. No stone flung up by a passing carriage can carry enough force to kill a man – and why should some trollop suddenly be possessed of an ability to resurrect? I met Annie Petwer

355

once; she loves money, and if she thought for an instant that she had saved Thomas, she would have demanded a massive reward. She never did. Hodgkinson is being fanciful.'

'Why would he fabricate such a story?'

She smiled. 'Well, it did make him a popular raconteur in the coffee houses for a few weeks. I imagine he has told the tale so many times that he now believes it.'

Chaloner supposed Mary had been telling the truth when she denied being Newburne's mistress. The alleged association was pure fabrication, although Chaloner suspected Mary Cade had had her reasons for calling herself Annie Petwer when the incident was supposed to have taken place. And he was sure they would not be innocent ones. 'When we last met, I asked whether you knew a Court musician called Thomas Maylord. You said you did not, but—'

'But you were actually talking about *Tom Mallard*,' she interrupted. 'I realised afterwards that I had misled you, although it was not intentional. It was just the way you said his name, and I was upset anyway, so not thinking clearly. Yes, my husband knew Mallard.'

Chaloner was annoyed with himself. He knew perfectly well that the musician had used a variety of spellings and pronunciations for his name, depending on the occasion. Many entertainers did, as a device to appeal to different kinds of audiences. 'In what capacity?'

'I suppose it does not matter if I tell you now, but he was secretly learning the flageolet. He wanted to surprise me with a tune on my birthday. Mallard was teaching him.'

'How did he come to choose Maylord as a tutor?' Chaloner was uncertain about her claim, because everyone else had said the decent Maylord would have had nothing to do with Newburne.

'He was the best, and my husband was determined to learn. Mallard refused at first, but Thomas could be very persuasive. He yielded in the end.'

So, thought Chaloner, perhaps whatever had driven Maylord into his frenzy of agitation was something heard or seen during one of these lessons. After all, Newburne had worked for three – and possibly more – very dubious masters. Any one of them might have embroiled the solicitor in business that Maylord would have found shocking.

'This is a fine house,' he said, moving on to his next quest: learning the way to Newburne's hidden jewels. 'And you have a pretty garden, too. Is that a sage bush?'

She beamed at him. 'I have worked hard to make this a decent home. Would you like to see it?'

When he accepted, he was shown every room from attic to basement. It was indeed a pleasant dwelling. Dorcus stood at the top of the stairs while he descended the cellar steps, and his eyes immediately lit on a patch on the beaten-earth floor that had been recently disturbed. Bulteel was right!

Chaloner took his leave, then doubled back to the garden. Now familiar with not only the house, but its servants and routines, he let himself in through the pantry door and made for the basement again. It was dark, but the light from the single barred window was enough to see by. He scratched away the soil with his dagger until he reached a layer of sacking. Wrapped within it was a box. The box was small, no larger than a pocket prayer-book, and was ornately designed. It was secured by a pair of locks that were far too large for it. Chaloner

357

stared at them for a moment, then, on a whim, inserted the keys he had taken from Maylord and Smegergill. They fitted perfectly, and he pushed back the lid to find the little container brimming to the top with precious stones. Newburne had indeed hidden himself a fortune.

Chapter 10

Chaloner gazed at the jewels, amazed that both finding the box and opening it had been so easy. But now what? Should he take it with him? It would be easy enough to steal, hidden in a pocket, but the problem was that he did not have anywhere secure to keep it. His rooms were no good, and he was loath to burden Thurloe with a second hoard to mind. However, he suspected it would be safe in Newburne's cellar – the solicitor had been dead for almost two weeks and Chaloner could tell by the state of the hole that no one else had been to inspect it. Then he could collect it later, when it could be taken straight to the Earl.

His mind made up, he replaced box and dirt, stamping down firmly when the hole was filled. For good measure, he dragged a barrel across it, too, to conceal evidence of disturbance. He even took cobwebs from the ceiling and draped them over the cask, and only left when he was sure no visible sign of his visit remained. He was just making his escape through the garden when he heard voices.

The back gate opened, and two people entered. One

was Dorcus, and the other was L'Estrange. Chaloner was just wondering why the editor should be with her when L'Estrange's hand slipped around her waist in a way that made her giggle.

'All right,' the spy murmured to himself. 'That answers *that* question.'

He was about to duck back inside the house and hide until he could leave without being seen when a servant came to the rear door. With weary resignation, he saw he was trapped. So he knelt next to the sage bush, and did not have to try very hard to feign awkward embarrassment when Dorcus and L'Estrange approached him.

'You have caught me red-handed,' he said with a feeble grin. 'I realised after I had gone that my wife would be furious if I did not take her a cutting of your splendid sage. I knocked at your front door, but there was no reply.'

'You did not tell me you were married,' said L'Estrange, earrings and teeth flashing as he grinned. 'What is the lucky lady's name and where do you live?'

'I am often complimented on my sage,' said Dorcus before Chaloner could reply. 'Please pick some, and tell your wife it is best with pork.'

Chaloner tried to look as though he knew what he was doing as he gathered several handfuls. While he did so, he noticed the maid was smiling prettily at L'Estrange, who was leering back at her.

'Take an onion, too,' suggested Dorcus. She grabbed one that had been overlooked when the rest of the crop had been harvested, and lobbed it. Her throw went suspiciously wide of Chaloner, and struck the servant in the middle of her white apron. The maid squealed her dismay at the mess.

360

'I brought the galingale you needed, Sybilla,' said Dorcus, brandishing a package rather menacingly. 'For the pie you are supposed to be making.'

'Thank you.' Sybilla turned to simper at L'Estrange. 'Will there be company for dinner?'

'There might,' said L'Estrange, waggling his eyebrows at her. 'It depends what is on offer.'

'Beef pie with galingale,' replied Dorcus. 'We thought we had plenty, but the rats had been at it.'

'Rats are all over the place these days,' said Chaloner, thinking L'Estrange's behaviour made him a particularly predatory one. 'It must be the weather.'

'It must,' agreed Dorcus. 'Especially now the river is on the rise. I met Roger at the market, and he escorted me home because the Walbrook has burst its culverts and water is gushing everywhere.'

'Phanatiques have opened secret floodgates,' explained L'Estrange, eliciting small squeals of alarm from both women. 'They are trying to drown us in our beds.'

'Most of us will not be in our beds at this late hour,' said Chaloner, suspecting the same could not be said of L'Estrange and his ladies. 'So this devilish plot to take the city by water is doomed to failure.'

'Here is your onion,' said Sybilla, tossing it to him. She turned to L'Estrange. 'Do come in, sir.'

L'Estrange entered the house like a king, the two women fussing behind him. Chaloner stuffed the onion and sage into his pocket, and supposed he was fortunate that Dorcus had been so credulous about his admiration for her herbs – and that L'Estrange had been more interested in recruiting Angels for his Army than in the curious behaviour of the Lord Chancellor's spy.

As he walked down the path, Chaloner thought about

361

the keys that had fitted the jewel box. Had Maylord and Smegergill stolen them from Newburne? Had that been the cause of Maylord's agitation? Obviously, it had not been Newburne himself that had worried the musician, because Maylord had written his urgent note on Friday night, and Newburne had been dead for two days by then. An unpleasant sinking feeling gripped Chaloner as he considered the possibility that Maylord had poisoned the solicitor.

He reached the back gate and stepped outside. And tripped over Giles Dury, who was kneeling with his eye glued to a crack in the wood.

'Damn it all!' cried the newsman as he went sprawling into the mud. 'What are you doing here?'

'Leaving,' replied Chaloner dryly. 'And you?'

'Following L'Estrange,' snapped Dury, trying to brush himself down. 'It is Saturday.'

'I see. You always follow L'Estrange on Saturdays, do you?'

'Of course. It is the day he collects the parliamentary summaries for his Monday newsbook. He always indulges in a dalliance on his way home, and . . .' He trailed off, angry at himself.

'And you take the opportunity to examine his papers while his attention is on his conquests,' finished Chaloner in understanding. '*That* is why the news-letters so often pre-empt the newsbooks! I thought someone was selling you his reports, but you just steal them for yourselves.'

'We do not steal,' objected Dury. 'We just read what happens to be left lying around. He usually goes to a brothel, which makes life simple, although his selection of Dorcus presents more of a challenge. And not all our news comes from the parliamentary summaries, anyway. Just some of it.'

'Your spy gives you the rest,' said Chaloner. 'Wenum.'

'Wenum,' echoed Dury with a sigh. 'I believed the rumour that said he fell in the Thames, but now Muddiman tells me he was probably Newburne in disguise. I never met Wenum, so had no reason to know – it was Muddiman who went to buy news from him, not me. Muddiman said the man was always careful to stick to the shadows, and now we know why: he did not want to be recognised.'

'By buying secrets from Newburne, and by reading the confidential summaries issued to L'Estrange, you have been undermining the government's newsbooks. I suspect that is treason.'

Dury started to draw his sword, but stopped when he saw Chaloner held a dagger and was ready to throw it. He sneered. 'What are you going to do? Take me to the Tower? I will scream if you try.'

Chaloner was thoughtful. Technically, he should escort Dury to the nearest prison, but he had no desire to deliver anyone into Spymaster Williamson's vengeful hands, and he was still uncertain about the shifting allegiances of the newsmen and their masters. He decided that arresting Dury was not the best course of action. At least, not yet.

'If I say nothing to Williamson about this, will you answer some questions?'

Dury was immediately wary. 'How do I know I can trust you?'

'You don't, but you are hardly in a position to negotiate. You can take my offer or you can go to the Tower. It is your choice, but you will reveal the information either way.'

Dury shrugged, feigning nonchalance but failing miserably. He was beginning to be frightened. 'What do you want to know?'

'Why have you been following me? I saw you in the Golden Lion.'

'That is easy.' Dury sounded relieved. 'Muddiman wanted me to make you an offer: five pounds plus a year's free newsletters if you feed bad intelligence to L'Estrange. We want him discredited and Muddiman reinstated. Will you do it?'

Chaloner laughed at the notion. 'No! Williamson would kill me for certain.'

'Do not be so sure. He is married, and L'Estrange has taken to visiting his home when he is out at work. I do not understand what women see in L'Estrange, personally. It must be the earrings.'

Chaloner wondered if he should buy Leybourn a pair. 'Have you seen him with Joanna Brome?' he asked, more from idle curiosity than a genuine need to know.

'I do not envy her position! If she yields, she betrays her husband, whom she loves. If she resists, L'Estrange might destroy her shop. As far as I know, she has managed to evade the choice so far by giving L'Estrange just enough encouragement to keep him keen, but not capitulating completely.'

'I saw you meet Ireton at the Rainbow Coffee House yesterday. Why?'

Dury shrugged again. 'Why do you think? To acquire information. A newsman is not particular about his sources, and Ireton offered to sell me a tale about the murder of a Court musician called Smegergill. I thought he might have some original intelligence, but I was wrong. All he wanted was to declare the Hectors innocent.

Unfortunately for him, our readers will be outraged if I write nice things about criminals, so I can use nothing of what he told me.'

It made sense, so Chaloner moved to another question. 'Why did you and Muddiman search Finch's room? I saw you there, so do not tell me you did not.'

Dury sighed resentfully. 'You certainly want your pound of flesh! You had better not betray me after all this. Williamson is not the only one who knows how to hire Hectors. I shall pay a few to visit you if you breathe one word of our discussion to anyone.'

'Just answer the question.'

Dury regarded him with dislike. 'We followed Hickes there – we saw him receive a note as he stood outside our house, and we thought it would be fun to see where he went. We watched him chase a thief, and laughed ourselves silly when he fell off the roof.'

'What did you find in Finch's room?' Perhaps Dury had removed the deadly lozenges.

'We had a quick look around in an attempt to understand why Hickes had been sent there so urgently, but there was nothing obvious. The first thief must have grabbed any pertinent evidence. So, although we had high hopes of a decent scandal – preferably one involving the government – we were disappointed. We already knew Finch was dead, so it was not as if we discovered the body.'

'How did you know Finch was dead?'

'Muddiman heard it in Robin's Coffee House, which is not far from Finch's home. He often frequents Robin's, because it is also close to Brome's shop, and so allows him to spy on L'Estrange. Do not look disapproving, Heyden – L'Estrange does it to us. Now, is there anything else, or am I free to go about my business?'

'You mean the business of reading L'Estrange's reports while he frolics with Dorcus?'

'And the maid. If you look the other way, I will make it worth your while. We need this intelligence, and it is too late to tap into other sources this week. Your interference will cost us dear.'

'Pity,' said Chaloner unsympathetically.

It was a gloomy crowd that braved the storm and circled the gaping pit in the graveyard for Maylord's funeral. Greeting came to stand next to Chaloner, both blinking rain from their eyes.

'I am soaked through,' grumbled Greeting when the dismal ceremony was over. 'Come to the Rhenish Wine House with me. I shall buy some cheap wine and we can drink to Maylord. You owe me for saving you last night, and I would not mind picking your brains about Smegergill in return. Williamson summoned me this morning, and was livid when I told him I had no luck in tracking down the killer. He ordered me to try again, so I need all the help I can get.'

It was not the most enticing of offers, but Chaloner accepted, thinking it would be a good opportunity to pass Smegergill's ring to its rightful owner, and thus be rid of the responsibility. They entered the fuggy warmth of the hostelry, clothes dripping. Landlord Genew was drying his bald pate with a cloth, and informed them that he would not have left his tavern for anyone other than dear old Maylord on such a foul day. He ushered them to a table near the fire, and brought a jug of spiced wine. Chaloner would have preferred something to eat, but Greeting was more interested in liquid refreshment, and he was paying. The musician drank one cup in a

366

single swallow, then poured himself another, listening intently while Chaloner related some of what he knew about Smegergill's death. He did not tell Greeting everything. No spy was ever that honest with a man who might later transpire to be an enemy – especially one who was working for Williamson.

'Were you aware that Maylord knew Newburne?' Chaloner asked, watching Greeting down his second cup and reach for the third. 'And both died of cucumbers?'

Greeting nodded. 'I recently heard from my colleague Hingston that Maylord was secretly teaching Newburne the flageolet, although it was like tutoring a goat, apparently. And then of course there is the Smithfield connection – something I uncovered just this morning, because Smegergill was Maylord's sole beneficiary, but I am Smegergill's, much to my astonishment.'

'What Smithfield connection?' Greeting did not look astonished, and Chaloner was not about to forget that the devious musician had been in desperate need of money, and now he had inherited a fortune. Was it really a coincidence? And there was another thing: surely, it was odd for Williamson to order Smegergill's heir to explore the circumstances of Smegergill's death? Or was the Spymaster unaware of the connection between the two men?

'Maylord owned a shop there. I vaguely recall him telling me that he had bought one from a distant cousin a few years ago, but he could not be bothered with it, so Newburne managed it for him. Apparently, it earned a respectable income, but Maylord recently became aware that Newburne had been less than honest with him.'

Chaloner's thoughts whirled while Greeting drank more

367

wine. Smegergill had said Maylord thought he was being cheated, and learning that Newburne was the culprit came as no surprise. The spy considered the likely outcome of Maylord's suspicions. He would have tackled the solicitor about the discrepancies, but Newburne would naturally have denied the accusations, so Maylord would have needed proof. He had begun to pry. His Thames Street house was near one of Newburne's properties, and perhaps it was there that the secret music lessons had taken place. But then what? Had Maylord uncovered more than he had bargained for, and had that knowledge driven him to write the agitated note to Chaloner? Or had he laid hold of the keys to Newburne's jewel box as an act of petty revenge, and then realised he had bitten off more than he could chew?

And what did Smegergill know about the affair? When Chaloner had asked, Smegergill said that Maylord had refused to confide on the grounds of ensuring his friend's safety. Was it true? There were a number of reasons why Chaloner now thought it was not. First, Smegergill had been in possession of a key to Newburne's box, and although it was possible he did not know what it was, Chaloner thought it unlikely – it would not have been on his person if he had considered it unimportant. Second, Smegergill knew some Hectors, and Chaloner was beginning to believe Ireton's contention that he and his cronies had not killed the man. Did that mean Smegergill and the felons were in league somehow? And finally, Chaloner had not forgotten Thurloe's instinctive distrust of the man. Smegergill was an enigma. Some people found him 'difficult', some thought he was losing his mind, and others considered him harmless. They could not all be right, so which was the real man?

'What do *you* know about Smegergill?' he asked, watching Greeting finish the wine in the jug.

'I have learned that he was actually French, although you would not know it to speak to him. He worked in Paris for years, but came here about a decade ago. He was musician to Cromwell, but that dubious connection was overlooked in view of his talent – along with the fact that he composed a rather nice Birthday Ode for the Duke of Buckingham.'

'Was he in England before the wars?'

Greeting shook his head. 'He arrived long after that. Why?'

'He said he knew me as a child. He remembered a particular tree on my father's estate.'

'Then he was mistaken – he could be confused on occasion.'

But Chaloner was becoming increasingly convinced that Smegergill was not as confused as he had let people think. He thought about the discussion in which Smegergill had claimed he was a friend of Chaloner's family. On reflection, it contained inconsistencies. One example was Smegergill saying that all Chaloner's siblings were talented musicians, which was untrue: his sisters were skilled, but his brothers were adequate at best. Then there was the May-day celebration under the oak on the Chaloner estate. *Maylord* had loved the occasion, and had probably told Smegergill about it. And then, Chaloner realised with a flash of understanding, Smegergill had passed off the memories as his own.

But why? The answer was chillingly clear. Maylord must have confided to Smegergill that he had written to Chaloner – an intelligence officer – about his troubles. But Smegergill had inherited those troubles, along with his friend's goods, and he had no one to help *him*. And then along came Chaloner, eager to learn the truth behind Maylord's death. The spy ran through more of the conversation in his head: Smegergill's forgetfulness and eccentricity had occurred later, *after* he had established that Chaloner was willing to help him.

So, what had Smegergill hoped they might learn together? Could it have been the location of the documents he had mentioned? Chaloner stared into his cup. Of course it was! Maylord had hidden them well enough to fool amateurs, and Smegergill knew the services of a professional spy were needed to locate them. Of course, Maylord had hidden them too well for professional spies, too, and all Chaloner had been able to unearth was music.

'Poor old Maylord,' Greeting was saying. 'Smegergill arranged for him to come here, you know. He suddenly became frightened in Thames Street, so Smegergill spoke to Genew on his behalf. Smegergill and I were the only ones who knew about Maylord's abrupt relocation.'

Chaloner stared at him. 'Smegergill told me he did not know where Maylord had moved.'

'Perhaps he forgot, although I confess I did not think his absent-mindedness had reached those sorts of levels. He must have decided he did not want to tell you for some reason.'

Chaloner nodded, while more solutions snapped clear in his mind. Smegergill's purse had been empty, so how had he intended to pay for the coach to the Rhenish Wine House? The answer was that he knew his Hector friends would be willing to give him a ride. And what would have happened after Chaloner had located the documents? The spy doubted Smegergill would have been willing to share. So what had gone wrong in St Bartholomew's churchyard, and why had Smegergill died? Chaloner already knew Greeting was the real target, and Ireton must have realised the mistake as soon as he recognised a man he knew. Smegergill had not called for help, which suggested he had not been overly alarmed at the time.

Unsettled by his conclusions, Chaloner handed over Smegergill's ring; the keys he decided to keep. 'This belonged to Smegergill, so it is now legally yours.'

'I thought the murderer had stolen that from his body.' Greeting regarded him warily.

'If I were the culprit, do you think I would give you evidence of my guilt in a crowded tavern? I have already admitted that I was with him when he died, and now I am telling you that I took his ring, too. I was not thinking clearly at the time, but I swear I never intended to keep it.'

'Then I shall give you the benefit of the doubt,' said Greeting, although there was uncertainty in his voice. 'My fortunes are on the rise today. I may even be able to buy my way clear of Williamson.'

Chaloner doubted it: Spymasters did not relinquish hold over their victims that easily.

Greeting stared at the ring. 'This was actually Maylord's, but Smegergill took to wearing it after he died. You think Smegergill was losing his wits, but Maylord was the one *really* worried about it. Look.' He prised up the stone, revealing a space inside. A tiny scroll of paper dropped out.

Chaloner caught it as it rolled to the edge of the table. 'What is it?'

371

Greeting smiled sadly. 'It is common knowledge that the keepers of Bedlam will not take you if you know the answers to two questions: your date of birth and the names of your parents. Maylord often told me he was anticipating a visit from the Bedlam men, and once confided that he kept the answers to both questions inside his ring, just in case the wardens arrived and his memory failed him.'

Chaloner wrestled with the minute scrap of paper, thinking it would not have helped Maylord, because it would have taken him too long to unfurl; the Bedlam men would have had him anyway. 'Smegergill was a shade mad, though,' he said as he struggled. 'He went around telling people he was Caesar.'

Greeting laughed. 'But he *was* Caesar. As a child, he was adopted by a dean called Caesar, and he often used the name for his compositions. I know it does not sound very likely, but it is perfectly true. Personally, I suspect he was as sane as you and me, and probably a good deal more clever.'

Chaloner had an uncomfortable feeling that Greeting was right, and that he had been a fool to let the old man deceive him so completely. He turned his attention to the paper, which comprised not a reminder of sires and birthdays, but a fragment of music – a scale with letters written underneath. He gazed at it with sorrow, assuming Maylord had been afraid he would forget those, too. Yet when he looked more closely, he saw the letters did not correspond with the names of the notes – for example, C-sharp had the letter T under it, while E-flat had a W.

'This is not answers for the Bedlam men.'

Greeting took it from him, regarded it with disinterest, then tossed it on the fire before Chaloner could stop him.

'Poor Maylord! It looks as though he really was losing his mind.'

Chaloner left the Rhenish Wine House and went home for dry clothes, selecting some of the better ones from the pile Maude had delivered. The cat was among them, having clawed them into a nest of its own design, and it was not pleased when it was ousted. It had deposited another rat by the hearth, which went to join the growing pile on the mantelpiece. Chaloner put the onion and sage next to them, and was reminded of his landlord's recipe for rat stew. He sincerely hoped it would not be necessary.

Wearing an old-fashioned cloak that was far better at repelling rain than any coat, he left for Monkwell Street. The altercation with Leybourn was preying on his mind, and he wanted to apologise to him for accusing Mary of being Newburne's whore. The streets were awash, and he abandoned any attempt to keep his feet dry; to do otherwise necessitated the kind of acrobatics for which he had no energy. The Fleet bridge at Ludgate was open again, although water lapped perilously close to the top of it, and a layer of odorous sludge along one side showed the level to which it had flooded the previous night.

He arrived at Monkwell Street, where Leybourn's brother told him the couple had gone to Smithfield. Chaloner was uneasy. Why would Mary take him there? Was she intending to have him murdered, then lay claim to his house on the grounds that they had been living as man and wife?

'I liked Mary at first, because she made Will happy,' said Rob Leybourn, as Chaloner prepared to go after them. 'But she has some very unpalatable friends.'

'Like Jonas Kirby?'

'He is among the better ones. She has invited Ellis Crisp for dinner tomorrow – the Butcher of Smithfield! I would assume she *wants* our business to fail by forcing Will to associate with villains, but then she only hurts herself. Did you know he lost all his money to burglars last night? Until he makes more there will be no funds for plays and soirées. She must be livid, and I would not want to be in the thief's shoes.'

'He is so bedazzled by her that he would probably go into debt rather than disappoint her.'

Rob sighed. 'Bewitched, more like. Still, he has not had a woman in years, so I suppose you cannot blame him for grabbing the one who hurls herself at him. I just wish it had not been her. Are you going to find him? Keep him busy, if you can – I plan to move his most valuable books to my house this afternoon. There are fewer than there should be, and I think she has been selling them off. I want the rest where she cannot get at them.'

When Chaloner reached Duck Lane, he saw a great gathering of people. To his consternation, their attention seemed to be focussed on Hodgkinson's print-shop. Crisp's henchmen were out in force, jostling people for amusement. No one had the courage to tell them to behave themselves.

'What happened?' he asked a disreputable-looking man with a patch over one eye.

'A death in the costermongery. Or maybe the print-shop. I cannot tell from here.'

'Someone else has died of cucumbers?' asked Chaloner uneasily.

But the man shrugged as he slunk away, grumbling

that there was nothing to be seen and that he was wasting his time.

Chaloner looked for someone else to question, and saw a number of familiar faces among the crowd. L'Estrange was grinning contentedly, and Chaloner supposed his good humour derived from the fact that he had enjoyed his morning with Dorcus. Joanna and Brome were with him, both looking thoroughly wet and miserable. Not far away, Leybourn was talking to the influential booksellers, Nott and Allestry. Mary kept tugging his arm to make him leave, but he had the animated expression on his face that said he was discussing mathematics, and all the tugging in the world would not budge him. Not far away, Muddiman was conversing with a pair of drovers, and Chaloner eased closer in an attempt to eavesdrop. What he learned made him smile, because it answered at least one mystery.

The rain came down harder still, driving some of the onlookers away. L'Estrange was among them. Chaloner watched him shoulder his way through the gathering, not caring who he shoved, and anyone who objected could expect to be called 'damned phanatique'. Unfortunately, Leybourn was in one of his feisty moods, and took exception to the remark. Chaloner hurried forward when L'Estrange's sword came out of its scabbard. Leybourn struggled to draw his own but, not for the first time, disuse and poor maintenance caused it to stick. Then it came free in a rush, almost depriving Nott of his peculiar hairbun.

'Come on, then,' the surveyor yelled, holding the weapon like an axe. Immediately, people began to form a circle around the combatants. 'Fight an honest bookseller, and let us see who God favours.'

There was a cheer from the onlookers, but L'Estrange responded by performing several fancy swishes that showed his superior training, and the applause faltered. Leybourn was about to be skewered. Chaloner looked around for Mary, expecting her to urge him to walk away from a confrontation he could not win, but she remained suspiciously silent.

'I shall defend myself in the event of an attack,' announced L'Estrange loftily, eyeing Leybourn with disdain when he attempted to duplicate the display and ended up dropping his blade. 'But I decline to debase myself by fooling about with amateurs. Is that your wife, Leybourn? She is a pretty lady.'

Leybourn was confused by the compliment. He bent to retrieve his weapon. 'Yes, she is.'

'Well, if she is made a widow out of this, you can trust me to comfort her in her sorrows,' said L'Estrange, winking at her. Mary smiled coquettishly.

'Tell him where to go, Mary,' ordered Leybourn icily. There was a pause. 'Mary?'

'Put your blade in his gizzard, Leybourn,' suggested Nott, jumping back when the surveyor made another of his undisciplined swings. 'God knows, he deserves it.'

'No,' said Chaloner, stepping forward to grab the surveyor's shoulder. 'Duelling is illegal.'

'Heyden is right,' said Brome, elbowing his way through the throng to join them. Joanna was at his heels, eyes wide with alarm. 'L'Estrange is an excellent swordsman, and you will certainly lose this encounter. Walk away while you are still in one piece.'

'You were insulted,' whispered Mary in Leybourn's other ear. 'Will you meekly accept it?'

Chaloner waited for Leybourn to realise she was

encouraging him to enjoin a brawl that would see him killed, but he seemed to have lost his senses as well as his heart. He shoved the spy behind him and held his rapier in a grip that would see him disarmed in the first riposte. Brome's expression was one of horror, but Joanna darted past him and punched L'Estrange in the chest.

'Leave him alone, you horrible man!' she cried. The editor regarded her in astonishment, which turned to rage when people began to laugh. Joanna's bravado began to dissolve. 'I am not saying you are horrible all the time, but you are horrible when you challenge weaker men . . . I mean, you are . . .'

Abruptly, she turned and fled, scuttling behind her husband. Several onlookers snickered, but Chaloner thought she had at least tried to conquer her fear and make a stand to help a friend, and he respected her for it.

'You are a phanatique, Leybourn,' declared L'Estrange, turning back to his prey. 'Why else would you be fined for the sale of unlicensed books?'

If L'Estrange had expected his observation to earn him the crowd's support, he had miscalculated badly. There were booksellers and printers among them, and their sympathies were clearly not with the Government's official censor. Leybourn found himself with growing support and, with alarm, Chaloner saw him draw strength from it.

'Run him through, Leybourn,' yelled Nott to accompanying cheers. 'Williamson will no doubt appoint another cur to do his bidding, but he cannot be as bad as this mongrel.'

'Please, Will,' said Chaloner quietly. 'Do not let them—'

'Ignore Heyden,' ordered Mary. 'He is a coward, afraid to fight for what is right. *You* are brave.'

Chaloner could easily have disarmed his friend, but he did not want to humiliate him by exposing his ineptitude. And he certainly did not want anyone thinking L'Estrange had won the encounter.

'Walk away, Will,' he urged. 'You cannot afford to let L'Estrange kill you. You have a wife to consider. What would Mary do without you?'

Mary's expression hardened. 'Actually, I would rather have a man who—'

'He is right, William,' called Joanna from behind Brome. 'Think of Mary, and put up your sword.'

Mary was furious when Leybourn's blade began to droop, but her rage was the cold kind, and she kept her temper admirably. 'Perhaps you should fight Heyden instead, sir,' she said prettily to L'Estrange. 'William is no phanatique, but Heyden is.'

L'Estrange moved his head in a way that made his earrings sparkle, while his teeth flashed in an appreciative leer as he looked her up and down; Chaloner thought he looked like the Devil. 'Heyden is a phanatique, is he? Would you care to tell me how you come by such information, dear lady?'

She smiled back, fluttering her eyelashes. 'He was in the New Model Army, fighting Royalists – such as yourself – during the civil wars. And more recently, he was spying in Spain and Portugal.'

L'Estrange regarded Chaloner appraisingly. 'I thought you had the look of a Roundhead about you. It is all to do with the boots. Was it you who made the Walbrook burst its banks?'

'He is *not* a phanatique,' shouted Joanna defiantly.

378

When L'Estrange whipped around to glare at her again, she managed to hold her ground, although her voice trembled as she spoke. 'And no one made the Walbrook flood. It is just something that happens when there is a lot of rain.'

'We should be about our work,' said Brome, boldly grabbing L'Estrange's arm in an attempt to pull him away. 'We have a lot to do, if Monday's *Intelligencer* is to be ready in time.'

'True,' agreed L'Estrange, sheathing his sword with a flourish. 'My time is too valuable to waste on skirmishing with old Roundheads. I can harm their cause much more deeply with my pen than a sword, anyway.'

Seeing the situation defused, Allestry tried to seize Leybourn's weapon, although Nott looked disappointed the fuss was over. When Chaloner saw Mrs Nott nearby, eyes fixed longingly on L'Estrange, he understood exactly why the bookseller had wanted a brawl. Predictably, Mary made no attempt to help Allestry; her attention was gripped by the smouldering invitations L'Estrange was sending with his eyes. Chaloner sincerely hoped Leybourn would not notice, or no one would be able to disarm him and there would be blood spilled for certain. He turned to find Joanna at his side.

'I see a solution,' she said. Her face was pale, and Chaloner suspected the set-to had taken a heavy toll on the timid rabbit. 'We shall arrange for L'Estrange to entice Mary away from William, and *that* is how we shall save him. I cannot think of a more deserving candidate for her affections. Can you?'

Chaloner had spotted Kirby, Treen and Ireton at the fringes of the dissipating crowd, and did not want a confrontation with them, especially in Smithfield, where they had access to reinforcements. He tried to take refuge in the costermongery, but it was still closed, and a notice on the door said it had suffered a flood, but would be back in business the following day. Inside, Yeo laboured furiously with a mop. Chaloner stepped into a butcher's shop instead, a bloody little emporium of glistening entrails, smelly meat and vats of grease. He was not alone for long, because Joanna and Brome followed him, having abandoned L'Estrange to the various Angels who clustered around him. Mrs Nott was among them.

'Why are you hiding?' asked Brome. 'L'Estrange will not fight you now, not while he has all those woman fussing over him.'

'Actually, I am hiding from Hectors. I have aggravated rather too many of them.'

Brome was appalled. 'That was rash! They are not just louts, you know – most are skilled fighters, and not all of them are stupid. And I hate to sound selfish, but we enjoyed your company the other day, and were hoping you might dine with us again.'

Joanna gazed at Chaloner with her huge brown eyes. 'I hope you have not done anything to annoy Crisp; his Hectors are one thing, but he is another entirely. I would not like you on the wrong side of the Butcher.' She shuddered involuntarily.

'I doubt I am important enough to attract his attention,' replied Chaloner.

'Do you think Crisp was responsible for attracting that crowd?' asked Brome of Joanna. 'I saw him when we first arrived, but now he is gone. Do you think he dispensed one of his "lessons"? Perhaps on a shopkeeper who declined to pay the safety tax?'

Joanna shuddered again. 'Lord! I knew we should have refused when L'Estrange suggested we come here to talk to Hodgkinson. I have never liked Smithfield, and it is a dreadful place now Crisp has accrued all that power. Perhaps we should all go home, before anything else nasty happens.'

'We had a crisis with the newsbooks,' Brome explained to Chaloner. 'The Thames Street print-house is knee-deep in water, so Hodgkinson cannot produce Monday's *Intelligencer* there. And this morning, blocked gutters flooded his Smithfield print-house, too. The situation was looking bleak, and we have all been sitting in St Bartholomew the Less, discussing solutions.'

'Fortunately, Hodgkinson's nephew has offered to print it instead, which is a relief,' said Joanna. 'We were just leaving, when L'Estrange saw the crowd and decided to investigate. He was hoping it might be a newsworthy incident, because we are short of material for the last page.'

They talked until Joanna said they should be getting back to the bookshop. Chaloner was sorry, because spending time in their company was infinitely more preferable to the other grim matters that beckoned to him that day. He waited until they had gone, then left the butcher's stall, pulling up his hood against the rain. Within moments, he realised that Brome and Joanna were being followed. It was by Muddiman, so he moved quickly to intercept the man.

The newsmonger did not seem at all concerned that he had just been caught doing something rather insalubrious. 'There is some sort of problem at the newsbook office,' he said breezily. 'So I have been spying on Brome in an attempt to find out what it is. Of course, we have a bit of a hiccup ourselves, thanks to you preventing Dury from reading those parliamentary summaries.'

'My apologies,' replied Chaloner. 'But it cannot be the first time your plans have been foiled. I do not imagine L'Estrange jumps into bed with someone else's wife every Saturday.'

'Well, you would be wrong, because he does. I suspect he will have Leybourn's before the day is out, too, despite the fact that he has already enjoyed Dorcus and her maid. He made a play for my wife once. He asked her to proofread the newsbooks, if you can credit his audacity. But he left disappointed, because she rejected his offer of work *and* his affections.'

So, Leybourn was not the only man to be blind in affairs of the heart, thought Chaloner. 'He does seem unstoppable where women are concerned. I overheard what you said to those drovers earlier, by the way. You have started a rumour that L'Estrange is responsible for the Walbrook flood.'

Muddiman's laugh was unpleasant. 'We shall see how he likes being regarded as a phanatique.'

'This is not the first time you have used your skill as a newsmonger – a gossip, in essence – to teach someone a lesson, is it?' said Chaloner, giving voice to the conclusions he had drawn before Leybourn's predicament had claimed his attention. 'You invented tales about Newburne, too.'

Muddiman laughed again, and clapped his hands. 'Extraordinary though it may seem, you are the first to guess that was me. Even Dury has not caught on. Arise, Tom Newburne! What *does* it mean? Does *anyone* know? Everyone thinks he does, but ask a dozen Londoners and they will all tell you different things. I amused myself by setting whispers and watching them ignite. Newburne was appalled, because it made him visible when he wanted anonymity. No defrauder wants to be famous.'

'You told me the phrase meant he was Catholic. Dury had a lewd interpretation. Hodgkinson thinks Newburne rose from the dead. Leybourn said it describes men who drink too much and miss church. L'Estrange claims it means a rapid rise to power. Bulteel believes it refers to promotion in the face of brazen dishonesty. The Earl of Clarendon uses it as a curse—'

'But my favourite is the one I told Newburne's wife – that business about knighting people with a wooden sword. He did nothing of the sort, of course.'

'You adapted the story to suit the recipient, playing on their superstitions, interests, fears and hopes. And you did it well, especially with Hodgkinson. The man actually witnessed Newburne's encounter with Annie Petwer, yet you managed to make him think he had seen something completely different.'

'Malleable minds. It is fun to shape them. Why do you think I became a newsmonger?'

'You said it was to make lots of money.'

Muddiman cackled. 'Well, there is that, too.'

'Hickes is following you,' said Chaloner, looking to where the hulking spy was making a bad job of pretending to inspect some sausages. 'So who is watching Dury?'

'I have no idea. We quarrelled today – because of you, in fact. I told him he should have taken firmer measures in Dorcus Newburne's garden, and he told me he is not that sort of fellow.'

'Firmer measures? You mean such as killing me?'

'It would have saved us a good deal of trouble, although we appreciate your Spanish reports. Why do you refuse to help bring down L'Estrange? Surely you must see his venture cannot run much longer? People are already complaining about the poor quality of his news, and I am offering you an opportunity to back the winning side.'

'I prefer not to work against the government when I can help it. Spymasters have a strange way of regarding such activities as treason.'

Muddiman smirked, an expression Chaloner found impossible to interpret. 'My newsletters are better written, more informative and more popular than the rubbish Williamson lets L'Estrange print. You are a fool to throw in your lot with them, when I can make you rich.'

Wealth would do no one any good if his head was on a pole outside Westminster Hall, Chaloner thought, as he watched the newsmonger slink away with Hickes on his heels. He turned his attention to Hodgkinson's print-shop, where the crowd had dwindled to a handful of crones. Like the costermongery next to it, water was trickling from under its door.

'It is still in there,' announced one old lady mysteriously, when he went to stand among them. 'People do not believe us, but we know what we saw.'

'A body,' elaborated another. 'We spotted its feet, but then Mr Hodgkinson came and hauled it inside, so no one else got to see it.'

'It will have to come out eventually, though,' said the first. 'And when it does, we will call everyone back. Folk will see we are no Bedlam-toms, seeing things that are not there. *We* are sane; it is the rest of the world that runs mad.'

Chaloner entered the shop. The floor was ankle-deep in water, and Hodgkinson, dirty, wet and agitated, was scooping it into buckets. Lying on a bench, covered with

384

a blanket, was indeed a body. Chaloner pulled the cover away, and was shocked to recognise Giles Dury.

'I have had a dreadful morning,' said Hodgkinson wearily, flopping into a chair and wiping his face with his inky fingers. He looked ready to cry. 'Both my print-shops are flooded, I had to arrange for *The Intelligencer* to be published by my nephew – and he is charging me a fortune for the privilege – and then Dury chooses my premises in which to die? I shall be ruined!'

'I imagine Dury is none too thrilled with the situation, either. What happened?'

'You can see the mess I am in, so when L'Estrange, Brome and Joanna came here to discuss the problem with tomorrow's printing, I suggested we talk in St Bartholomew's Church instead. I must have forgotten to lock my door, because when I came home, there was Dury – dead on my floor.'

'Murdered?'

'No! I brought all the broken guttering inside after it collapsed last night, to prevent it from being stolen. He must have bumped into it in the dark, causing some to slip and hit him. What shall I do? Those harridans are waiting like vultures, and I cannot carry him out when they are watching. One is sure to start a rumour that I killed him – and I never did!'

Chaloner inspected the body again. Dury had certainly been hit with something heavy, because his skull was badly crushed. He glanced at the offending guttering, and supposed it might well have caused the damage. Of course, any other weighty implement would have done the same, and there was no way of telling whether there had been an unfortunate accident or something else entirely.

385

'What was he doing here in the first place?' he asked.

'He must have come to spy,' said Hodgkinson. Tears of frustration, self-pity and anger began to flow. 'He and Muddiman are short of material for their next newsletter, so obviously he came to poke about here, to see what he could find. It was certainly his own fault, but what am *I* going to do?'

Hodgkinson was right to be worried, thought Chaloner. People would wonder why one of the newsbooks' enemies should end up dead on his premises. There was not much he could say to comfort the man, so he settled for advising him to contact the proper authorities before his dallying really did begin to look suspicious. Hodgkinson had made a few half-hearted enquiries, but no one had seen Dury enter his shop. People had remembered L'Estrange, Brome and Joanna arriving – and then leaving moments later for the church – but Dury had apparently taken care to remain invisible.

Chaloner's mind teemed with questions as he left the print-shop. Had Dury died in an unfortunate accident, or had someone assisted him into his grave? Hodgkinson, L'Estrange, Joanna and Brome could not have harmed him, because they had all been in the church together. Of course, it was possible to buy anything in London, including the services of assassins, so alibis meant little. Or was the culprit Muddiman, because he and Dury had quarrelled? Or was Williamson taking measures against the success of the newsletters? Chaloner was still weighing up the possibilities when Leybourn accosted him. The surveyor had been waiting for him at the end of Duck Lane.

'I do not recall telling Mary you were in the New Model Army, or about Spain and Portugal,' he said sheepishly.

'But I suppose I must have done. Please do not be angry with her for blurting it out.'

'Well, we are even with our wrongful accusations now,' said Chaloner. 'Hers almost saw me attacked for being a phanatique, and mine had her in the distasteful role of Newburne's mistress.'

'Do not worry. I did something that has soothed the hurt of your unkind words: I have made her the sole beneficiary of my will. She will have my house, shop, books and mathematical instruments.'

Chaloner regarded him in horror. 'What about your brother? Surely some of that belongs to him?'

'Actually, it is all mine – we share the profits, but that was only ever a temporary arrangement. However, times change and I have a wife to consider now. Rob will not mind.'

Chaloner suspected Rob would mind very much. With a sick feeling, he recalled Mary's eagerness for Leybourn to fight L'Estrange: she already wanted him dead. 'Are you sure that is wise?' he asked lamely, suppressing the urge to tell Leybourn he was a damned fool.

'Quite sure,' said Leybourn. 'You think she wants me for my money, but you are wrong. If she did, she would have left when my sack was stolen. She will do anything for me, even asking you to break the law by stealing me a Gunter's Quadrant. She is a true friend. Here she is now.'

Chaloner saw Mary approaching – and L'Estrange walking in the opposite direction with a distinct bounce in his step. He was appalled. Mary would not risk being disinherited for infidelity, so her obvious course of action would be to kill Leybourn before she began wooing her next victim. And as L'Estrange clearly represented a far more lucrative catch, Leybourn's time was fast running out.

'There you are, William,' said Mary coolly. 'Still keeping bad company, I see, despite my advice.'

'He wants to apologise,' said Leybourn. Chaloner blinked at him. He did not mind apologising to Leybourn, but he was damned if he was going to do it to Mary. 'Over what he said about Newburne.'

'It is too late. He declared war on me, and I spit on his truce. Come, William. Mr Kirby is waiting for us near Mallard's Costermongery, and I want to confirm the arrangements for tomorrow's dinner. He has agreed to tell Mr Crisp what time to come.'

'Near where?' asked Chaloner sharply. 'Mallard's what?'

'I was not talking to you,' said Mary icily.

'Mallard's Costermongery,' supplied Leybourn. 'You must know it. It sells excellent cubebs.'

'Mallard's? You mean Maylord's?'

'The Court musician,' said Mary impatiently. 'Some folk called him Maylord, but his cousin – who sold him the shop – referred to himself as Mallard, so that is the name we continue to use. Apparently, Newburne cheated the poor fellow mercilessly. And *that* is the man you accuse me of seducing! You are a foul-tongued rogue, Heyden, and I hope L'Estrange runs you through one day.'

Clues were coming faster than Chaloner could process them, so he went to a grubby coffee-shop on Long Lane to think. The stench of burning beans, the sewage-laden mud that had been tracked inside, and the ever-present reek of tobacco was so potent that it made him nauseous.

He had no money to buy coffee, but he had information. When the proprietor greeted him with 'What news?' he offered some in exchange for a hot drink and a quiet table. The owner was regaled with a detailed account of the plague that was raging in Amsterdam, and the Dutch physicians' prediction that it might soon break loose to afflict other major cities.

The coffee house was full of talk about the near-flooding of White Hall. One man was arguing the case for moving the royal residence to Hampton Court, to be safe from such disasters, but most customers thought the King should stay where he was. With luck, they said, he would be seized by the Thames and carried back to France where he belonged, and if a few courtiers drowned on the way, then so much the better.

Chaloner sipped the hot coffee, feeling it sear his empty stomach and turn it to acid. He would not have drunk it at all, had he not been so cold. He thought about his investigation. Maylord had owned a shop that sold cucumbers. Was that significant? Had Maylord learned his wares featured in some peculiar deaths and *that* was the cause of his agitation? And had the killer then turned on him? Chaloner knew his first step should be to question the people who worked in the costermongery. He abandoned the coffee house and retraced his steps.

'We are closed,' called Yeo, when Chaloner hammered on the door. 'Come back—'

'Does Thomas Maylord own this shop?' demanded Chaloner, forcing his way inside. 'You said last time I was here that the proprietor was someone at Court.'

'Yes, sir,' said Yeo, puzzled. 'Originally, it belonged to Simon Mallard, but he sold it to his cousin, Thomas. Thomas never came here, though. Not once.'

'He had an aversion to greenery. He thought it gave him hives.'

'That is right,' nodded Yeo. 'His solicitor, Newburne, handled the business for him, and Mallard received the profits at the end of each quarter-year. After the September payment, Mallard claimed he was being cheated, and that the amount paid to him should have been higher.'

'Was he right?'

Yeo shrugged, but his expression showed he thought the answer was yes.

Chaloner regarded him thoughtfully. Many questions relating to Maylord were now answered. Newburne had been defrauding him, and during the process of exposing the solicitor's dishonesty, Maylord had become frightened by something. He had appealed to Chaloner for help when Newburne had been murdered, but two days later he had followed the solicitor to the grave. Then Smegergill had become involved, and he had been killed, too. Yet although Chaloner had a clearer understanding of what had happened, he still had no idea about the identity of the killer.

When he arrived home, he found a letter had been left for him at the Golden Lion. It was from the linen-draper, Richard Bridges.

Sir,

I am compelld to telle the Truth, becaus the lie sitts heavye on my conscience. Annabel Reade was more than cooke=mayde to me; she lived as my Wyfe. When I learnd she was Marryed to Another, we argued and she was gone the next Day with sylver. The consta=bles sett after her, she was tooke to Hange. But Hectors compelld me to buye her Freedome. Synce then they have demanded infor=mations – mostly Gossyp from cofye=howses – and I Feare they

use the Intelligences for Theevery. I saile for Tangier tonyght, and
there they cannot reach mee, althou you must Watche for my hous
and my Servants. Leybourn is a goode man, so save hym.
Yr servt Richd Bridges.

That evening, Chaloner sat in his attic trying to make
sense of all he had learned. Rain pattered on the roof,
which was leaking in several places. He lit a fire with a
log he had found on his way home, and attempted to
review the new information, but he was so hungry, he
could not concentrate. He glanced up and saw three tails
dangling off the mantelpiece. Sighing, he drew his knife,
supposing that what he had eaten during the wars was
good enough for now. He skinned and filleted the rats,
then dropped them in a pot with the onion and sage
from Dorcus's garden. There was salt and dried peas in
the pantry, so he added them, too, along with the
cucumber and the spices he had bought from Yeo.

While the concoction simmered, he thought about his
investigations, although answers continued to elude him,
and he was distracted by the notion that Leybourn might
be in grave danger. But eventually, a plan began to take
shape, and he decided to implement it the following day.
He shot to his feet when he heard a noise on the stairs.
It sounded like a lone man, coming openly with no effort
to disguise his approach. His dagger dropped into his
hand when there was a sharp knock.

'Heyden? It is Hickes. I need to talk to you. I came
earlier, but you were out.'

Wondering what Williamson's best spy could want,
Chaloner opened the door warily, and gestured for him
to enter. The cat came to sniff at him, and Hickes picked
it up, ruffling its fur in a way that made Chaloner relax

a little. Hickes would not be fussing over an animal if his intentions were too unfriendly.

'This is nice,' Hickes said, looking round appreciatively. 'Cosy.'

'The roof leaks, there are cracks in the walls, and the whole thing might tumble down at any moment,' Chaloner replied. 'Apart from that, it is a palace.'

'It is just the rain,' said Hickes, going to stand by the window, still cradling the cat. 'It is doing all manner of harm, but when the ground dries, these old buildings will shore themselves up.'

Chaloner suspected the weather was going to bear the blame for a great many future evils, whether it was guilty or not. He closed the door and went to kneel by the fire. Hickes came to squat next to him, stretching his hands towards the flames. The cat squirmed in a way that said it wanted a lap, so Hickes obligingly arranged himself for its comfort. Chaloner supposed the man would not place himself in such an indefensible position if he intended to launch an attack, and allowed himself to relax his guard a little more.

'I brought some oil for your lamp,' said Hickes, producing a flask with a genial smile. 'You so seldom light it, that it is difficult to tell if you are in or not. Shall I fill it for you?'

'Thank you, but there is enough light from the fire. So, you have been watching me, have you? Dury has, too. Did you work together? I cannot see Williamson being pleased with that arrangement.'

Hickes was shocked by the suggestion. 'We most certainly did not! I work alone. It is better that way, because then I do not need to worry about who can be trusted.'

Chaloner could not argue with that premise.

'I do not like L'Estrange,' said Hickes, somewhat out of the blue. 'He asked my wife to proof-read his newsbooks, but she can barely write her name, so I cannot imagine what use she is to him. She still helps him twice a week, though.'

Chaloner was not sure what to say. 'He seems to employ a lot of women.'

Hickes was shaking his head. 'I cannot believe you thought I was working with Muddiman and Dury! They did offer me a bribe to leave them alone, but these things get back to Williamson, and I have no wish to die. You know what he is like when crossed – dangerous, vindictive and persistent.'

'So I have been told. Do you spy on anyone other than Muddiman and Dury? L'Estrange, for example, perhaps by paying one of his colleagues for information?'

Hickes looked like a deer caught in a bright light. 'No,' he blurted, in a way that made it clear the answer was yes. 'And I do not want to talk about L'Estrange. As I said, I cannot abide the man.'

Chaloner shrugged. The clumsy denial was an answer in itself. Clearly, Williamson did not trust L'Estrange, either, and Brome was being paid to monitor him. He wrinkled his nose in disgust, thinking that all the intrigue and scandal in the foreign courts he had visited had nothing on London.

'That smells good,' said Hickes, indicating the cooking pot with a flick of his thumb. 'What is it?'

'Rat stew. Would you like some?'

Hickes laughed; he thought Chaloner was joking. 'If you have enough.'

It felt almost companionable, eating with someone by the fire while the weather raged outside. The stew tasted better than Chaloner remembered, and he supposed the spices made the difference. When they had finished, Hickes pulled a pipe from his pocket and began to tamp it with tobacco. Chaloner fetched his viol, feeling like music now he was full. Hickes grimaced in disapproval when he began to play, but listened quietly, cat in his lap, and it was some time before he spoke.

'Did you know Dury is dead?' he asked.

Chaloner nodded. 'Killed by guttering.'

Hickes seemed about to spit in disgust, but remembered where he was and settled for making a hawking sound instead. 'He took a blow to the head, but I saw his neck before they took the body to the church. His collar had been arranged just so, but *I* noticed the bruises at the sides of his neck. Someone took his throat in their hands and squeezed. Would you like me to demonstrate?'

'No, thank you.' Chaloner was surprised – yet again – that Hickes had thought to look beyond the obvious, especially as it had not occurred to him to do so. He stopped playing, better to concentrate, because he was disgusted with himself for his negligence. 'Why did you inspect the body?'

'Because he died on my watch. Williamson thinks I was careless, and has ordered me to find out what happened – although it is unfair of him to expect me to watch Dury and Muddiman at the same time. So, I looked at the body, although I cannot imagine how I will prove whether L'Estrange or Hodgkinson is the guilty party.'

'What makes you think it is either of them?'

'Because they are the ones with motives. L'Estrange wants to get back at Muddiman for being a better newsman. And Hodgkinson is a printer, so hates men who *handwrite* their news. It is obvious.'

It was not obvious at all, and Chaloner thought Hickes was an odd man – thorough and dogged on one hand, but apt to draw false conclusions on the other. 'L'Estrange and Hodgkinson were doing business with Brome and Joanna when Dury died. Thus they have alibis in each other, although that does not mean they did not hire someone to do their dirty work. Is this why you came to see me? To tell me your suspicions about Dury's death?'

Hickes looked sheepish. 'Actually, I came to give you this. It is the music I found in Finch's room. You asked whether I had collected any documents. Well, this was all I could find. By the time I managed to return for a more thorough search, everything else had been removed.'

Chaloner took the proffered sheet. It was, without question, the same kind of music that had been in Maylord's chimney, and that L'Estrange had asked him and the Bromes to play. He kept his expression carefully neutral. 'Did you know Muddiman and Dury followed you to Finch's house the first time you went there?'

Hickes gaped at him. 'They never did! I would have noticed – I am a professional spy.'

'Right.' Chaloner held up the piece of paper. 'Why do you think I should want this?'

Hickes shrugged, and looked more uncomfortable than ever. 'It is a sort of peace-offering – like the oil. I am confused and worried, and no longer know who to trust. I think Dury's killer might be after me now.' He showed Chaloner a small box with a label declaring the contents to be Theophilus Buckworth's Personal Lozenges. Inside were several green tablets.

'I hope you do not expect me to eat one of these.'

'Of course not – they are an example of the poisonous

395

pills I was telling you about last time. They were sent to me today, along with a note saying they ward off chills in men who stand around in the rain a lot. My wife encouraged me to swallow a couple, because my chest has been bothering me.'

'But you know better than to consume gifts from anonymous donors,' said Chaloner, wondering whether Mrs Hickes was aiming to clear the field so she could pursue L'Estrange unfettered.

'Hodgkinson is missing,' said Hickes, while Chaloner was still mulling over the implications of the pills. 'He disappeared not long after Dury was killed. Do you not think that is suspicious?'

'No, because he summoned the constables.' Chaloner ignored the nagging voice in his head that told him the printer might only have sent for them because he had been caught with a body, and that to do otherwise *would* have looked suspect. He continued less certainly. 'And how do you know he is missing? Perhaps he went with the constables to make an official report, or has gone to stay with friends because his properties are flooded. You are not "missing" after such a short period of time.'

'When I found him gone, I searched his Duck Lane print-house,' said Hickes. He handed Chaloner another piece of paper with music on it. 'I found this. Will you play it?'

Chaloner started to oblige, but Hickes soon held up his hand for silence.

'I thought so,' said Williamson's man disapprovingly. 'It is that nasty, disjointed stuff that Finch said he found in Newburne's room. He played it for me on his trumpet.'

Chaloner compared the two pieces. 'They are almost certainly by the same composer.'

'Hodgkinson is a dangerous, devious fellow,' Hickes continued. 'And I must speak to him about Dury as soon as possible. Do you have any idea where he might have gone?'

Chaloner did not think the printer was missing, devious or dangerous, and Hickes's conclusions said his judgement could not be trusted. 'No, but I will tell you if I find out.'

'You should, because you may need *my* help soon. First, a lot of very unpleasant men are after you, and you need friends. And second, your friend Leybourn is keeping bad company.'

'Mary Cade,' said Chaloner unhappily.

'Annie Petwer, Annabel Reade, Mary Cade. Call her what you like. Her real name is Anne Pettis.'

'Pettis? But that is the name of the horse-trader who died of cucumbers.'

'He was her first husband. However, if he died a natural death, I will dance naked in St Paul's Cathedral. She killed him – I would stake my life on it.'

Chaloner regarded him in alarm. 'You said you found some of these green lozenges on Pettis's body. If Mary killed Pettis, then it means she must have dispatched Newburne, Finch, Beauclair and all the others, too. And she is in Will's house.'

'She will not kill him tonight – not the same day he changed his will. He is safe for a while yet.'

Recalling how eagerly Mary – he could not think of her as Anne – had encouraged Leybourn to fight with L'Estrange, Chaloner was not so sure. 'How do you know so much about her?'

'Williamson sends me to watch various Hectors sometimes. I knew it would not be long before she found another victim. Bridges managed to extricate himself, although it was expensive, but the fellow between him and Pettis ended up floating in the Thames. His name was Nobert Wenum.'

'Wenum?' echoed Chaloner, bewildered. 'But he was Newburne.'

Hickes gazed back, nonplussed. 'He was not! He was a totally different man, I followed him several times after he met Muddiman, and he was not Newburne. I am totally certain of it. I can see why Muddiman might have thought so, but he is wrong.'

'I see,' said Chaloner, not seeing at all.

Chaloner waited a few minutes after Hickes had gone, then left via the back door. He sent a message to Thurloe about Wenum, then trudged through the deserted streets towards Smithfield. He wore an oiled cloak against the foul weather, and Isabella's hat against attack. He did not think anyone would be following him, but he was cautious by nature, and took a circuitous route across the city, using alleys that would have been dark during the day, but that were pitch black at night. He crossed the River Fleet farther north than usual. It was a vicious torrent, and the bridge creaked as he used it, low and deep. He suspected it would be washed away by morning.

When he reached Smithfield, he headed for the Bear alehouse, making the assumption that it was one of Kirby's regular haunts. He took up station behind a water-butt, but did not have long to wait, because it was already late and even Hectors needed to sleep. First out was big-nosed Ireton, who emerged to saunter fearlessly up Long Lane. Chaloner had intended to waylay Kirby, but decided Ireton would do just as well. He trailed the

398

felon to a pleasant little cottage, and watched him unlock the door. He waited until the lamp was doused in the upper chamber, then let himself in. He saw a lute on the table downstairs, which served to confirm some of the conclusions he had drawn.

Ireton was fast asleep when Chaloner stepped into the bedchamber, but woke fast when a knife was pressed against his throat. He opened his mouth to yell for help, but closed it sharply as the blade begin to bite. He lay still, and waited to hear what his assailant wanted of him.

'Maylord,' said Chaloner softly. 'What happened to him?'

'Oh, it is you,' said Ireton, immediately recognising the voice. He sneered, confidence returning now he was facing an opponent he knew. 'Mary Cade told me about you, but I am confused. Who *do* you work for? It is not Williamson, and I doubt the Lord Chancellor would dare send a man against the Hectors. He, like most sensible politicians, treats us with respect.'

'If you tell me the truth, you will live to see tomorrow. If you lie, I will cut your throat and drop your body in the Fleet. So, I repeat: what happened to Maylord?'

There was something in Chaloner's low, purposeful tone that convinced Ireton he meant business. 'Maylord?' The Hector realised his voice was a bleat, and struggled to compose himself.

Chaloner began to test the theory he had so painstakingly deduced. 'You killed him on Smegergill's orders. You smothered him with a cushion – using enough force to break teeth – and left the cucumber to cause confusion. Did Smegergill tell you to do that?'

'A confession will see me hang,' said Ireton slyly. 'But if I keep quiet, you can prove nothing.'

It was answer enough for Chaloner, and he itched to

punch the man – or shove a pillow over *his* face. 'Smegergill was teaching you the lute – Greeting said he had taken on some dubious pupils.'

'Am I more dubious than a man who breaks into houses and threatens their occupants with knives?'

Chaloner ignored him. 'You talked a lot during your sessions together. He told you how Newburne's dishonesty was depriving Maylord of the profits from his costermongery. Perhaps it was you who suggested something should be done about it. Regardless, Smegergill encouraged Maylord to watch Newburne, and possibly convinced him to poke about in Newburne's house.'

Ireton's voice dripped contempt. 'Prove it.'

'The proof lies in the fact that Maylord suddenly elected to give Newburne – a man he despised – lessons on the flageolet; it is clear there was a reason for his abrupt acquiescence. Both owned houses on Thames Street, and I imagine the lessons took place there. During one of these tutorials, something happened to unnerve Maylord, so Smegergill helped him move to a different part of the city. Smegergill said he did not know where Maylord had gone, but he was lying.'

Ireton regarded Chaloner with contempt, but the temptation to gloat was stronger than his desire to say nothing that would help the spy unravel the mystery. 'Of course, he was lying! He knew where Maylord went, although he could not find where he hid his valuables. Maylord kept that from him.'

'And that is why he wanted me to go to the Rhenish Wine House with him. He anticipated that a professional spy would have better luck.'

'So, what did you find?' asked Ireton, curious despite himself. 'Documents?'

400

'Music. I have assumed it is irrelevant, but perhaps I should not have done. Maylord understood its significance, even if I do not – at least, not yet. Who wrote it? And who is it for?'

Ireton laughed derisively. 'Music? Do not be a fool! Smegergill wanted a key, not music. He said it would pave the way to a box of priceless jewels. Why do you think I went to the Rhenish Wine House the day after he died? It was not for music, I assure you!'

Chaloner frowned. Locks could be smashed, so why had Smegergill wanted Maylord's key? 'Proof of ownership,' he said in understanding. 'Whoever has a key can show the hoard is his.'

Ireton inclined his head, but made no other reply.

'Did you know there were two keys?' asked Chaloner. He could see from Ireton's expression that he did not: Smegergill had not been honest with his accomplices, either. 'He already had one.'

'You lie! Maylord stole the only one when he was teaching Newburne the flageolet. Then, because Newburne had been cheating Maylord for years, Smegergill told him to say the box was his. The key was proof of ownership, as you said. But then Maylord got cold feet, and began to baulk at carrying the plan through.'

'So you killed him,' said Chaloner.

'I decline to say,' replied Ireton, although the uneasy flicker in his eyes told Chaloner that he had. 'And you can prove nothing. After Maylord was dispatched, Smegergill was going to retrieve the key and claim the treasure in his stead. He offered me a share for my silence.'

'So, who killed Newburne? Smegergill?'

'We were both at a musical soirée when Newburne died. You can check, if you like – a dozen people saw us.' Ireton could not resist a brag. 'Smegergill's idea of leaving that cucumber with Maylord was a stroke of genius. No one except you is remotely suspicious. Do you know *why* he devised the plan that would see Maylord the owner of Newburne's hoard?'

Chaloner nodded, aware that Ireton's boast about the cucumber was guilty knowledge of Maylord's death. 'He wanted Maylord rich, because he was the sole beneficiary of Maylord's will. He intended to kill his friend from the start – not to squander the money on wild enjoyment, but to support him in his old age. His joints were stiffening, and he knew it would only be a matter of time before he could no longer earn a living from the virginals. Now, tell me what transpired between you and Smegergill in the churchyard the night he died.'

'We did not—'

Chaloner tightened his grip on the dagger.

'All right!' snarled Ireton, trying to flinch away. 'There is no need to decapitate me. We made an arrangement, while Kirby and Treen dealt with you. How did you guess?'

'Because of your actions in Smithfield last night. Treen was right when he said Crisp would want to interview the man who everyone believes killed Smegergill, but you were eager to kill me anyway. The reason is obvious: you knew Crisp would learn the truth from me – that I had nothing to do with Smegergill's murder. So, what happened? How did he die?'

'As soon as I saw him, I realised we had waylaid the wrong pair of musicians. He assumed you were dead when you fell to the ground, and was furious, because

402

he said you were going to locate Maylord's key for him. He had made plans: he was going to ask *me* to drive you to the Rhenish Wine House, and I was to knock you over the head once he had the key.'

'What next?'

'The graveyard ambush was a mess, and Kirby and Treen have loose tongues. He was worried about what people would think when you were bludgeoned to death, but he escaped unscathed.'

'So he asked you to hit him, to make it look as if we were both victims?'

Ireton pointed to his mouth. 'I tapped him softly here. I saw him walk towards you *after* I struck him, ready to raise the alarm once we were safely away. He tripped over you – you must have felt it.'

Chaloner recalled being kicked in the side, and slowly he began to understand what had happened. Dizzy from Ireton's blow, Smegergill had stumbled in the dark and landed face-down on the flooded ground. And that had been that. Stunned, he had been unable to rise, and by the time Chaloner had regained his own senses, Smegergill had drowned. And yet it was hard to feel sorry for the old man. He had betrayed his friendship with Maylord by arranging his murder. He fraternised with Hectors, and put his future comforts above all else. In all, Smegergill had been a selfish, odious man, and Chaloner knew he should stop feeling guilty about his death.

There was no more to be said, and the spy was just considering the best way to deliver Ireton to the constables, when he heard a creak on the stairs. Someone was coming.

Ireton smirked. 'Nothing happens in Smithfield without the Hectors knowing. Here is my rescue.'

403

Swearing under his breath, Chaloner knocked Ireton out cold with the hilt of his dagger and made for the window. He clambered on to the sill just as the door flew open and Kirby and Treen stood there, swords at the ready. More Hectors were hurrying up the stairs behind them. Chaloner dropped out of the window, rolling as he landed in an attempt to lessen the impact. He staggered to his feet and saw a carriage rattling towards him. Certain it was the Butcher, he jigged away, colliding with Kirby, who had followed him out of the window. The felon grabbed him by the throat, so Chaloner felled him with a punch that hurt his own hand.

'Thomas!' hissed a familiar voice as the coach's door swung open. Chaloner dived through it, and Thurloe banged on the ceiling with the butt of his handgun. 'Go!'

'What are you doing here?' gasped Chaloner, struggling to hang on as the vehicle lurched away.

Thurloe raised his eyebrows. 'The same as you, I imagine. Trying to find a way to prise Mary away from William before she slits his throat.'

Chapter 11

Thurloe said it was not safe for Chaloner to sleep at Fetter Lane that night, but agreed to let him collect the music, keys and Wenum's ledger before going to Lincoln's Inn. While the ex-Spymaster waited in the carriage, Chaloner ascended the stairs to his room.

The fire he had lit earlier was out, and he could no longer see. Then he remembered Hickes's gift of oil. He groped in the darkness for fuel, lamp and tinderbox, and was about to fill the lantern's reservoir, when he detected a faint odour that should not have been there. He stoppered the flask in alarm. It did contain oil, but there was also a sulphuric scent, and there would be an explosion if he tried to light it. It might not kill him, but it would certainly cause him injury. Who would do such a thing? Wryly, he acknowledged that there was a whole host of people who wanted him indisposed.

His first thought was that Hickes was responsible, but then he recalled how Hickes had offered to light the lamp for him. Did that mean Hickes had not known what would happen once a flame was set to the substance? The more he considered Hickes, the more he became sure he was the innocent instrument of someone else's plot. But which one of Chaloner's many enemies was to blame? Crisp? Muddiman? Williamson? L'Estrange? Mary? A Hector? Or was it Greeting, a man of whom he was becoming increasingly wary?

Quickly, he gathered what he wanted and left, first making sure the window was ajar for the cat – it was off hunting, and he did not want it to find itself locked out when it returned. As the carriage rattled to Lincoln's Inn, he told Thurloe what he had deduced regarding Smegergill. The ex-Spymaster sighed.

'I am not surprised to learn he would kill a friend to secure himself a comfortable retirement. What was the alternative? Teaching men like Ireton until he died? Performing for critical patrons like L'Estrange while his hands became ever more crabbed? But you have done enough on that case. I will arrange for the parish constables to arrest Ireton in the morning, assuming he has not fled the city.'

'Will they do it? They are not too frightened of Crisp?'

Thurloe rubbed his chin. 'True. Perhaps I had better visit the Lord Chancellor instead, and arrange for a contingent of soldiers to do it. It is a pity your reckless enquiries have not provided you with answers about Newburne, though. How much longer do you have?'

'Until Monday – the day after tomorrow. All I learned tonight was that Newburne probably cheated Maylord out of a fortune. No wonder he was rich.'

'And you think it was Smegergill's plan to defraud Newburne of his jewels that turned Maylord so anxious in the last two weeks of his life?'

Chaloner nodded. 'He had his revenge, though. He hid his key, and Smegergill never did find it.'

406

Thurloe was thoughtful. 'And yet there is something about this explanation that does not ring true. I think Ireton may have been lying to you – at least in part. I do not doubt that having your dagger at his throat rendered him more willing to confide, but can you trust what he told you?'

'Which parts do you not believe?'

'The business with the key, mostly. I do not see Maylord being so single-mindedly venal over a box of jewels, and originally, Smegergill did say he wanted you to locate documents.'

'But the "documents" were only that strange music,' said Chaloner. He rubbed his eyes tiredly. 'Or, more likely, I found the wrong hiding place.'

'I doubt you made such a basic mistake – you were trained by *me*, after all. You say this music has been cropping up in all sorts of odd places, so perhaps we should consider it more carefully.'

Chaloner tried, but answers still eluded him.

Thurloe sighed. 'Then let us go back to Maylord, and what might have frightened him. I do not think he would have gone to pieces over the notion of defrauding Newburne of jewels – he was stronger than that. I think something else was responsible for his agitation.'

'What?' asked Chaloner, wracking his brains.

'Hodgkinson's print-house is near Maylord's cottage. The news business is a dangerous one, and it would not surprise me to learn that Hodgkinson is engaged in something illegal. And now Hickes says he is missing. Perhaps Maylord's unease had nothing to do with Newburne, but a lot to do with another neighbour.'

'It is possible, I suppose. After all, Hodgkinson prints items for L'Estrange and Muddiman. And Dury *was* murdered on his premises.' But that solution raised its own set of questions, and Chaloner could not see the answers to save his life. He rubbed his eyes again, defeated. 'What did you learn this evening?'

'That Mary Cade is the widow of a Smithfield horse-trader, who also happened to know Crisp—'

'Valentine Pettis.'

Thurloe regarded him balefully. 'You *have* been busy. When I was Spymaster, the Hectors were just a band of brutish felons whom we periodically crushed. Now they are a highly organised clan, and some are even intelligent. Williamson turns a blind eye to their dealings on the understanding that they will supply appropriate manpower when he needs something done.'

Chaloner's unease intensified. 'What are we going to do about Will? We cannot leave him in that woman's clutches. We may arrive tomorrow and find it is too late.'

'He will not appreciate being kidnapped, if that is what you have in mind. But I doubt anything will happen tonight – the Hectors will be too busy looking for you, for a start. We will act in the morning.'

'And do what?'

'I will think of something. You concentrate on solving Newburne's murder for your Earl.'

Thurloe's servant made up a bed for Chaloner in Thurloe's sitting room, but although the ex-Spymaster swallowed a sleeping draught and retired immediately, Chaloner was too unsettled for rest, despite his bone-deep weariness. He sat crossed-legged in front of the dying fire and made piles of the four sets of music; the one from Maylord's chimney, the one L'Estrange had given him, the one Hickes had taken from Finch's room, and the one Hickes said he had found in Hodgkinson's print-shop. The light was poor, but it was enough to work by.

He compared them minutely, his curiosity piqued by Thurloe's suggestion that they should not be too readily dismissed. All were penned by the same hand, and when he picked them out on Thurloe's virginals – certain the noise would not bother Thurloe after whatever medicine he had taken – they sounded unpleasantly similar. Then he recalled the tiny scroll that had been in Smegergill's ring. The brief glance he had been allowed before Greeting had destroyed it had put him in mind of a cipher key – a crib for decoding secret messages. He recalled that a C-sharp was a T and an E-flat was a W. Could the music actually represent a message, and it was not the *tune* that the composer was trying to communicate to his listeners, but something else? Obviously, there were only seven note-names to twenty-six letters in the alphabet, but there were sharps and flats that could be taken into consideration, along with beats of different duration – minims, crotchets and quavers.

He started with the music from Finch's room, because it was the shortest, working on the premise, familiar to all spies, that some letters were used more frequently than others. It was a sequence Thurloe had drilled into him years ago, and had enabled him to break into many a secret. The most commonly occurring letter in English was E, so he went through the music, and determined that the most commonly occurring note was a B. The next most common letter was T, followed by A, the latter of which seemed to correspond to a G, but one that was two beats in duration.

He made mistakes, and had to keep reworking what

he was doing, but eventually a pattern began to emerge, and the idea was so simple that he wondered why he had not seen it before. Words began to appear, although they were interspersed with meaningless letters, a device to ensure the tune was not too outlandish. He began crossing out the extraneous ones, until he had a message that made sense – or rather, he had a collection of words in a rational order, which was not the same thing.

BE WARY. TOO MANY HORSES.

Too many horses for what? He moved on to the compositions he had recovered from Maylord's chimney, barely aware of the watchmen calling two o'clock, and then three.

SHERARD LORINSTON. GROCER OF SMITHFIELD. LARGE SAD BAY MARE. MOTHER FIRST NEWE MOON WEATHER PERMITTING.

The next one read:

JAMES BRADNOX. VINTNERS HALL. THURSDAY FOLLOWING. GUILD MEETING.

And so it went on, message after message Heart pounding, he turned to L'Estrange's piece.

RICHD SMITH. BELL SMITHFIELD. BRIGHT BAY MARE. SAINTE LUKE DAY EVE. THEATER.

Chaloner stared at it. He had met Richard Smith in Brome's shop. The man had been placing an advertisement in *The Newes*, because his 'bright bay mare' had been stolen, and he wanted its safe return. Chaloner consulted Thurloe's almanac, and learned that the Feast of St Luke was the fifteenth day of October, which was roughly when the man said the horse had been stolen. With a start, Chaloner also recalled him say that the thief was Edward Treen, who had been spotted in the very act of stealing the beast. The music was telling someone

410

that on the eve of St Luke's Day, Richard Smith had been planning to go to the theatre.

Chaloner chewed the end of his pen. Was that the essence of the messages? That someone was gathering information about the movements of men with horses, and was arranging to have them stolen? Had Pettis the horse-trader and Beauclair the equerry been part of the operation? Or had they been killed because they had worked out what was going on? And if Treen, one of the trio that was causing Chaloner so much trouble, had stolen Smith's horse, then were his fellow Hectors responsible for the other thefts, too? Chaloner imagined they were.

He finished decoding the messages, grinning his satisfaction when one contained a note about Beauclair's black stallion, then searched Thurloe's bookshelves until he found back issues of *The Newes* and *The Intelligencer*. It did not take him long to learn that most of the men mentioned in the music had bought notices in the newsbooks, offering rewards for their animals' return. So, what did that tell him? It certainly confirmed what he had heard in the coffee houses: that if a valuable animal was taken, then the best way to ensure its recovery was to advertise in the newsbooks.

Maylord had owned a horse. Had it been stolen? Chaloner trawled all the way back to L'Estrange's very first publication, but Maylord had never placed an advertisement if it had. Was *this* the secret that Maylord had learned about Newburne, and Thurloe was right in that it had nothing to do with Newburne's jewels? Chaloner lay on the mattress, but there were still far too many questions to allow him to sleep.

* * *

411

Events were beginning to spiral out of Chaloner's control. It was only a matter of time before the Hectors tracked him down and tried to kill him, and he only had one more full day left to solve Newburne's murder. He rose long before dawn with a sense of foreboding, thinking about what had happened, what he had learned, and the questions he still needed to answer. He woke Thurloe, sitting on the edge of the bed to regale the drowsy ex-Spymaster with an account of what the music meant.

'And the fact that Smegergill started to wear the ring after Maylord's death means *he* knew about the music, too,' he concluded.

'You are almost certainly right. Smegergill must have been determined to feather his nest at any cost. Perhaps he even helped with the encoding or decoding – he made money from these horse thefts, as well as aiming to get Newburne's jewels and Maylord's inheritance. I never did like the man.'

'So, he had two reasons for smothering Maylord,' mused Chaloner. 'He wanted his inheritance *and* he was afraid Maylord would expose the horse-theft business.'

'It explains why Ireton was ready to commit murder with him – he was protecting Hector business, as well as doing a favour for his friend and music-master. So, at last you know what frightened Maylord: it started with a hare-brained scheme – probably devised in the heat of the moment and later regretted – to defraud Newburne of his jewels, but it ended with him stumbling into the Hectors' latest venture.'

'He must have found the coded music while acquiring Newburne's keys and, being a musician, it piqued his interest. He must have taken some, and become worried when he realised its significance.'

412

'Do you think Finch was translating the music when he was murdered?' asked Thurloe.

'No, because he was playing it at the time. You do not need to play it to translate – in fact, it is better if you do not, because the melody is irrelevant. But there was a second person in the room when Finch died, someone eating a pie. I suspect *he* knew what the music entailed, and killed Finch to make sure he never worked it out.'

'That particular missive said there were "too many horses". Do you know what that means?'

'Yes, I think so. The music directs Hectors to prey on specific victims, but it has been too successful. The message from Finch's room is a warning, urging the perpetrators to cut back before their activities become obvious.'

Thurloe was uncertain. 'Obvious?' he echoed doubtfully. 'Obvious to whom?'

'To anyone reading the newsbooks, had the operation been allowed to continue at such a furious pace. It is not obvious *now*, because the warning was heeded.'

'If advertising means the return of these valuable beasts, then it is small wonder that so many men are clamouring to buy newsbook notices.' Thurloe frowned. 'Horse-thievery has always occurred around Smithfield. I see all manner of connections emerging here, and I imagine you do, too.'

Chaloner nodded. 'The music is directed at Smithfield-based men like Ireton, who plays the lute and so has an understanding of notation. Of course, it was the one thing I did not bother to ask him last night. He and the Hectors – Treen was actually seen taking Smith's mare – steal these beasts, then Smithfield horse-dealers, such

413

as Valentine Pettis, help to sell them. Pettis was Mary Cade's husband, so I doubt his role in the business was an honest one.'

'Rewards are offered for the safe delivery of most of these animals, so if Pettis could not effect a sale, the thieves could still profit from their crime by returning them to their grateful owners.'

'Perhaps that is why Pettis was killed: he preferred a sale to a reward, because it would be more lucrative. He became greedy, and someone was obliged to stop him before he spoiled everything. Did I tell you that the night Greeting was supposed to have been ambushed, he was carrying *music* between L'Estrange and Spymaster Williamson?'

'Yes – but that does not mean Greeting or L'Estrange are actively involved. L'Estrange might have somehow acquired the music from the villains, and was dutifully passing it to Williamson for investigation.'

'Then why did Williamson toss it on the fire as soon as it was delivered? It is not impossible that L'Estrange wrote the music himself – he *is* an accomplished violist – for Williamson to pass to the Hectors. Williamson often hires Hectors, and we should not forget that he has allocated a singularly stupid agent to investigate this particular case.'

'One who might have died giving you exploding oil for your lamp,' mused Thurloe. 'You said there was music on Wenum's windowsill, too, but that is to be expected, given that Wenum is Newburne. And Newburne would certainly have involved himself in this, you can be sure of that.'

'Hickes would not agree with you about the Newburne–Wenum connection. According to him, Wenum was one of Mary's victims, found floating in the Thames.'

414

'Then he is mistaken. I set my servant to work when I received your note earlier. Records are kept of drownings, but Wenum is not among them. Wenum *is* Newburne, which explains why Wenum has not been seen since the solicitor died. And, more to the point, we cannot overlook the very obvious fact that the names are anagrams of each other. Hickes must have been listening to unsubstantiated gossip, and he is not intelligent enough to know the difference between fact and speculation.'

Chaloner supposed he might be right, although an element of doubt remained. 'He is an odd combination of credulous and astute.'

Thurloe was not interested in Hickes. 'I visited "Wenum's" attic in the Rhenish Wine House the other day, and I saw the book – Galen's tome on foods – that you mentioned. That edition is actually rare and very expensive, so I took it to Nott the bookseller, and asked him to find out who bought it. He undertook similar tasks for me during the Commonwealth, so I have high hopes that proof will not be long in coming. I fully expect the owner to be wealthy old Newburne.'

Chaloner nodded vaguely, unwilling to commit himself one way or the other. He did not know what to think about Wenum.

'What will you do today?' asked Thurloe, when the spy made no other reply. 'Other than keep your distance from Smithfield, of course.'

'Speak to Hickes, ask who gave him the oil. Then question Muddiman about what Dury was doing in Hodgkinson's print-house.' Chaloner was not very enthusiastic, because he did not think either would provide him with the answers he so desperately needed.

415

'You said Hickes wanted information about Hodgkinson's whereabouts. If he refuses to cooperate, you can persuade him with the intelligence that Hodgkinson has a sister in Chelsey.'

'How do you know that?'

Thurloe's smile was enigmatic. 'Hodgkinson is a printer. Such people have the means to flood the streets with seditious literature, so naturally, he was of interest to me during the Commonwealth.'

'Hickes said he was dangerous. Is *that* what he meant?'

'Hodgkinson *is* dangerous. He may seem amiable and pleasant, but he has a core of steel – and iron fists to go with it. He associates with insalubrious men, too. Why do you think he has a print-shop at Smithfield, of all places? It is not to sell cards and advertisements, believe me.'

Chaloner stared at him. 'Have I underestimated him?'

'You have if you think he is some harmless innocent. Why? Did you cross him?'

'Not as far as I know. So that explains why he was willing to "help" Greeting search for Smegergill's killer in Smithfield. He is a Hector himself!'

Chaloner returned to his rooms to don different clothes before going to see Hickes, hurrying because he could not afford to waste time. Bells were ringing to call people to church, but it was pouring with rain again, and those who did brave the weather did so resentfully. His cat was still out, and he hoped it had not come to grief in the swollen runnels and streams that gushed to join the bloated Thames.

He strode to The Strand, in the hope that Hickes would be at his customary spot outside Muddiman's

416

house, but even the regular street-traders seemed to have given up the battle against the elements, and the city felt strangely deserted. The only other place he could think to look was White Hall: if Hickes was Williamson's spy, then someone there would know where he lived. He asked Bulteel, whose bloodshot eyes and rumpled clothes indicated he had been working all night. The clerk leaned back in his chair and massaged his back.

'Hickes lives in Axe Yard, Westminster, but I doubt he will be accepting visitors today. There is a rumour that he has been poisoned. Rat stew, apparently.'

'I had rat stew last night, and I am not poisoned,' said Chaloner, wondering if Mrs Hickes had persuaded her husband to swallow one of Theophilus Buckworth's Personal Lozenges after all.

Bulteel shuddered. 'You old soldiers! I have heard them wax lyrical about the lost delights of rat stew before, but I did not think they would eat it when more pleasant alternatives were available.'

'I would not have to eat it at all, if the Earl paid me,' said Chaloner, not without bitterness.

Bulteel stared at him. 'You are that impecunious? You should have said! I administer a small fund for emergencies, and you should have some expenses for your work. Here is ten shillings. I cannot give you more, but it should last until you bring about a successful resolution to your enquiries.'

Chaloner accepted it warily. 'Are you sure this is legal? I do not want the Earl accusing me of theft.'

Bulteel looked hurt. 'Of course it is legal! Do you think I would risk my career with a new child on the way? Now you must sign my ledger, to say you have received the said amount.'

417

Chaloner bent to write his name in the book Bulteel had pulled from his desk, and saw the clerk was telling the truth, because it did contain a list of minor expenditures incurred on the Earl's behalf.

Bulteel lowered his voice. 'Your reasons for leaving Newburne's hoard where it was were sound at the time, but the situation has changed. If his cellar floods in all this rain, it will almost certainly be discovered by the workmen who come to clean up. I think you had better bring it here – today, if possible – and I will find somewhere to hide it. I have a feeling you are going to need it soon. The Earl is expecting his answer tomorrow, and you do not seem overwhelmed with solutions.'

Chaloner did not want to waste precious time on treasure, but Bulteel was right – a chest of coins might well appease the Earl in lieu of a solved case. Because he now had plenty of money, he took a hackney to Old Jewry. It raced recklessly towards its destination, spraying water so high that it splattered over the buildings on both sides simultaneously. It also drenched other road-users, and their progress was marked by waving fists and curses. The driver swore back, and Chaloner was not surprised when someone brought the journey to an abrupt end by hurling a clod of mud. It missed the hackneyman, but the ensuing altercation looked set to last for some time, so Chaloner ran the rest of the way.

When he arrived, Dorcus Newburne was leaving. A carriage waited outside her house, and L'Estrange enticed her into it with one of his leers. The maid stood sulkily in the doorway, and Dorcus gave her a jaunty wave as the coach rattled away. Sybilla made a gesture that was far

418

from servile, then left herself; Chaloner had the impression she was playing truant as an act of rebellion. He waited until she had gone, then hurried around to the back of the mansion, and fiddled with the door until it came open. Then he trotted quickly down the cellar steps, intending to unearth the jewels and leave with them as fast as possible.

The first thing he saw was that the barrel he had placed over the hoard had gone. The second was that there was a hole where the box had been. He stared at it in dismay. Had his act of moving the cask precipitated the treasure's removal? If so, then it meant someone else had been monitoring it. He thought about L'Estrange's sudden interest in Dorcus, and could not help but wonder whether the editor might have another reason for courting the widow of his colleague.

'You think L'Estrange has the jewels?' asked Bulteel, when Chaloner reported the bad news back at White Hall. 'How will we get them back? Or shall we just forget about them? It is one thing invading Dorcus Newburne's domain, but another altogether taking on L'Estrange. *He* knows how to use a sword.'

'So do I,' said Chaloner, wondering if the secretary really was nervous of L'Estrange, or whether he had his own reasons for wanting to pretend the hoard had never existed. Chaloner rubbed his head, and thought he had been a fool to think anyone at White Hall could be trusted.

'No, it is too dangerous. Leave them. We will have to think of another way to appease the Earl.'

'Leave them?' echoed Chaloner. 'I thought they represented your chance for better working conditions, as well as seeing me reinstated.'

'They do, but they are not worth your life. I am a religious man, Heyden. I do not want a soiled conscience,

419

and you have always been decent to me. You let *me* take credit for finding the Earl's lost pendant when most men would either have kept it or given it to him themselves, to earn his favour. Allies are few and far between at the palace, and I do not want you dead.'

'I am glad someone does not,' murmured Chaloner, finding it hard to imagine that a simple act of honesty – and laziness, if the truth be known, because he had not wanted to be bothered with the Earl's baubles – should have resulted in the making of a friend. In fact, it was so difficult to believe that he was more wary and suspicious than ever.

'You do seem to have accrued a lot of enemies. Yesterday – before he was poisoned – Hickes told me some of the Hectors were asking after you, wanting to know where you live. He did not tell them, but they are resourceful, and it is only a matter of time before they find someone else to question.'

And Bulteel was a coward, who would probably tell them what they wanted to know at the first asking. Time really was running out, because Chaloner could not dodge them, uncover Newburne's killer and watch Leybourn, all at the same time.

'What will you do now?' asked the secretary, when Chaloner said nothing.

The spy did not want to discuss his plans – and he certainly had no intention of confiding that he intended to search L'Estrange's house to see if he could find a chest of jewels. 'Visit Hickes.'

'Be careful, then. I do not want to lose you just yet.'

'Just yet?' echoed Chaloner.

Bulteel smiled his uneasy smile. 'Just a figure of speech.'

* * *

Axe Yard was not far from White Hall. It was a cul-de-sac of twenty-five houses around a cobbled yard, and although the entrance to it was small and mean, the court itself was pleasant. The houses to the north overlooked St James's Park, and were occupied by ambitious men who wanted to be near White Hall. In the south, the homes were rather more shabby, and the one rented by Hickes was the shabbiest of all. Its paint was peeling, and its plasterwork in desperate need of a wash.

Chaloner knocked several times, then let himself in when there was no reply. He heard male voices from the further of the two ground-floor rooms; Hickes had company. He eased open the door, and was surprised to see Greeting, violin at the ready. Meanwhile, Hickes lay on a bed groaning.

'We can try it again,' Greeting was saying. 'But if it was going to work, I think we would have noticed an improvement by now. Perhaps we should call a physician, and—'

'Please,' moaned Hickes. 'Just once more, and if I am still no better, you can fetch Mother Greene from Turnagain Lane. She is a witch, and knows some remedies.'

Greeting began to play, and Chaloner recognised an old tune called the Sick Dance. Some people believed singing it would protect them from the plague, and Hickes obviously had even greater hopes. When he had finished, Greeting lowered his bow and looked expectantly at the ailing man.

'Mother Greene, did you say?' he asked, when Hickes gripped his stomach.

Hickes had seen the movement in the doorway. 'Heyden! What was in your damned stew? I *knew* I should not have touched it when I offered some to your cat and it turned up its nose.'

'You said Heyden ate the same food you did,' Greeting pointed out, 'and there is nothing wrong with him, so you cannot blame his cooking. Nor would he have let you offer some to his cat, if it was tainted. No man takes risks with his own cat.'

'No,' groaned Hickes, white-faced and unhappy. 'I suppose not.'

Suspecting that if Hickes had been suffering for a while, then he was probably over the worst, Chaloner fetched milk from the pantry and mixed it with charcoal, which he collected from the hearth and ground into a powder with the handle of his knife.

'Where is Mrs Hickes?' he asked as he worked.

'Proof-reading,' replied Greeting, when Hickes only moaned. 'With L'Estrange in Ivy Lane.'

Chaloner helped Hickes sit up and sip his concoction. 'My sister uses this for upset stomachs.'

'She is not the one who taught you how to cook, is she?' asked Hickes weakly. 'Why are you here?'

'You asked last night if I knew where Hodgkinson might be. He has a sister in Chelsey.'

'We know,' said Greeting. 'Williamson sent *me* there to look for the wretched man, but she has not seen him in weeks. However, it is good of you to come and tell us, and in return, I have something for you. I learned it last night, and planned to track you down today anyway.'

'You mean about Butcher Crisp?' asked Hickes, gagging slightly when Chaloner made him drink too fast. 'What Williamson told us before I was taken poorly? Yes, tell him all that.'

'Actually, I was thinking about Smegergill,' said Greeting.

'When I went through his belongings – which are now mine – I found documents telling me three things. First, Maylord was definitely being cheated by Newburne. Second, Smegergill was teaching the lute to a Hector called Ireton. And third, I was astonished to discover that Smegergill owned several magnificent horses currently stabled at the Haymarket. Unfortunately, I have a bad feeling he did not come by them honestly.'

'What makes you think that?' asked Chaloner, thoughts churning.

'Because records show he acquired them *after* Maylord had accused Newburne of cheating him. I think there was extortion going on, and he was given these nags to keep him quiet. However, if you black-mail felons, you should not be surprised when you are presented with stolen property. I took Bayspoole with me – as Surveyor of His Majesty's Stables, he knows horses – and he said one of the stallions belonged to Colonel Beauclair.'

And Beauclair was one of the men who had been poisoned with Personal Lozenges and a cucumber left to disguise the fact, thought Chaloner. Ends were begin-ning to come together, to make sense at last. He knew from the encoded music that Beauclair's horse had been stolen by Hectors.

'What did Williamson tell you about Crisp?' he asked Hickes, moving to another subject.

'That he has taken to killing his own people. He is now more than just an underworld king: he is a despot, who gains in power every day.'

'I asked Williamson why he did not crush the fellow,' added Greeting. 'He is Spymaster, after all. But he said something I did not understand: that he needs to weigh the advantages first. What advantages? Surely, there are none to having such a man loose in our city?'

Chaloner suspected that Williamson had allowed himself to become more closely allied to Crisp than most respectable citizens would consider appropriate. He said nothing, and Greeting packed up his violin and left, saying he was due to play in the Chapel Royal for Sunday prayers. When he had gone, Hickes claimed he was feeling better, and that the Sick Dance had finally worked its magic.

'My stew did not make you ill,' stated Chaloner firmly. 'What else did you eat?'

'Nothing, other than what I had at your house,' replied Hickes, rather shiftily.

Chaloner analysed the words with care. 'Last night, you said you had visited me earlier in the day, but I was out. So, when you say you have had nothing other than at my house, are you actually saying you ate something more than the stew?'

Hickes flushed scarlet. 'I was hungry, but I was going to replace it. Honestly.'

'Replace what?'

'The cake outside your door. I thought I would just sample a piece while I was waiting, but you did not return, so I had another. And suddenly the whole thing was gone.'

'You ate food that just happened to be lying around?' Chaloner was disgusted. 'I thought you knew better. You had no problem rejecting the Personal Lozenges.'

'Yes, but this was *cake*,' insisted Hickes earnestly. 'Cake is different.'

Chaloner suspected there was no point trying to convince him otherwise. 'Who was it from? Was there a letter with it? A message?'

'I threw it away when I accidentally finished the cake. It could not have been from whom it said, anyway, because he is missing.'

'Hodgkinson?' Chaloner was confused.

'It must have been from him, because it was a beautifully printed letter. However, I made up for eating the cake by giving you the oil.'

'Ah, yes,' said Chaloner, removing the flask from his pocket and holding it in the air. 'The oil. It contains something volatile, so it was fortunate we did not use it. Where did you get it from?'

Hickes grabbed it, sniffed its contents and regarded him in horror. 'You are right! It was another gift. So, there were two attempts on us in one night?'

'One on each, I imagine: you should be blown up, I should be poisoned. Who gave you the oil?'

'I do not know. It was left for me on my doorstep.'

'And you did not question it?' Chaloner was amazed Hickes had survived so long in the treacherous world of espionage, given that he seemed not to take even the most basic of precautions.

'Why would I? Lamp fuel is not food, to contain poison. It did not occur to me that someone might make it explode. Why am I a target, anyway? Watching Muddiman is hardly dangerous.'

'Right,' said Chaloner, lacking the energy to explain that a good spy considered every situation dangerous. He turned his attention to analysing the current situation, replacing the oil in his pocket as he did so. 'The perpetrator is becoming worried, and is taking precautions to protect himself.'

'But who is it?' asked Hickes fearfully. 'And how do we stop him?'

Chaloner had no idea. 'Just answer a few more questions before I go. I saw you with Henry Brome on Friday, and you were giving him money. You lied about it when I asked. Why?'

'Damn! We are always so careful, too. Brome is a decent man – truthful and loyal to the government – but Williamson says L'Estrange is not very trustworthy. So, he pays Brome a small salary for information about L'Estrange.'

'What sort of information?'

'Anything and everything. Williamson is not a good Spymaster – Thurloe did not have to pay men to spy on his own people, because *he* knew whom he could trust. Williamson does not.'

'What kind of things does Brome tell you?'

'That L'Estrange charges five shillings for each advertisement placed in the newsbooks, but tells Williamson it is only four.'

'So, L'Estrange is dishonest?'

'He is a government official, so of course he is dishonest! Upright ones are few and far between, and extremely poor. Take Bulteel, for example. He is honest, and it costs him a fortune in bribes.'

'What else did Brome tell you about L'Estrange?'

'Nothing much. Personally, I think Williamson is wrong to distrust him. He has his faults – more than most men – but his loyalty to the government is total and absolute.'

'He cheats it of money.'

'That is different – petty. It is hardly worth the risk for Brome to reveal these things. His wife is after him to stop, because if L'Estrange ever found out, there would be a terrible scene, and she says it is not worth the pittance

426

Williamson pays. Or *would* pay, if he were not tardy with settling his bills.'

'Do you believe Brome tells you the truth? He passes you everything he finds out?'

Hickes nodded grimly. 'Oh, yes! You see, Williamson discovered that, as a youth, Brome wrote a pamphlet praising the Commonwealth. He says it is treason, and has poor Brome so frightened that he would never dare hold anything back.'

'Poor Brome indeed.'

'But even so, it is better than what is happening to the other booksellers – fined so heavily they will spend the rest of their lives in debtors' prison. Where are you going?'

'To see L'Estrange.'

The foul weather meant there were no free hackneys, so Chaloner travelled to Ivy Lane on foot. On The Strand, he met Muddiman, who invited him to read a draft analysis about the proposed Spanish marriage contract. The spy did not want to dally, but Muddiman remained a suspect for Newburne's murder, and he could do worse than ask the newsman a few questions.

'You must be shocked by Dury's death,' he said quietly.

Muddiman's expression was bleak. 'It started as a game, but it has now become something infinitely more deadly. Whose side will you back?'

'Fortunately, I do not need to make such choices. All I need do is learn who murdered Newburne – and he *was* murdered.'

Muddiman sighed. 'So much has happened since Newburne's death that I had all but forgotten about it. However, I can tell you that it had nothing to do with

427

politics and struggles for power. It did not even have anything to do with controlling the hearts and minds of London through the news. It was about horses.'

Chaloner nodded. 'I know. Coded messages are passing between criminals, telling them which ones to steal on which nights. It is all contained in music.'

'I suspected it would not take you long to work that out, especially when I learned L'Estrange had given you a copy of one of the messages. You spies are trained to notice that sort of thing, I believe.'

Chaloner did not like to admit it had taken him longer than it should have done. 'How do you know about the code? Are you part of the deception?'

Muddiman gave a wan smile. 'I am not, although I would not mind a share of the profits. The perpetrators must be making a fortune, and I envy them.'

'I would not recommend an association with Hectors – look what happened to Newburne. And I suspect it was they who recently sent me a poisoned cake, too. Hickes ate it and is lucky to be alive.'

Muddiman looked shocked. 'Hickes is not a bad man. I am sorry he is a casualty of this war.'

'Do you know the identity of the killer?' asked Chaloner, not bothering to mention the exploding oil. 'If so, then please tell me. Too many people have died already, and he needs to be stopped.'

'I would rather not ally myself to someone in the Earl of Clarendon's retinue, if it is all the same to you. It would spoil my reputation as an independent observer.'

'I want to stop a murderer, not rule the country. Talk to me. Tell me what you know.'

'You talk to *me*. Tell me what *you* know. We have both worked out that the horrible music that is sailing rather freely around London contains orders to horse thieves – and to answer your earlier question, I learned about it from my search of Finch's room. I doubt he had put the pieces together, but I am far more clever. Start from the beginning. Explain how you think this operation functions.'

Chaloner resented the squandered time, but was also aware that he desperately needed any answers the newsman might be willing to share. 'Very well. Coffee houses are places to exchange gossip – such as who is away from home, or perhaps who plans to ride alone on a lonely road. These tales are carefully culled, and passed to the Hectors.' He thought about the letter Bridges had sent him, revealing how he had been forced to pass such chatter to Hectors after his accusations had almost seen Mary hanged for theft.

Muddiman inclined his head. 'I concur. Butcher Crisp is a powerful criminal, who has a network of people listening in coffee houses. The intelligence is passed to him, and he sends instructions to villains such as Ireton in the form of music.'

'Why music? Why not a simpler system? Or why not word of mouth?'

'Because the music code is very secure – only a few people can decipher it – and it totally conceals the identity of the sender.'

This did not seem right. 'But you and I both know the sender is Crisp.'

'Yes, but we cannot *prove* it, can we? You will have to catch him writing the music in order to be sure of his guilt. And using music means the recipients of these orders never meet the man who issues them. *Ergo*, they can never testify against him. So, what happens after the horses are stolen?'

429

Chaloner was still unconvinced, but he pressed on. 'If the victims advertise in *The Newes* or *The Intelligencer*, their property is often returned. L'Estrange has five shillings for every notice printed, and perhaps even a share of the reward when the thieves restore the horses to their rightful owners.'

Muddiman laughed humourlessly. 'He gains from the paid advertisements, but I doubt he knows about the music. He plays it from time to time, but I suspect its real meaning has eluded him.'

Chaloner was not so sure. 'You have a tendency to underestimate him, because of his campaign against phantom phanatiques, but that is a mistake. Even if he does not understand how the music relays messages to thieves, he knows the meaning of an increased demand for newsbook notices.'

Muddiman gazed at him. 'Are you saying these thefts benefit him, by encouraging people to buy his newsbooks? The advertisements actually improve circulation?'

'That is exactly what I am saying. Victims have their property returned after buying these notices. They discuss it in the coffee houses. More horses are stolen, and more notices bought. More people purchase the newsbooks to see which of their friends have lost animals – or had them recovered. And once the newsbook is bought, people read the other stories, too. It *is* about gaining hearts and minds.'

Muddiman shrugged. 'You may be right, although L'Estrange still has a problem in that people take his "news" with a pinch of salt. If he limited himself to writing reports, rather than indulging in rants, his publications might be a threat to me. But they are not, not as they stand.'

430

'Do you know how Dury died? Hickes thinks Hodgkinson did it.'

'When I saw Hickes examine Dury's body, I waited until he had gone and went to do the same. I saw the bruises on his throat, so I know he was strangled. But they were *bruises*, not dirty marks.'

Chaloner understood what he was saying. 'Hodgkinson's hands are always inky, and he would have left traces of dye on Dury's neck. But if Hodgkinson is not guilty, then who is?'

'L'Estrange?' asked Muddiman with a shrug. 'Not Hickes – he would not have inspected Giles's neck, if he had been responsible. Crisp? After all, Dury *did* die in Smithfield. Wenum, perhaps.'

'Wenum is Newburne.'

'I doubt it, as I have told you already. I appreciate it is odd that Nobert Wenum should happen to spell Tom Newburne, but perhaps it was Wenum's private joke.'

Chaloner was not sure about anything connected with Wenum. 'Then who is he? He abandoned his room about the same time that Newburne died. And you told me he drowned in the Thames.'

'But his body was never recovered, was it? Maybe he realised the stakes were being raised, and ran while he could. Spying is a dangerous business, as I am sure you know all too well.'

The streets were so badly flooded that it was difficult for Chaloner to move very fast through them. Many were solid sheets of water, under the surface of which lurked potholes and other hazards. The continued rain made no difference to his clothes: he could not have been more wet had he jumped in the river. Everyone

431

was the same, and he could even hear some houses groaning, as if their waterlogged timbers were beginning to buckle. Then people started to yell the news that a roof had collapsed in Canning Street, and three people had been crushed to death.

When Chaloner arrived at Ivy Lane, L'Estrange was not there. Brome and Joanna, removing hats and coats after Sunday church, said he had gone out but added that he had declined to say where. Brome ventured the opinion that his errand had almost certainly not been religious, and that one of the Angels was probably involved. Chaloner had been ready for a confrontation, and L'Estrange's absence was an anticlimax. He experienced an overwhelming weariness, his sleepless night beginning to catch up with him.

'Then I should speak to Hodgkinson. It is urgent.'

'He is not here, either,' said Brome. 'I have not seen him today, but that is not unusual for a Sunday. Can we help?'

'You are soaking,' said Joanna kindly. 'Come and sit in the pantry and take some hot wine.'

Chaloner was loath to lose yet more time, but he did not know where else to go for answers. He accepted the wine, burning his mouth when he tried to drink it too soon. He felt like dashing the cup against the wall in frustration, because everything seemed to be taking too long, even wine to cool.

'Do you know who writes that discordant racket for L'Estrange?' he asked, trying to calm himself. 'The stuff we tried to play on Friday?'

'I do not think he commissions it,' said Joanna, seeming to sense his brewing agitation, and speaking softly to soothe him. 'And it is not delivered, as far as we know;

432

he just acquires it. Henry believes it is some kind of code, and that he is communicating with someone.'

Chaloner regarded Brome sharply. 'Why do you think that?'

'Because the tunes are not real music,' explained Brome. 'The harmonies are wrong, and there are too many flats and sharps. He obtains information for his newsbooks from so many sources, that I have wondered whether these airs contain snippets of foreign intelligence, sent to him by spies.'

'I disagree, though,' said Joanna. 'I believe it is just bad music. What do you think, Mr Heyden?'

'That I prefer more traditional melodies,' replied Chaloner noncommittally.

'Well, I do not really want to know how L'Estrange gathers his news,' said Brome with a shudder. 'It is bound to be distasteful, and all I want is a quiet life with Joanna.'

Chaloner was afraid he was not going to have it. He disliked upsetting a man who had been friendly and hospitable towards him, but he needed to know for certain that Hickes had told the truth about Brome being in the Spymaster's pay. He took a deep breath and launched into an attack.

'I understand you spy on L'Estrange for Williamson,' he began baldly.

Joanna's sweet face crumpled into a mask of dismay, and the cup she had been holding clattered to the floor. 'How dare you say such a thing! We have never—'

Brome silenced her by laying a hand on her shoulder. 'Do not try to mislead him, dearest. It will only make matters worse, and if someone at White Hall has been indiscreet, then the safest course of action now is for us to tell the truth. Do not forget that Heyden is the Lord

Chancellor's man – and we cannot afford to be on the wrong side of *another* powerful member of government.'

'No,' said Joanna, regarding Chaloner with a stricken expression that cut him to the core. 'I will not forget that. Not again.' She turned and buried her face in her husband's shoulder.

Brome's voice shook slightly. 'I had no choice but to do what Williamson asked, because he discovered something about me that I would rather was kept quiet.'

'You wrote seditious pamphlets,' said Chaloner.

Joanna's head jerked up, eyes brimming with tears. 'He wrote *a* pamphlet, when he was fifteen. It praised the Commonwealth when Cromwell was Protector, so was regarded as patriotic at the time. But now it is treason. It is unfair! Who did not do things then that he would never consider now?'

'Who told you about the pamphlet?' asked Brome hoarsely. 'Surely not Williamson? He gave me his word that he would say nothing if I did as he asked.'

Joanna stood suddenly, and grabbed a poker from the fire. Her hands shook so badly that she was in danger of dropping it. 'It does not matter who told him, but we cannot let him tell anyone else. The government will say we are phanatiques. They will seize our shop and we will be disgraced, ruined.'

'What are you going to do?' asked Brome uneasily. 'Dash out his brains? In our sitting room?'

Tears slid so fast down Joanna's cheeks that Chaloner imagined she was all but blinded. 'I will not let him destroy you. I will not! They can hang me for murder, but I will protect you with all I have.'

'Joanna, please,' said Brome, making an unsteady lunge towards her. Joanna raised the weapon and he

434

flinched backwards, stumbling into Chaloner. 'This is not helping.'

Joanna aimed a blow at Chaloner, but he evaded it with ease, and grabbed the iron when she was off balance. She tried to resist, but it was not many moments before the poker was back in the hearth.

'I doubt anyone will care about a pamphlet published so long ago,' said Chaloner gently, helping Joanna into a chair. She was shaking violently and sobbing as if her heart would break. 'Williamson has played on your fears – terrorised you into thinking he has uncovered a darker secret than is the case.'

Brome gazed miserably at him, and when he spoke, his voice was low with shame. 'I penned a sentence that mocked the old king's beard, and Williamson said I would hang if he ever had cause to show it to anyone at Court.'

It was Chaloner's turn to stare. 'He said *that* was seditious?'

Brome nodded, red with mortification. 'I did not mean it. The King's father had a very nice beard, and I imagine I was jealous of it at the time, because I did not have one.'

Chaloner rubbed his head, wondering how the Spymaster could sleep at night when he took advantage of such easy prey. 'How did Williamson find out about it in the first place?'

Joanna was still crying, great shuddering sobs that wracked her body. Brome knelt next to her and held her tightly. 'I believe someone sent it to him for malice, but I do not know who.'

Chaloner had his suspicions. 'Muddiman. Or Dury. They produced the Commonwealth's newsbooks, and

probably have a fine collection of Parliamentarian literature between them.'

'Muddiman has an excellent memory,' conceded
Brome slowly. 'He must have recalled me writing something and looked it up. But why would he do such a
spiteful thing?'

'To sow the seeds of discord between L'Estrange and
his assistant,' explained Chaloner. 'A weakened L'Estrange
is a good thing for him.'

'Oh, God!' said Brome shakily. 'Of course! I should
have seen it weeks ago. I do not think I am cut out for
this sort of subterfuge.'

Chaloner was sure of it. 'So what have you told
Williamson about L'Estrange?'

'Nothing!' cried Brome. 'Because there is nothing to
tell. Believe me, I would have uncovered something if it
was there to find, given the pressure Williamson puts me
under. L'Estrange is cantankerous, greedy, irritable and
not always scrupulously honest with money, but these are
minor faults, and he does nothing brazenly illegal.'

'He is a rake,' said Joanna. Her eyes had swollen from
tears, and she gripped Brome's coat so hard that her
knuckles were white. 'Mean and selfish. And likes to
seduce other men's wives.'

'He has been after Joanna for ages,' added Brome.

She gave him a wan smile, then turned back to
Chaloner. 'What will you do now? Inform L'Estrange
what we have been doing? Or tell the Earl how I almost
killed his spy with a poker?'

Chaloner was amused that she thought she had posed
a danger to him. 'It takes a ruthless, resilient kind of
person to succeed in the news business. Perhaps you
should revert to plain bookselling. But do not worry about

L'Estrange. He will not learn what you have been doing from me.'

'You are kind,' sniffed Joanna. 'And I shall tell you a secret in return. When L'Estrange refused to tell us where he was going, I set my maid to follow him. He went to Monkwell Street. I suspect Mary Cade is already priming her next victim, so it will not be long before she relinquishes her hold over William. It is good news.'

Chaloner did not think so; he was appalled. 'She needs Will dead first, to inherit his property.'

Joanna's jaw dropped. 'Then we must make sure she does not succeed. I shall visit him at once—'

'No,' said Chaloner sharply, suspecting she would get herself hurt if she tried to interfere with Mary. 'Leave them to me.'

'We are not cowards,' said Brome with quiet dignity. 'We are not afraid to go to his rescue.'

'I know,' said Chaloner tiredly. 'But trying to reason with him will do no good, and might even make the situation worse. We must devise another way to foil her.'

'How?' demanded Brome. 'Will you let us help?'

Chaloner nodded, but had no intention of doing so. They would be a liability, and he could not look after them and Leybourn at the same time. He wished they would just leave London while they were still relatively unscathed. Joanna accepted his acquiescence without demur, and he saw it had not occurred to her that he might lie. She really was too innocent for her own good.

'Very well,' she said, 'but I insist you borrow my gun.'

'Your gun?' Chaloner was not sure he had heard her properly.

'It belonged to my father.' She went to a chest and removed a small dag. The firing pin was broken, so it

437

would not work, but Chaloner took it anyway, loath to hurt her feelings by refusing. 'It is loaded. Well, I think it is loaded, but I am not really sure how it works, so . . .'

She trailed off helplessly, and Chaloner checked it was not before he tucked it in his belt. 'I had better see if I can find L'Estrange.'

'Then be careful,' said Joanna, following him to the door. 'And do not forget to tell us when you require help with Mary.'

'Please do as she says,' said Brome softly. 'You need someone you can trust in this wicked city.'

Chaloner left the bookshop despising Williamson for dragging the Bromes into the murky world of espionage, especially on such a flimsy pretext. He found himself wanting to avenge them somehow, and hoped with all his heart that he would uncover evidence to prove the Spymaster did indeed hire Hectors for his dirty work. If so, then Chaloner would do all he could to see it included in Muddiman's newsletters, with a view to creating a scandal that would see Williamson disgraced and dismissed. He set off towards Monkwell Street, but had taken no more than two or three steps before he heard his name being called. It was Nott the bookseller, whose premises were opposite.

'Thurloe asked me to identify the owner of that Galen,' he said when Chaloner went reluctantly to see what he wanted. 'He said when I had my answer, I was to tell either him or you. I just happened to spot you coming from Brome's house, and I thought—'

'You know who bought it?' interrupted Chaloner impatiently.

438

'Oh, yes,' said Nott. 'Its binding makes it unique, you see, because it is—'

'Who?'

Nott told him, and Chaloner felt the situation become more urgent than ever.

'And there is something else,' the bookseller burbled on. 'Jonas Kirby was here earlier. He knows you and I are acquainted, because he asked me to give you a message.'

He handed Chaloner a folded piece of paper. When the spy opened it, all it contained was a crude drawing of a cat with a gibbet beneath it.

Daylight was fading by the time Chaloner reached Leybourn's house. Door and windows were closed, and Leybourn's colleague Allestry was loitering outside. Allestry was peeved because the surveyor had shut shop early after making an appointment with him. He had struggled all the way from St Paul's in the teeming rain, and now would have to walk all the way home again for nothing. Concerned, Chaloner went to see Leybourn's brother.

'I have not seen him all day,' said Rob. 'Did you know he changed his will? I could not believe it! Mary says she will look after my family, but I do not trust her. I wish I could expose her as the lying cheat she is, but Kirby came to see me this morning, and said that if I did anything to malign her, he will hurt my children. She has won this war, Tom. We cannot fight her sort of battle.'

Chaloner thought about his missing cat. 'They think they can intimidate us by striking at the things we hold dear. But they are in for a shock – I do not like bullies.'

Rob was alarmed. 'There are too many of them to take on, and while I appreciate your loyalty to Will, there is no point in squandering your life. Do you know who is due to dine with him today? Ellis Crisp! Go home, Tom, and try not to think about it.'

'The Butcher of Smithfield,' mused Chaloner. 'I have been wanting to meet him for some time.'

The wind drowned any sound Chaloner might have made as he climbed up the back of Leybourn's house and let himself in through an upstairs window. The door to the main bedchamber was closed, and when Chaloner opened it, something furry emerged to rub around his legs. He smiled, and spent a moment petting his cat, allowing it to purr and knead his shoulder with its claws. He wondered how Mary had explained its presence to Leybourn. It objected when he shut it in the bedroom again, but he could not risk it tripping him when he was trying to move stealthily, and it was safer where it was.

He crept downstairs, hearing voices raised in laughter. He smiled grimly: he had known someone was in, despite the air of abandonment outside. The reek of tobacco wafted towards him, along with the scent of new bread and roasting meat. He reached the bottom of the steps and peered through a gap in one of the door panels.

Leybourn was sitting at the head of his table, and Mary was at the foot. Between them were a number of familiar faces, including Kirby and Treen, both in their finest clothes. The Hectors were clearly on their best behaviour, but even so, their lack of manners showed in the clumsy way they used their silver table forks. Long-nosed Ireton was watching them with amused disdain. Next to Leybourn was a man Chaloner did not know. He was huge, with a heavy, brooding face and eyes so deeply set they were almost invisible. On Leybourn's other

side was a tiny fellow with a red face and pale eyes, like
a pheasant. Prominent on the table was a dish of cucumbers and a huge pie. Chaloner supposed the latter had
been furnished by the Butcher of Smithfield, and
wondered whether it contained anyone he knew. Mary
picked up the cucumbers.

'Try one of these, William,' she said. 'They are delicious.'

'No, thank you.' Leybourn's voice was strained, and
Chaloner was under the impression he was not enjoying
the party. 'Galen says cucumbers are bad for the diges-
tion.'

'Piffle,' said Mary. Even Chaloner was surprised by
the curt tone of her voice, and Leybourn looked posi-
tively distraught. 'Eat one.'

'I would rather not,' said Leybourn plaintively. 'It might
make me ill.'

'Then I shall cut it up for you,' said Mary, going to
stand behind him. She held a knife, and Chaloner was
not entirely sure what she intended to do with it. He was
not prepared to stand by while she slit his friend's throat,
though. He stepped into the room with his sword in one
hand and Joanna's useless gun in the other.

'He said he does not want it.'

'You!' snarled Ireton, surging to his feet. Mary made
a hissing sound, and he sat again, albeit reluctantly. As
he did so, he picked up the knife he had been using to
cut his meat.

'Tom!' said Leybourn uncertainly. 'Where did you
come from?'

'From upstairs,' said Mary. She did not seem disconcerted by the spy's sudden appearance. In fact, she seemed
inexplicably pleased about it, and Chaloner had the

441

sudden sense that something was about to go very wrong. He glanced around quickly, trying to assess what it might be. 'He regularly burgles your house, as I told you before.'

'He took your money sack off me,' added Kirby, eager to support her claim. 'I recognise his voice now. He came at me with a dag . . .' He trailed off when he realised the implications of what he had said. Ireton was not the only Hector who rolled his eyes.

'Yes, I took it from you,' agreed Chaloner pleasantly. 'After I saw you steal it from Will. I cannot imagine how you knew where to look for it – unless someone told you its whereabouts, of course.'

'Where is my money, Tom?' asked Leybourn, hurt and bewildered.

'That is a good question,' said Kirby, standing slowly. There was a dagger in his hand, and several Hectors grinned at each other, anticipating some entertaining violence. 'And you will answer it.'

'Before or after I paint the wall with your brains?' asked Chaloner, aiming the gun at him.

Kirby sat quickly, but Ireton was less easily intimidated. 'And then what? You shoot Kirby, but how will you tackle the rest of us? You cannot win against us all.'

'No one is going to kill anyone,' said Leybourn. His face was white with anguish. 'What is wrong with you all? Mary told me you were civilised.'

'It is all right, Jonas,' said Mary, as Kirby's fingers tightened around his dagger. Her eyes flicked towards the fire, passing him a message. Chaloner glanced at the hearth, where there was a merry blaze. Over it was a cauldron-style pot containing something that bubbled, along with a side of pork on a spit. Chaloner had eaten nothing all day, but there was something about the

442

situation that robbed him of his appetite. Something was definitely not right.

'Do not worry about his gun,' said the pheasant-faced man to Mary. He grinned merrily at her. 'The firing pin is broken, so it is quite harmless.'

'So it is,' said Ireton, suddenly gleeful. 'That puts a different complexion on matters!'

Treen laughed jubilantly, and several of the Hectors produced daggers.

'No!' breathed Leybourn in a strangled voice. 'Stop!'

Chaloner saw his situation was fast becoming hopeless, and knew he should have taken more time to assess the situation before acting. What could he do against a dozen armed men? He could eliminate some with his sword, but it would only be a matter of time before he was overwhelmed. And then what would happen to Leybourn?

Mary smiled coldly at him. 'I have been saying for some time that you should meet Mr Crisp, and he has honoured us with his presence at dinner this evening. So, I am delighted you came.'

Chaloner expected the large, menacing man to reply, and was startled when Pheasant Face looked up and beamed at him.

'Are you a bookseller, too?' he asked cheerfully. 'I like booksellers! They are an erudite lot, and there is so much to learn these days. I read an English translation of Galileo's *Dialogo* just yesterday, although I prefer the original Latin. Leybourn tells me you were at Cambridge.'

Chaloner was bemused. A cheery gnome who read Latin was not what he was expecting from the Butcher of Smithfield. He recalled glimpsing a round, smiling face at Newburne's funeral, and supposed it was the same man. Then he remembered the catlike grace with which Crisp had moved when he was with his Hectors at Smithfield and in Old Jewry, and was not so sure.

'Who is your father?' Chaloner asked, somewhat abruptly. Ireton sniggered – he knew the line Chaloner's thoughts had taken.

'This *is* Crisp,' said Leybourn in a small voice. 'I have known him for years.'

But something was awry. And why were the Hectors not attacking him when they could overpower him with ease?

'My father is Sir Nicholas,' replied Crisp genially. 'Have you read my piece on inshore winds and climate, by the way? Leybourn was good enough to say it was a significant contribution to navigation.'

'But I did not know *you* had written it, not until tonight. It was published anonymously.' Leybourn sounded as confused as Chaloner felt.

'I am a modest man,' said Crisp. 'Where are you going, Ireton? I hope it is not to fetch your lute. I dislike music. This pork is excellent, incidentally. May I have some more?'

'In a moment,' said Mary, dismissing him carelessly. 'We are celebrating.'

'Celebrating what?' Chaloner was watching Ireton, who had gone to lean against the far wall with his hands tucked into his belt. The spy was growing more bewildered by the minute. Ireton did not seem to be moving towards a weapon, so what was he doing?

'William and I made wills today, leaving all our property to each other,' said Mary. Her voice was smug, and Leybourn settled back into his dazed state. 'Thurloe threatened to apply some devious legal ruling that would see me disinherited, but Ireton is a lawyer, too, and he worked out a way to prevent that from happening.'

Ireton removed a pipe from his pocket, the picture of insouciance. 'Thurloe's ploy will not work now she has signed *her* property over to *Leybourn*. And she owns a small house near Uxbridge, before you say she has the better end of the bargain. She is not poor.'

'You are very wet, Heyden,' said Mary, shooting Kirby another unreadable glance. 'Stand by the fire, to dry off. But drop your sword first.'

Chaloner frowned. The table had been placed in such a way that Leybourn was nearest the hearth, and Crisp, as his right-hand guest, was not much further away. What was she going to do?

'Yes, drop it,' said Kirby, fingering his dagger. He drew back his arm when the spy continued to hesitate, and prepared to throw it.

With no choice but to comply, Chaloner let the weapon clatter to the floor.

'I want more pork,' declared Crisp. He banged on the table with his spoon, more in the manner of a petulant child than a man who held a city to ransom with his evil deeds. 'Now.'

'Wait!' snapped Mary. 'Stand by the fire, Heyden.'

But Chaloner was beginning to understand. 'Will, come to me,' he ordered.

'Stay!' barked Mary, when Leybourn started to stand. Conditioned to obey, the surveyor sank down again. 'And go to the hearth, Heyden, before Kirby knifes you.'

'I shall have a cucumber, then,' said Crisp sulkily. He gnawed off a chunk and tossed the rest towards Kirby, who flinched away violently. It touched his hand before falling to the floor, and he began to scrub it on the side of his coat.

'Will,' said Chaloner urgently. 'Come here.'

'He stays where he is,' said Mary harshly. She backed away, and suddenly she, Kirby and Treen dived to the floor and put their hands over their heads. Leybourn gaped at them.

'Are you going to fetch the pork?' asked Crisp. 'These cucumbers are—' He stopped speaking, and both hands went to his throat.

'He is choking,' said the big man next to him, alarmed. 'He took too big a bite.'

'Good bye, William,' shouted Mary exultantly. 'Thank you for everything.'

Chaloner leapt towards Leybourn, hauling him from his chair just as there was a tremendous explosion that turned the room into a chaos of sound and light. And then there was only darkness.

Chapter 12

There was a dull roaring in Chaloner's ears, which gradually resolved into a single voice. He opened his eyes to see Leybourn's frightened face looming over him, speaking indistinctly as though he was underwater. He sat up slowly, taking in the carnage around him.

Ellis Crisp was dead, lying on the far side of the room like a broken doll, and there were three other bodies, too. One was Treen, while Mary lay gasping at his side. Chaloner scrambled upright, and grabbed Kirby, who was in the process of crawling towards the door. But before the spy could stop him, Leybourn had dealt the felon a vicious blow with a skillet, which laid him out cold.

'Mary set an explosion,' said Chaloner hoarsely, thinking for one horrible moment that Leybourn might assume *he* was responsible. 'She and her friends threw themselves to the floor to avoid the blast, leaving us sitting like ducks on a pond.'

'I know,' said Leybourn brokenly. 'It took the near-demolition of my home and a close brush with death, but my eyes are open now. I struggled to keep them closed too long, and look what it brought.'

Chaloner was not sure what to say, so resorted to a practical analysis of what had happened. 'Unfortunately, she miscalculated the amount of gunpowder needed, and she used too much.'

'She added nails to her mixture,' said Leybourn, shuddering when he saw what they had done to Crisp. 'She must really have hated me.'

'She did not hate you. She just wanted your money.'

Leybourn was not listening to him. 'She would have killed you, too, if you had followed her orders and stood by the hearth.'

'I should have known,' said Chaloner, angry with himself. 'There were slops under the stairs – not left for slovenliness, as I assumed, but because they are a component of gunpowder. She made her own, so no purchase of the stuff could be traced back to her. That is why she miscalculated. Powder is always unpredictable, but it is even more so when an amateur manufactures it.'

'What was she thinking of? Crisp is dead, and so are some of his Hectors. Surely, that cannot have been what she intended?'

'I suspect it was exactly what she intended. The explosives were in the pot over the fire, and Crisp was positioned to bear the brunt of it when it went up. So were you. I imagine she planned to have you blamed for Crisp's death – you invited him to dinner for the express purpose of assassination. And to be doubly sure of success, she included poisonous cucumbers in her feast, too.'

Leybourn gazed blankly at him. 'Why would she want Crisp assassinated?'

'Because that is not Crisp.' Chaloner put his fingers in his ears and shook his head in an attempt to stop them ringing. He saw Leybourn's bemusement, and tried to explain. 'That is to say he *is* Crisp, but he is not the underworld king. I have seen the Butcher of Smithfield walking about twice now, and this Crisp is too short to be him – and nor would he have the agile, soft-footed gait of the man I saw.'

'I confess I was surprised when Mary introduced us. I knew he *was* Crisp, because I met him years ago, but the more we spoke, the more I thought that little fellow could never have ruled Smithfield.'

'Someone took his identity and turned him into something he is not. Also, Crisp claimed he did not like music, but the horse stealing is based entirely on music. He would not have made that comment, had he been the real Butcher.'

Leybourn still looked as though he had no idea what Chaloner was talking about, and it was a testament to his shock that he looked as though he did not care, either. 'So, who is the Butcher? One of the Hectors, who rose through the ranks and decided to succeed to the whole operation?'

'I imagine we will find out when this Crisp is declared dead, and his successor steps forward to take his place.'

'But who?' pressed Leybourn. 'Ireton is a cunning fellow; Kirby is stupid but strong.'

Ireton's position against the far wall had allowed him to flee the carnage, and Chaloner wondered whether he had gone to rally his forces – perhaps to march on Leybourn's house and accuse him or murder. If so, then he would be doing it without help from Mary. She had left herself too close to the blast, and Chaloner had seen enough battle-field wounds to know she was unlikely to survive. He knelt next to her, but could tell from her eyes that she had been blinded by the flash, and could not see him.

'Crisp said only people near the fire would die,' she whispered. She sounded indignant. 'He lied.'

Chaloner regarded her askance. 'Crisp told you how to kill him?'

Her expression hardened. 'Go away, Heyden. Why did you have to survive? You should be dead, along with your pathetic friend.'

Chaloner glanced at Leybourn, but the surveyor was wandering around the remains of his kitchen, and was not listening. He showed no inclination to be at his lover's side during her last moments.

'Crisp told you how to kill him?' Chaloner asked again.

She smiled, and there was blood on her teeth. 'You want to talk? Very well. He did not tell us how to kill *him* – he told us how to make powder and set an explosion that would only kill selected victims. He was fond of theories, but he was not a practical man.'

'I have no idea what you are talking about.' Chaloner knew why she was deigning to speak to him: she was hoping to keep him occupied until one of her cronies rallied, at which point he would be killed. Because she could not see, she did not know her accomplices were either dead or had fled.

'We picked that pathetic, grinning little man – Ellis Crisp – and we built a legend around him. It worked for a while, but it is becoming difficult to maintain the illusion, and the real Butcher wants to claim the kingdom he has forged. So, we decided to kill Crisp in a spectacular way – one in keeping with the flamboyant character we have created for him. And as there are a few Hectors I dislike, I decided to get rid of them, too, as well as our surveyor friend.'

'How did you keep the real Crisp from the public eye? Lock him in a dungeon with plenty of books?'

'In a country house, visited only by his father.'

'Who is Crisp's successor?'

'Someone who will make us rich. We communicate by music, but we have never met. We shall call *him* Crisp when he takes his throne. The creature I killed tonight does not deserve the name.' She shifted slightly and blinked, trying to see how much longer she needed to talk.

'Will you tell me about the horses?'

She swallowed. 'Some we returned for the reward; some we sold. It was all carefully planned, so no one would be suspicious. And no one is. Everything is working perfectly. Newburne tried to take more than his due, but he learned what happens to disloyal people. He was quietly poisoned.'

'Like your husband – Valentine Pettis? And Colonel Beauclair? And James Hickes?'

'Hickes was getting too inquisitive, and he acquired some of our music from Finch. Meanwhile, Val tried to do business at Crisp's expense, and I never cared for him anyway. I wanted to marry Jonas – and I did. Why do you think I could not wed William?'

Chaloner was bemused. 'Murder, theft and extortion are all right, but bigamy is not?'

'It would have meant lying in church, and I have my scruples.' She blinked again, still trying to clear her vision. 'The Butcher is a genius, so do not think you can defeat him.'

'And the horses?'

'Beauclair returned home unexpectedly when we went to steal his stallion, so Ireton made him eat lozenges. We took his body to White Hall in a sedan-chair. The carriers promised to keep quiet, but who takes unnecessary risks? They were given lozenges, too. The Butcher ordered us to leave cucumbers with them all, so their

451

deaths would be deemed natural. He has a talent for deception.'

'He certainly does,' agreed Chaloner. 'Where is he now? I would like to meet him.'

Her hissing laugh was distinctly malevolent. 'Oh, you will, Heyden. You will.'

People had been awoken by the explosion, and were massing outside. The parish constable arrived, but promptly disappeared when he saw several of the victims were Hectors, and so did some of the onlookers. Then soldiers came, and placed everyone under arrest until they were satisfied with the stories they were being told. The government did not like gunpowder in the hands of private citizens, being of the belief that its only use was for armed rebellion. Chaloner chafed at the ponderous questions put by a thickset sergeant. Every moment spent repeating himself was another moment for Crisp to assume his mantle of power, and Chaloner had the sense that unless he struck before the man was fully enthroned, he might never have another chance.

'I have to get away,' he said urgently to Leybourn, when the sergeant had gone to see whether there really was a cat in an upstairs bedroom. 'We are wasting time here.'

'You knew from the start,' said Leybourn softly. His face was grey with shock, and he looked away when Mary's body was carried past. 'As soon as you set eyes on her, you saw something I did not.'

Chaloner glanced at the door, and wondered if he could disappear into the darkness before the guards outside opened fire. 'You are not the only one she deceived. Bridges had a similar experience.'

'Do you think she really does own a house near Uxbridge?' asked Leybourn. 'If so, and it is proven to be mine, I shall give it to you.'

'I do not want it,' said Chaloner in distaste. 'Besides, I suspect Kirby might have something to say about that. He is her real husband.'

'He is dead. I hit him on the head with a pan.'

'Unfortunately, he recovered and is now at large. The only way we shall catch him is by going after the Butcher. Of course, we have no idea who the Butcher is, or where to find him, but find him I must. He killed Newburne. Mary told me.'

'I will help,' offered Leybourn. 'And when we locate him, I shall put a ball in his black heart.'

'Crisp did not order Mary to prey on you,' warned Chaloner, knowing exactly why the surveyor wanted to meet the Butcher of Smithfield. He smiled when the sergeant handed him his cat; it did not seem any the worse for its experiences. 'That was her own idea – her way of earning a living.'

'No, they were in it together,' said Leybourn bitterly. 'Ireton, Kirby and Treen were always visiting, and I believed her when she said they were her cousins.'

'Did you?' asked Chaloner, wondering how he could have been so gullible. 'How did they explain bringing my cat to your house?'

'I did not know you had a cat,' said Leybourn acidly. 'You are far too secretive to reveal such a personal detail, remember? And I am going with you when you challenge the Butcher, no matter what you say. I am sure it was he who put her up to hurting me.'

'You cannot come if you intend to murder him,' said Chaloner firmly. 'That would not be helpful. And such

453

recklessness is likely to see us both killed, anyway. If you will not go to stay with your brother tonight, then I will take you to Lincoln's Inn.'

Leybourn glared at him. 'Thurloe will help me bring down the Butcher's evil empire. *You* can go to the Devil!'

He stamped to the far side of the room, and Chaloner put his head in his hands in despair when the sergeant sat at the kitchen table and took a pen in one of his heavy hands. He was going to write a statement, and judging from the way his tongue poked out when he concentrated, it was going to take a very long time. Casually, the spy walked to the hearth, and removed from his pocket the bottle of oil Hickes had given him. Surreptitiously, he dropped it into the still-glowing embers of the fire.

It was not a huge blast, although it would certainly have maimed anyone using it in a lamp, but it had the desired effect. Yelling that there were probably more explosions in the offing, to cause enough panic to cover his escape, Chaloner grabbed his cat and ran. He reached the end of Monkwell Street and headed south. He was not pleased when he glanced behind him and saw Leybourn hard on his heels. He did not have time for him – not until the Butcher was eliminated.

Trusting Thurloe to ply the surveyor with enough wine to render him insensible for the night – the ex-Spymaster would not want him racing around London like an avenging angel, either – Chaloner hired a carriage to take them to Chancery Lane. They did not get far. The back wheels caught in a rut, and then the whole thing became bogged down in mud. They walked to the Holborn Bridge, which groaned and shuddered as the Fleet River roared underneath it. Warily, they started to cross, but a large tree was being borne downstream, and it crashed into the structure before they were halfway over. Part of the balustrade was carried away, so Chaloner grabbed Leybourn's arm and hauled him back the way they had come. The guard promptly declared it closed until the flood had abated.

'We shall have to use the Ludgate bridge,' said Chaloner, determined to see Leybourn in Thurloe's care that night.

'Closed since dusk,' said the guard. 'And the one at Bridewell is washed away altogether.'

'What about the two upstream?' asked Chaloner, seeing Leybourn brighten.

'I saw both float past in pieces about an hour ago. You will have to stay in the city for the night, although it will not be easy. Every inn is full, because lots of people are stranded.'

'You have no choice now, Tom,' said Leybourn grimly. 'You cannot foist me on Thurloe. You cannot even deposit me in Temperance's brothel, because the Fleet stands between us. And I am sure you do not want me wandering Smithfield alone. You have no alternative but to let me help you. So, what shall we do first?'

'Christ!' muttered Chaloner, standing calf-deep in flood-water with a cat in his arms and a friend determined to avenge himself on the man he needed to question. 'This is turning into a difficult night.'

Leybourn drew his sword. It stuck halfway out, and the extra tug he needed to free it from its scabbard forced Chaloner to jump back. 'The Butcher will be sorry he ever meddled with me.'

'He may not be alone,' said Chaloner unhappily.

*　*　*

Because Leybourn had a waterproof coat, Chaloner persuaded him to carry the cat, on the grounds that it would keep the animal dry. It did not occur to the surveyor that an armful of moggy would also slow him down and prevent him from racing into a situation that might see him killed. Before that, Chaloner had seriously considered hitting him on the head and leaving him in an alley, but water was gushing everywhere, and he was afraid he might drown. Reluctantly, he conceded the surveyor was right: there was no choice but to accept his 'help' and hope for the best. While they walked, he told him all he had learned about the murders.

'So,' said Leybourn when he had finished. There was a cold, flat light in his eyes that said he was going to be dangerous company. 'Where first? How will we unmask this evil Butcher – a man who has been so careful to keep his face concealed that no one knows what he looks like?'

'He is someone fit and agile – someone who moves with feline stealth.'

'L'Estrange? He moves with feline stealth, especially when he is in pursuit of a woman. You should have seen him stalk Mary earlier . . .' He trailed off.

'I am sorry Will,' said Chaloner gently. 'I know she was dear to you.'

'She could not cook, though. My ideal woman must be able to cook.' Leybourn took a deep breath and changed the subject. 'You must have other theories about the Butcher's identity. A stealthy tread is not much on which to accuse L'Estrange.'

'What about Hodgkinson as the culprit? Both Hickes and Thurloe say he is dangerous – that his pleasant façade is a ruse.'

'Well, there you are, then. Hodgkinson. He works for L'Estrange *and* Muddiman, so he obviously has no conscience. And now he is missing. Perhaps the reason he is 'missing' is because he knows his predecessor is due to die in an accident, and he needs to be ready to take his throne.'

It was good logic, especially in light of what Nott had told Chaloner earlier. 'You may be right, Will. I learned this evening that *he* bought the book on cucumbers I saw in Wenum's room. He is definitely involved in something sinister.' He broke into a trot, heading for the Thames Street print-house.

Leybourn tried to stop him. 'He will not be there. He will be at his Smithfield shop, which lies at the heart of the domain over which he is about to assume control.'

'I am sure of it – especially as the Thames is on the verge of flooding again, and only a fool will want to be near the river when that happens.'

'Then why are you going the wrong way?'

'We need solid evidence to convict him, but all we have is supposition and theory. It is a good time to search his main lair. So I will look, while you keep watch and make sure he does not catch us.'

'All right,' agreed Leybourn, albeit sulkily. 'But if he appears, I *will* fight him.'

Thames Street was now more the domain of its name-sake than of the land, and Chaloner and Leybourn ploughed through water that was well past their knees. A candlelit boat rocked its way up the black waters in the opposite direction, and Chaloner did not like the way familiar sights were being turned on their heads by the deluge.

457

'Perhaps I should find a second cat,' grumbled Leybourn as they paddled towards the dark mass of Baynard's Castle. 'Then we would have two, and I could pretend to be Noah.'

They reached the print-house, which looked dark and forbidding amid the flood waters.

'Stand in that doorway and keep a tight hold of my cat,' ordered Chaloner, prepared to resort to devious means to keep Leybourn's hands occupied. 'If anyone comes, whistle. No fighting – you may tackle the wrong person, and we have to be sure before we attack.'

Leybourn stepped into the alcove Chaloner indicated. 'Go on, then. And when you are finished, we will go to Smithfield, and assault this den of thieves – like crusading knights against the infidel.'

Chaloner had a vague memory that most of the crusades had ended in disaster, and hoped Leybourn's words would not prove to be prophetic. He picked the print-house lock and stepped inside. The basement was a black, deserted cavern full of peculiar groaning creaks, as if water had seeped into its very foundations and rendered them unstable. Sloshing sounds indicated the Thames was already bubbling into it. He lit a lamp and saw the great presses standing in a lake of dirty water that rippled softly in the waves made by his feet. Bales of paper had been suspended from the ceiling in rope nets, and all written records had been removed, to save them from the impending flood. Chaloner was about to leave empty-handed, when he saw something had been left on the press nearest the door. It was the little box containing Newburne's jewels, apparently abandoned.

The spy stood still and listened hard, but the only sounds were those of water. A rat swam across the room, heading for the door, leaving a v-shaped trail of ripples in its wake. Chaloner opened the box, expecting to find it empty because the locks had been smashed. Therefore, he was astonished to see the gems still glittering within it.

'Step away and put your hands in the air,' ordered Hodgkinson, emerging from behind the largest of his presses. He held a gun in his right hand, which he was shielding from the wet with his left. Chaloner did as he was told, hoping Leybourn would not hear their voices and come to investigate.

'What are you doing with Newburne's hoard?' he demanded. He was not really in a position to interrogate the printer, given that he was not the one holding the dag, but the box was the last thing he had expected to find in the print-house and he was hopelessly confused. 'And what are you doing here?'

'Where else would I be?' snapped Hodgkinson. 'I had a feeling villains would come to see what they could steal while my premises were underwater.'

'I am not here to steal,' said Chaloner tiredly. 'Unlike you, it seems. I repeat: how did you come by Newburne's treasure?'

Hodgkinson kept the gun trained on Chaloner's chest. His face was shadowed, and the spy could not see it well enough to read its expression. 'I knew where he hid it – I saw it once, when I visited his house. And I also knew someone recently dug it up to look at it. So, I retrieved it and brought it here. I should have guessed you were the one who tampered with it when L'Estrange told me about your strange behaviour in Dorcus's garden. He did not understand it at all, but now I do.'

'What do you mean?' asked Chaloner, bemused.

'It is really very simple: *you* are Newburne's killer. You

459

have been pretending to investigate, but all the time you are the guilty party. I am shocked, because I thought you were honest. You gave me back my silver pen, but you are a thief and a killer.'

Chaloner's mystification increased. 'What?'

Hodgkinson sighed impatiently. 'Everyone knows about Newburne's treasure, and it is obvious that someone murdered him in order to steal it – to visit all his houses and search them one by one.'

'But I was not even in the country when he died. I was on a ship, travelling home from Portugal.'

'I do not believe you. As soon as L'Estrange mentioned your peculiar conduct in the garden, I went straight to the cellar and saw how someone had dragged a barrel over the place where the gems were hidden. The culprit – you – knew exactly where to look.'

'Yes, I did. However, I think Crisp killed Newburne, although the original Crisp has just been dispatched in an explosion. Whoever steps forward to claim his kingdom will be the real villain.' Chaloner shrugged. 'I assumed it was you.'

'Me?' Hodgkinson was indignant. 'How dare you!'

'Do not believe him, Hodgkinson,' came a voice from the shadows. Chaloner had sensed another person hiding there, but was shocked – and dismayed – to see Brome emerge. The bookseller also held a gun, although his hand shook and he looked acutely uncomfortable. He had, however, a far better weapon than the one Joanna had lent Chaloner. 'He is lying.'

Chaloner tried to reason with him, his thoughts tumbling chaotically as he struggled for answers. 'Please put the gun down, Brome. You know I am no danger to you – we resolved that last night.'

'That was before I learned you went after the jewels,' said Brome unsteadily. 'Hodgkinson was right.'

'There are serious flaws in his logic,' said Chaloner to Brome, trying not to sound desperate. While he wasted time trying to convince them of his innocence, the Butcher was stepping ever closer to his new throne. He saw now that Hodgkinson was not the culprit, because he would not have spent half the night loitering in his flooded basement if he were – he would have had more important matters to attend. 'There is no reason to assume that whoever killed Newburne also knew where he kept his treasure.'

Hodgkinson sneered. 'He is trying to confuse us, to worm his way out of my trap. If he had eaten that cake I sent him—'

'*You* tried to poison me?' exclaimed Chaloner. 'Did you send Hickes the exploding oil, too?'

Brome glanced uneasily at the printer. 'What is he talking about?'

Hodgkinson started to deny the accusation, but then shrugged, exasperated. 'Heyden keeps asking us awkward questions. He always seems hungry, so I sent him something to keep him quiet.'

Brome's jaw dropped in horror. 'But it is his duty to ask questions! We have nothing to hide – not now he knows about my pamphlet. He can ask whatever he likes, as far as I am concerned.'

'And the oil?' asked Chaloner.

Hodgkinson shook his head firmly. 'I know nothing about any oil, and why would I want to harm Hickes? Muddiman said he had him under control.'

'Did you hear that?' said Chaloner to Brome. 'Why would Muddiman make such a comment to Hodgkinson, unless they were in league together? It is revealing, and

461

should tell you how Muddiman lays hold of L'Estrange's news – or some of it, at least. Do you remember the ledger I showed you, which contained details of sales written by one Wenum? Well, Wenum is Hodgkinson.'

'Lies!' spat Hodgkinson. 'It was Newburne. Tom Newburne and Nobert Wenum are the same name – the same letters arranged in a different order.'

'You made a mistake,' Chaloner went on. 'You wanted to read about cucumbers so you bought a book by Galen. It was in "Wenum's" room in the Rhenish Wine House. Unfortunately, Wenum did not buy the book: *you* did. Nott told me.'

'Hearsay,' snapped Hodgkinson. 'And I—'

'Wenum's neighbour talked about his scarred jaw,' Chaloner continued, 'but Newburne's face was unblemished. Remove your false beard, Hodgkinson, and show Brome what lies beneath.'

Furious, Hodgkinson pulled the trigger. Chaloner ducked instinctively, but there was a resounding click and no more – the powder was damp. Taking advantage of the printer's brief moment of surprise, Chaloner made a grab for his beard, while at the same time trying to prevent him from hauling a second dag from his belt. The hair came off in the spy's hand, but Hodgkinson managed to draw his weapon.

'Stop!' yelled Brome, brandishing his own gun wildly. 'Stand away from each other. At once!'

Chaloner complied, afraid the bookseller might shoot him just because he was agitated and afraid. Meanwhile, Hodgkinson's free hand was pressed to his ravaged face. His expression was murderous, and Chaloner braced himself, sure the man was going to kill him where he stood. But the printer lowered the weapon.

462

'No.' His voice shook with rage, but he was holding himself in control. 'I want answers before you die. How did you know about my skin?'

Brome gaped in shock: Hodgkinson's response was a clear admission of guilt.

'Because you wore a darker beard to Newburne's funeral,' explained Chaloner. 'I assumed you had blackened the real one as part of your funeral attire, but you had actually donned a completely different hairpiece. I was a fool not to have understood its significance straight away.'

'*You* are Wenum?' asked Brome unsteadily. '*You* have been betraying us?'

His accusatory tone drove Hodgkinson to greater anger. The gun came up, and Chaloner hurled himself behind one of the presses.

'All right,' snarled the printer, moving to get a clear shot. 'I am Wenum, although I constructed my character in a way that meant Newburne would be blamed. I even kept a few law books in the Rhenish Wine House, should anyone ever search it. And why not? He was corrupt, anyway.'

Desperately, Chaloner tried to make Brome see who was the enemy. 'It meant that when Newburne died, "Wenum" had to disappear, too. Hodgkinson was forced to abandon the Rhenish Wine House and spin a tale about Wenum throwing himself in the river. To confuse matters further, he started a rumour that Wenum was a victim of Mary Cade.'

Hodgkinson sneered, crouching with the firearm clutched in both hands as he pointed it towards where he thought Chaloner was hiding. 'What choice did I have? Men like you were prying into affairs that were none of their concern, spoiling everything.'

'Hickes believed your tales, and so did Spymaster

463

Williamson, which is why they never looked very closely at Wenum – a man they believe to be dead.'

'Put down the gun, Hodgkinson,' said Brome quietly. 'Selling L'Estrange's news to Muddiman was dishonest and stupid, but when we explain—'

'No,' grated Hodgkinson. 'L'Estrange will not appreciate that printing is a hard business and that profits must be made where they can. He will accuse me of being a phanatique.'

Brome's mouth snapped shut, telling the printer he was right. Chaloner rolled his eyes, wishing Brome was endowed with a little more strength of character. Hodgkinson's guilt had been irrefutably exposed, but Brome still hoped for a happy ending.

'What do you intend to do with Newburne's hoard?' Chaloner asked, dodging to one side when Hodgkinson took aim again. 'Share it between you?'

'Of course not!' cried Brome, shocked. 'Hodgkinson brought it here for safekeeping, and we intend to see it returned to its rightful owners – the people Newburne defrauded. I cannot imagine how we will locate them all, but we shall do our best.'

Chaloner suspected Hodgkinson had a different plan in mind, and he saw neither he nor Brome were going to be allowed to leave Thames Street alive. The printer's crimes were simply too great to allow witnesses to live.

'Stop!'

A dark shadow streaked from Leybourn's arms as he struggled to draw his sword. There was a deafening bang, and something grazed Chaloner's hat as he threw himself to the floor. He said yet another silent prayer of thanks for Isabella's gift. A second boom followed the first. Water surged into his ears, and spray was everywhere. Then all was silent.

* * *

Cautiously, Chaloner clambered to his feet and saw Hodgkinson floating face-down and unmoving in the water. Brome stood with his gun dangling from his fingers, while Leybourn, alarmed by the sudden discharge of deadly weapons, had raced back outside, and was taking shelter in the street.

'What have I done?' whispered Brome, appalled. 'Oh, God, what have I done?'

Chaloner spat foul water from his mouth. 'It was not your fault. Hodgkinson—'

But Brome was full of anguish. 'It *was* my fault! I took his life with this . . .' Repelled, he flung the dag away from him, and stood wiping his hand on his coat, as if trying to clean it. When he next spoke, his voice was flat and expressionless. 'I will take Newburne's jewels to L'Estrange and ask him to return them to their rightful owners. Catching whoever tried to steal them from his cellar seems unimportant now. Why did you come here, if it was not for the treasure?'

'To find evidence of Hodgkinson's guilt.' Chaloner did not explain that he had had the printer in his sights as the Butcher of Smithfield. 'Why take the jewels to L'Estrange? You of all people know he is not always honest.'

Brome shrugged. 'He is my master, and ethical in his own way. If I ask him to track down the victims of Newburne the phanatique, he will do it with all the fervour of an avenging angel. He is the best man for the task, other than perhaps your Earl. Unfortunately, though, Clarendon is on the other side of a flooded river.'

Chaloner gestured around the dark print-house. 'Why did you come here tonight?'

'Because Hodgkinson sent for me, and he was my

friend.' Brome's voice trembled as he looked at the printer's body. 'I see I was wrong, and his betrayal emphasises the fact that I have no place here in London.'

'You intend to run?' asked Chaloner uneasily. 'Don't. It will look as though—'

'I do not care what it looks like,' said Brome in the same numb tone. 'The situation has escalated out of control, and a prudent disappearance is the only option open to me. Will you give me a hour's grace, for friendship's sake? To collect Joanna and flee this horrible city? If you do not trust me to give the jewels to L'Estrange, then take them yourself.'

Chaloner declined to accept the proffered box. 'I must go to Smithfield before the Butcher – whoever he is – assumes power. I cannot waste time with treasure.'

'It is reckless and stupid to go to Smithfield without knowing the identity of the man you think is responsible for so much evil,' said Brome, seeming to come out of his daze a little. 'You need more information. Talk to Muddiman. He knows more about London than anyone else, and might be willing to help you prevent a catastrophe.'

'All the way back to The Strand?' Brome's suggestion made sense, but it would take far too long.

'The bridges are closed, so he cannot have gone home. Try his favourite coffee house – the Turk's Head at St Paul's. And while you are there, ask him about this exploding oil, too. He bought a pamphlet from me on the subject just last week.'

Leybourn emerged from the shadows to make a lunge for Brome as he left the print-house, but the bookseller flinched away from the clumsily wielded weapon and disappeared into the night.

466

'Why are you letting him go?' demanded Leybourn. 'He just shot Hodgkinson. I saw him!'

Chaloner was too weary to explain. 'He saved my life, Will. The least I can do is return the favour.'

Leybourn waved his sword again. 'He is irrelevant, anyway. Our first duty is to stop the Butcher from realising his nefarious plans. So, shall we go straight to Smithfield, or shall we do as Brome suggested and see what Muddiman is prepared to tell us?'

'Muddiman,' replied Chaloner, hurrying into the street. 'Brome is right: knowledge is power, and we do not have enough of it to tackle the Butcher yet.'

'What about your cat?' asked Leybourn, as the spy set off towards St Paul's. He looked sheepish. 'I am afraid I dropped it.'

Chaloner grimaced, wishing Leybourn had looked after the animal, as he had been told.

'It will find its way home.' Leybourn was trotting to keep up with him. 'But I am not sure I understand what happened in there. Newburne's treasure—'

'I will explain later,' said Chaloner, not wanting to waste breath that could be used for running. It was still dark, but the first glimmerings of dawn were lightening the night sky. It would come late, because of the rain, but at least he could see where he was going. 'Hurry!'

'So the Butcher was not Hodgkinson?' said Leybourn, beginning to pant.

Chaloner ran harder, splashing through water and oblivious to the spray that flew around him. 'No.'

'Maybe Muddiman is, then,' gasped Leybourn. 'For several reasons. He gave exploding oil to Hickes, to dispatch him before he reported something *really* incriminating to Williamson. He hired Hodgkinson to betray

467

L'Estrange's secrets. He probably killed Dury, because they argued. He bought cucumbers from Covent Garden the day before one was left at the scene of Newburne's death. And he is bitter because he lost control of the newsbooks to L'Estrange.'

'No,' said Chaloner tiredly. 'Muddiman is not the Butcher.'

'Yes he is,' countered Leybourn firmly. 'And *that* is why he is at his coffee house and not at home tonight. He is on this side of the Fleet River, because he is preparing to seize his Smithfield throne.'

Lights burned in the Turk's Head Coffee House. The windows had steamed up, so it was impossible to see inside, and the distinctive reek of burned coffee wafted into the street, combining unpleasantly with the stench of overloaded sewers. Chaloner was about to go in, when the door opened and Muddiman himself bustled out. He carried a bag, and behind him were two servants bearing boxes. The newsman raised his arm and a cart immediately rattled towards him, loaded with goods and covered with a sheet of oiled canvas.

'Going somewhere?' asked Chaloner softly, stepping in front of him.

Muddiman jumped in alarm. 'The river is set to burst its banks, and I do not want to be here when it does. Besides, I meet L'Estrange everywhere I go these days, and he has a nasty habit of drawing his sword. Without Dury to protect me, I am safer in the country.'

'L'Estrange is in there?' asked Leybourn, trying to peer through the glass. 'Have you considered the fact that he may have good reason to grab his weapon when you appear? You are a killer, and thus a dangerous man. You

468

murdered Newburne with poisonous lozenges, and left one of the cucumbers you bought by his side.'

Chaloner winced.

'I did no such thing,' objected Muddiman indignantly. 'My wife used those fruits to make me a remedy for wind. Ask her, my servants *and* my apothecary. They concocted the potion together.'

Chaloner suspected he was telling the truth, because it was a tale that could easily be verified, and Muddiman was not stupid.

'You gave a flask of exploding oil to Hickes,' Leybourn went on, going for his suspect like a dog with a rat.

'Did I?' asked Muddiman coldly. 'Do you think me a fool, then, to blow up the Spymaster's best agent? Besides, Hickes is no threat to me. He is incompetent.'

'But now Dury is dead, Hickes will concentrate all his attention on you, and that will be inconvenient,' said Leybourn, shaking off the warning hand that Chaloner laid on his arm.

Muddiman sighed. 'You might have a point, *if* I was doing something I do not want Williamson to know about. But I am not.'

'How about buying secrets from Hodgkinson?' asked Chaloner, shoving Leybourn hard in an attempt to make him shut up. 'Secrets that have damaged Williamson's newsbooks?'

'Hodgkinson has confessed to being Wenum, so do not deny it,' added Leybourn.

'You are lying,' said Muddiman dismissively. 'Hodgkinson is not Wenum. Wenum had something wrong with his face, and Hodgkinson has a beard—' He stopped speaking as he saw how the two facts fitted together, but quickly rallied. 'You cannot prove I sent Hickes the oil.'

469

'Actually, I can,' said Chaloner. 'When I visited your office on Monday, I saw a pamphlet on such devices, and Brome just said he sold you one. It is not a subject a man reads about for fun, as I am sure Williamson will agree when he searches your home and finds it. But that is not your only crime. You are also responsible for Brome spying on L'Estrange. You sent Williamson some silly broadsheet Brome wrote as a child, knowing Williamson would use it to force him into turning informer.'

Muddiman sneered. 'You call that a crime? Besides, it was Williamson who resorted to blackmail, not I. All I did was send our noble Spymaster an anonymous gift. It was a waste of time, though. I wanted Brome to discover something so unsavoury about L'Estrange that it would see him ousted, but he learned nothing we do not know already. And neither of them had the wits to work out the business with the music and the stolen horses.'

'I have decided you are right: Muddiman is not Crisp,' whispered Leybourn in Chaloner's ear. His voice was hard and cold. '*L'Estrange* is.'

'He is not,' said Chaloner irritably. 'He cannot be, because—'

He broke off when the door to the coffee house creaked, and the editor himself stepped out.

'Hah!' yelled Leybourn in savage delight.

'Christ!' sighed Chaloner, bracing himself for yet more trouble. 'What wretched timing!'

L'Estrange grinned when he saw Muddiman talking to Chaloner and Leybourn, and gave a bow that was intended to be insulting. 'All the phanatiques together. What are you plotting this time?'

'Your downfall,' replied Leybourn bitingly. 'I was just

about to explain to Tom how you send coded messages to criminals, telling them when to steal horses, so you can collect five shillings when the hapless victim is obliged to advertise the loss in your nasty little newsbooks.'

'It is a fascinating theory,' drawled Muddiman. 'And I wish Dury were here to hear it. However, I shall be sure to repeat it in my next newsletter, so others can enjoy it, too.'

Chaloner was not surprised when L'Estrange's sword was whipped from its scabbard, or when Leybourn struggled to do the same. He drew his own and stood between them, wishing L'Estrange had stayed in the coffee house for just a few moments longer. He had just missed a second night of sleep, and his wits were not as sharp as they should have been – he was not sure he was alert enough to prevent the brewing skirmish by trying to reason with them.

'I am no horse thief,' snapped L'Estrange. He ignored Leybourn and lunged at Muddiman, furious when his blow was parried by Chaloner's blade.

Muddiman jerked into Leybourn, who promptly dropped his weapon in the water that lapped around their feet.

'No?' demanded the newsmonger, rashly provocative. 'Then tell Heyden why you wanted Newburne's death quietly forgotten. Dury was looking into the matter for me, but you warned him *and* Heyden to leave the matter well alone.'

'Of course I did,' exploded L'Estrange. 'Newburne died of cucumbers. There was no need for an investigation, because cucumbers kill people all the time. I am a newsman, so party to this sort of information. I could name half a dozen people who have died of cucumbers this year alone.'

'And it did not occur to you that this is odd?' Muddiman grabbed Leybourn and cowered behind him, as

471

L'Estrange brandished his sword and Chaloner tried to keep it from landing on someone. Leybourn was desperately scrabbling around in the water for his lost weapon, and Chaloner might have laughed at the ludicrousness of the situation, had he not been so tired or so worried about what might be happening in Smithfield.

'Of course it is not odd. People die of peculiar things all the time. Besides, if you must know the truth, I was paying court to Dorcus Newburne when her husband breathed his last, and I knew what Dury would have made of *that* – he would have said it was motive for murder. Damned phanatique!'

'Hah!' exclaimed Leybourn, as he found his blade at last. It came out of the water like Excalibur. 'And you, Muddiman? Why did you order Tom not to investigate Newburne?'

'Because Dury was doing it,' replied Chaloner, when Muddiman realised he was in more danger from Leybourn's undisciplined swipes than L'Estrange's determined lunges. The newsman ducked and weaved, more interested in protecting himself than in answering questions. 'And he did not want us tripping over each other in the search for clues.'

'Let me at him,' ordered L'Estrange, advancing purposefully on his rival. 'I do not want to kill you, Heyden, so step aside before you are hurt. Muddiman, prepare to die! London will not mourn a phanatique of your standing.'

Muddiman shrieked as L'Estrange fought his way past Chaloner, whose attention was half on keeping Leybourn out of the fight, and he suddenly found himself exposed.

'Stop him! I will tell you everything if you save me. *Dury* was investigating how messages in music helped

472

criminals to steal horses, and *Crisp* slaughtered him when he came too close to the truth. He went to Hodgkinson's print-shop in Smithfield for answers, and was strangled for his pains. A gutter was dropped on his head to conceal what really happened.'

'The music is nothing,' snapped L'Estrange, scowling when Chaloner grabbed his coat and spun him around, forcing him to halt his relentless advance. 'Greeting takes the stuff to Williamson for me, because Williamson thinks it contains a code, but he is wrong. I have played it every way imaginable, and it is just music – from China, probably, which is why it is difficult for western ears to understand.'

L'Estrange was the one who was wrong, thought Chaloner, falling back quickly when the editor went on the offensive. Williamson knew exactly what the music meant. But why had the Spymaster tossed the music on the fire when Greeting had delivered it? He realised the answer was clear: Williamson had no intention of interfering with Hector business. And why? Because they obliged him with manpower when he needed something shady done.

Leybourn had been about to stab L'Estrange in the back while the editor's attention was on Chaloner, but he lowered the weapon slowly as he considered the claims. 'You are not Crisp, either,' he said, sounding startled. 'You cannot be, if you are passing the music to Williamson.'

Chaloner had had enough of dancing around with L'Estrange. He abandoned the fancy sword-play of Court and reverted to more brutal tactics – ones he had learned during the wars. In seconds, L'Estrange's elegant weapon lay on the ground and the editor was nursing a bruised hand. Muddiman did not wait to see what else happened;

473

he dashed to his cart, screaming at the driver to whip the horses into a gallop. Boxes dropped from the wagon as it careened away, and shadows emerged from nearby alleys to claim them.

'How *do* you come by the music you send to Williamson?' asked Chaloner, standing next to L'Estrange as they watched the newsmonger rattle away.

'Brome keeps it hidden in Joanna's virginals,' replied L'Estrange sullenly, inspecting his fingers in the gathering light of dawn. 'You must have noticed the instrument's muted tones when we played together? Well, I looked inside it one day, and it was full of this odd music. Brome frets when a few pieces go missing occasionally, but I do not see the harm in taking a couple now and then. It pleases Williamson, and that should be reward enough.'

'Brome,' said Chaloner. He exchanged an appalled glance with Leybourn as the truth finally dawned. They had had the Butcher of Smithfield in their hands, and they had let him go.

'I tried to tell you I did not trust Brome,' said Leybourn, as they raced through the sodden streets towards Ivy Lane. 'But you would not stop to listen, and I was overly ready to believe Muddiman was the culprit. Brome had *two* guns. He aimed at Hodgkinson with one, and you with the other. I saw him. Obviously, he sent us to the Turk's Head to make us waste time.'

'He did not make much attempt to disarm Hodgkinson, did he,' said Chaloner, wondering why he had not seen it at the time. He supposed he was simply too tired. 'He *wanted* him to shoot me.'

'Because he could not tackle two fairly dangerous men at the same time,' explained Leybourn. 'If Hodgkinson

474

had dispatched you, then he would have been left with only one. He might be the Butcher, but he does not do his own dirty work. He has Hectors for that. And Mary.'

'He did not know Hodgkinson was Wenum, though. His surprise over that was genuine.'

'And so was his retribution,' said Leybourn. 'Hodgkinson did not live long after that little secret came out, did he!'

The streets were light now, although it was a grey, sullen dawn that oppressed the spirits. People were sweeping water from their houses, and everywhere, buckets were being emptied. It was all to no avail: rain kept falling as if it intended to drown London and every living thing in it.

They reached Ivy Lane, and Chaloner skidded to a stop. He wished he was not so tired, and that he could think properly. Leybourn had not sheathed his sword; he was holding it like a battleaxe, and unless Chaloner devised some sort of strategy, his friend's determination to avenge himself was going to cause some fatal problems.

'We cannot just burst in,' he said. Exhaustion slurred his words. 'His Hectors will kill us.'

'You have a plan?'

'No,' admitted Chaloner. He pointed to where Kirby was guarding the bookshop door. 'But it looks as if Brome has already asserted control over his Hectors. Of course, they will be eager to do his bidding – I let him take Newburne's treasure, so he has the wherewithal to pay them. I should have been suspicious when he offered to take the box to L'Estrange in the first place. He was supposed to be running for his life, and who cares about delivering stolen property under such circumstances?'

'We must smash his vile empire,' declared Leybourn.

'And the only way to do that is to strike off its head. Once it is leaderless, it will founder, and hopefully Williamson will be able to crush the rest of it before someone else steps up to accept the challenge.'

'Williamson? He is more likely to appoint a new Butcher – the Hectors are too useful to lose.' Chaloner tried to rally his fading strength. 'We cannot do this alone, Will. We need help.'

'Unfortunately, that will not be coming. The only man I trust is Thurloe, and he is on the wrong side of a flooded river. And if you say Williamson will turn a blind eye to the Hectors, then there is no point in sending for him, either – he will probably arrange for us to die. The best option is for us to storm the bookshop and stab Brome before he realises what is happening.'

'Kirby will shoot us long before we reach the door. How many coffee houses are there nearby?'

Leybourn gazed uncertainly at him. 'Why?'

'*How many?*'

Leybourn shrugged. 'Half a dozen or more.' He began to list them.

Chaloner shoved him towards the closest. 'Go to the ones by St Paul's. Say the vicar of Wollaston has complained to the government about his prayer-book being smeared with grease, so the government is giving him a solid gold lectern as compensation. It will cost a thousand pounds, and will be paid for by a tax imposed on Londoners.'

Leybourn gaped at him. 'What for? It will cause all manner of trouble.'

'Of course it will. And you can say a public announcement of the facts will be made from the newsbook offices within the hour. I will do the same along Cheapside.

476

Carry your sword, and say people are massing in Ivy Lane to voice their objections.'

'What is to stop them marching on White Hall?' asked Leybourn uneasily.

'A flooded river and no bridges. Hurry, or we will be too late.'

Chaloner darted towards Cheapside without waiting for an answer, praying that the coffee houses would be full of their usual early-morning patrons. People saw his drawn weapon and gave him a wide berth as he ran. He shouted that there was to be a great announcement at Ivy Lane in a few moments time, and although some folk ignored him, others started to move towards the newsbook offices.

It was easier to inflame the occupants of the coffee houses than he had anticipated, and he was startled when he reached the third one to find his tale had preceded him. Someone had run ahead, and men were streaming out of the door, heading westwards through the pouring rain. He glanced east, and saw coffee-boys racing to the next establishment and the one after that. The rumour was now well out of his control, so he turned back to Ivy Lane.

He arrived to find a crowd of about fifty people milling in the street, and more were flocking to join them with each passing moment. Kirby was declaring that there would be no announcement, and that they should go home, but Kirby was a Hector, and his very presence in such a place was unusual enough to fuel speculation. People refused to budge. Then someone threw a stone at a window, and the sound of smashing glass brought a triumphant cheer. It was time to act.

Chaloner ran around the block, and let himself in

477

through Brome's back door. It was locked and there was a guard, but one he picked with his customary deftness, and the other he felled with a sharp blow from Joanna's otherwise useless pistol. He made his way along the corridor towards the bookshop. Brome was there, looking out of the window, and with him were Ireton and several Hectors. There was another cheer, and Kirby suddenly raced through the front door, slamming it behind him.

'They are throwing rocks at me now,' he yelled indignantly. 'Give me a gun. There is only one way they will be driven off.'

'Order them home,' instructed Brome. 'They will go if you tell them properly.'

'I *have* told them properly,' shouted Kirby, 'but they will not listen. They are saying there is to be an announcement about some new tax. If you do not believe me, *you* go out and try to convince them.'

'Someone is trying to obstruct us,' said Ireton thoughtfully. 'Where is Joanna? This is an important day, and I do not want her wandering about and spoiling everything.'

'She will not spoil anything,' said Brome icily.

Ireton raised his hands and backed down at the fierce tenor of the bookseller's voice.

Chaloner took a deep breath, and stepped into the room. He levelled the dag at the group by the window. 'The King's troops will be here any moment, and you are all under arrest. Put up your weapons.'

Ireton sneered. 'What will you do when we refuse? Shoot us all? With one gun? I would have thought you had learned that lesson already. Grab him, Kirby.'

Chaloner lobbed the dag hard enough to knock Kirby cold, then took a firmer grip on his sword. Ireton drew his own blade, while Brome hurled a dagger. It went wide, and stuck in the doorframe near Chaloner's head.

'You summoned that crowd,' snarled Ireton, lunging at him. 'You are the one trying to sabotage what we have worked for all these years.'

Chaloner jumped away from him, noting that Brome was making no further attempt to fight. Leybourn had been right: he did prefer others to do his dirty work. He stood with his arms folded and indicated with a nod of his head that his men should make an end of the spy who was such a thorn in his side. Obligingly, several Hectors closed in on Chaloner from behind, restricting the space he needed to wield his sword.

'I should have known,' Chaloner said to the bookseller. 'You warned me away from "Crisp" the first time we met. You pretended to be afraid, to frighten me into abandoning my enquiries. You knew they would lead to me discovering not only the identity of Newburne's killer, but also your plans to take control of Smithfield.'

'And you ignored me,' said Brome wearily. 'I tried to keep you out of it, but you did the exact opposite of whatever I recommended. You know little that can harm us, but it is a pity you meddled.'

'I know enough. For example, I have deduced that you killed Finch. You admitted to hating the trumpet when we played with L'Estrange, and you showed your ignorance of the instrument when you put cucumber inside it – you put the chewed piece in the wrong place. Callously, you ate a pie while you watched Finch die.'

'I was listening to him play,' acknowledged Brome. 'He had acquired some of the music I send to Ireton, to say where and when to procure certain horses. I needed to know whether he had decoded the messages, but I could

479

tell from his playing that he had not. I offered him a lozenge anyway.'

'Yesterday, you told me the music might be code,' said Chaloner, jerking away from a riposte from Ireton that almost removed an ear. Once again, the hat came into its own. 'You were testing me, to see if I had worked it out, too.'

'You were good,' acknowledged Brome. 'I confess I had no idea at the end of the discussion whether you had guessed our secret or not. I decided your days were numbered regardless, because loose ends can be dangerous.'

'Was Newburne a loose end?'

'He was cheating us, which was unacceptable. I sent him some lozenges – the same as the ones I fed to Pettis, Beauclair and anyone else who did not fall in with our plans.' Another stone hit the window with a crack, and Chaloner could hear people yelling that they wanted the news.

'And it was all for horses?' he asked.

'Horses are a lucrative business,' replied Brome. 'And do not think the government will stop us, because Williamson knows all about it. L'Estrange got hold of a few tunes somehow, and sent them to him. He understood their significance immediately, but he turns a blind eye.'

'And why not?' asked Ireton. 'He has nothing to lose and a great deal to gain – more advertisements sold; more people wanting to buy the newsbooks for tales of lost nags; more people reading the news *he* decides should be released. If you think Williamson is going to put an end to that, you are a fool.'

'Why do you think he set Hickes and Greeting to solve Newburne's murder?' added Brome, gloating now. 'A half-wit and a novice, neither of whom was going to discover anything. He even sent Hickes to Finch's room on my behalf, when I foolishly left the music behind. Of course, Hickes neglected to collect the lozenges, so I was obliged to go back myself anyway.'

'And you pretend to be his reluctant spy,' said Chaloner, disgusted. 'You let him think he has a hold over you with that pamphlet you wrote, but the reality is that the information you send him is carefully designed to benefit your own cause.'

Smugly, Brome inclined his head.

'Enough talking,' snapped Ireton, lunging again. 'The Butcher will be here soon.'

His comment startled Chaloner anew. 'What do you mean? Brome is the Butcher.'

Ireton laughed as the spy's lapse in concentration allowed him to perform a fancy manoeuvre that saw the sword wrenched from his hand. 'Do not be ridiculous!'

The door opened. 'Joanna!' exclaimed Brome. 'You should not be here.'

'I heard there was trouble,' said Joanna. She looked furious. 'And since I cannot trust you to do anything properly, I am here to sort out the mess. I cannot take Crisp's mantle as long as there is a mob outside, baying for blood.'

Chaloner gaped at Joanna, scarcely believing his ears, and was sufficiently astounded that Ireton came close to running him through. It was only an instinctive twist that saved him. As he turned, he saw Kirby had crawled to a cupboard and had pulled out a gun. He was priming it, and Chaloner knew he would be shot as soon as it was ready. He was running out of time, and facing insurmountable odds.

Joanna smiled prettily at Chaloner, but he did not think he had ever seen eyes so cold. There was no trace of the

rabbit now – the prey had turned predator. 'I understand I owe you my thanks,' she said pleasantly. 'You
relieved me of a certain problem.'

'Crisp?'

'Hodgkinson – Henry tells me you unmasked him as
a traitor to the newsbooks. Mary must take the credit for
Crisp, although I was furious when I learned she had involved
poor William in our plan to be rid of the fellow. I was angry
when she set her sights on him at all – he is popular, and
their relationship attracted the wrong kind of attention.'

'You were keen to separate them.' Chaloner performed
an agile leap across a table to avoid Ireton, and managed
to retrieve his sword at the same time. He found himself
facing two more Hectors. They did not possess his skill
with a blade, but beating them off took too much of his
failing strength.

'I *did* want to separate them,' she agreed, with the
same icy smile. 'I ordered her to leave him alone, but
she could not resist stupid men. Still, she is gone now,
which is just as well. The gunpowder was a foolish idea,
and the whole affair was hopelessly bungled.'

Chaloner's muscles burned with fatigue when Ireton
resumed his attack, and he was not sure how much longer
he could fight. Then Joanna gestured for her henchman
to hold off. Chaloner was amusing her, and she did not
want him killed just yet. Meanwhile, Kirby sat on the
floor, feverishly loading his gun.

'You have been pretending to be Crisp for some time
now,' said Chaloner, wondering why he had not associated the Butcher's slender grace with Joanna before. 'The
real one has been in the country with his books and
experiments, seen only by his father. When you are out,
you are surrounded by Hectors – not to protect Crisp as

482

I assumed, but to keep anyone from coming close and seeing you. And you decline invitations—'

'Like the Butchers' Company dinner,' said Ireton. Chaloner remembered Maylord's neighbour mentioning Crisp's abrupt cancellation. 'I told you to let me go. I could have carried it off.'

'I am sure you could,' said Joanna coolly, and Chaloner saw Ireton was too ambitious for his own safety. He would not last long under the new regime. She turned to Chaloner, laughing at him. He wondered how he ever could have thought of her as sweet and meek. 'How can *I* be the Butcher? You saw him the morning you went to Haye's Coffee House with Henry, but I was with Mrs Chiffinch, consoling her over her husband's infidelity.'

'I doubt your company could have compared to that of L'Estrange,' countered Chaloner. 'He would have occupied Mrs Chiffinch, giving you ample time to don a disguise and make an appearance. Besides, how do you know I saw the Butcher that day? It was an insignificant event, and not the sort of thing most husbands would have mentioned to their wives. But of course it *was* significant, wasn't it? Brone deliberately dallied as he gave alms to that beggar, which gave you time to change and leave the house. You wanted me to see "Crisp" at a point when I would think he could not be either of you.'

'Yes,' agreed Brome, rather boastfully. 'It was a precaution, lest you later—'

'We are wasting time, and this is no longer fun,' snapped Joanna, turning to anger fast enough to be disturbing. 'I should have killed you yesterday, but I thought you might be a useful source of information. You have now outlived that usefulness.'

'I will shoot him.' Kirby had finally finished preparing

483

the gun, and he stood with triumph in his face. 'I have been wanting to do this ever since he attacked me outside the Bear.'

'You have not loaded it properly,' said Ireton, rolling his eyes when Kirby squeezed the trigger and nothing happened. 'And a sword is better for this kind of work anyway.'

'News!' came a yell from outside. 'We want news.'

Joanna grimaced. 'Make a speech, Henry. Tell them the government has no intention of raising another tax. Diffuse the situation. It will please Williamson, and make him more willing to look the other way while we grow rich.'

Ireton came after Chaloner with a series of concerted sweeps. Two more Hectors weaved behind the spy, and he stumbled when one stabbed his leg. His boot saved him from injury, but he felt himself losing ground.

There was a roar of massed voices, and a heavy missile crashed through a window, sending glass spraying across the room. The mob cheered, and through the broken pane, Chaloner could see Leybourn, urging them on. The surveyor prised a rock from the sodden ground, but it was the windows of the house next door that paid the price. The crowd laughed, and suddenly more stones were being hurled. The room was awash with them, and one struck Chaloner's shoulder. Then Kirby took aim again.

The gun's blast was deafening in the confined space, and Chaloner saw the felon drop to the floor with blood on his hand. In his haste, he had used too much powder. More stones pelted the windows, and Chaloner noticed Brome and Joanna had gone. His momentary lack of concentration saw Ireton on him, and he was hard-pressed to defend himself. Someone hit him from behind, and he fell heavily. Ireton's sword plunged downwards,

484

and he only just managed to twist away. Then the room was full of shouting. The crowd had stormed inside. Leybourn was at the front, blade in his hand.

'Hectors!' he yelled furiously. 'Run them through! Proud Londoners are not afraid of Hectors!'

Not everyone rallied to his battle cry, but enough did. The Hectors turned and ran. It was the worst thing they could have done, because the mob became braver once it smelled a rout. Chaloner saw several criminals disappear under a flailing mêlée of fists and knives.

'Bastard!' yelled Ireton at Leybourn, seeing the surveyor as the cause of the disaster. He gripped his weapon and prepared to make an end of him. Leybourn was whirling his blade around his head like a madman, but he neglected to maintain a proper grip. It flew from his fingers, and its hilt caught Ireton in the centre of the forehead. He went down as if poleaxed.

'I did not mean to—' began Leybourn, startled.

Chaloner staggered to his feet as two burly apprentices advanced on the senseless Ireton. He put out a hand to stop them, but they knocked him away.

'Joanna and Brome have escaped,' he said to Leybourn, looking away from the carnage.

'Does it matter?' asked Leybourn, grabbing his arm and making for the door. The people who had not chased Hectors were busily looting the shop, stripping it of anything that could be carried. 'They are toothless now their henchmen are on the run.'

'We do not want them loose in the city. They will avenge themselves somehow.'

'I saw them heading for the river, but they cannot escape because the bridge is closed. Brome was carrying a box – Newburne's treasure, presumably.'

485

The rain had stopped, but everywhere was running with water. It was so deep in Paternoster Row that it was above Chaloner's knees, and flowed fast as it headed for lower ground. His progress was agonisingly slow. Joanna looked behind, and he could hear her urging her husband on. Brome was slower, and she would have made better time alone, but she would not leave him. When he dropped the box, she screamed at him to leave it.

'Gather it up,' ordered Chaloner, pushing Leybourn towards the abandoned hoard. 'Or it will wash into the Thames, and the Earl will dismiss me for certain.'

Leybourn did as he was told, grabbing mud as well as gems, while Chaloner struggled on, trying to ignore the burning exhaustion that threatened to overwhelm him. Joanna reached Ludgate Hill, skidding and sliding down towards the Fleet. There was a barrier across the road to stop people from approaching, but she dodged around it, dragging her husband after her. She gained the bridge, ignoring the yells of people who shouted that it was ripe for collapse.

Hands reached out to prevent Chaloner from following, and he lost his footing. Joanna and Brome were a quarter of the way across when the structure began to sway. They tried to move faster. Chaloner punched his way free of the people who were holding him, and staggered towards the balustrade. It shuddered, and there was a tearing groan. The pair were more than halfway across, and he saw they were going to escape. Joanna turned and gave him a jaunty wave.

Chaloner took another step, but someone came from nowhere, and he felt himself hauled backwards just as the bridge tore away from its moorings. He managed to lift his head in time to see Joanna and Brome carried with it. Brome's mouth was open in a scream, and Joanna's face was white with horror as they were swept downstream. Then the whole structure rolled, and began to crack apart. Chaloner closed his eyes and fell back, exhausted.

'Well,' drawled L'Estrange. 'There is an end to *them*! You are lucky I followed you, or that pair would not be the only ones heading for a watery grave. I always knew Brome was a phanatique. Joanna, too, or she would have let me bed her when I made my advances. But you are in my debt now, Heyden. I saved your life, and in return, you will say nothing to Williamson about my inadvertent role in this affair.'

'I shall say nothing to Williamson at all,' said Chaloner fervently, not liking to imagine what would happen to him if the Spymaster ever discovered that he knew about the blind eye that had been turned to the Hectors' thievery.

'Very wise,' said L'Estrange. 'Shall we seal our arrangement with some music?'

'I do not know about that,' said Chaloner. There were limits.

'Tomorrow, at three o'clock,' said L'Estrange comfortably. 'And do not be late.'

Epilogue

The Lord Chancellor rubbed his plump hands and chortled in delight as he inspected the box Chaloner had given him. He made no attempt to soil his fingers with its contents, of course, stained as they were with the filth of the street. Chaloner could have rinsed the jewels before presenting them to his master, but he had not done so, and he had refused to let Bulteel do it, either. Money was a dirty business, and he did not see why the Earl should be spared that knowledge.

'And this is all of it?' asked the Earl.

'Yes,' said Chaloner shortly. 'It is.'

The Earl sighed. 'I am not accusing you of dishonesty, Heyden. I was just wondering whether the Bromes had spent any before you managed to retrieve it.'

'They did not have time. Is there enough to pay Dorcus Newburne's pension?'

'I have been relieved of that particular obligation,' said the Earl smugly. 'Newburne *was* working for me, and that why I was determined to have the truth about his death. However, he was killed because he was a thief, and I cannot be held financially responsible for that sort of thing. Dorcus has agreed to forget about the pension.'

'How did you persuade her to do that?' Chaloner was startled.

'Bulteel suggested I offer her an official government post instead – Assistant Editor. She is an educated lady, and said she would relish the opportunity to use her intellect to benefit her country. So, we are both happy.'

Chaloner glanced to where Bulteel was labouring over his ledgers in an antechamber. 'It means she will be spending a lot of time with L'Estrange.'

'That is what I said. It was only fair to point out the downside of Bulteel's recommendation, but she said she did not mind at all. In fact, she said it would be a pleasure.'

'Bulteel is a clever man,' said Chaloner, impressed by the coup the clerk had staged for his master's benefit. 'You would not have had this treasure without him.'

'So you have said, at least a dozen times. I have rewarded him with a pleasant house in Westminster – his wife presented him with a son last night, and I do not want him wasting hours travelling between here and his old home in Southwark, when he could be working for me.'

Chaloner smiled, pleased the clerk's loyalty was being acknowledged at last.

'I have reinstated you,' the Earl went on. 'I have also arranged for you to be paid for the time you were in Portugal, and I have informed Williamson that you are a vital member of my household. I do not think he will risk my wrath by harming you now.'

'Harming me for what reason?' Chaloner had not told the Earl about Williamson's role in the Hectors' dark business, so the Spymaster should have no need to resort to sly daggers.

'For tossing a bottle of exploding oil on a fire, and throwing his soldiers into a panic. He is furious that you exposed them as incompetent to the general populace.'

'I needed to leave, and they were dithering. You would not have been pleased if I had allowed Joanna to assume control of the Hectors – or if she had used Newburne's hoard to do it.'

'That is what I told him,' said the Earl, closing the box and patting it contentedly. 'You should avoid antagonising him in the future, though – he has a nasty habit of dispatching people he does not like. But time is passing, and I have a lot to do. The floods did much damage, and my organisational skills are needed to put all to rights. Incidentally, London is not the only city to suffer from an excess of rain. So did Oxford, and I want you to go there and solve a theft that took place in my old College when the waters were up.'

'Oxford?' asked Chaloner unhappily, wondering if he would ever be granted the opportunity to stay in London and learn about its customs and politics.

The Earl ignored his disgruntlement. 'The day after tomorrow will do, though – you have earned a few days of leisure. Perhaps you can use them to purchase some better clothes.'

Chaloner congratulated Bulteel on the birth of his son, and stayed to enjoy a piece of celebratory cake. Then he walked to Lincoln's Inn, taking a few moments to look at the green stain on the buildings around White Hall, which showed the height of the flood. The rain and a gale in the North Sea had combined to produce one of the highest tides anyone could remember, and water was still seeping from damaged buildings.

Lincoln's Inn's new astrological device had been bent

491

during one particularly fierce downfall, so it would never track the movements of the stars accurately again, but the foundation was otherwise intact. Chaloner knocked on the door to Chamber XIII, and was admitted by Leybourn. The surveyor had still not gone home, despite his brother sending word that all signs of the explosion – and Mary – had been eradicated.

Thurloe suggested a walk in the garden. The sun was shining, a weak, watery orb in a misty sky, and birds sang in trees that dripped. The ground squelched underfoot, a morass of mud and sodden leaves. Gardeners were out in force, gathering fallen branches and sweeping paths. One sang a song about love, and Leybourn snorted his derision.

'So, you have answers to all your questions, Tom,' said Thurloe, to distract Leybourn from bitter thoughts. 'Brome and Joanna – but mostly Joanna – conceived the notion of listening in coffee houses for details of valuable horses and the movements of their owners. This information was converted into a code in music, and was sent to Ireton and the Hectors.'

'The Hectors stole the horses,' said Chaloner. 'And most victims bought notices in the newsbooks. Some nags were returned and the rewards claimed; others were sold.'

'Why did they sell some of them?' asked Leybourn. 'Why not return them all?'

'Because that would have aroused suspicion,' explained Chaloner. 'In fact, at one point, Joanna thought they were returning too many, and wrote a note telling Ireton to hold back. Somehow Finch got hold of it, probably through Newburne. Anyway, the horse thefts fulfilled two functions.'

'First, making money from the rewards or the sale of

these stolen horses,' said Thurloe. 'And second, making money for the newsbooks. Those advertisements cost five shillings a time.'

'Three functions, then,' said Chaloner. 'They also made the newsbooks popular, which meant an increased circulation – more copies printed and more sold.'

'*Four* functions,' said Thurloe with a smile. 'An increased circulation means the government has better control of the news – and therefore of the hearts and minds of the people. Everyone believed that tale about the vicar of Wollaston's soiled prayer-book, but it was almost pure fabrication. Apparently, the book was accidentally left open when a bird flew past, but L'Estrange reported it in his own inimical way to make a point about religious phanatiques.'

'Because L'Estrange is something of a phanatique himself, Williamson does not trust his judgement,' Chaloner went on. 'He recruited Newburne *and* Brome to spy on him.'

Leybourn gave the ghost of a smile. 'Williamson is almost as stupid as his lumbering Hickes. He chose two men who were deeply involved in the horse business *and* with the Hectors.'

'Joanna and Brome killed Newburne when he tried to cheat them,' said Thurloe. 'They killed Finch because he was interested in the coded music. They killed Colonel Beauclair, because he caught the horse thieves in the act. And they killed the two sedan-chairmen, because they carried Beauclair's body to White Hall.'

'Meanwhile, Smegergill decided he wanted to inherit his best friend's property sooner, rather than later,' said Chaloner. 'But first, he wanted to add to it. He worked Maylord into a fury of indignation over Newburne's dishonesty with the profits from the costermongery, and devised a plan to steal the solicitor's jewels. It entailed Maylord teaching Newburne the flageolet.'

Thurloe took up the tale. 'Unfortunately for everyone concerned, Maylord learned about the horse thefts when he happened across some of the odd music in Newburne's house. The knowledge that he had unearthed Hector business terrified him.'

Chaloner frowned. Here was something that did not quite ring true. 'Did it? I thought we had agreed that he was stronger than that.'

Thurloe shook his head. 'Going to the authorities with what he knew was equal to signing his own death warrant. Of course he was afraid.'

'Was Smegergill involved in the thefts?' asked Leybourn.

Chaloner nodded. 'Yes, but I am not sure whether he demanded a piece of the action after Maylord made his discovery, or whether he was in it from the start. However, I know he was presented with some stolen horses for his services, because Greeting told me so.'

'And he was prepared to go to considerable lengths to retrieve the incriminating "documents" from Maylord's room,' added Thurloe. 'I suspect Ireton involved him long before Maylord stumbled across the secret.'

'I imagine you are right,' said Leybourn. 'Everything I have heard about him indicates he was not a man to let a lucrative opportunity pass. And he and Ireton were friends, after all.'

'So, poor Maylord had to be silenced before he could reveal what the Hectors were doing,' said Thurloe. 'Ireton was quite happy to oblige, and Smegergill helped. Foolishly, though, neither of them thought to ask where

494

Maylord had hidden the music before they smothered him.'

'Or the key to Newburne's box,' said Chaloner. 'The second of the pair that he thought – wrongly, I imagine – would allow him to claim Newburne's jewels. Smegergill was doubtless delighted that his friend's riches would soon be his, but was concerned about how Maylord's death would look, too.'

'Because he would be the obvious suspect for the murder?' asked Leybourn.

Thurloe nodded. 'So he and Ireton left a cucumber at the scene, to conceal what had really happened. He would have knocked you over the head as soon as you had provided him with what he wanted, Thomas. You felt guilty about his death, but he brought it on himself.'

'What about Dury?' asked Leybourn. 'Who killed him?'

'One of the Hectors, on Joanna's orders,' said Chaloner. 'He was investigating them too, and was coming close to the truth. He was lured to Smithfield and strangled in Hodgkinson's print-shop. Hodgkinson was probably complicit in the affair, although his role is a murky one. I have no idea who owned his real allegiance.'

'I am sorry about your cat,' said Leybourn, after they had walked in silence for a few minutes. 'It survived the flood and made its way back to your room, but I heard it died in the explosion that took place there.'

'What explosion?' demanded Thurloe, shocked. 'You have not mentioned this before.'

'I forgot,' said Chaloner.

'You *forgot* an explosion?' asked Thurloe incredulously.

'Secretive,' said Leybourn to the ex-Spymaster. 'I told you, he is secretive. But *I* shall tell you about it. It was set by Brome and Joanna. After using Hodgkinson to find out what Tom had learned about his operation, Brome tried to shoot him, but missed. Brome killed Hodgkinson, though, then fled, because he had no more ammunition for his gun and knew he could not defeat Tom in a sword fight. However, he had already set the trap in Tom's room – he must have done it early, because otherwise the bridges would have been closed, and he would not have been able to get there.'

'Fortunately, the powder was damp,' said Chaloner, wanting an end to the tale. 'The "explosion" was reduced to a very loud hiss, according to my landlord.'

'What was *he* doing in your rooms?' asked Thurloe curiously.

'He went to let the cat in. The device was set to ignite when the fire was lit, which my landlord did to dry off the cat.'

'But the landlord survived,' said Thurloe. 'Does this mean the cat did, too?'

'It hissed back, apparently. It is alive and well, and making the most of London's rats.'

'But you will not be joining it for rodent repast now you are gainfully employed with the Lord Chancellor,' said Thurloe. 'At least, not until you annoy him the next time.'

A mile away, in White Hall, Spymaster Williamson left his office. As usual, he donned a heavy cloak and a broad hat, so he would not be recognised. It had been several days since the Hectors' empire had collapsed so spectacularly, but no one had come knocking on his door, demanding to know why he had maintained such a close association with it. Somehow, the Earl's spy had failed to see the connections, although it had been a tense time, and he was glad it was over.

'And the Lord Chancellor is happy with Heyden's explanation?' he asked the small man at his side, just to be sure. 'He does not think there are questions that remain unanswered?'

'No,' replied Bulteel. 'He is not naturally curious about matters of espionage, and Heyden's report has satisfied him completely.'

'Good,' said Williamson, relieved. 'Newburne was stupid to have left the music lying around for Maylord to find – and Maylord might have become a serious problem, had Ireton not acted when he did.'

'Ireton was just in time,' agreed Bulteel.

They walked in silence for a while, until Williamson spoke again, 'I trust *you* did not go empty-handed from the affair? I know about your new house in Westminster, but Newburne's hoard was worth a good deal of money. I imagine you and Heyden took a little, and shared it between you?'

'Not Heyden,' said Bulteel. 'I do not think it even occurred to him. But a few gems happened to fall into my pocket when I was given the task of washing them. Here is your half.'

Williamson raised his hands. 'Please!' he demurred, although an acquisitive gleam flared in his eyes. 'I would not dream of it.'

'I insist,' said Bulteel, pressing the pouch into the Spymaster's ready palm. 'It is only fair – I would not have known where to tell Heyden to look, were it not for you.'

Williamson patted the purse with pleasure. 'Giving up Newburne's hoard was money lost to a good cause – I did not want the Lord Chancellor to set Heyden after me. I could kill him easily enough, but there is Thurloe to consider.'

'Thurloe is nothing,' said Bulteel contemptuously. 'His powers have waned.'

'They are not gone yet, though, and he is not a man I want as an enemy. But thank you for your help, Bulteel. Can I assume we shall work together in future?'

'I think you may,' said Bulteel comfortably. 'Just as long as you continue to make it worth my while for declining all the bribes that come my way.'

'Come with me to Smithfield,' said Williamson. 'The remaining Hectors are gathering, and I could do with your help.'

'Will you tell them you were the real Butcher all along, and that Joanna was working for you? That Maylord discovered it, which is why he died in such terror? Fear is always a good way to keep the troops in order.'

Williamson considered the question. 'No,' he said eventually. 'I do not think so. We shall keep that as our little secret.'

Historical Note

Londoners in 1663 endured some terrible weather. There was a long, wet summer, with so much rain that prayers were said in Parliament for a reprieve. In December, there was an unusually high tide, which corresponded with a gale in the North Sea, and White Hall and Westminster were flooded. Although these were two areas that were especially prone to flood, there were almost certainly problems in other parts of the city that were low lying, too, and rain would have turned the Thames's tributaries into raging torrents. The Fleet and the Walbrook are culverted now, and most Londoners are unaware of their presence, but they were major geographical features in the seventeenth century, and bridges were important lines of communication.

A piece of political skulduggery in September 1663 saw the experienced journalist Henry Muddiman ousted from editing the government's official newsbooks, and Roger L'Estrange appointed in his place. The Spymaster and Under Secretary of State Joseph Williamson was behind the coup, and was determined to see the new-style publications – *The Intelligencer* (Mondays), and *The*

Newes (Thursdays) – succeed. He was alarmed when people began to complain almost immediately about the fact that L'Estrange included so little domestic news. This should have come as no surprise, as L'Estrange is on record as saying that such information 'makes the multitude too familiar with the actions and counsels of their superiors, too pragmatical and censorious, and gives them not only an itch, but a kind of colourable right and license to be meddling with the Government.'

L'Estrange – passionate royalist, inveterate womaniser and talented violist – was very interested in providing domestic news on some subjects, though. In October and November 1663, his newsbooks were full of editorials about the Farnley Wood rebellion, in which a few desperate Parliamentarians thought they could oust the newly installed monarchy. These 'dreadful phanatiques' were the subject of numerous bigoted rants, and the name of every rebel was gleefully published in *The Intelligencer* on 16 November. Besides details of the thwarted uprising, the newsbooks for November and December 1663 carried reports about the movements of foreign courts, the damage to the vicar of Wollaston's prayer-book, advertisements for lost and stolen horses, and several notices praising Mr Theophilus Buckworth's Personal Lozenges and Mr Turner's dentifrices, some of which have been used verbatim in *The Butcher of Smithfield*.

Besides editing the newsbooks, L'Estrange was also Surveyor of the Press, which meant nothing could be printed without his permission, and he did indeed hire spies to look for booksellers who sold unlicensed tomes. It was also rumoured that some authors were granted licenses if they had pretty wives willing to spend a little time in his company.

L'Estrange was assisted in his work by a man called Henry Brome. Brome had a bookshop in Ivy Lane, and L'Estrange's office was above it. Brome's wife was Joanna, who was said by contemporaries to be proud. The news-books were printed by Richard Hodgkinson, whose premises were on Thames Street, at the back of Baynard Castle. Baynard Castle was destroyed in the Great Fire of 1666, along with Hodgkinson's print-house.

Muddiman, meanwhile, was not about to take his dismissal lying down, and immediately exploited a loophole in the law. L'Estrange had a monopoly of all *printed* news, but handwritten 'newsletters' were another matter. Muddiman's weekly manuscript sheets (which had a circulation of about 150 at an annual charge of between £5 and £20 each) contained plenty of home news and were very well received. Because he did not have a government telling him what to write, and because he was not a censor, his letters were generally regarded as a far more reliable source of news than the official rags. They quickly became a huge financial success, allowing Muddiman to purchase Coldhern, an elegant country mansion at Earl's Court (an echo of it survives today in streets called Coleherne in the Earl's Court area).

Williamson was furious and jealous, and hired James Hickes, a clerk at the Letter Office, to spy on and attempt to circumvent Muddiman. Williamson's correspondence at this time also suggests he commissioned the services of mercenary gangs, perhaps for intercepting the letters; he may even have hired members of the famous gang called the Hectors. As Muddiman's enterprise grew, Hickes used increasingly more brazen methods to destroy him. He even stole the addresses of the people who subscribed to the newsletters and wrote to them himself, offering to sell them circulars of his own. Although Hickes was promised great rewards for his shady activities, Williamson weaselled his way out of them all, and Hickes slid out of the public records a bitter and disappointed man.

In 1665, public disapproval of L'Estrange's management of the newsbooks became so great that Williamson was obliged to act. In his usual sleazy manner, he waited until the Court was in Oxford, where it had gone to escape the plague, and founded *The Oxford Gazette* as the official government's mouthpiece. He asked Muddiman to edit it. L'Estrange, who had loyally remained at his post in the disease-ravaged capital, suddenly found himself deposed, and wrote several letters of dismay to Williamson, which the Spymaster probably ignored. It was not long before Williamson and his new editor fell out, though, and Muddiman soon resigned and reverted to his more popular newsletters. Muddiman's early assistant was named Giles Dury.

Court records of 1663 describe a devious character called Anne Pettis, who stole silver from the linen-draper Richard Bridges, and was sentenced to hang. Her aliases included Cade, Petwer and Reade, suggesting she had had previous trouble with the law. She was later acquitted.

There is no record of William Leybourn marrying, and eventually, he moved out of his bookshop on Monkwell Street in Cripplegate, and went to live in Southall, between Uxbridge and Acton. In 1667, he wrote a book on the use of Gunter's Quadrant.

John Thurloe, Cromwell's Spymaster General and Secretary of State, was living quietly in Lincoln's Inn in 1663, and the Earl of Clarendon's secretary was named John Bulteel. Court musicians in the 1660s included

Thomas Maylord (or Mallard), William Smegergill (a Frenchman whose alias really *was* Caesar), John Hingston and Thomas Greeting, the latter of whom may also have been involved in espionage.

In 1663, the diarist Samuel Pepys recorded that two men were dead from eating 'cowcumbers'. It was generally acknowledged that ingesting raw fruit and vegetables could be dangerous, and both the apothecary Nicholas Culpeper and the ancient Greek physician Galen warned against the perils of cucumbers in particular. One of the deaths was Thomas Newburne, a corrupt solicitor who lived in Old Jewry, and the other was Ellis Crisp. 'Arise, Tom Newburne' was apparently a 'nick-word' associated with the lawyer, although its meaning has been lost in the mists of time.